MISTRUST

NEW YORK TIMES BESTSELLER

MARGARET MCHEYZER

Interior Formatting by Tami Norman, Integrity Formatting

IT TAKES COURAGE
TO HIDE A SECRET FROM
THE PEOPLE YOU LOVE.
BUT IT TAKES STRENGTH
TO FINALLY TELL THEM.

**FOR ALL SURVIVORS
OF SEXUAL ASSAULT.**

PROLOGUE

TRUST IS SOMETHING that has to be earned. It's not freely given.

There are some people in our lives we automatically trust. We believe everything our parents say and do. We know their actions and instincts are always to protect and teach us.

We learn to trust those with whom we develop a bond of friendship.

Strangers don't have our trust. We're wary of them; we keep them at arm's length until they prove themselves to us.

Trust, once earned, can also be ripped away. That can happen over a period of time or in an instant.

Tonight I'll discover how cruel the world can be when trust is brutally torn away...

CHAPTER 1

STANDING IN FRONT of the full length mirror, I look myself over. My emerald green gown sweeps the floor while my long, dark brown hair is twisted back into a simple, yet elegant chignon.

"You look beautiful, darling," Mom murmurs, leaning against the door frame.

Looking to her, I see tears glimmering in her eyes. "Mom," I say walking toward her.

Her arms open and she folds me into a warm 'mom' hug. "Oh look at me! I'm being so silly, Dakota. It feels like it was only yesterday I was watching you crawl around the house in diapers and today, you're the most beautiful sixteen-year-old young lady my eyes have ever seen."

Smiling broadly at her, I can't stem the wetness beginning to well up in my own eyes. "Mom," I whisper as I blink crazily, trying to hold back the tears.

Mom steps back and holds me at arm's length. "Let me look at my gorgeous daughter all ready for her junior prom." She looks me over as I do a small spin for her, showing off my dress and my hairstyle. "Oh darling," she whispers while shaking her head. "I've never seen anyone as beautiful as you."

"You have to say that; you're my mom."

"No, I don't." She's shakes her head. "I'm so blessed to have you as my daughter." Suddenly the few tears Mom's let escape have escalated to more and before I know it, her whole face is drenched in salt water. I move to hug her again, but Mom pushes me away. "Don't, I'll ruin your dress," she says wiping her tears from her face. "I'm just being a silly old lady."

"You're not silly, and it doesn't matter about my dress." I hug Mom, and she holds me close to her body.

"Thank you, sweetheart. It means so much to me to be able to hug you today." Mom's body relaxes and she takes a deep breath. "You have to finish getting ready before Levi arrives to take you to prom."

"I need to touch up my makeup and I'll be out."

"Okay, I'll go get the camera ready. Dad said he wants heaps of photos, because he won't be home from work in time to see you leave."

"It's okay, I understand," I tell her. Truthfully, I'm a little hurt Dad can't be here, but I know he wants to be and he can't get any time off from work because he's taking two weeks' vacation over the summer break so we can go to Canada to visit Mom's sister and our cousins.

"You look so beautiful." Mom lovingly smiles at me before turning to leave my room.

I sit back down in front of my dressing table, and carefully touch up my hair and make-up. When I'm finally ready, I pick up my small clutch and head out to wait for Levi.

My heels make a clicking sound as I make my way down the hall and into the family room where Mom is already waiting with the camera. My younger sister, Sam, is standing beside her, eagerly watching me walk toward them.

"Dakota," she gasps as her eyes follow my dress up and down. "You look so . . . wow!"

Sam has recently turned fourteen and I know she idolizes me. It's obvious in the way she tries to style her hair like mine and copies what I wear. It used to bother me when I was younger, but it doesn't anymore because I know she loves me and wants to be exactly like her big sister.

I'm considered to be one of the 'popular' girls at school. I'm on the cheerleading squad, have great grades, and I'm dating Levi Matthews, who's on the basketball team. We're the couple everyone wants to be.

"Let me take some photos out back by the pool," Mom says.

"You look so pretty, Dakota," Sammy says again. "I can't wait for my prom, but you have to promise you'll help me look like a princess, too."

"Of course I will. Come on, let's go," I call to Sam, who's sitting on the sofa watching me and Mom.

"You want me to come too?" Her eyes light up as if I've given her the best news of her life.

"Well, you *are* my little sister, and I can't exactly be in these photos all by myself."

Sam's face brightens with joy at being included. She leaps off the sofa and runs straight at me, just stopping before she falls into my arms. "I don't want to ruin your dress so I'll just stand beside you," she says, excitedly bouncing on the spot.

When we get out to the pool, Mom has already positioned herself, ready to take a million or so pictures. "Stand over here, Dakota."

Sam follows me as I walk to where Mom's pointing, already snapping pictures. Before long, I have Sam in the photos with me, and Mom continues with the broadest, proudest smile she can muster. "I think I've got about three hundred," Mom says. "I'm certain Dad will love them. Come on, let's go inside and wait for Levi."

"Are you nervous about tonight?" Sam quietly asks me.

I'd confided in her that maybe Levi and I would finally go all the way tonight. He's booked a hotel room, and without Mom and Dad knowing we're planning to leave the prom early to go there. But I've been having second thoughts, and I just don't think I'm ready for it. "I don't know if I can," I whisper to Sam as we keep an eye on Mom to make sure she's not listening.

"If you're not sure, then don't do it. You don't want to regret it. Just talk to Levi. He loves you, and if you're not ready, tell him." She brings her arm up to drape around my shoulders and pulls me in close for a hug.

"Who made you so responsible? You're supposed to be fourteen, Sam, not logical and level-headed." We both giggle, because we know Sam has always been the super smart one, the one who can look at a situation and instantly know what's right and wrong. She's been like that for as long as I can remember. As I lean in to kiss her cheek, there's a knock on the door. "Eeeek," I squeal happily and Sam jumps up and down, clapping.

Mom answers the door, and Sam leans in to whisper, "Just talk to him, okay?" Nodding my head, I bring her in to give her another tight cuddle.

"Hello, Mrs. Bennett, how are you?" I hear the deep gravel of Levi's voice.

"Don't you look handsome tonight, Levi? And I'm very well. Please come in. Dakota is waiting for you." She opens the door further and Levi enters looking so hot. He's wearing a black suit with a green tie that perfectly matches the color of my dress. His dark hair is nicely styled back, and his suit really emphasizes his broad shoulders. *I'm so lucky to have him.*

"Oh my God," Levi breathes when his gaze falls on me. Hungrily, he looks me up and down, and I see him gulp while his eyes appear glued to me. "You look . . ." He shakes his head and shoves a hand in his pocket. Seemingly speechless, he leans in close and under the guise of kissing my cheek, he whispers, "You look good enough to eat." My heart beats quicker and my cheeks burn with an obvious flush. Pulling back, he smiles at me and hands me a corsage. "I can't talk, I'm blown away by how gorgeous you are."

"Thank you," I say while looking down at the vibrant pink rose. "Will you pin it on me?" Taking it out of the clear plastic container, I hand it to Levi to pin on my dress.

"You two look so cute together," Mom gushes and I hear the camera clicking.

Both Levi and I turn to look at Mom, who's busy staring at us from behind her active lens. "Okay, well, we should get going," Levi announces once the flower is pinned to my dress.

"Have you got your keys?" Mom asks. I double-check my clutch and nod my head. "If you can't get home, call me and I'll come to get you. And no drinking," she says the last part in her firm 'mom' voice, while pointing her finger.

"I won't, Mom." Levi opens the door while I give Sam and Mom another hug.

We walk out the door hand in hand and head toward the car Levi hired. "Oh wow," I squeal excitedly. "A limousine!" The long black car waits out on the street in front of my house, and the uniformed driver is standing beside it with the back passenger door open for us. "Oh my goodness," I murmur as I excitedly clasp my hand to my mouth.

"Nothing but the best for my girl." Levi holds me close against his body. "I love you." He leans down and brushes his lips across mine. "I'd do anything to put a smile on your gorgeous face." His fingers flex against my hip as he makes me a silent promise about tonight.

My heart is pounding inside my chest, and I feel as if a swarm of butterflies have taken up residency in the pit of my belly. When we reach the car, he holds out his hand to help me slide in first. Once I'm settled inside the back of the car, Levi slides in beside me and the driver gently closes the door, then goes around to the front to get into the driver's seat.

"How are you feeling?" Levi asks quietly. I know the question is more about our plans for *after* the dance, rather than the dance itself.

I lift my head to see the privacy partition is up, separating us from the driver. "I'm not sure I'm ready, Levi," I openly admit. With my blood thrumming loudly through my veins, I hold my breath and watch Levi's reaction to my words.

"Oh." The hopeless defeat in his voice makes me squirm in my seat with guilt.

"I'm so sorry. But I don't think I can give you *that* tonight." This is the first time I'll be having sex, and even though I know I love Levi, something is telling me to wait.

"Yeah, okay," Levi responds dejectedly and sits back in his seat. He turns his head and looks out the window, while his left leg bounces up and down. "I thought you loved me, Dakota." He doesn't turn his head to look at me, and the knot in my stomach tightens even more. He's disappointed in me, but I'm not ready to give him my virginity. I can't do something that doesn't *feel* right.

"Can you please wait for me?" I move my hand to touch his arm, hoping he won't hate me.

He takes a deep breath and slowly his shoulders move up and drop as he expels the air. Levi turns to look at me. His features don't seem harsh, "Of course I can wait," he responds and leans in to give me a small kiss on the forehead.

Suddenly the butterflies leave my stomach and I let out a ragged breath. "I'm sorry if I've lead you on." I slide my hand down to his so we can link our fingers.

"Don't worry about it. We've been together for seven months now and I thought it was time. But I can wait, I suppose." He trails his fingers up and down my bare arm while leaning in to kiss my temple. "It'll be fine," he mumbles against my forehead.

We arrive at the prom and can hear the thumping of the music from the street. As we walk in, I let out a soft gasp, taking in the brightly colored decorations transforming our usually drab gym into a place of magic.

"Let's get a photo together," Levi says as he pulls me toward one of the four photo booths already set up.

"Like we haven't had enough." I laugh, referring to the scene with Mom as Levi leads me to a booth.

We spend a few moments taking pictures, and head over to where our friends are sitting.

"Hey," Jordan sings out as she stands and gives me a hug. "You look beautiful."

"Thanks, Jordan, but your dress is killer! Crap, check out how low that V is." I point to where the point of the V stops, inches above her navel. Jordan is one of my best friends. There are four of us in our group;

Jordan, Lindsey, Mariah, and me. We're incredibly close, and have no secrets between us.

"I know," she coyly responds. "Aaron can't keep his hands off me." Aaron is Jordan's boyfriend and one of Levi's friends from the basketball team.

"Hey." I look over to Levi and see Reece has arrived. Reece is Levi's best friend and those two do practically everything together. They hang out all the time and play ball after school and even on weekends. Reece's gaze slowly roams over me, and I feel a rush of heat travel up my spine. "You look breathtaking, Dakota," he says as he leans over to give my cheek a light peck.

"Thank you." I glance behind him. "You're not here with anyone?"

"Nope." He smiles. "The person I like doesn't even know I exist." His words are full of sorrow. The worst part though, is that he's clearly accepted this as fact.

"You should fight for what you want," I respond.

"Yeah, fight for it," Levi adds, then turns to give me a wink.

"Anyone want a drink?" Reece asks and moves from foot to foot, suddenly looking uncomfortable being here.

"Grab me a Coke," Levi says. "Want anything, babe?" he asks me.

"Any type of soda please."

Reece looks at me, then Levi. "One soda coming up." He smiles at me. "You can get your own," he says, playfully punching Levi's shoulder as he turns to get us a drink.

"Get me a drink, dick!" Levi yells at Reece and Reece turns to flip him off. "Asshole," he mumbles before jogging after him to catch up.

"Oh my God. Look at Mr. C." Jordan stares over my shoulder as I sit next to her. Just as I turn to look, Lindsey comes to sit with us. "Hey." Jordan and I smile at her.

"Who are we looking at?" Lindsey asks.

"Mr. C," Jordan answers.

Lindsey shivers but looks toward Mr. C, who's over in the far corner staring at us. "Oh crap," Lindsey says and looks away. She giggles and her hand covers her mouth as her shoulders come up, looking like she's been caught staring at the cute guy at the mall.

"He creeps me out." A shudder of grossness and revulsion runs over me. "There's something off about him."

"Last week, Aaron and I went to the movies and he was there. It's freaky," Jordan says as she sneaks a look over at Mr. C.

"That's why we call him Mr. C and not Mr. Collins. The C is for creepy." Both Lindsey and Jordan laugh.

"You know, I went to the mall the other day, and I swear to God, I saw him sitting in a car in the parking lot just outside the mall. It wasn't his car, it was another one. He was just sitting there, not doing anything. I waved to him, and he looked right through me. It was like he didn't see me, but I know he did," Lindsey says, her face contorting with disgust.

"Yuck." I pretend to gag and can feel my forehead scrunching.

"Here's your drink, Dakota." Reece hands me a cup of soda and sits opposite me. Levi sits beside him.

I thank him and place the cup on the table in front of me.

"Oh I love this song! Let's go dance." Lindsey eagerly stands and seductively moves her body on the spot. "Come on, this is our prom!"

As Jordan and I head out to the dance floor, I turn back to see both Levi and Reece staring at us. Blowing a kiss to Levi, he catches it and sends one back. "You two are so cute together," Lindsey says when we get to the dance floor.

"Yeah I know," I respond with a smile, because really, I do know how lucky I am to have him.

"You two are going to finally have sex tonight, right?" she asks in a lower tone.

Shaking my head I look down at the floor to avoid the look I know she's giving me. "I'm not ready."

"How can you not be ready? You've been with him practically forever. Even Aaron and I have done it. Just do it and get it over with." Lindsey nods in agreement with Jordan's words.

"Hey, what are you girls talking about?" Mariah asks as she joins us on the dance floor.

"Dakota doesn't want to have sex with Levi." Lindsey fills her in. "Hell, if you're not going to have sex with him, I certainly will," she playfully taunts. But I know she'd never betray me like that. We're all tight, like sisters. "He's mighty fine, he is." She looks at me pointedly.

"I know. But, I'm not ready," I say again for all their benefit. "Anyway, we talked about it on the way over here. He was really good about it and said he understood."

The girls all nod and sigh, telling me how lucky I am that he's so understanding. The discussion about Levi and me finally wraps up and we spend the next four songs dancing and having the best night of our lives. Mr. C is around, standing in the corner looking creepy, and a few other teachers are all walking around ensuring the night is problem-free. Mrs. Walker, our English teacher, is standing by the drinks table making sure no one is spiking anything with alcohol.

"I'm really hot, I need a drink," I say to the girls while fanning myself.

"I'm going to keep dancing," Mariah says and the other two agree with her.

I leave the dance floor and head toward our table. Everyone's gone, and the table is completely isolated. Picking up my soda I look around the gymnasium, checking everyone out. Mr. C has moved from the corner and is mingling around the students dancing. I see Levi over on the other side talking to some of the guys on his basketball team. He sees me, and blows me a kiss. *He's the cutest, sweetest guy ever.*

I'm so thirsty I down my soda all in one go.

Putting my cup back on the table, I sit and watch the others dancing for a few minutes. Still feeling thirsty, I make my way over to the drinks table and grab another soda.

Mrs. Walker watches me as I pour a drink into a new cup. "Having fun?" she asks once I've had a sip. "You're not dancing?" she questions, looking from me and my friends.

"I was dancing with the girls, but I'm so hot and thirsty I'm taking a few minutes out. Then I'm going straight back out with my new dancing shoes." I lift my dress slightly to show her my gold strappy heels.

"Very cute," she responds with a smile, staring at my heels. The music changes into another fast track and Mrs. Walker does a small shuffle on the spot. I have a giggle at her because she's getting into the music.

Heading back to the table, I decide to relax for a few minutes before I join my friends back on the dance floor. I'm sitting, sipping my soda, when suddenly I'm overcome with an awful queasy feeling of lightheadedness. "What the hell?" I mumble to myself. I must've overdone it on the dance floor. I grip the edge of the seat as my head starts spinning. Trying to swallow through my parched throat, I grab my first empty glass and get every last drop out of it, then lift the second empty glass and try to get every drop from that, too.

I bring my hand up to my forehead to wipe away the sweat forming and notice my face is on fire. My body is still heating up and my head spins around and around. The music begins to blur while colorful spots are forming everywhere I look. *I don't know what's happening to me.*

I need to get some water on my face and some fresh air in my lungs. My stomach churns as my head whirls, losing my grip on what's going on.

Making a beeline for the bathroom, I push through the door and go directly to the sink. Splashing cold water on my face, I try and focus on the girl's reflection in the mirror, but I can't see her clearly. She's jumbled and doesn't look anything like me. Her face is pasty and white, her eyes are bloodshot, and she looks like a shadow of the girl I'm used to seeing.

Air . . . I need air. My lungs feel like they're starving for it; my throat is closing on the air I'm attempting to breathe. *I can't get enough air into my lungs.*

As carefully as I can, I open the door and try to walk out of the bathroom without seeming like I'm stumbling. The teachers will think I'm drunk. I'm not, and I don't want them to call my parents.

Bracing myself against the first chair I find outside the bathroom, I steady myself. *What the hell is happening to me?*

"Are you okay, Dakota?" I hear a man ask. Turning I notice Mr. C standing beside me. Looking at him, I try and speak, but my voice fails me. "I said, are you okay?" he asks again while reaching out to grab onto my elbow.

"I need some air," I finally manage to mumble.

Mr. C looks at me, and then looks up and away from me. "Just wait here, I have to go deal with a situation," he says as he drags a chair out and points for me to sit in it. Something's off with him and I don't want him to come back to find me. "I'll be back in two minutes, don't go anywhere." He looks to his left and when I try to focus, I see there are a couple of guys from my class about to get into a fight. I'm trying to focus on them and see what they're doing, but Mr. C's back blocks everything out.

I need air. My body is burning up, my head is fuzzy, and my stomach is roiling with a desperate need to vomit. *Air . . . air . . . air.*

Dragging myself out of the gymnasium and down the hall, I move toward the side doors. But with no one here to help me once I'm outside, I will need to sit for a moment out on the steps leading to the back field and gather myself.

My legs become heavier as I get to the doors. The cyclone taking place inside my head is whirling faster, and my vision is so unclear I can barely make out objects.

Stumbling down the first step, I hardly recognize where I am.

"What's happening?" I think I question.

There's a cacophony of dense sounds; a combination of white noise, mumbling, and a beat which doesn't make sense.

My eyes are now so heavy I can barely keep them open. My legs are completely useless as I attempt to make my way down the stairs. I think I'm going to pass out.

"Well, well, well. What do we have here?" the familiar yet unrecognizable deep male voice says. "Let me get you home." *I know this voice, but it's muffled by fuzz.*

Trying to focus, I start to turn to see who's here with me, but my eyes close.

CHAPTER 2

THERE'S SOMETHING WARM on my face. My mouth is dry and my entire body hurts. Slowly blinking my eyes open, I gaze around me. A bright light coming over the horizon is blinding me, and I can hear the chirping of birds singing to one another.

"Where am I?" I mumble, but no one answers. Turning my head to the left, my eyes try to focus on my surroundings, but I can't make out anything but the color green. "What the hell?" As I blink wildly, the cloud obscuring my vision begins to lift. I finally realize I'm out behind the school, hidden in some shrubs about fifty yards away from the bleachers. The sun is slanting at an angle that tells me it's still early morning. "What?" I sit up slowly, and a spike of pain shoots up my back and into my abdomen at the exact same moment.

My body tenses with fear and confusion. I have no idea what the hell I'm doing out here, or even how I got here. Finding some strength in my legs, I manage to maneuver my body so I'm on all fours. Once I finally find my balance and stand, I'm keenly aware of the intense pain shooting through various parts of my body.

Brushing my fingers against my face, I wince in pain when I reach the side of my neck. "What is going on?" I repeat to myself as I look down at my now torn and tattered green gown. I wiggle my toes and notice I'm only wearing one shoe. I feel the soft, lush, green grass beneath my sole while the ankle strap is still attached, the shoe loose behind me.

Trying to think back to last night, clouds fill my mind. I remember getting ready, Mom taking a lot of photos, and Levi coming to pick me up. I remember dancing with the girls, but I can't remember anything after that.

Did I drink? Is this me hungover? Or am I still drunk?

Did I do something?

As I stumble to where my clutch is tossed, I feel a distinctive pain shooting up from between my legs. I lift my dress to see what could be hurting, and I notice all the blood on the inside of my thighs. My panties are gone, and my legs are heavily bruised with marks I know won't be fading any time soon. "Oh my God!" I gasp as vomit rushes up to burn my throat.

I barely make it back to the shrubs before I start throwing up. Once, twice, three times . . . it keeps coming up, over and over again. I can't stem the nausea.

When the vomiting finally ceases, I'm left with an unsteady panic vibrating through me.

Tears are falling while I lean down to take off my remaining shoe, get my clutch, and start walking home. I'm so embarrassed by what must have happened. I'm not ready to look at my phone and the phone calls and messages I know I must have. I know my parents must be going out of their minds looking for me, but I'll be beyond humiliated to tell them I got so drunk I passed out on alcohol I don't remember having. They're going to be ashamed of me, and disappointed.

I walk home, all the while praying they fell asleep early last night and think I'm home and in bed already. *Please God, don't let them notice I'm not home yet. Please God, please.*

It takes me about fifteen minutes to walk home and when I do, I use my key to open the front door. My heart tightens in my chest as the opening door makes a low creaking sound. I hold my breath, hoping no one has heard me. I feel a rush of blood in my ears as I listen for any slight sound in my house. I finally realize everyone must still be asleep.

Closing the door softly, I scurry to my room as quietly as I can and lock my door behind me. With my back against the cool timber, I slide down until my bottom finds the hardwood floors beneath me. Bringing my legs up, I hug my knees and begin to silently cry again.

Raw feelings of helplessness and anger choke me. *How did this happen to me?*

The handle rattles, and I hear Mom whispering, "She must still be sleeping. Let's go make breakfast; she'll be up when she's ready."

"Okay, sweetheart," Dad answers.

Dad mumbles something about blueberry pancakes as their footsteps go down the hall toward the kitchen.

My thoughts scatter, trying to build a timeline of last night's murky events. But my eyes shift from wall to wall, the haze of the evening is screaming at me preventing any kind of focus. My mind is telling me I'll probably never know the truth. *My heart agrees.*

I stay on the floor trying to figure this out for minutes, or hours. I don't know. But what I *am* sure of is the fact I have no idea what happened last night.

Finally I stand and unzip my dress, and let it fall to the floor. It's covered in blood and grass stains, torn and shredded around the hem. Taking a deep breath shaky with trepidation, I gingerly walk to my full-length mirror. I'm not sure I'm ready to see whatever will face me in the reflective glass. When I'm finally positioned in front of the mirror, I don't dare make eye contact. I'm not ready to see the horrific sight which will be staring back at me.

Taking in and releasing a deep breath, I lift my head to see what the girl in the mirror wants to show me. Clapping a hand to my mouth, I hold in a scream. I want to yell that it's not me. She's nothing more than a figment of my dark imagination, not real.

But she blinks the moment I blink and the tears stream down her cheeks, reflecting the ones running down mine. A pained, muffled cry escapes my swollen lips as I look at the broken girl in the mirror.

Her body is heavily bruised. There are marks all over her legs, with specks of dried blood stuck to her skin. There are bruises around the base of her neck and on the tops of her arms. She looks beyond broken, she looks . . . destroyed.

"My God," I whisper as I look around the room, fearful that someone came in without me noticing. "What happened to me?" Of course the question is rhetorical. No answers appear.

Turning from the girl in the mirror, I grab my dress and scrunch it up, stuffing it in a box as far back in my closet as I can get it. Then I wrap a towel around myself and go to the door. Placing my ear up against it, I listen to the sounds of the morning. I need to make sure no one is near so they don't see me when I come out of my room. When I know Mom and Dad are in the kitchen, and I can't hear Sam, I open the door and quietly pad down the hall to the bathroom Sam and I share.

My senses are in overdrive, and I try to remain invisible. When I get to the bathroom, I quickly close and lock the door behind me. Taking a deep breath I feel my legs become solid again. I can't even move anymore. I'm so scared Mom and Dad will know something has happened by looking at me that my entire body is on high alert. Swallowing hard, I try to calm my pulse as it hammers violently through my veins. "You can do this, Dakota," I encourage myself.

Double- then triple-checking the door's locked, I'm finally able to get into the shower, knowing I'm safe in here. Turning the water to as scalding hot as I can get it, I drop the towel and step into the continuous stream of boiling water. The moment it touches my bruised and painful skin, I let out a small yelp of pain. But I welcome the heat, and hope it has the power to wash the night off me.

Looking around the shower I try and find a cloth to wash my body, but there's nothing in here. Dripping wet, I get out and look under the vanity to see what mom's got here. I find a scrub brush with hard bristles I've seen mom use to clean the bathtub, and I bring it into the shower. Squirting liquid soap on it, I begin by scrubbing my fingers, which leads to my hands, and then all the way up my arms. I can't stop; I need to make sure everything is removed, scoured clean so I have no trace left of what happened last night.

Every body part I touch hurts; every bruise I scrub makes me wince in pain. I dread washing my vagina, but I know I have to. "Oh God," I say to myself as I squirt more soap on the scrub brush. Totally bracing myself I move my hand down. "Ahh," I cry out as I wash off whatever the hell is on me. The heat of the shower is pounding on my back, and tears are flowing down my face.

This hurts so bad. But I have to do it. I have to wash away whatever happened to me. No one can know; no one can suspect. I don't want to know, I don't want to even think about what might have happened. It's too embarrassing. If anyone finds out, they're going to think I'm a slut, and that I was asking for it. I can't have that. I can't let anyone find out. It's beyond humiliating.

Shaking, I continue to clean myself, making sure any trace of what happened is long gone. The only problem is the more I scrub, the dirtier I feel.

"Get off me," I howl while squeezing more soap on the rough bristles. "Get off me!" I keep crying as I try my hardest to clean the filth away.

I stand in the shower for so long that the water begins to cool. I look down at my body to see exactly what I've done to it. I'm completely raw from the hard brush, and some spots are red from where I've scrubbed enough to break skin. "Oh my God," I gasp as I look at the parts of my body which are covered in crimson drops.

Suddenly everything changes while I'm standing under the now cool water. I go from feeling crushing shame and humiliation, to staring blankly at the wall. Small blurring dots dart in front of my eyes as I continue to glare at the tiles on the wall. Not a single thought enters my mind, not even a hint of feeling.

My tears stop and the compulsion to make sure I'm thoroughly clean dissipates at a rapid rate. The cold fingers gripping my throat have melted away. I can't feel anything. I can't think. There is nothing for me to hold on to. I'm icy cold and numb.

As I stand under the shower a realization washes over me. A part of me died last night. Something was taken from me, and I know I didn't give permission for it to be taken. I know what happened now.

I was raped.

CHAPTER 3

I'VE LOCKED MYSELF in my room and pretended I wasn't feeling well, which is the only reason I got away with it. Mom was concerned when I came out in jeans and a long-sleeved sweater, but when I told her I'd danced too much and hadn't drunk enough water, she put it down to me being exhausted.

I don't have the courage or the heart to look at my phone to see who has messaged or called me. I don't want to lie to anyone, so I simply won't look. Instead, I've been in bed all morning with the blankets pulled over my head, trying to forget. But trying to forget isn't easy, especially considering I know what happened, even though I wasn't conscious for it. I keep replaying the evening in my head, looking for any clues that could lead me to the truth. They say knowledge is power, but as I lay in bed, I keep fighting with myself. Do I really want to know, or should I forget about it all and move on with my life?

I'm stuck. My heart is telling me to forget about it, but my head is telling me to try and find the answers. But then, if I do find out what happened, what do I do with the information? Do I go to the authorities? Or do I keep my mouth shut? If I tell the police, will they believe me? What happens if my friends find out? Or worse still, what happens if my parents find out, or even Sam. *My God, Sam.* I would hate to see the disappointment in her eyes if she ever found out. I'm sure Sam would still accept and love me, but what if she didn't? I don't think I could live with myself if I saw anything in her eyes other than the worship she shows me now.

Knock.

Knock.

I don't want anyone coming in, but I know regardless of who is on the other side of the door, they'll start questioning me and will want to know why I'm so withdrawn. "Come in," I call with as much enthusiasm as I can muster. My voice sounds strained and cautious, even to me. Sitting up in bed, I fix my hair, pretending everything is fine while I wait to see who's coming in.

"Hey." Sam excitedly bounces into my room. "How was the prom?" She sits on the end of my bed, and eagerly waits for my answer.

"It was good," I answer, but avoid her eyes.

"Did you and Levi . . . ?" I shake my head, and pick a spot on the blanket to look at. "Phew. I was scared he'd try to pressure you into it."

A soft smile plays at my lips, although I'm only smiling to hide the real feeling of shame. I start picking at a loose thread on the white cotton blanket on my bed. "There was no pressure. He was really good about it."

"I heard Mom and Dad saying you got in late. Tell me all about it. What happened? What were Lindsey, Mariah, and Jordan wearing? Did you look the prettiest? I bet you did. Oh my God, was Reece there? He's sooooo cute." Sam's talking so fast and enthusiastically all her sentences are blending into each other.

"Sam," I say, finally working up the courage to look her in the eyes for the first time since she came in here. "Everyone looked great." Although I try to feign enthusiasm, my tone is flat and dry and Sam immediately picks up on it.

Her shoulders drop and her eyebrows knit together in question. "Did something happen, Dakota?"

Every single hair stands on end and my entire body shivers as a cool breeze touches my exposed skin. "No, why?" I automatically respond, defensive. I close my eyes for a second and regroup. "I mean, no, nothing happened. I just . . ." Crap, what do I say? "I'm really tired. You know dancing and things like that."

"Levi called earlier looking for you, and I told him you were still asleep. He sounded funny, too."

"What do you mean?" I sit up further in bed and painfully cross my legs. *I'm so sensitive.*

"He sounded like he was worried about you. What happened last night? You're acting all weird and he sounded strange. Did you two have a fight or something? Is it because you told him you weren't ready to have sex? You know, you can tell me anything; I promise not to tell Mom and Dad." She reaches out and rubs her hand on my leg. The moment she touches me I flinch, moving my leg away from her hand reflexively. Sam notices and pulls her hand straight back.

My bedroom fills with awkward tension as she looks at me in confusion "Sorry, I'm just tired," I say, dragging my gaze away from the hurt she's obviously feeling.

"Dakota?" I don't dare look at her. "Dakota!" she says again in a stronger voice.

"I'm really tired, Sammy. Can we talk later?" I don't give her an option to say anything more. I turn over on my side, my back to her, and pull the covers up to my chin.

I'm hyperaware of her still sitting on my bed, but I have to keep my shit together until she leaves. My heart breaks. I'm so angry, not at Sam for her questions, but at myself for treating her so badly. She's my little sister and all she wants to do is talk to me. I wish I could tell her, but I just can't. I can't tell anyone.

I feel the bed move, and a few seconds later I hear Sam say, "I don't know what's going on with you, Dakota but you know you can tell me anything, I'll always love you." Then the door quietly closes behind her.

I want to scream at her, to call her back so I can hug her and tell her what happened. But I know I can't. It's too shameful.

Instead I lay perfectly still and my eyes finally close, giving me some peace and quiet.

Knock.

Knock.

Startling awake, I grab the blankets and pull them close to me. "Come in," I call out in a croaky voice.

"Sweetheart, are you going to sleep the day away?" Mom asks as she comes and sits beside me on the bed. "Are you feeling okay?" She puts her hand to my forehead and feels for a fever. "You don't feel warm. What's wrong?"

I look up at her and smile weakly. Degradation and humiliation fills every part of me. I want to burst into tears and tell her what's happened. But I can't, because then she'll look at me differently. She'll think badly of me, and I don't think I could take it. "I'm okay," I finally whisper, choking back the tears threatening to fall.

"You sure?" Mom asks as she strokes the hair off my face. "You look tired." I nod to her and try to paste a smile on my face, though of course it's a fake and sickly sweet. "You must have had a great night last night."

"Yeah," I finally respond after a few seconds of quiet. Better I say very little than risk my voice deceiving me and Mom looking at me as if I'm crazy. No matter how much I want to tell her, I know I can't.

Mom's naturally golden hair is falling gently over her shoulders, her deep brown eyes examining everything about me. I have to put on my 'happy face' and pretend I'm okay. "You sure?" she asks again, trying to determine whatever's bothering me.

I swallow down once, and smile again. "Yeah, Mom, I promise. I'm good."

Mom takes a deep breath and stops playing with my hair. "Okay, I trust you." The moment the word 'trust' is said, I have to hold back the strangled cry of shame. "We're going out for dinner tonight. Just down to Henry's Pizza House. We're leaving in about half an hour."

"I'll be ready," I say, though inside my soul is dying.

"Okay." Mom leans down and gives me a kiss on the forehead. She then leaves my room, and I bury myself back under the covers.

A few moments pass, and I know if I don't get up, Mom will know something is really wrong. So I reluctantly push back the blanket, and get up out of bed. "You can do this, Dakota," I encourage myself. Stumbling over to my mirror, I look at my body where I can see every scratch, bruise, and mark made last night. If I can see them, everyone else will see them too.

Looking at my make-up arranged on my small table, I pick up the concealer and dab it all over the glaringly obvious marks on my face and neck. "Oh my God, I look terrible," I mumble to myself. I begin to layer the make-up on my skin, masking the horrible marks beneath.

By the time I finish, I look halfway like my normal self. Almost like the sixteen-year-old version of me before *last night* happened. But my eyes tell a different story. They tell of sadness, humiliation, betrayal, and guilt. The rock lodged in the pit of my stomach confirms the shame I'm carrying.

Examining myself, I make sure there are no visible marks and that I look somewhat normal. Putting on an air of fake happiness, I take myself out to the family room where Dad is sitting on his usual chair, reading on his tablet. He looks up when I enter the room and a huge smile brightens his face. My throat tightens knowing how deceitful I am being.

Man, now I feel even worse.

"Hi there, princess. How was your prom last night?" he asks as he sits up in his seat and leans forward in anticipation of me retelling my evening.

"It was great," I lie. *Oh God, Dakota.*

I should tell them, get it over with. But, it's too late. I should've done it when I got home instead of waiting for hours.

Everyone will think I'm making it up. Besides, I can't remember anything, so what *can* I say?

More guilt consumes me. I've lied to everyone who loves me. A colossal wave of remorse overtakes me and suddenly I can feel my heart clamoring to get out of my chest, bile sits in my throat, and I shove my hands in my jeans pockets so Dad can't see them shaking.

"Tell me about it. Did you dance a lot?" Dad smiles at me.

"Yeah, too much. I've been really tired all day."

Dad nods. "Was the food nice?"

"Uh-huh. Great. Um, I've got to go to the bathroom before we go for dinner."

"Okay, we'll talk more later."

"Yep," I respond and run to the bathroom. When I get there, I let out a huge breath and drag myself to the mirror. "What are you doing?" I ask myself. Shaking my head I look away from the lying eyes of the girl in the mirror. I can't stand looking at her anymore. She's such a liar. "I'm not a liar; I'm protecting them. I'm protecting me, too," I tell myself.

Finally I'm able to calm myself down enough that I can leave the bathroom. I'll just keep quiet and only answer questions I'm asked. I won't say anything, and tomorrow will be better.

Tomorrow will be a new day. Won't it?

CHAPTER 4

HONEY, ARE YOU okay?" Mom asks when I come into the kitchen to get a juice.

"Yeah I'm fine, Mom." Quickly and discreetly I adjust the long sleeve sweater I'm wearing. Averting my eyes, I pour a glass of juice and turn to leave the kitchen.

"Hey," she calls. Stopping dead in my tracks, I take several deep breaths, plaster a fake smile on my face and turn to Mom. "Are you sure you're okay?" she asks again, this time with worry clouding her words. "You're looking really pale, and you're not wearing what you usually wear to school."

I knew this morning when I woke, everything is going to be different. "Yeah, I know. I just feel like jeans and a sweater." I try to force myself to make eye contact. Instead, I'm looking at the fridge door to the right and behind Mom.

Mom takes a couple of steps toward me, and I have to force myself not to retreat, and not to flinch when she reaches out to tuck some hair behind my ear. "If something's bothering you, you know you can talk to me, right?" her voice is soft and earnest, and I know she's genuinely concerned for me.

"Nothing's bothering me. I'm good." God, I wish I could tell her. To yell and scream at the top of my lungs how what was supposed to be the best night of my life, turned into the scariest nightmare any person could ever go through. The worst part though, is not remembering. "Really, Mom, I'm good. I promise." I lean in and give her a kiss, although I know I'm lying to her.

"Okay. But if you need to talk, I'm always here for you." Smiling at Mom, I step around her, place my glass in the sink and get out of here so I don't break down and cry in front of her.

"Bye," I shout as I close the door. Walking down the garden path I try and get away before Sam catches up to me, because we always either walk or catch the bus to school together.

"Dakota." Crap, she heard me leaving. Speeding up, I pretend I didn't hear her. "Dakota!" I hear her footsteps as she runs to catch me. "Hey, I was calling you," she says once she's caught up to me, puffing.

"Were you? Sorry, I didn't hear anything." I don't dare look at her, she may see my lie.

"You sure you're okay? You're kinda different." Sammy shoots me a sideways look as she ties her light brown hair back in a ponytail. "You've been a bit off since yesterday."

"What the hell is wrong with everyone?" I snap and immediately regret my outburst. "Sorry I shouldn't have said that." Gosh, this is so hard. So much more difficult than I could've ever imagined it would be.

Sammy looks at me sideways again, and takes a step away from me, looking down at her shoes. "S'okay." But her actions speak much louder than her words do.

I have to make this right with her, although I still can't tell her what's happened, I can pretend I'm the way I was before prom night. "How about after school today we go to the mall and we get some frozen yogurt?"

"I'm not ten anymore, Dakota," she teases with a smile. "But, if you insist."

The lightness of Sam and her gentle personality makes me think there's hope for me. But the instant I start to forget, the nightmare returns with the force of a blow and reminds me that I'll always remember.

"Where the hell have you been?" Levi accosts me the moment he sees me and Sammy walking in to school.

"I'll catch you after school," Sam says as she walks ahead of me.

"'Kay," I reply then look to Levi. "I've been at home." I start walking toward class as Levi keeps up with me.

"I know that, Dakota. But what happened to you?"

Putting my head down, I try and make an exit without Levi chasing after me. "Nothing," I answer with no conviction.

"Dakota!" He yells at me. But I pretend not to hear him. I've been doing a lot of that lately. "Fucking hell." He grabs my upper arm and pulls me back against his rock-solid body. "Stop walking away and tell me what the hell happened to you on Saturday night."

I can't bring myself to look at him. There's no truth I can tell him, only lies, lies, lies. *Just like I've been feeding everyone else.* "I felt sick," I finally manage to mumble while keeping my eyes on a piece of chewed gum stuck on the floor.

"You felt sick? So what, you thought you'd leave and not say anything to anyone?" I can see now he's moving from foot to foot, clearly agitated with me. "Why didn't you tell me? I could've taken care of you? Or is this all because you didn't want to have sex with me?"

"What? No." I look up at him for a second, and see the hurt etched across his beautiful face. But as quickly as I looked at him, I avert my eyes again so *he* can't see the secret I'm hiding. "I started feeling really woozy, and I took myself home. I didn't want to ruin anyone else's night." I shrug and chance a quick look at Levi. His face is full of hurt, which makes my stomach roil with guilt and my heart leap into the back of my throat.

"You could've told me, Dakota. I would've taken you home." He takes a hesitant step toward me, and slings his arm around my shoulder. I brace myself, and mentally will my body not to flinch and move away from him. *This is Levi, he loves you.* "Promise me you'll never do that to me again." He leans in and brushes a light kiss to my temple.

Swallowing hard, I nod my head but I can't say the words. It'll make me even more of a liar than I already am.

"Meet at lunch?" he asks as we walk toward our first classes for the day.

"Yeah."

"'Kay, bye, babe." He gives me a chaste kiss on the lips and heads off down the hall toward where Reece is standing by his locker.

The moment Levi's lips land on mine, bile quickly rises to the back of my throat and instantly my stomach knots as I hold in a heave.

Quickly I run to the bathroom, check there's no one in here and lock myself in a cubicle. "Oh my God," I whisper to myself while I sit on the lid of the toilet. Holding my book bag close to my chest I rock back and forth with tears springing to my eyes. "I can't do this."

I sit alone in the cubicle, holding in the tears threatening to fall. It would be a tell-tale sign that I'm not okay. And I can't take anyone asking me, or even suspecting there's something wrong with me.

Taking a few deep breaths, I manage to pull myself together. I know in the next couple of minutes the bell will ring, and I'll have to take myself to my first class of the day, which, unfortunately, is Mr. C's math class.

Standing, I leave the cubicle, wash my hands and head toward class.

"Dakota," I hear his rough voice call me from behind. An icy chill snakes up my spine and I freeze on the spot. "I need to speak with you."

Rooted to the spot, I wait for him to catch up to me. "Mr. Collins," I say in a nervous, small voice.

"What happened on Saturday night? I told you to wait for me and you left. I went looking for you and couldn't find you anywhere."

"I was feeling ill," comes my rehearsed, stoic answer. "I took myself home." I look up to Mr. C's dark, inquisitive eyes.

"How did you get home?" I feel like he's interrogating me. "Did you call your parents?"

"I walked."

"By yourself, at night?"

"Yes, sir."

I see his jaw flex and he runs his hand over his short, crew-cut hair. "You're telling me you walked home on your own?"

"Yes." I look away from him and defensively tighten my grip on the book bag against my chest. "I did."

"I came back to the office, found your number and tried calling you. You didn't answer your phone. I even got in my car and drove to your home."

Shit. "Why would you do that?"

"Because you looked like you were going to pass out, and I was concerned for you. I looked everywhere, Dakota. I went out to the bleachers, checked there, I asked your friends."

He was at the bleachers? They're only a few feet from where I woke. "You went to the . . ." I stop myself in time, because if I say 'bleachers' he may know something more than he's letting on. *Oh God, could it be him?* "You went looking for me?" I regain my composure and try to watch him for any signs. Signs of guilt, sorrow, something. But his eyes are steely, and don't give anything away.

"I did go looking for you," he finally says. "But I couldn't find you."

"I was fine."

"You didn't look fine to me." He reaches out to touch my elbow, and automatically I retreat with my gaze falling to his outstretched hand. Quickly he shoves it in his pocket and his left eye twitches as he presses his lips to form a thin, strained line. The bell sounds and I cautiously back away from Mr. C. There's a look of confusion on his face, as his eyebrows knit together. "Get to class," he calls after me.

Breaking into a run I get to his class, and sit in the back far corner, not really paying attention to anyone in the class. Mariah's in this class with me, and although she said 'hi' to me when I came in, I haven't acknowledged her yet.

Mr. C is damn creepy. He knows something, and isn't saying what.

He waltzes into class, closes the door and his eyes go directly to me. "Good morning, class. I trust you all had a good time at your prom? Considering there's only a couple of weeks of school left, I could go easy on you and give you light work to do."

There's happy chatter in the class.

"But I'm not that nice. So open your books, page one hundred and fifty-five."

The chatter turns to groans. Opening my book, I focus on the work and ignore everything and everyone. I have to get through this class, then I can get out of here. And hopefully breathe easy again.

CHAPTER 5

"**WHAT HAPPENED TO** you?" Lindsey asks when I sit at our table at lunch. "Huh? When?" I play dumb and hope they'll drop the questioning.

"On Saturday night. Where did you disappear to? I tried calling you, and someone said they saw you walking home."

My head instantly turns to Lindsey. "Who said they saw me walking home?"

She shrugs her shoulders. "I don't know. I was asking around to see if anyone had seen you, and people were saying they hadn't. Levi was going out of his mind looking for you, and Reece took off running toward your place. Mr. C even asked where you were."

I shudder when Lindsey mentions Mr. C's name. "I went home to sleep. I started getting sick, and I knew I had to get into bed."

"You ignoring me?" Mariah asks as she sets her lunch tray down and sits opposite me.

"What? No."

"I was trying to get your attention in math, and you were ignoring me. What's up with that, Dakota?"

"I'm sorry, my mind's been wandering all day."

"She went home on Saturday," Lindsey says to Mariah.

"Oh," Mariah responds and lifts her eyebrows at me. "Why?"

Before I have a chance to answer, Lindsey says, "Because she was 'sick'." And actually uses air quotes as if to emphasize her disbelief.

"Did you get drunk?" Mariah leans in to listen to my response. "Why didn't you tell me you were bringing alcohol? How did you sneak a drink and not get caught?"

"I wasn't drunk. I just felt like I was going to be sick." I leave it at that, because the less I say the better it is. "So I walked home."

"In those killer gold heels you were wearing?"

"Um, yeah." I nod and look down at my food tray, pushing everything around and not really eating anything. I lie about them too, because I have no idea where one is, and the other is shoved in the back of my closet, along with my dress.

"Hey, babe." Levi sits beside me, hooking his arm over my shoulder. "What's for lunch?" He grabs the banana from my tray, peels it and eats it.

"I don't know. I'm not really hungry. Here, I haven't touched it." Sliding the tray in front of Levi, he takes it and starts inhaling the food as if he's never eaten before.

Reece sits beside Mariah and clunks his tray down while watching me. I quickly glance at him then back down to my knotted hands. "Are you okay?" he asks quietly once everyone around the table starts talking.

Not saying anything, I simply nod. "Are you sure?"

"Yep." I look up at him and weakly smile. "I'm sure."

Reece's penetrating gaze holds me captive. His strong brown eyes don't let me go. He's looking at me as if he wants to say something, but can't. *Oh God, it's not him is it?* He brings his hand up to his face, and looks sideways at Levi before he whispers, "You look different, Dakota. I can tell something's wrong."

My stomach jumps when he speaks the words, but I calm myself down and try to keep anything from becoming visible. "I'm good." I smile. "I need to go to the bathroom. Excuse me." I stand and grab my bag.

"Hey, where are you going?" Levi asks with a mouth full of food.

"Bathroom." I don't wait to hear if he has anything to add. Instead I get out of there.

As I'm walking out of the cafeteria I see Sophie, a girl in my year sitting at a table near the bin on her own. Her nose is stuck in a book, and she's concentrating hard on not being seen. I recognize it now as how I've been feeling ever since the prom.

I don't know why, because I've never said more than a handful of words to her. But something inside is telling me to go over and talk to her. I plonk my bag on the empty seat opposite her and sit, waiting for her to acknowledge me. Sophie slowly peers over her book at me, and then brings her book back up to cover her face.

"Hi, Sophie," I say. I'm met with complete silence. "I'm Dakota." I stop and wait again.

"I know who you are," she answers without lowering her book. "What are you doing over here? Why aren't you with your *popular* friends, sitting at the *popular* table, talking about all the *popular* things you all do?"

My mood drops as my shoulders slump to reflect how I'm feeling. "I'm sorry." I stand and grab my bag. "Sorry to have bothered you."

I start to walk away when Sophie calls me back. "No, I should apologize. You haven't done anything wrong. Come back." Halting my steps, I turn to her to see she's put her book down. "Come on." She warmly smiles at me.

"Thanks." I sit again and now an awkward silence engulfs both of us. "Have I done something to upset you in the past?"

"Not you . . . but some of them." She flicks her chin in the direction of where I was sitting. "They're not nice. You've only ever ignored me."

Heaviness tightens every pore of my body and ice trickles down my spine as I shamefully avert my eyes. "I didn't realize I'd been ignoring you. I'm sorry."

"It's okay." She shrugs. "At least you know now."

I'm beyond ashamed of the way I've treated her. I know how bullying can effect someone, but I've never stopped to think what silence can do too. "Why aren't you sitting with your friends?" I ask trying to move away from my own embarrassment to something more positive.

"Wow." She lets out a chuckle while looking around us. "You really know how to ignore a person." I feel myself look at her questioningly. "I don't have any friends. No one wants to hang out with me. Usually I spend my time in the library, but sometimes I come in here or go sit out under a tree."

"By yourself?"

"Well, yeah."

"Why don't you have any friends?"

"Doesn't matter why. And don't feel obligated to pretend to be one now." Tears are filling her eyes, and I can tell how hard those words must be. She must be desperate to have someone to hang out with, worse still, she must be hurt that she doesn't. "I haven't had a friend in such a long time, to have one now seems . . . I don't know. Kind of like too little too late." Her shoulders come up as if she doesn't really care. But I can hear the ache in her voice, and I can see the loneliness behind her dark eyes.

"Well, from today, you and I are officially friends. I promise."

"Don't say something you can't follow through on. I'd rather it go back to you pretending I don't exist. I can't deal with any more hurt than I already have."

It's then I see something familiar in Sophie. Her eyes are the same as the ones reflected in the mirror.

Can she be a victim too?

CHAPTER 6

"**YOU READY, LITTLE** sis'?" I ask Sammy as she walks out of school and heads my way.

"I am. Have you let Mom know?"

Damn it. I've left my phone at home, and haven't turned it on since I got home the other night. I can't stomach to look at the messages and phone calls, so I let the battery die and left it at home. I figure, my phone didn't save me from what happened on Saturday, then what's the use of having one? "I forgot my phone at home. Have you got yours on you?"

Sammy takes it out of her pocket and holds it up triumphantly. "Sam to the rescue." She smiles as she dials Mom's number. "Hey, Mom, Dakota and I are going to catch the bus to the mall to get some frozen yogurt." She listens intently to whatever Mom's saying, while I catch myself worrying my lip between my teeth. "I'll tell her." She listens again. "We won't." Sammy rolls her eyes at me and smiles. "We will." She takes a few breaths and I turn, starting to walk toward the bus station. "I love you too, Mom. Bye."

Looking over my shoulder, I see Sam jog toward me. "All good with Mom?"

"Yeah, she said for us not to be too late, and to call her so she can pick us up."

"Cool."

We reach the bus stop in a few minutes and only have to wait a few more for the bus to come. There are lots of kids from school catching the same bus to go to the mall. "Guess what I heard today?" Sammy says in a hushed tone.

Immediately I freeze and the hairs on my arms stand to attention. *Crap, did someone see something? Say something, Dakota!* "What?" I say once the dryness in my mouth is gone.

"Taylor Johnson has the hots for me!" she squeals as quietly as she can.

"Who?"

"Oh my God, Dakota. Taylor Johnson. You know, he's in my grade at school, super cute, wears glasses, kind of really dorky, too. Loves to read." She keeps looking at me as if I've grown two heads. Maybe, that's how I look to her. "You seriously have no idea who he is, do you?" I shake my head and scrunch my mouth. "I've been crushing on him since before Christmas."

I look away for a moment and mentally scan everything she's said about any boy. "Oh, yeah. Taylor. I know who you're talking about now. I thought his name was Calvin."

"Where did you get Calvin from?" She looks at me blankly.

I can't help but start laughing. "You pointed him out after Christmas, and he was wearing Calvin Klein underwear; I know that because you could see the elastic above his jeans. I don't know why, but Calvin has stuck ever since. I know you've spoken about Taylor, but my brain automatically changes it to Calvin."

Sammy shoulders into me and starts to laugh. "You're such a dork, Dakota."

The bus gets to the mall fairly quickly, and most of the students from school file off and go in their separate directions. Sam and I walk toward the frozen yogurt shop, and when we get there we fill our cups with what we want, pay, and sit to eat it.

"So, tell me about the prom," Sam says as she eats some of the yogurt.

"It was fun." The good part I can remember, not the bad part I can't.

"That's it? It was fun? Nothing to add to that?"

"What do you want to know?" I stir the yogurt, mixing all the flavors with unwarranted concentration to avoid looking at her.

Sam has left the spoon in her cup and is twirling her light brown hair around her finger. "Just tell the truth." Those words cut right through to me. It's as if she knows what happened, but is waiting for me to tell her. I can't risk it though. If she doesn't know and I tell her, she'll stop looking at me with so much love.

Shrugging my shoulders I quickly dismiss anything she may be thinking. "There's not really much to tell you. It was fun. The girls and I danced, and had fun. That was it."

"Hmmm," she mumbles, giving me an assessing look. She picks up her spoon and starts to eat her yogurt.

"So tell me about Calvin."

"It's Taylor, Dakota." She rolls her eyes and smiles. The mood swiftly changes and we're back to sisters and the awkwardness disappears. "He's cute. Anyway, Jasmine told me in class today she heard Taylor and Curtis talking in the library and Taylor said he was going to ask me out on a date. He wants to take me to that new movie coming out, you know the one? It's got Rebel Wilson in it. Um, crap, I forgot the name . . .." She palm slaps her forehead as she tries to remember the name of the movie.

"Oh yeah . . . um . . . it's on the tip of my tongue." My gaze turns to outside while I try to recall the name of the movie, and I see a man sitting in a car, talking on his phone, staring right in to the window of the store we're in.

Mr. C.

My body goes clammy while the arctic hand of suspicion blankets me "Crap," I mumble. Sharp thunderbolts of fear rip through my body.

"What is it?" Sam asks as she turns her head to gaze in the direction I'm looking.

I'm paralyzed with fear. Why is he here? "Nothing," I respond as confidently as I can. But I know my tone suggests there's something very wrong.

"Hey look, it's Mr. Collins. Let's go say hi to him," Sam innocently says.

"NO!" I shout so loud a hush falls over everyone in the yogurt store as they all turn to look in our direction. Sam's own features are questioning, as if I've freaked out for no reason. "I mean no, we'd better not. This is his time. He wouldn't want us to disturb him." *Phew, good save.*

"Yeah, I 'spose." Casually she goes back to her yogurt as if I hadn't just had a minor freakout. "Anyway, about Taylor. What do you think, should I go out with him when he asks me?"

With Mr. C in my thoughts, I didn't really understand the question Sam asked me. "Huh?"

"Are you even listening to me? I said, should I go out with Taylor when he asks me, and would you help me with my outfit for the movies? I mean, I don't want to come across . . . you know . . .." She leans in so no one can hear us and looks around before she whispers, "Easy." Sam scrunches her nose in response to her own word.

"If that's what he wants you for then I'm sorry, Sammy. There's no chance in hell I'll let you go." I'm not going to let her go through what I'm going through.

"He's not like that, but I also don't want to give him the wrong impression either. I mean, I'm into him, but I'm not into him enough to do *that* with him."

"Sam, you're fourteen, you shouldn't even be thinking about sex. Just promise me something."

"What?" She scoops the last of her yogurt out and pops it into her mouth.

"Don't give it to the first guy who wants it. There'll be lots more to come along, and besides, you don't want to be known as *that* girl, either."

"I have no intention of having sex until I'm at least sixteen. So you don't have to worry about me, Dakota."

Lord. "Sixteen? You can wait longer; there's no rush."

"How long are you going to wait?"

Cringing, my pulse quickens and I know sweat is beginning to form on the back of my neck. I say the only thing I can, without telling her about what's happened. "Until the right guy comes along."

"So, Levi?" Staring at her across the booth, I simply lift my shoulders. "Are you saying you're not going to have sex with Levi?"

My blood boils as every possible emotion floods me. "I don't think so," I finally manage to say. "I don't think we're right together."

"What? Now I know something's happened. Did he try to force you on Saturday? Because I swear to God, Dakota, if he did . . ." A cherry color floods her face.

"No. God, no. He didn't force me." I close my eyes while shaking my head. "No, he didn't try to force me," I say again with a sigh. It takes me a few seconds to gather my strength and open my eyes. "I'm just saying, it's not something you should do because you're a certain age, or because it's the thing everyone's doing. Have sex when *you* are ready, not when everyone else says it's time."

"Yeah, I know."

"Hey, babe. I didn't know you were coming to the mall," Levi says as he slides into the booth beside me, while Reece sits next to Sam.

"Hey." Reece greets us together. "How are you, Sam?" Once I smile at Reece to acknowledge him, he turns to face my sister and talk to her.

"Yeah, we're just having yogurt then going home," I reply to Levi.

Levi lifts his hand to cup the back of my head, and moves his face down to kiss me. But I pull away and don't let him get the kiss in. "What's wrong?" he asks as he sits back in the seat and stares at me bitterly.

"Nothing." I look over to Sam, and although she's talking to Reece, she's still looking across to Levi and me. "Not here," I whisper as I tell him with just shifting my eyes how my little sister is watching.

Levi stands and straightens his shoulders. "Tomorrow, we gotta talk," he says. "You staying?" he asks Reece. "Bye, Sam." Levi takes off without waiting for Reece.

Reece stands, but before he leaves to go with Levi, he comes around my side of the table, and sits beside me. "You okay?" he asks. His dark brown eyes hold nothing but concern for me.

"I'm fine." I turn to smile at Sam, and avoid Reece's powerful gaze. If I look at him right now, I know he'll see straight through me, and he'll start asking questions.

"You sure?" He stands and slings his school bag over his shoulder.

"Yep." I nervously tuck some fallen hair behind my ear. "I'm good." I quickly look up, smile then look back to Sam.

"See you at school tomorrow. See ya,' Sam." Reece leaves and I suddenly realize a knot has been sitting in my gut. A nervousness, in a calming way, not a bad way.

"He's into you." Sam flicks her stare in the direction of Levi and Reece.

"He's my boyfriend, but I think after that 'we need to talk,' he probably won't be for long."

"Not Levi. I'm talking about Reece."

"What?"

"Reece. He's into you."

My brows pull together in question. "Whatever." Shaking my head and rolling my eyes, I stand and grab my bag. "Come on. Call Mom and tell her to meet us out the front near the cab stand."

"He's into you," she says in a high, sing-song voice. "I'm telling ya,' Reece Hendricks is into you."

"Doesn't matter." We start walking out of the yogurt store and toward where Sam and I will meet Mom.

Sam grabs her phone, and gives Mom a quick call, telling her where we'll be. When she ends the call, she taps me on the shoulder as we near our meeting spot. "Why doesn't it matter?"

"Huh?" I try and play dumb hoping she'll drop the subject, but Sam is so stubborn and she'll keep going until she finally gets an answer.

"Reece." She encourages me with her happy smile.

"What about him?"

"Hello, girls. What are you doing here?" My heart skips a beat when

I turn and come face to face with Mr. Collins.

"We were having frozen yogurt, Mr. C," Sam sweetly responds.

Instinctively I step into her, pushing her to behind me so his eyes are on me and not her. "Mom will be here in a minute to pick us up," I retort while trying to shield Sam.

"I'll walk with you," he says and steps around me to stand beside Sam.

Fuck . . . My mind is turning rapidly as I try and think of something, *anything*, to get him away from us. *And away from Sam.* "Actually, Sam and I need to go into Target to grab a few things before she gets here," I say and tug on Sam's bag to go toward Target and away from Mr. Collins.

"We do?" Sam naïvely asks.

"Yeah we do. Thanks for the offer, Mr. Collins, but we'll be okay."

"I'd feel more comfortable if I waited with you," he says while trying to get us to leave the mall.

"No, we're okay. See you tomorrow at school. C'mon, Sam." I start walking so fast that Sam is almost jogging to keep up with me.

"What happened? We don't have to go to Target."

"Just keep walking, and don't look behind you."

"What? Why?"

"Shhh." We get into Target, and I lead us to where the check-out counters are. There are people milling about here, and if he comes in, I'll have a clear line of sight. The other advantage is the number of people around will make it difficult for him to try anything, whereas the cab stand is more isolated and anything can happen there. I can't take any chances with Sam.

"What's going on?" Sam asks clearly confused and frightened.

"Mr. C freaks me out. Haven't you noticed he's always around and staring. I've got a really bad feeling about him, Sam." My hand flies to my stomach and I can feel the panic etched deeply inside me. "Please, just trust me."

"Of course I trust you, but if there's really something wrong, you need to tell Mom and Dad."

"No! Jesus, Sam, what do I say, 'Hey Mom and Dad, a teacher at school freaks me out, but I have nothing to go on except he seems creepy'? Yeah, good one."

"Then you have to tell Mr. Preston, the principal."

"You're not listening, I can't tell anyone. There's nothing but a feeling in my gut that screams at me that Mr. C isn't who he says he is. Something's really off about him."

I have Sam on edge now, because she keeps looking from me to the entrance of Target as though measuring the distance. I shouldn't scare her like this, but she needs to be vigilant because I don't want for her to be hurt like I was. "Okay, Dakota. We won't tell anyone, but if anything happens, you have to promise me you'll tell Mom and Dad."

"'Kay. I promise." We're interrupted by Sam's ringing phone, and it's Mom to say she's waiting for us. "Listen to me; we make our way out to the car, and don't stop no matter if we see Mr. Collins or not."

"Alright, alright."

We head straight out of Target and speed walk to where Mom's waiting for us. When we get in the car, Mom starts talking to us about school. Sam replies to everything Mom's asking. She's an absolute star, talking to Mom normally as if I haven't completely spooked the crap out of her.

Mom pulls out of the parking area and I keep an eye on everyone around us. I half expect to see Mr. Collins somewhere, staring at us.

Instead I lock eyes with Levi as he's leaning against an outside wall talking to Reece and a few others from school. He holds my gaze as we drive past him, and keeps holding my stare until we're out of sight.

CHAPTER 7

"HEY, SOPHIE," I say when I go to the library at lunch to return a book I've borrowed. "You're in here today?" She's sitting at a table, quietly eating a sandwich while flicking through a book.

"Hi, Dakota," she whispers and then looks around her.

I pull out the chair opposite her, and slide in. She looks at me and squints her eyes. "What?" I ask.

"Truthfully, I thought you wouldn't bother with me again. I thought yesterday was 'let's pretend to like the girl with no friends' day, and by today you'd have gotten over it."

Man that hurts. Like an arrow piercing my heart, and it also shatters my own perception of how I used to be. "Was I really that bad?"

Sophie lifts her shoulders and looks away. It's enough to tell me that's *exactly* how I was. "Anyway, what are you doing here?" She takes another bite of her lunch and waits for me to answer.

"Had to check a book in, and I saw you. Thought I'd come over." I offer her a smile, and pray she sees it's genuine.

"Cool." She looks back down at her book.

I have a feeling she thinks I'm being fake, that I don't care about her. "Whatcha' reading?"

Sophie raises her eyes without lifting her head. A smirk pulls on the corner of her mouth and her left eyebrow arches with derision. It takes her a few moments before she holds the book up for me to see the cover.

"*To Kill a Mockingbird?* Harper Lee? I read somewhere that until recently everyone thought this was her only book. It wasn't until recently they discovered she'd written a sequel called *Go Set a Watchman.*"

Sophie looks at me in wonder, her eyebrows high on her forehead with her mouth partly open. "How do you know that?"

"I remember reading *To Kill a Mockingbird* a few years ago. And I liked it. I haven't read *Go Set a Watchman,* though. Life gets in the way, you know."

"Who knew?" Sophie says. I tilt my head to the side, silently questioning her remark. "Who knew you're kinda cool?"

I can't help but laugh aloud. "Apparently I'm cool."

"Yeah, who knew? Up until this conversation I thought you were one of those girls who drank diet soda and ate two peas so as not to put weight on. Now, I think you're okay."

"Ate two peas? Really?"

"You know what I mean. *One of them.*"

"No, who is 'them'?"

"The girls who don't see anyone except whoever is in their clique. Have the latest of everything, and don't talk to anyone unless they're one of the popular kids."

"Is that how you see us? Or worse, how you see me?"

Sophie lifts her right shoulder. "It's hard not to when I walk past, say hello, and I barely get acknowledged and never spoken to."

Slumping in my seat I can't help but look away, embarrassed. "Sorry, we're like that. I never realized. If I knew I would've . . ."

"Well you know now, so let's move on. Anyway, shouldn't you be at cheerleading practice?"

"I didn't feel like going. I told the girls I wasn't feeling well. There's only a couple of weeks of school left so it doesn't make that much of a difference." If it does, they'll probably give me a warning before telling me they no longer want me on the cheerleader squad. But in all honesty, I don't think I care anymore.

"Whoa, we got a rebel on our hands."

"Something like that." I half-heartedly smirk.

"Hey, what are you doing here? I've been looking everywhere for you. Why aren't you down in the cafeteria?" Levi says as he leans against the table Sophie and I are sitting at. He looks over to Sophie, scans her dismissively then looks back to me.

"Levi, this is Sophie, Sophie this is Levi."

"I know who she is," he says flatly, quite rudely.

"Pleased to meet you," Sophie adds with a fake smile.

"Whatever. C'mon, babe, let's go 'cause I wanna talk to you."

Taking a deep breath, I stand and push my chair in under the desk. "I'll catch you later, Sophie."

"Yeah, I'll see you around," she says while giving Levi a look I can only describe as a 'stink eye.'

When Levi and I leave the library he turns to me and asks, "What's her problem? And why the hell are you hanging out with her and not at our table? Don't you know Slutty Sophie has a reputation? You don't want people to associate you with *her.*"

"What?" I look up at him as we walk down the stairs toward the cafeteria. "That's a horrible name, why would you call her that?"

"That's the name the guys call her because she got so drunk at a party one night, she was letting guys do whatever they wanted to her."

"What?" I question as we keep walking. "That's not the girl I know."

"And you know her real good, do you?" He snarls at me over his shoulder, his face morphing into disgust. "What the hell's happened to my girlfriend? What happened to you, Dakota?"

"What?" My fingers begin to tingle as I become hyperaware of my reaction to Levi and his statement. I can't let him know about Saturday night. "I'm still me," I say with a shaky tone. *You can do better, Dakota.*

"Look." He stops walking and takes a step closer to me. We're in the isolated hallway leading up to the cafeteria. Dehydration hits my mouth instantly and I try to keep swallowing through the dryness. Levi leans into me, and I take a step back. He keeps coming toward me, and I keep moving back. My back hits the exposed wall, and my thin t-shirt does nothing to shield me from the cold bricks. My body shivers as Levi cages me against the wall by bringing both his arms up to lean against the wall on either side of my head.

I start to breathe heavily and my heart is hammering, desperate to rip through my chest wall. *Oh God, what is happening?* "What are you doing?" I manage to whimper. Even to me, I sound pathetic; as if I'm frantically trying to hold onto the sane part of me.

Levi gets within an inch of my face. His breath touches the tip of my nose, his wild eyes looking straight through me. *Please don't let him see.* Closing my eyes, I move my head to the side. "I knew it," he says, still really close to me. "I fucking knew it." His tone changes as he almost spits the words out. "You were never going to have sex with me, were you, Dakota?"

My eyes spring open and I turn to look at him. "That's not true. Honestly, I was going to, but I got so nervous and I couldn't because it didn't feel right." Levi is shaking his head, while his face and angry eyes scream at me without using any words. He pushes off the wall and starts pacing in front of me. "I'm sorry, Levi. I'm not ready." *And now I'm not sure I ever will be.*

"So that's it? I just have to wait? We've been going out for months, seven of them to be exact, and you're still 'not ready'? I've never once pressured you, I've never once given you an ultimatum, have I?" he spits toward me.

"No, you haven't," I whisper and look down at my feet. Regret washes all the way through me. "Maybe, if you can give me more time . . ." I offer, although I don't think I'll ever be ready. Not after what's happened.

"More time?" He stops pacing and turns to look at me. Of course, my head is still lowered, but I can see his Nikes in front of me. "You want more time? Everyone else is having sex with girls who've been going out with them for far less time than you and I have. What makes you so special that I have to wait?"

Anger slowly rises through me, and I can't help but notice how he's now trying to pressure me. "You know what, Levi?" I lift my head, pull my shoulders back and take a step off the wall. "I'm not ready and I'm not sure when I will be. If you want to wait, wait. But if you don't, then find someone else, because I'm not having sex with you until *I'm* ready."

Levi's shoulders sag slightly, as he takes a step back from me. "Maybe I will," he says in a way that is intended to make me quiver. "How do you like that, Dakota?" he spits toward me.

"Fine, then. Go. Enjoy yourself," I say sarcastically. "Have fun, and remember to wrap it up or it'll fall off." I step away from him and go toward the cafeteria.

"We're over. You hear? We. Are. OVER!" he yells toward my retreating back.

I shake my head and go straight toward the cafeteria, but make a pit stop in the bathroom. Locking myself in one of the cubicles I do the only thing I can.

I cry.

CHAPTER 8

"HEY, I HEARD Levi broke up with you today?" Sam says as she leans against my open bedroom door.

"Something like that." I sit up in bed, pat the covers for Sam to come and sit down with me. "I was going to tell you."

"Yeah, I don't like really hearing things about you second hand from others. Makes me think we're not friends." She scrunches up her mouth and looks down at her knotted hands. "We *are* friends, aren't we?" She looks up at me, and I see her eyes are brimming with tears.

"We're more than friends. We're *best* friends, Sammy" I say as I move to engulf her in a hug.

"Then why can't you tell me what's going on?" Her words hurt me. They tear me apart, and I can't look at her. I'm filled with so much shame, and so much remorse that I just can't tell her what happened.

"I don't know what you're talking about," I say with no conviction whatsoever. We both know, by my tone, I'm holding something back from her. The words I should tell her are stuck. They're firmly wedged in the back of my throat because telling her I was . . . *assaulted* brings so much shame. I can't even bring myself to think about saying the 'R' word. There's a stigma to it, and an even worse one attached to the knowledge that it happened to someone you know.

"One day, Dakota, I hope you can trust me enough to tell me." She stands from my bed, gives me a weak, hurt smile and leaves closing the door quietly behind her.

There's only one emotion dominating me right now—sadness. I'm completely heartbroken to be pushing away the one person who had always had my back.

I should tell her, get it out there and let her know what happened to me, so she knows what to do. But if I tell her, she'll act differently around me, as if I'm wounded . . . broken. No, I can't tell her. I need to keep her from knowing. Once she knows, it'll be a huge responsibility on her shoulders. And what if she tells Mom and Dad? She'd never betray me on purpose, but knowing your sister has been assaulted? That's a whole different burden.

Pulling the covers over my head I close my eyes and pray. Pray for the world to disappear forever. But that's being selfish. I can't wish that on everyone else, all I can do is wish these things for myself.

Maybe if a sinkhole formed under my bedroom I could disappear and never have to look anyone in the eye. Shame would never surface again, and neither would the emptiness and self-loathing that hasn't left me since I woke on Sunday morning.

I'm still trying to hold on to any part of the old me, but it's all been ripped away. Taken, stomped on, and tossed aside as if I was never really worth anything to begin with.

My Mom often says to Sam and me, "The sun will rise and the sun will set." Up until today, I never really knew what she meant by it. Of course the sun will rise and set; it's inevitable. No matter what happens in the world, there's always going to be a tomorrow. I can't help but wonder if I should let this go and get on with my life as if nothing happened.

Or should I trust in myself, in my family, my friends, and the law and tell them all what happened Saturday night?

Is it too late?

Of course it is.

I should've said something earlier; I shouldn't have waited. If I tell them now, they'll think I had a willing part in it, that I was asking for it, they'll think I'm trying to lay blame elsewhere, when the blame lies with me. They'll think I'd been drinking, and because of that, I was definitely asking for trouble. But I hadn't been drinking. I can't remember having anything but soda. All I remember was dancing, feeling weird, then waking up outside near the bleachers.

Dear God, please help me. Help me remember or help me forget. Just please, help me.

"I can't do this anymore," I whisper to myself. "I just can't."

"Dakota!" Sammy bursts into my room as if a nationwide crisis is unfolding.

"What?" I snap while pulling myself up into a sitting position. I try to wipe the stray tears from my cheeks before she sees them.

"Are you crying?" she asks coming further into my room.

"It doesn't matter." I notice her phone in her right hand, the screen bright. She's obviously come in to show me something. "What is it?" I move my eyes to her phone then back to look her in the eye.

Sammy looks out my bedroom door, then closes it quietly. "Is there something you want to tell me?" She's holding her phone and my body stiffens at the way she's holding it. There's something on there she doesn't want me to see, but she's not telling me what it is.

"No," I mumble. But what I want to do is scream, at the top of my lungs. To yell and shout and cry. I want to tell her, but I can't.

"Dakota." Her shoulders slump, and her face falls.

Oh no, she knows.

Instantly I lower my head, and don't let Sam see the truth behind my lying eyes. "No," I repeat. My voice is strangled and no actual sound comes out, just a muffled groan.

"Dakota." She sits next to me on the bed. Reaching out, she places her hand on my leg and gently squeezes. "I know."

Those two words cause an avalanche of emotions to erupt. They have the power to rip a person's soul apart, or to put them together again.

I purse my lips tight, fearing if I open my mouth nothing but a pained cry of raw hurt will escape. Tears are dripping down and I use my hair to cover my face, a veil protecting me from the disgust I'm sure is etched deep on my sister's face.

"Dakota," she softly whispers.

I shake my head and don't say anything. I don't want her to know. I hate that she does. I hate knowing she'll look at me like I'm less than nothing. I hate it. Hate everything. Hate myself. Hate my life. Hate this happened to me.

Throwing my covers back, I spring out of bed, and run. I run out of my bedroom, out the front door and down the street. I keep running, completely unaffected by the fact I'm running with no shoes. My hair is swinging from side to side and, as the cool night air smacks me in the face. The cold asphalt is coarse against the soles of my feet, and I have no doubt that soon, my feet will be bleeding.

But, I don't care. I need to get away from Sam. *From her knowing.*

Hot tears stream down my cheeks. From the outside I must look like a girl jogging, on the inside, though, I'm a broken girl trying to get away from herself.

My breath rasps in my throat as my feet take me far away from where I once thought I belonged. The streets are dark, isolated and though it is early evening the night sky is blacker than normal.

My legs take me to a park a few blocks over, and when I get to its secluded green gardens I fall to my knees. Bringing my hands up to cradle my face I do the only thing I can do. I cry. A storm of emotions keeps building, a whirlpool of rage and hurt mix together.

My tears cease and I look up to the full moon in the dark sky. "ARGHHHH!" I yell. The scream so deep, the sound so forceful my ribs vibrate against my chest. I keep screaming. My throat dries out, and my chest heaves as I gasp for air. With every part of me exhausted, I collapse to the ground. My body is spent. My rage has been consumed by so many other emotions, and I curl into a protective ball.

Shame.

Self-hatred.

Embarrassment.

Fear.

Laying on the grass, the heaviness that was so prominent earlier lifts from my body, replaced by a warm body whose arms tighten around me.

"I love you, Dakota," the girl whispers. The girl, of course is Sam. "I'm so sorry." She kisses my forehead while her arms tighten around me.

We lay on the grass, with our arms wrapped around one another. No words are spoken. No promises are made; no lies are told. *We just are.*

Wetness is soaking my t-shirt, and I know Sam's crying too. Not for herself, but for me. She hasn't asked any questions yet, but I'm sure she already knows. *She's always been the smart one out of the two of us.*

When her tears have stopped, and we are still wound around each other, I feel her chest heave a huge breath. "I got two messages," Sam finally says. I don't respond, I simply listen as I pet her hair and hold her tighter to me. "The first one said, 'Your sister is a whore.'"

Swallowing the huge lump in my throat, I attempt to hold back the tears because I really need to hear what she has to say.

"I wouldn't usually reply to anyone who'd say something like that, but I did. I said to them, 'I don't know you, you have the wrong number.' Because it came from a cell number I didn't know. Right away, I got a reply."

My heart jumps wildly, goosebumps crawl all over my skin and my eyes prickle with barely-contained tears. "What . . ." I cough to get the roughness out of my throat. I take a huge breath, close my eyes and ask the question, "What did the second message say?"

"It didn't say anything, Dakota."

My eyes snap open, while my eyebrows furrow tightly together. "I don't understand."

"It was a photo."

What the hell? "A photo? Show me." Encouraging Sam, I move her off me and sit up on the grass. Sam positions herself so she's sitting opposite me, our knees touching while we both huddle over her phone.

"I wanted to delete it, but I already saw it. I can't get that image out of my head. It's scary. It made my stomach churn."

Oh God, please, please don't let it be bad.

"Show me." I watch as her finger hovers over the bottom of the screen so she can slide it open. She's hesitating. I know she is by the way her finger is lingering over her phone. "Just show me," I say again softly.

"I didn't believe whoever it was, but then . . . this came through." She swipes the phone on, and goes to her message icon. "Here." She hands me her phone and immediately looks down at the triangle of grass caught under her crossed legs.

"Oh," I gasp as I take the phone and see what it is she's seen. My hand comes to my mouth as I hold in the screams threatening to break through. "Shit," I whisper.

"I want to beg you to tell me it's not you, but there's no denying it is."

Even with blurred vision, it's obviously me. There I am, lying on the grass, in my beautiful green gown with my arm thrown over my face, my dress hitched up, with my lower half exposed. Dropping Sam's phone I bury my head in my hands to cover my shame, and my tears. "Shit," I whimper between my heavy tears.

"What happened, Dakota?" Sam rests her hand on my thigh and rubs it in gentle circles. "You had sex? You could've told me."

Gathering my strength, I shake my head. "It's not that," I say. Swallowing down the bile and trying my hardest to hold onto the little pride I actually have left, I lift my head from my hands.

"What is it?" Sam tilts her head to the side and offers me a reassuring smile. "You can tell me anything."

"Promise me you won't tell anyone, including Mom and Dad."

"I promise," she quickly agrees.

"No, Sam. Not like that. *Promise me.*"

"I promise," she repeats herself.

"Sam. This is serious. I don't even want to tell you, I would never have said a thing if it wasn't for that disgusting picture."

"You're scaring me, Dakota. Just tell me." She squints her eyes as she knits her eyebrows together.

"You have to promise me."

"Sister first and always." She crosses her heart. "I promise I won't say a word."

"On prom night, I blacked out and woke up early the next morning out by the bleachers. My panties were missing, and so was one shoe. I don't remember anything at all, except I had, and still have bruises all over my body. And I had dried blood on the inside of my legs."

"Oh my God, Dakota! We *have* to tell Mom and Dad."

"NO!" I yell, but quickly try and calm myself. "You promised me, Sam. You can't say anything."

"You said you don't remember anything. What exactly *can* you recall?"

"Um." I look at her and notice the pleading look in her eyes. "The last thing I remember is dancing with the girls."

"Nothing after that?" I shake my head and look down at my now knotted fingers. "I have to ask. Were you drinking alcohol?"

"Don't be stupid, Sam. There were teachers everywhere. Anyway, I only had a soda." An epiphany hits. "Oh my God. A soda. I remember there was the soda Reece brought back for me." Standing I begin to pace.

"Reece gave you a soda? I don't get it."

"He asked if anyone wanted a drink." As if I'm watching my prom in rewind, I see him hand me a drink. "He asked and I said I'd like a soda. Levi told him he wanted a Coke but Reece flipped him off. They came back a few minutes later and Reece gave me my soda before the girls called me over so we could dance."

"Is that all you had? One soda?"

I rake my left hand over my face and through my hair, tugging on the silky strands as I reach the ends. "That's all I remember. Everything else is hazy. Until I woke, I can't remember anything else."

"What do you mean by hazy?"

"More like blank. Like a sheet went over me after I had the soda Reece bought over, and it didn't lift until I woke the next morning."

"Dakota, that's not right. Something isn't adding up." Sam is on her feet now and leaning against a park bench. "You didn't drink, so you can't say you were drunk. Maybe you were drugged."

"I don't know how. I didn't take anything anyone gave me."

"Dakota?" she says in a serious tone and looks at me with her chin tipped up and her eyebrows high.

"I didn't!" I protest. "I swear, I didn't take any drugs."

"Not voluntarily," she says quietly. "But you did have a drink."

It all comes crashing down, answering the 'how' question from my prom night. "Crap," I whisper. Sam's face tells the story rumbling around inside me.

"You must have been drugged. It was in your drink."

"I was drugged." My feet suddenly stop pacing and I freeze on the spot. "Shit."

"Yeah, Dakota . . . shit."

CHAPTER 9

"**L**ET'S GO OVER this again," Sam says when we get back to my room and have closed the door.

"We've been going over it for the last half hour. I can't remember anything else." I sit cross-legged on my bed, and Sam sits opposite me.

"Reece went and got you the drink."

"Yes," I confirm.

"And did you have some straight away?"

Scrunching my eyebrows together I try to recall what happened that night, step-by-step. "I'm fairly certain he handed it to me, then Lindsey said we should dance. I put it on the table and then, Jordan and I went out on the dance floor." My hands are going through the motion of accepting the drink and putting it on the table. I'm staring at the corner of the bed as I replay what happened from my clouded memory. "Yeah, that's what happened." I look to Sam as she's watching me closely.

"So, Reece handed you the drink. He got it for you? And you said at the park Levi went with him. And you didn't have any of it before you went to dance."

"Yep, that's right."

Sam takes a deep breath, the right side of her mouth pulls up in an agonizing grimace. "Something's not right, Dakota. It's off, like weird, you know?"

"Tell me about it. Reece gave me the drink, but Levi was with him."

"Yeah, which means they'd be in it together if it was one of them."

I balk at the thought of either of them doing anything like this. "It makes no sense, why would Levi do this to me considering I was going to have sex with him."

"Did you tell him you wanted to wait, like you said you were going to?"

"Yeah, I told him in the limo on the way to the prom and he was understanding. Well, he was kinda pissed to start, but got over it quickly."

"What about Reece?"

"What about Reece?" I repeat the question to Sam. "Reece is super sweet, there's no way he'd do this." Frustrated, I jump off the bed and pace around my room. "Listen to us. We're trying to accuse everyone, when it really could've been anyone." Suddenly I stop and turn to look at Sam. "Oh my God, Sam. What if it wasn't meant for me? What if it was meant for someone else?"

Sam shakes her head. "How many times have we watched the news to see a girl's been attacked, Dakota? Whoever did this knew exactly what they were doing and targeted you specifically."

I begin pacing again and there are a million thoughts running through my mind. "Crap."

"What?" Sam looks at me questioningly.

"If what you say is true; if it *was* a targeted attack, then who's to say it was a student? It could just as easily have been a teacher."

"A teacher?" She scratches her chin with a look of absolute disgust on her face. "But that's . . ." She shudders and grimaces. "That's seriously messed up. Ugh."

"I'm thinking about a specific teacher."

Her gaze is fixated on the corner of my bed then slowly she lifts her eyes to meet mine. Realization quickly sets in. "You mean Mr. Collins?" I nod my head. "You can't go saying things like that about a teacher, Dakota."

She's right I can't but something about Mr. C isn't right. "I know, I know," I sigh. Taking a huge breath, I go and sit beside her on the bed. "I haven't looked at my phone since Saturday night. Maybe I should see who's tried calling and messaging." I get up and go to the nightstand where my phone is still plugged in and charging. "Damn it, Sam, I don't want to look at this."

I hold my phone in a feeble attempt not to buckle under the pressure of what might be on it. "I'll do it," Sam offers. "There's nothing on here that can shock me. So . . . I'll do it."

"You know what I'm scared of, right?"

"Whoever sent me *that* picture, has probably sent it to you too."

I desperately want to look but I'm terrified of what might be there. Dread is bubbling away inside me, and panic prickles from my scalp down to my toes. "I'm not sure I can do this," I whisper while still holding the weightless phone to my chest. "It hurts, Sam." I look at her and see the same pain I'm feeling reflected in her eyes.

"I know it does, but it has to be done." I nod, agreeing with her. "I'll do it." She holds her hand out to me, silently asking for the phone.

Hesitantly, I unfold the arm hugging my phone close to my chest. It takes me forever to find my courage, so long that I'm sure the moon is at its highest point for the evening. I know it's not. Reality is outside of time for me now. "I'm not sure I can do this." Gripping the phone I pull my hand back hastily. "I can't."

"You have to know what's going on. We don't want to be surprised if anything is said in there." Sam points to my phone. "Let's get this over and done with."

She's right. She's *always* right. "I'll do it," I say taking a huge breath. "Okay." I move to sit on my bed, and Sam sits beside me. She puts her hand on my thigh and gives me a gentle, reassuring squeeze. I turn my phone on, wait until it's powered up, and enter my PIN.

Messages upon messages, a register of countless missed phone calls all brightly display on the screen. First, I scroll through the missed calls. There are over forty of them, from practically everyone I know. There are also four calls from an unknown number which corresponds with what Mr. C said at school.

"You need to look at all the messages too," Sam says encouragingly.

"Yeah, I know." I meet her eyes for a moment before turning away completely consumed by shame. "Here goes." My body violently reacts to the knowledge of what may possibly be on my phone. "Oh God," I mumble as I roll through the messenger app. There's a vast catalogue of communications, mostly my friends asking where I am and what's happened to me. I've got messages from Levi, Reece, Jordan, Mariah and Lindsey as well. A few from Mom asking if I'm having a good time, and even one from Sam.

Then there's an unknown number with an attachment in the body of the message. My finger hovers over the message. I want to click and see what it is, but at the same time, I'm scared too. "It's okay," Sam says. She moves her hand from my thigh, and drapes it over my shoulder, bringing me in close to her. "No matter what it says, we're going to get through this together."

I nod and offer her a weak smile. "Okay," I worriedly sigh while letting out a huff of air. "I can do this."

"You can."

I touch on the message from the unknown number and it takes me to the top, the very first message. It's from the night of the prom and it reads, 'You're a whore.' The next message says, 'You're a lousy lay.' My heart is frantically pounding, and my entire body is vibrating so violently I can barely control my hand as I try to get to the bottom of the message. The third message is the worst so far. It says, 'You were moaning like a two-dollar hooker, but I'll never fuck you again.' There's still more, but I can't bring myself to look at it. "Oh shit." I feel the phone slipping from my fingers and hear the quiet thud as it hits the floor. "What the hell happened?" I ask, but know there's no one in this room who can give me an accurate answer.

Sam leans down and picks up my phone. She stands and leans against my bedroom door. "I'm going to see what's happening." I turn away from Sam. *Out of sight out of mind, right?* But there's nothing 'out of mind' about this. It's completely consuming me. My life has been dramatically altered. This has changed me forever and no part of me will ever be the same. "It's the same picture that was sent to my phone. And one more message which says 'Enjoy the show, I have plenty of pictures with you as the star.'"

"Oh." Sitting on my bed, I'm numb. Completely dazed, and non-responsive to whatever the hell happened. Something died inside me the night of prom, and now, another piece of me has cascaded down to the pit of eternal darkness.

"It's okay, Dakota, we'll get through this."

With no expression, and absolutely no emotion, I simply nod at whatever Sam said.

"Dakota." I can hear her calling my name, but I can't bring myself to respond. I'm powerless. "Dakota," Sam's tone has now taken on a sense of urgency. "Dakota!" she almost shouts at me. Blankly I turn my face to where her voice is calling me. "Screw this," she says. She looks down at my phone, does something then lifts it to her ear. "Damn it, the number has been disconnected. Hang on." Vaguely I register what she's doing. I think she opens her messenger, compares the number, then brings her phone to her ear. "Bastard," she spits. "Different number and they've both been disconnected."

"It's okay," I say in a detached tone. My voice reflects my lifeless emotions. On the inside, where no one can see, I've . . . departed. That's exactly how everything inside of me feels. Empty, cold . . . *extinct.* "You tried." My stomach churns with those two words stumbling out of my mouth. "There's nothing else we can do."

"Like hell there's not. We're not going to give up on this, Dakota." Sam is igniting a tiny spark deep down in the pit of my stomach. "We may not know who the hell this person is, but we're not going to let them rule your life either."

I collapse on the bed and absolutely hate myself. "I'm so damned weak. I'm not sure I can get through this." Hugging my pillow, I bury my face in it, completely ashamed of myself.

"Jesus, Dakota. Weak? Are you serious?" The bed dips beside me. "Weak is not the word I'd use."

"I can't do this."

"Then we have to tell Mom and Dad."

"NO!" I say with authority. "You promised me you wouldn't say anything." I look to where she's sitting.

"Then you can't blame yourself either." Sam takes a deep breath and moves her hand out, silently asking for my mine. "I don't know what you're feeling. But I can imagine how painful, and . . ." She looks off into the corner of the room, trying to find the words she wants to use. "And humiliating this must be to you. But you didn't bring this on yourself, all you did was go to your junior prom, expecting to have fun with your friends. There's nothing you could've done differently, and if it wasn't you someone else would have been targeted at the prom."

"That makes me feel sick. The thought of someone else waking up in the back field. I can't even imagine it. I don't wish this on anyone, Sam."

"Come on." She pulls me up from my bed. "We'll get through this," she says as she engulfs me in a hug. "Together."

"Together," I say, though really, I feel so alone.

CHAPTER 10

"**WHAT HAPPENED TO** you two last night?" Mom asks as she sits down opposite Sam and me with a cup of coffee.

My hand freezes, with my spoon mid-air and my stomach nervously churning as a cold wave covers me. Sam elbows me, and her gaze goes to my spoon. "Dakota bet me she'd win in a race down to the park, but she cheated. She took off before I even had a chance to put my shoes on. She cheated, because she went barefoot." Sam lifts her eyebrows and looks at me.

Crap, she's good at lying. "Yeah, I did," I confirm and smile at Sam's story. Taking another spoonful of my cereal, I block out the sound of Mom and Sam's insistent chatter.

"Did you hear what I said, Dakota?" Mom asks while Sam kicks me under the table.

"Sorry, what?"

"What's happening with you? I could swear you just transported somewhere else, like you weren't even here," Mom says, standing to take her cup to the sink.

"Just thinking about cheerleading practice." *Great, now I'm lying too.*

"I said when you're ready, let me know. I'll take you two to school today because I need to head over to the mall."

"Thanks, Mom," I say and go back to my cereal.

"You have to watch it, Dakota. She's going to know something's not right if you're always spacing out and not being here." Sam says in a low voice, pointing to the floor, trying to tell me to be more aware of what's happening around me.

"I know. I'm trying."

"You have to try harder." Her voice of reason screams at me. Her stern features tell me she's right, I do have to try harder. Not to forget, but to hide the truth and the shame. I hate the fact Sam knows, but there's not much I can do about that now. She's involved because of a malicious, gutless person hiding behind their phone. But I need to protect Mom and Dad from what happened. I'm not sure I would be able to bear their judgment if they knew.

"Okay, I'm going to make more of an effort. But you need to let me know if I go weird."

Sam's lips turn up in a quirky smile. "Like more weird than normal?"

Playfully smacking her arm, I smile at her. "Thanks, Sam," I say, standing to take my bowl to the sink.

"Don't forget it when I want to borrow something of yours to wear." Rolling my eyes, I simply nod. "Including that cute red sweater, and black knee-length pencil skirt." This time I shake my head, but smirk. "Oh, and that purple dress."

"How about I give you free reign over my entire wardrobe?" I say sarcastically and turn on my heels to look at her with raised eyebrows.

"Yay!" She claps her hands together and brings her bowl over to the sink. "I knew you'd see it my way." Her smile is cheeky, and her eyes reflect the playfulness of her words. "Now, let me see, what should I wear on my date?" She rubs her hands together and leans against the counter.

"With Calvin?" I tease. "Has he even asked you out yet?"

She pushes on my shoulder and laughs. "His name is Taylor, not Calvin. And noooooo," she draws out her response. "He *hasn't* asked me out yet, but he will." She does a little jiggle on the spot. "I just know it."

"How about we wait for him to ask you first, then we can pick what you can wear."

Sam stops dancing and gives me the funniest look. It's a cross between 'how dare you' and 'he's so asking me out, sister.' "Whatever." She flicks her hand at me. "He's asking me out."

Her features turn serious, and for a split second I think she's mad until she starts laughing. I can't help but join her with my own chuckle.

"You ready, girls?" Mom calls while slinging her handbag over her shoulder. "Hurry up, we're going to be late." Mom's already at the front door, and Sam and I grab our book bags.

"Hey," Sam shouts from her room. "I call shotgun."

With my bag on my shoulder, I run past Mom, and out to the car. "Hurry up, Mom!" I yell for her to unlock the doors so I can get in the front.

"I called it," Sam pushes by Mom who's now locking the house. She bolts over to me, and with her hips, shoves me out the way.

"Hey," I protest.

"I called it."

"So?"

"I called it." She stands guard over the front door, like an offensive lineman ready to block me from getting near the front passenger door.

"You two," Mom sighs as she unlocks the car and gets in.

Smiling, I get in the back and Sam slides into the front, not before turning around and poking her tongue out at me. I was going to let her have the front regardless.

It's a quick ride to school, and when we pull up, Mom lets us know she can pick us up after school if we want. Sam jumps in and tells her we can catch the bus home. I'm really grateful for Sam and her quick responses, it means I don't have to think of anything.

"Hey, thanks for everything," I say to her as we walk up the steps into the corridors of school.

"We're sisters, we're supposed to stick together. Anyway, I gotta go. I want to see if Taylor's around." She fixes her hair then runs her hand down over her jeans. "Do I look alright?"

"You look cute."

"Cute? I don't want to look cute, I walk to look, hmmm." She pushes her chest out. "Like a woman."

"Well you're not, and don't rush trying to be one."

Sam nods, then looks down at her shoes. "You know what I mean," she whispers. "I didn't mean anything by it. Sorry."

"I know. Anyway, I'll meet you out front. See ya. Oh, and good luck with Calvin."

"Taylor," she corrects immediately.

I get to my locker, open it and put in my bag, taking out the books I need for my morning classes. When I close it, Mariah is walking toward me. "Hey," I say when she reaches me.

"Did you and Levi break up?" She leans against a locker and eagerly looks at me. "'Cause he's telling everyone he broke up with you."

"Yeah, we broke up yesterday."

"Why didn't you call me? Oh my God, are you going out with someone else?"

"What? No. I wasn't feeling my best yesterday. I went home and crawled into bed, I wasn't really up to calling or talking with anyone."

"You should've called me. Anyway, why did you guys break up?"

We both start walking toward our first class for the day. I shrug and choose to remain quiet. "We just did," I finally say after a few moments.

"You just did? What kind of lame answer is that?"

We get to Mrs. Walker's class and sit in our usual seats. Levi walks in, with Reece a step behind him. Levi looks at me, his gaze travelling all over me, then his top lip curls up into a snarl. "You don't belong here. These seats are reserved for my friends."

"What?" I snap toward him. "This has been my seat all year."

"You're no longer welcome to sit here anymore. Go sit somewhere else." He hovers over me, trying to intimidate me with his size.

"Levi," I hear Reece call him. "What's going on?" Reece comes to stand beside Levi and looks between us.

"I was just telling her she's no longer welcome to sit here. These seats are reserved for my friends."

I watch Reece's left eyebrow rise as he looks at Levi in a disgusted way. "Dude, since when are those rules in place?"

"Since we broke up," Levi barks at Reece.

"Don't be a dick, man. Just leave it alone."

Levi looks down at me, then back to Reece. "Whatever, but next class, you're not sitting there." He thumps his hand on my desk, causing me to jump back in my seat and my heart to startle with fright.

"She can sit wherever she wants." Reece pushes on Levi's chest to get him away from me. It's not an aggressive gesture, just one basically saying to leave me alone. "You can sit there again if you want, Dakota." He smiles at me, and pushes into Levi to get him to leave.

"Thanks."

When Levi and Reece are on the other side of the room, Mariah leans over to me and rubs her hand up and down my arm. "What's gotten into him?" she whispers in a voice only I can hear. Lifting my shoulders and shaking my head I opt to not answer. I know why he's being a jerk, because I haven't had sex with him.

Mrs. Walker enters the room, and everyone goes quiet. She starts talking about the book we've studied but her voice becomes a persistent hum in the background. Nothing holds my attention because the only thought drumming through my mind is the way Levi is acting toward me. I try and not look over in his direction, but I can feel his intense gaze boring into me.

I'm fighting myself, because as much as I know I shouldn't look, I almost can't stop myself. As the class continues, the frustration builds and my hands become clammy. A nervous knot in my stomach grows. I can feel my shattered nerves, tension building to a point where I think I'm about to lose my mind.

Suddenly everything starts blurring as my throat closes and I can barely breathe. Sweat snakes down my damp skin, creating an uncomfortable sensation. "Damn," I whisper, lifting the hem of my t-shirt to wipe away the moisture gathering at my temples. Everything inside me begins to seize. Panic is rapidly rising and choking every one of my senses. "What's happening?" I mumble and try to stand from seat.

"Miss Bennett, sit back down," I vaguely make out Mrs. Walker yelling from the front of the class.

"I'm not feeling well . . ." Crap, my legs go completely weak and wobbly as the room spins in every direction.

"Miss Bennett?"

"Dakota," someone calls in a desperate voice.

"I . . ."

"Dakota." A warm hand gently strokes my face. "Can you hear me?" Blinking my eyes open, the first face I see is Reece. He's holding me against his chest with one arm, and his other hand is slowly stroking down my cheek.

"What happened?" I try to sit up but Reece holds me even tighter to his chest.

"Don't try to move," he orders me. "You passed out, Dakota. You stood up and started swaying, mumbled something, and collapsed."

"Did I?" I ask as I look around to see all my classmates' faces staring back at me, not even trying to hide the whispering behind their hands.

"You did. I noticed how you were unsteady on your feet and got to you just as you collapsed."

"You did?" Reece comforts me by smiling. "Thank you."

"Any time."

"Dakota, can you stand?" Mrs. Walker asks.

"I think so."

"You need to go to the nurse. Reece, can you help Dakota?" Mrs. Walker asks him.

"Yes, Ma'am." Reece moves me away, and jumps to his feet. "Here, take my hand." He stretches his arm down and offers me his hand so I can pull myself up.

"Thank you," I say and turn to grab my books and clear my desk.

"Here you go." Mrs. Walker holds out a slip for us to take to the nurse.

Reece and I leave and he grabs my books. "I can carry them," I say while we slowly walk down the hall.

"I'll take them."

"Thanks." I pull my hair out of the now messy ponytail and fix it. "I'll stop off at my locker first so I can get my bag."

"Okay." We walk in an awkward silence until we get to my locker. "So."

"So." I say the same time Reece says it.

"What happened back there?" He points toward the classroom. "Are you okay?"

"I forgot to have breakfast," I lie. I'm not going to tell him I got so wound up that I pushed myself to breaking point and passed out. Because if I say I panicked, then a whole new line of questioning opens up, and I don't want *those* questions to be asked.

"Can I ask you something else?"

"Um, sure."

"Why did you and Levi break up?"

Sighing, I figure I may as well tell him the real reason, because the way Levi's been acting toward me, I dare say he would've told Reece whatever he wanted. "Because I wasn't ready to have sex with him."

"What?"

"We were supposed to have sex after the prom, but then I . . ." I stop myself in time before I confess the truth to him. Reece is easy to talk to, which means it's even easier for me to slip up and tell him exactly what happened.

"You what?" he pushes me to finish what I started.

"I felt sick and I went home. But, besides the fact I left, I'd told him on our way to the prom how I wasn't ready. I thought he understood and accepted it, but I guess not." I shrug my shoulders and look down at the floor in the corridor.

"Hang on a minute." He stops walking and reaches out to grab my elbow so I stop walking too. I've been jumpy and jittery when people have come close to me, but I'm strangely okay with Reece's touch. "You're telling me Levi broke up with you because you wouldn't have sex with him."

"That's exactly what I'm saying." I nod.

"His attitude toward you sucks, Dakota."

"I don't know what to say or do. He's being a jerk."

"You say and do nothing. He doesn't deserve you. You should be with someone who appreciates and respects you. And if you're not ready to have sex, then he should accept how you're feeling. Not go around telling all us of how you're . . ." Reece stops talking, obviously he too started saying something I shouldn't really know.

"I'm what, Reece?"

He looks away from me, and I feel like a knife has been plunged into my heart. "Nothing," he says in a small voice. The knife gets twisted and I feel so sick at the thought of what reasons Levi might be giving about our break up. My heartbreak must be completely obvious to Reece, because his shoulders tense up and he takes a step closer to me. In an innocent move, he engulfs me in a hug. "I'm sorry, Dakota."

His warm embrace feels right. There's nothing creepy or wrong about his arms around me. Considering everything I've been through, I'm surprised at myself for being able to accept his touch and not freak out.

Reece lets go and takes a step back from us. "Sorry, I shouldn't have done that." He runs his hands through his sandy hair. His brown eyes find mine, and I can see the apology screaming at me.

"It's okay, don't worry about it." We continue toward the nurse's office in an awkward silence. When we get there, the nurse takes my slip from the teacher, and sits me down while she reads the note.

"I'll go back to class," Reece says in a strained and hesitant voice.

"Yeah, okay. See you at lunch."

"Lunch . . . right. See ya."

I watch his retreating back leave the office, and suddenly loneliness overtakes me.

CHAPTER 11

WALKING TOWARD THE cafeteria, I spot Mariah and Lindsey ahead of me. They haven't noticed me yet and they appear to be oblivious to everyone around them. They're talking, pointing, laughing and carrying on. I can't help but wonder if this is how I come across too? Do I walk like them, with an air of superiority? Do I discreetly point at others and giggle behind my hand all the while saying mean and hurtful things?

God, I hope not.

When I get into the cafeteria, Jordan and Aaron are already sitting at our table. Lindsey and Mariah join them, quickly followed by me.

"Hi everyone," I say while sitting down on a spare chair.

"Oh my God, I heard you passed out. Are you okay?" Jordan asks as she leans over the table to give my hand a light squeeze.

"Yeah, I didn't eat breakfast and I kind of just . . . well, you know." This story is much easier to tell then the actual truth.

"Hey, how are you feeling?" Reece folds his tall body into the seat next to mine.

"Yeah, good. Just needed to eat. The nurse gave me some juice and a couple of cookies and I felt fine so she sent me back to class."

"But you're okay, right?"

There's an unusual concern coming from Reece. It's quite intense. I bring my arm up and lean my head down, essentially creating a barrier blocking out everyone else at the table. "I'm okay." I take a deep breath and narrow my eyes in question. "Are you okay? You seem kinda weird."

"Yeah, I mean it's nothing. Just making sure you're okay and it wasn't anything serious."

"Are you trying to say something, Reece?" I caught the tail end of some conversations behind me, and they seemed to be quite interested in why I'd passed out in English.

"What are you doing here?" I hear Levi boom over everyone else at the table.

Blinking a few times, and taking several deep breaths, I slowly turn to find Levi standing on the opposite side of the table, his hands on his hips leering down at me. "I'm talking to Reece, and if you don't like it, you can leave," spurts uncontrollably out of my mouth.

"You don't get it, do you, Dakota? This area . . ." He does a circular movement with his finger than places his fists back on his hips, " . . . is for people I like. And I don't like you."

I look over at the girls, who are quietly nibbling on their lunch with their eyes downcast. They're listening, though not saying anything. "So you're saying you have a problem with me?"

"That's exactly what I'm saying." He gives me a fake smile while narrowing his eyes at me.

"Hey, man. What's your problem?" Reece stands and puts his fists on the table in an obviously aggressive move. "She always sits here, just like she's always sat in English class. Just leave her alone. You're being a dick."

"Are you two going out now? Figures. Well, good luck with that." Levi's looking at Reece but points to me when he says 'that.' "She's like a dead fish."

"You're a damn jerk, Levi. What the hell did I see in you to begin with?"

"You mean, what did *I* see in *you?*"

"Leave it alone, Levi. You're acting like a real prick," Reece says to him.

"Whatever. You're all a bunch of losers." Levi turns his back to us, and looks over at Lindsey. He motions for her to go to him, and she stands and obediently follows. "Let's go," he says as he slings his arm over her shoulder.

I can hear her giggling as they walk away.

"What the hell?" I say, looking at someone who was supposed to be my one of my best friends, walk off with my ex-boyfriend who's turned out to be nothing but a jerk.

"Don't worry about it." Reece sits back down and I watch Levi nuzzle into Lindsey's neck. "She's made no secret of the fact she'd go out with him if you two ever broke up."

"She said she'd have sex with him because she thought he's hot, but

I honestly thought she was kidding. I never, in a million years, believed she'd actually do it." With a shake of my head, I look down at my lunch, confused and completely astonished. "I really can't believe she's gone with him."

"Don't worry about them."

"It'll be easier if I find somewhere else to sit at lunch. This is going to get crazy, and besides, I can't handle looking at them together."

"Why? Is it because you still love him?" Reece questions me.

I look blankly at him. I know my face is void of any emotions, because frankly, I don't feel anything toward Levi, except he's not the person I thought he was. Lindsey on the other hand, she's hurt me more than Levi ever could have. "I'm more upset at Lindsey than Levi. She's supposed to be one of my best friends." Standing I grab my lunch and smile weakly at Reece. "I need some air." Turning away from Reece, I walk out of the cafeteria and head toward the library.

"Hey, Dakota," Reece calls out to me. But I keep my head down, and walk away as quickly as I can.

Pulling out a chair in the library, I sit and open the book I picked from the shelf. I chose it absentmindedly, not really looking at the selection. My eyes gloss over the title, but I don't register anything it actually says.

Instead of the book holding my interest, I keep replaying the image of Levi and Lindsey. He told her to get up and go to him, and she went like a well-trained puppy. I can feel myself losing faith in the friendship I thought Lindsey and I had. Tears quickly well up in my eyes, and my stomach churns at the betrayal I've witnessed.

"Dakota, what are you doing here?" Sophie asks as she drags out the chair opposite me. I lower my head so she can't see the tears, but I know she saw. "Why are you crying?"

"It's nothing." The tears are rolling down my cheeks and onto the book I'm holding.

"Then why are you crying all over the Bible?"

I actually look at the book and bark a humorless laugh. That's what I get for grabbing the first book I came across. "It's nothing, okay?" I muffle my sobs and try to hide the tears.

"Nothing, huh? Doesn't look like nothing to me. What happened?"

Shrugging my shoulders, I keep my focus down on the leather-bound pages I've now placed on the table. "Yeah, don't worry about it."

"Okay then, I won't. But you've gotta stop crying. Especially considering it looks like you're crying over this." She leans over and taps the book with her fingers.

My churning stomach settles somewhat within a few moments, and the tears recede enough for me to be able to look up at Sophie. "I'm okay," I finally manage to say, and mean the words.

"Good." She takes a deep breath and smiles at me. "How come you're in the library again?" I notice her blonde hair is pulled back tight in a high ponytail, and she's wearing a touch of make-up.

"You look really pretty today." I ignore her question but try to keep eye contact so she doesn't clue in.

"Avoiding giving me an answer?" *No such luck.*

"Yeah, I'm in the library again. Seems things are different now."

"You can tell me if you want, don't feel bad if you don't want to." She's so easy to talk with, and seems so carefree too.

"It doesn't matter; it's stupid stuff. But, seeing as you're insisting, you know my friend Lindsey?" She nods her head. "Well, Levi and I broke up and now she's with him."

Sophie's expression is impassive. She doesn't look surprised or upset or even amused. Nothing . . . zilch . . . nada. "And this surprises you? Seriously, this surprises you?" she asks, completely devoid of emotion. "Because the way I see it, those girls will turn on you in a heartbeat. I've seen it before and I know I'll see it again." She turns her head to look away and whispers, "They turn on anyone, and *everyone.*"

Scrunching my forehead, I look at Sophie and silently question her. I don't want to ask her what she means by her statement, but I do want to know if what she said is a warning, or an observation.

Instead I turn back to my book and pick it up. "You know, I've never really read this."

"Neither have I. How many people have read it in its entirety and actually understood it?" She lets out a laugh, and I know she's attempting to break the seriousness which has suddenly fallen over us.

"Ms. Bennett, may I have a word with you?" Mr. C's smarmy voice instantly chills my blood and my heart drops down into my stomach. With wide eyes I look at Sophie and silently plead with her to not leave me alone with him.

I look over my right shoulder to where Mr. C is standing about two feet away. "Um, sure," I answer him, but my voice comes out all croaky and rough. He takes a step back to wait for me to follow him. I slide out of my chair slowly and try to breathe through the panic creeping throughout my entire body. I follow Mr. C to the back of the library but I keep looking over my shoulder at Sophie. I want to maintain eye contact with her in case I need her to come over and rescue me.

"I heard you passed out today," Mr. C starts saying while attempting to discreetly look me over. However, it's obvious to me. "Are you okay?"

I nod my head, too scared to open my mouth and say anything; fearing my voice will let me down and I'll either scream or worse still, not be able to speak.

"Why did you pass out?"

Holy crap, now I have to respond, I have no choice. I look over to Sophie who's watching us with an eagle eye. "I . . ." my voice is scratchy. "I forgot to have breakfast."

"Did the nurse call your parents?" He furrows his brows together, and runs his beady eyes over me once again.

I nod, but again don't dare say anything.

"What happened?"

I clear my throat and look down at my shoes. Finding the courage, I look back into his inquisitive gaze. "I spoke to my mom and she said she'd come to pick me up and take me to the doctor, but I asked her not to and told her I was feeling fine. It was just this morning I wasn't feeling great, I'm fine now."

"You sure you're okay?"

Mr. C has been showing an unusual interest in me. He's always been creepy, but since Monday his attention has been much more intense. "Yeah, I'm sure." I look him straight in the eyes so he knows I'm okay. A long moment passes between us. The stifling air makes it difficult for me to breathe, and suddenly a tingle of raw nervous energy shoots through my body. However I ignore the warnings from my weary mind and fight to hide the secret I so desperately hold on to. "I'm sure," I confirm again, ensuring Mr. C believes me.

Tilting his head down to look at me with a keen eye, Mr. C nods his head once but also purses his lips together. "If you need anything, Dakota, come to my classroom and find me." He steps away from where we were at the end of library and turns his back leaving me to consider his words.

Mr. C is by far the creepiest, weirdest person I've ever met. And I never want to be alone with him.

"What was that about?" Sophie innocently whispers when I make my way back to our table.

"He wanted to talk to me about some homework due."

"Homework? Now? It's almost the end of the year? That's weird." Her words sound as if she doesn't believe what I said. And truthfully, I wouldn't believe me either. "Looked like he was almost angry with you."

My face turns up in a grimace and I shake my head. "Nah, nothing like that." I try to downplay the seriousness of the situation, and more specifically, the accuracy of her words.

CHAPTER 12

"ARE YOU GOING to the charity basketball game tonight?" Sam asks as we walk home from school.

"I don't know. Maybe. What happened with Calvin?"

"Taylor," she corrects me with a wide smile on her face. "Well, he kind of asked me to the game tonight."

"Oooh." Deliberately I step into her and bump her shoulder with mine. "Really? Are you going to go?"

"I want to. He asked me if I want to go to the movies with him on Saturday night, too."

"Wow. He must be serious to ask you out for tonight's game and tomorrow night too. Two nights in a row."

Sam squeals in delight, and bounces as she's walking. "I know," she excitedly says. "Dakota, will you help me find something to wear? Like maybe I can borrow that really nice green sweater you have and maybe your black knee-length skirt?" I turn to look at her, and she flutters her eyelashes at me as she brings her hands together as if in a prayer. "Puurleeeeaaasse?" she draws out.

"So you want to borrow something of mine to wear?" I'm teasing her, making her beg for it while I already know I'm going to say yes.

"Oh please, Dakota, please can I?"

"Maybe." I shrug my shoulders noncommittally at her.

"Come on," she teasingly whines. "Please?" Sam gives me a sickly sweet smile, her wide brown eyes gazing softly at me.

"Fine," I grumble playfully.

"I told Taylor I'd meet him at the game. You should come."

"I don't know. I'm not sure where I stand with Jordan, Mariah and the rest of them. Obviously I can kiss my friendship with Lindsey goodbye."

"Lindsey? Why? What happened?" Sam stops walking to grab my upper arm.

"Let's just say, she's not who I thought she was." I start to walk away, but Sam makes a grab for my arm again.

"What happened?"

Telling Sam what happened at lunch today I watch her reaction as it quickly morphs from shock, to irritation, then anger. "Are you serious? She walked off with him after he was being horrible to you?" I nod my head. "Man, I'm so . . ." she pauses, but her features give away exactly how she feels. Her eyes are wide with anger as she paces up and down the sidewalk.

"I know," I add.

"How can this not make you angry? *He's* being a dick and *she's* just— I can't even say what I want to about her. Grrr," she growls as she starts marching toward home.

"Hey, it's my own fault. I thought she was like a sister to me. Obviously, not."

"She's not me, Dakota. No one can replace me," she huffs angrily. *She's hurt.*

"No, that's not what I meant." It's my turn to stop her walking. I throw my arms around her and hug her. "You are the best person I know, Sam, No one could ever replace you, I just thought she'd always have my back, you know? Clearly, I was mistaken. I don't know what else to do. Up until last week I thought everything was perfect. Now, it's like nothing is as it seems on the surface."

Sam pulls out of the hug and we walk the final few blocks in silence. When we get home, Sam sits on the front lawn under one of the willow trees we have in the yard. Evidently she wants to talk or she wouldn't be looking at me, and then pointedly staring to the spot beside her. I sit cross-legged next to her and let out a sigh.

"I've been thinking about what you said that nothing seems the same. And that's because nothing *is* the same."

"I know," I say while running my hands over the lush green grass, avoiding her stare.

"It's been less than a week, Dakota, and nothing is ever going to be like it was. You'll never be the same, and neither will any relationship you've had or will have. Especially considering we have no idea who slipped you the drug. It could've been anyone, you yourself said you came back to the table and your drink was there."

"I'm trying to push it out of my mind, Sam. I don't think I can handle it if I allow myself to think about it."

"Pushing it out of your mind only means it'll fester."

I smack the ground in frustration. "Stop it, just stop it. I don't want to face it, or deal with it." Standing I brush the grass off my legs and butt. "I'm not ready." I sling my bag over my shoulder and run up the few steps in front of our home. "I'll get those clothes ready for you, Sam." Opening the door, I head straight into my room.

"Hi, darling," Mom calls out as I pass her in the hallway.

Hot tears burn my eyes, and I know I'm about to lose it and cry. "Hi," I mumble and quickly close my door before Mom sees the tears slipping down my cheeks. I take myself over to my bed, and lay on it, bringing my pillow in to hug. "This is bullshit," I say to myself.

I've gone from being a popular girl, confident and outgoing, to becoming an introvert who avoids everyone. I used to be able to trust people, but now I've tightened the circle of who I can depend and rely on. Sam's at the top of the list of people I have unconditional faith in. Since she found out about, *that night,* she's had my back and hasn't faltered in her loyalty to me.

My friends, or my so-called friends, are showing me their true colors. Levi has let me down, and as for Lindsey, she's clearly not the person I thought she was.

Knock, knock, knock.

I sit up in bed, wipe my face and call out for whoever it is to enter.

Sam opens the door with remorse and pain written all over her face. "I'm sorry," we both say together.

I can't help but go to her and hug her. "I'm sorry, Sam," I finally manage to say. "I know you're trying to help and I shouldn't have snapped at you."

"I'm sorry for pushing you. It's just . . . this is really scary, Dakota. I mean if it happened to you, then it must've happened to someone else and I wonder who else will become a victim, too?"

My stomach churns in fear, because these questions are haunting me. But I try and push them down, as far into the darkness as I can. I'm nowhere near ready to attempt to answer them or even *begin* to understand them.

"I know, and trust me when I say I think about those exact questions every moment I'm awake. I'm even having panic attacks, and I'm not sure if I can handle them."

"This is big, Dakota. Like huge. You should consider telling Mom and

Dad. They'll be devastated that you haven't told them if they find out by someone else. And before you freak out and think I'm going to tell them, that's not what I meant."

My throat tightens and I feel nausea quickly rise. I'm ashamed to admit I did panic because I thought Sam would tell. "You have all the power, Sam and I won't lie. I'm terrified you may accidently slip."

"You know I'd never." She unfolds herself from my hug and goes to sit on my bed. "I swear, I would never betray you." She places her right hand over her heart. "I promise," she says in the most serious tone I've ever heard come from her. Dropping her hand she places both of them in her lap and begins to nervously wring them together. "One day, Dakota, you have to tell them. It'll eat you up alive if you keep it to yourself. How much do you think you can handle before the cracks break open and everything spills?"

Slumping my shoulders I nod my head. "I know," I say in defeat. "Just not yet. I'm not ready."

"Promise me though, when you're ready, we'll tell Mom and Dad together."

Sam's beautiful, gentle nature makes my heart ache, because she sees the beauty in everything, and loyally wants to protect me. "I feel like I'm letting you down, Sam."

"Why?"

"You're *my* little sister, not the other way around. I should be protecting you and giving you wise advice, instead, you're the one who's looking out for me. It's not right. I'm not doing a very good job as your older sister."

Sam laughs out loud which causes me to look into her amused eyes and smiling face. "Sometimes, Dakota, we find the strength we need in others. My time will come when I'll need you and you'll be my strength, so for now let me be yours."

Christ, I'm a damn mess. Everything about me has completely fallen apart. "How about I get you those clothes you want to borrow?" I try and drag my mind away from the imminent darkness waiting to consume me.

"Are you and Levi going out afterwards?" Mom asks as she drops me and Sam to where the charity game is being played. "And you're not cheering tonight?" Mom looks me over.

"Nah, there isn't any cheering tonight. It's just a charity game." I know there will be cheering, but I haven't put in any effort this last week. Because of that I don't think it's fair for me to show up tonight and try to be involved. Besides, I truly don't care if they throw me off the squad or keep me.

"Are you and Levi going out after?" I was hoping she'd forgotten the first part of her question.

"Levi and I broke up." I look out the window to avoid her stare, but catch it in the reflection of the window.

"You broke up?" she gasps in disbelief. "When did this happen? Why didn't you tell me? What happened? My gosh, Dakota, you have to tell me when these things happen! It explains a lot actually; you've been quite withdrawn the last few days. You broke up with him on Saturday at the prom, didn't you? Since then you've been quiet and not saying much."

Taking a deep breath I simply sit in quiet and not say anything. "Hey, Mom, I'm meeting Taylor at the game tonight." Sam interrupts so I'm not the recipient of Mom's inquisition.

Discreetly reaching my hand back I feel for Sam's. She sees what I'm doing, and holds my hand, giving it a reassuring squeeze. It's my way of saying 'thank you,' and her way of saying 'you're welcome.'

Mom and Sam chatter about Taylor, AKA Calvin, and I watch the scenery go by as we near our school.

"I'll call you when we're ready to be picked up," Sam says as she closes the door. I'm already waiting for her by the curb, far enough away that Mom can't easily say anything to me.

It doesn't stop Mom from rolling the passenger side window down, leaning over to call me back. "Dakota." I feel the tightness strangle my chest as I approach the car. "Tomorrow we need to talk about you and Levi."

"Okay, Mom," I answer her but secretly hope she forgets about it.

"Come on, big sis, let's go. Bye, Mom." Sam waves and Mom leaves.

And I quietly freak out about our pending conversation.

CHAPTER 13

W HEN SAM AND I walk into the gymnasium, I immediately notice Jordan, Mariah, and Lindsey sitting on one of the bench seats at the front of the bleachers. I smile at them, but they look right through me. Obviously I'm not welcome to sit with them.

"It's okay, you can sit with us," Sam says and drags me up the steps toward where Taylor is sitting.

As I glance up at Taylor, I catch Sophie's eye and she waves me over. "I'll sit with Sophie," I say and make my way over to her while Sam heads straight to Taylor.

The first half of the game is fun. Both teams were all about having a good time, not really playing hard. Reece even grabbed the ball from Levi and dribbled it over to the opponents' side of the court and shot a hoop for them. It got them up to even the score and the crowd all cheered as Reece took a bow in the middle of the court.

Now it's half time, and there's a charity auction to raise money for a shelter in the area that houses women and children fleeing domestic violence situations. It's all small things, like double movie passes, dinner at local cafés and restaurants and even a few brand name clothing pieces. All in all, it's crazy and fun.

"It's a good idea, what the school's doing. It brings attention to things we wouldn't usually think about. Like domestic violence," Sophie says. "I mean it's good to start at this level, so we're aware of it."

"Do you know anything about it?"

"Unfortunately I do."

Crap, it's not the answer I was expecting. "Sorry," I say awkwardly, not really knowing what else to say.

"My mom was beaten really badly by my dad until he was arrested."

"He was arrested for beating your mom? Holy shit." I look away, because well, just because.

"Nope, my dad wasn't arrested for beating my mom. He was arrested for an armed hold-up. Beating my mom was something he did all the time, but Mom never wanted to say anything because she was scared she wouldn't be able to look after me on her own. So she stayed and never did anything about it. But when Dad was arrested for the hold-up, it was a godsend for us. We packed up and moved here. Mom even found the courage to get a divorce. We've had to change our names and everything so he doesn't find us, but things are better now."

"Oh my God," I say looking at Sophie. "That's got to be horrible."

"We've been here for three years. It wasn't good walking on eggshells around my own home. You know, before Dad was arrested, I'd hate going home. I'd do everything I could to stay away."

"It must be nice to feel safe."

Sophie's head whips to the side. Her right eye twitches as her lips turn up in a wry and hurt smile. "Safe is subjective, Dakota. There's pain everywhere. Even when you think you're out of danger, it has a way of finding you."

My gut wrenches as every hair follicle on my arms stands to attention. My palms become sweaty, just from the way Sophie's looking at me. She's trying to tell me something. I'm not sure what yet, but I'm hoping in time she'll tell me.

"What the . . . ?" I hear someone yell. I look over toward where the noise came from, but I don't see anything.

"Fuck, Levi Matthews and Reece Hendricks are fighting," someone else yells.

My gaze goes to the sideline and I see the two of them going at each other. "What the hell?" I jump up and bolt down the bleachers, across the court to where Reece has a thrown and landed a punch directly on Levi's nose. Blood spurts out and Levi stumbles back creating a cup with his hand to catch the blood.

"You can have her; she's nothing but a slut," Levi yells at Reece as he retreats and heads toward the locker rooms.

Reece looks over at me, and so does half the basketball team. I'm left stunned, not being able to say anything. "You're a sick fuck," Reece yells as Levi storms off.

Levi turns around, walking backward and flips Reece the bird, but his hate-filled eyes single me out. His face is flooded with disgust and judgement as he spits the word, 'whore.' I now realize their fight had to do with me. The energy in my body multiplies as the thrumming beat of my heart intensifies.

Reece steps in front of me shielding me from Levi, but it's too late, he's already said his piece, called me a 'whore,' and made me feel as if I'm nothing more than trash carelessly strewn aside. "You don't get to talk to her," Reece yells while still guarding me from the malicious and obvious hatred radiating from Levi.

I inhale a sharp breath and look around me. Some of the guys are laughing and pointing at me, while others are desperately trying to not make eye contact. A whirlpool of emotions all smash into me at the same time, fear is the biggest.

Reece's broad shoulders are in front of me, shielding me as he and Levi sling insults at each another, Levi a lot more vitriolic in his hatred for me. I try to look over Reece's shoulders, but he must feel me, because he steps back and puts his arm out protectively, almost in an on-court defense maneuver.

Levi's loud and venomous mumblings are heard as he leaves the gym. Reece still has his back to me, his arm out and shoulders high ready to fight anyone who comes our way. The entire gymnasium is quiet, except for a few teachers, including Mr. C, who are trying to calm down the volatile players.

Reece keeps watching the doors Levi left through, and when some time has passed, he swings around to look at me. His eyes have a furious intensity to them, as his mouth is drawn into a tight and pained line. Reece's chest is heaving while he makes an obvious effort to calm himself down.

"Reece," I mutter and immediately look down to the ground. I'm afraid if I look into his gaze, he'll see through me to the secrets I'm desperately trying to hold on to. Worse still, I don't know who it was that slipped me the drug, and considering he's the one who handed me the drink, I can't forget how it might have been him.

But if it's not him, then I don't want him to know the shameful, revolting secret I'm concealing. "I shouldn't have come," I whisper, too afraid to look anywhere but the dirty, sweat-damp floor. "I'll leave."

"You're not going anywhere until you tell me what the hell is going on." Reece grabs my arm, and storms to the side doors like a man on a mission, dragging me behind him. When we get out into the hall, he starts pacing the corridor in front of me.

Sinking back I try and flatten myself against the wall, hoping it'll open up and swallow me whole. Panic rises through me and a sheen of perspiration touches every part of my exposed skin.

"Do you know what he was doing?" Reece points toward the locker rooms and angrily spits at me. "Do you know?" he shouts.

Flinching away, I close my eyes and brace myself for the blow I'm positive is about to follow. "Please don't hit me," I plead with him.

But the seconds pass and I don't feel anything. Opening one eye, I squint toward Reece. He's puzzled by my reaction, and the distance between us is so great, there could be a parade in the vast void. "Why would you think that?" he asks and takes a slow step back, putting an even bigger gap between us.

Truth be told, I have no idea. So many things have happened over the past week that I don't know who I can trust, other than Sam and my parents. I feel shame claw its way through my body. It wants me weak and frail, frightened of everything and everyone. *And I am.*

"Dakota," Reece says quietly after yet another agonizingly long pause. "What's going on?"

"Nothing," I immediately answer. "Nothing at all."

"Then why was Levi telling everyone you're a slut? You told me you didn't have sex with him, and I took that to mean you haven't had sex with anyone."

Ice cuts through the part of me which believes one day I'll be okay. The tension in the air mounts between us, and I'm sure Reece is leading up to more questions. Questions I simply can't answer. "I haven't." My voice is small and scratchy and filled with humiliation.

"Then why was he showing everyone a picture he got from someone, of you laying on your back, your arm up over your face with your dress hitched up above your waist?"

My eyes fly up to his, and suddenly vomit forces its way up and sits like a lump in my throat. It's taunting me, wanting me to make a further fool of myself. "Oh my God," I whisper. My hand shoots up to my mouth and I do the only thing I can. I take off and don't look back.

My lungs hurt as air refuses to enter them, and the bile threatening its way out is now knocking loudly. I'm about to lose the meager contents of my stomach.

I push through the outside doors and run toward the half-filled car lot. Falling to my knees I hang my head low and bring my arms up over my head. I'm trying to shield myself, but all I can do is kneel here and allow the degradation and shame to further mortify me.

I hear heavy footsteps approaching, but I try with all my might to ignore them and hope that whoever it is doesn't see me.

"Dakota?" Reece quietly says. He kneels beside me, and I feel the warmth of his hand gently touch my back.

"Please, go away." Choking back the tears scorching my face, I try with everything I have left in me to retain the small shred of dignity I still have. "Just . . . please leave."

"Tell me what's going on," he tries to push for answers.

Shaking my head, I let the tears fall. My shoulders are shaking as I struggle with everything.

"Dakota?" I hear Sam calling for me. "Dakota?!" her voice becomes more urgent.

"She's here," Reece responds when he notices my lack of response.

I hear her running toward me, and she throws her arms around me. "Move," she screeches at Reece.

"I was trying to help." He sounds so defeated and worried.

"Move," she snaps again. "Are you okay?" She tries to shift the veil I've created with my hair to look at my face. Shaking my head, I can't say anything. "Let's go. I've called Mom and she'll be here soon." Sam helps me up, and then holds me as she guides us to wherever she told Mom to meet us.

I look over my shoulder and see the hurt on Reece's face. He's rooted to the spot as his left hand is raking through his hair. I look forward, and do what I've been doing since Saturday night. I push everything into the part of me where I can pigeon-hole it and safely shut it away.

"Are you okay?" Sam asks as we get further away from Reece.

"I think so."

"Let's go to the bathroom and get you cleaned up before Mom sees you like this. I think she's already suspicious and we don't want to give her any more reason to think something's wrong."

When we get inside the girls' bathroom, a few girls are applying lipstick and adjusting their boobs. The moment they notice me though, the talking turns hushed and their gazes become completely judgmental. "What?" Sam half-yells at the obvious ones glaring at me. They look back at the mirrors and keep doing whatever trivial thing they were doing. "Come on. Splash some water on your face." She pushes into a tight spot, but the two girls—who I don't recognize—leave the bathroom. Within seconds, we're alone.

"They left because of me."

"Who cares? They're not worth your time or energy, Dakota. Let's get you cleaned up and looking somewhat normal before Mom picks us up."

"Oh crap, Sam." A sudden surge of regret for my selfishness

bombards me, because I've totally forgotten about her date with Calvin.

"What?" She stands in front of me and looks around, as if there's a threat right here and now.

"Calvin. You should go and be with him. There's still half the game left and you should spend time with him." I try to push her out the door, but she crosses her arms in front of her chest and tilts her head to the side.

"No way, sis. Boys don't come between us, ever. Anyway, Taylor pointed out which way you went, because I was getting a soda. He knows you're upset."

Once I splash some water on my face I feel somewhat better. I know next week at school will be grueling, but I'll have to deal with situations as they occur. "I'm sorry," I say to Sam, bringing her in for a hug. "I'm a damn mess."

"Of course you are. It's been less than a week since it happened. What are you supposed to do? Just skip away and forget it happened? No one could do that, not even the strongest person."

"You have to stop, because I'm going to cry again. I've never cried so much in my life."

"Trust me, there's a lot more tears yet to be shed," she solemnly sighs.

I hope she's wrong, but deep down inside, I *know* she's not.

CHAPTER 14

SAM'S ROPED DAD into dropping her off at the movies for her date with Taylor/Calvin. Sam made me promise to call him Taylor, although I said I'd try, Calvin seems to have stuck.

She looked so excited when she was getting ready, but I couldn't share her enthusiasm. I tried, really I did, but last night's charity game turned disastrous for me. Sam told Mom she had a headache which is why she called and got her to pick us up early.

I hate how Sam's having to lie for me. It rips me apart piece by piece.

Now I'm lying on my bed, staring up at the white ceiling thinking too much about everything. My mind is a jumbled mess, I can't stay calm and I can't get past everything. Thankfully, next week is the last week of school, then it'll be summer vacation. Three months of not seeing anyone from school. But better still, two weeks in Canada visiting with my cousins.

There's a rap on my door and I sigh, fully aware it's Mom's to talk to me about Levi. There's no way of avoiding it. Last night when she picked us up, she kept a watchful eye on the rearview mirror all the way home, but thankfully Sam distracted her while I had a shower and got myself in check.

Mom opens the door enough to poke her head inside. "Can we talk, sweetheart?"

"Sure, I was just listening to music." As I lean over to mute it, Mom comes in and sits at the foot of my plush mattress.

"I'd like to talk to you about Levi."

Internally I wince while I plaster a fake half-smile on my face. "What is it you want to know?" I look away from Mom and hope she doesn't ask me any of the hard questions.

"You two broke up?"

"Yeah."

"What happened?"

"You know, just stuff." I offhandedly shrug, trying to telepathically tell her I don't *want* to tell her.

"What kind of stuff, sweetheart?"

"Just, you know, stuff. We kind of weren't working out."

"Honey," she says and rubs her hand on my thigh, reassuringly giving me a gentle squeeze. "What happened?" she pushes.

"Nothing." *God Mom, please stop.*

"Did he want sex?" I feel my face cringe at the question and I can't help but look at her, then quickly look away. "And you must've said no." She's filling in what she thinks happened.

"Something like that."

"He didn't put pressure on you did he? He didn't try the old line of 'if you love me you'll have sex with me.'?"

"No! Nothing like that. He asked, and I said I wasn't ready." That's true, as far as it goes. No one in the world knows what happened except Sam and whoever did this to me.

"I know that eventually you'll have sex, and I hope we have an open enough relationship that you'll feel comfortable enough to talk to me about it."

Cringe. I feel like a bad person because I can't tell her what happened. She'll look at me differently and besides, it's way too late to tell her now. It's been an entire week. "Yeah, of course."

"Is that all that happened? He didn't do or say anything else did he?"

"No, Mom. Nothing else."

"When I was sixteen all I wanted to do was be taken seriously and for everyone around me to treat me like an adult. I know that's how you must be feeling, but I really want to tell you, Dakota, don't be in a rush to grow up. Growing up comes with so many responsibilities, and sometimes this whole adult thing, isn't what it's cracked up to be."

I rub my palms over my face and try to not show Mom how dead I am inside. My soul has been trampled on and any flowering part of me has been crushed and destroyed by something of which I have no recollection.

"I don't know what I want, Mom," I truthfully respond. I try to think of something to give her, anything to take the worry out of her stressed voice and her tense face. "I don't even know who my friends are anymore." That's as much as I can say without giving anything away.

"Is this because of Levi?" I shrug my shoulders. "There's going to be plenty more boys out there. He obviously wasn't meant to be *your* boyfriend."

"Lindsey and him are now an item."

"Lindsey? As in your best friend, Lindsey?"

"Ex-best friend," I correct her. "And yes, her."

"That's going to happen in life too, Dakota. And it'll happen throughout every milestone. It sucks, but the people we trust sometimes turn out to be the people who we should push furthest away." I look at Mom. Her cautionary words have struck a chord with me. They sing to my very soul. It's as if a light has been sparked inside the darkness of my heart. "Not everyone in this world is good."

I breathe out a strained breath. "I'm learning that."

"It hurts the same no matter how old you are. But if there's anyone you can trust, it's me, your father, and Sam."

"I know that." I give her a sweet smile. "Anyway, sorry to offload all this onto you. It's probably the last thing you want to hear." I try to downplay how I'm feeling, because I can't tell Mom. It's been too long. A whole week has passed, and I've kept this secret, only granting Sam access to my darkness.

"Don't let Levi take you away from yourself, sweetheart. I know it's sad. He was your first real boyfriend, and I'm sure you had a lot of feelings for him. But don't give him all that power. It's only been a week."

My heart jolts to a stop as my pulse suddenly spikes. "What . . . what do you mean?" I stumble over my own sentence.

"Since breaking up with Levi. I knew it happened at prom, because you haven't been the same since. Speaking of which, where's your dress so I can take it to the dry cleaner?" She looks around the room searching for my dress.

A new wave of nausea overtakes me, and suddenly I'm petrified and beyond speechless. *Crap, what am I going to say?* "I took it into the dry cleaners when Sam and I went for frozen yogurt the other day."

Mom looks at me and tilts her head to the side, arching a perfect eyebrow at me. "Hmm," she huffs. "Let me know when to pick it up, and I'll go get it."

Double crap. "I think it's one day next week. I have to find the slip and check, I told them there's no rush on it." God, I despise lying to her. But the alternative is so much worse. If she sees the dress, how it's ripped and has grass stains all over it, she'll know something's not right. I don't want her to assume Levi was the cause.

"Alright, sweetheart." Mom stands and makes her way to the door, opening it before she swings back to look at me. "I know there's another week of school left, just try and put everything behind you and push past it."

"I will. It's the only thing I can do." *Ain't that the truth.*

Mom leaves, closing my bedroom door behind her. I lean over and put the music back on and close my eyes. I try to push the fact I lied to Mom out of my mind, but it's just not leaving. I hate how I can't tell her.

But I know she'll be disappointed in me for so many reasons. Mostly because she'll think I was drinking and I put myself in a dangerous situation. And also because I didn't tell her the morning it happened. God, I hate this.

Dread seeps out of my pores, as hopelessness surrounds every part of my sane mind. It screams at me, and tells me no one will believe me. No one will trust me again. I'm stupid and irrational.

"So irresponsible." They're the words I expect everyone to taunt me with. "You must've been asking for it," will be on everyone's lips. "You must've been flirting." Or, "It's the clothes you wear." Or, "I've seen you hanging off that boy, no wonder it happened." Eyes will roll; gossip will be poured from whispering mouths, getting worse the wider it spreads.

Just get through the week, Dakota.

My body is preparing for the worst, the definition of pain and raw humiliation. Every part of me began to shut down on the morning I woke stranded and alone near the bleachers. Subconsciously I think I'd known what had happened, but consciously I tried to push it out of my mind. But once I'd stripped and washed myself, I couldn't *not* believe it.

My soul is bleeding. It's oozing blood, while I slowly drift toward a place I don't want to be.

Lying on my bed, I close my eyes and wish for a better future.

"Well, well, well. What do we have here?" the familiar, yet unrecognized, deep male voice says. "Let me get you home." I turn to see who's standing behind me.

"Why are you out here?" I ask. But my voice is laced with unease and tightness. It sounds garbled, like my pitch has been altered.

"Let me help you. You can lean on me; I'll take care of you." The voice belongs to someone I know, I've heard it before even if I can't yet place it. The veil draped over my perception has changed my sense of reality—of who's here with me.

"Can you take me home?" Did I speak or am I thinking it?

"Shhh, I'll take care of you. I'll take care of you real good."

Opening my eyes I bolt straight up in bed. Energy pulses through me. My heart beat thrums loudly, and my eyes burn as I try to blink the tears away. Rubbing my hands over my face, I find I'm absolutely drenched in sweat. A raging fire is burning inside me, the smoke telling me of the familiarity of the person who found me outside.

Tangling my fingers in my long hair, I pull hard to remind myself I'm alive. The pain catapults me back into the now; the nightmare slowly sinking in as I begin to visualize every moment.

I was there, in my gown, feeling groggy while standing outside, breathing in the crisp night air. My vision blurred while my body desperately screamed at me. Something wasn't right. A flash of hysteria was urgently trying to overtake me. It was warning me, but my reflexes were slowed and my mind was fogged over by a hazy blindness.

Standing from my bed, I begin to pace and try to remember more of the night that altered my life. But no matter how hard I try, I can't see a face or even place the voice.

I go over to my desk, power up my laptop and open up a blank page. I start jotting down everything I *do* know. When I finish I read over everything. It reads like a novel, a book about a young girl who was once confident, who had been damaged and torn apart on the night when her innocence was stolen.

"Fuck!" I breathe while rereading the scorching words.

I sit and stare at the document, my miserable life for the last week on three pages.

CHAPTER 15

I 'VE BEEN SPENDING my days in the library with Sophie and this Wednesday is no different. She asked me what happened on Friday night at the charity game, but I shrugged and told her I had no clue.

It's the last class of the day and I'm walking toward Mr. C's classroom. Aaron, Jordan's boyfriend is walking toward me while speaking to one of the other guys Levi and Reece play basketball with. Aaron doesn't play, but he knows everyone. He's more into surfing and hanging out at the beach rather than team sports.

"Hey there," I greet him as I walk past.

"Slut," he mumbles under his breath and chuckles. David, the other guy laughs too.

I should ignore it, and keep going. My brain is saying how summer vacation is almost here and I shouldn't rock the boat. But someone I thought was my friend has trampled on my heart and I can't let it go.

"What did you say?" I ask once they've already passed me and are sniggering down the hall.

Aaron looks over his shoulder at me and smirks but doesn't stop walking.

I run back toward him and grab him on his shoulder, stopping him from going any further. "What the hell's your problem, Dakota?" he shouts at me.

"What did you call me when you walked past?"

By now there are few people gathered around, watching the interaction between Aaron and I. David's standing shoulder to shoulder with Aaron; they look menacing standing together.

"I called you a slut." His shoulders straighten and he juts his chin out defiantly. He's daring me to say something, anything to him. David howls with laughter and Aaron turns and gives him a high-five while smirking at the small crowd.

"Do you even know what the hell you're talking about?" I spit toward him.

"Yeah, I know you wouldn't put out for my boy, but you're happy to put out for some random guy."

"Not that it's your damn business, but I'm still a virgin, you jackass." Tears spring to my eyes while my chest expands with a deep breath. I will *not* let them define the person I am, I'll stand up for myself in front of everyone.

Aaron falters and his face falls momentarily before a condescending chuckle escapes his mouth. "Not according to the pictures."

In the midst of my humiliation, I attempt to hold onto my dignity, it's being savagely hacked away from me. "Photoshop," I say as I arch an eyebrow at him. I'm desperately praying my bluff works, because if it doesn't I'll just be feeding more fuel to the fire.

You're such an idiot, Dakota. I scold myself. *You should've kept your mouth shut and walked away.*

Aaron's smirk quickly fades, and David's chuckle stops. I dart my eyes to the small, imposing crowd and already it's diminished in size. A few of the students have already walked away. This gives me hope I can retain some pride.

"Whatever," Aaron barks, rolling his eyes and turns to leave.

Quickly the remaining horde dissipates, leaving me with my shoulders firmly squared and my head proudly lifted. The hallway becomes eerily calm with nothing more than my ragged breath filling the walls.

I get to Mr. C's class and peek in through the window on the door. I see everyone looking up as Mr. C's sitting on the edge of his desk talking to the class. Freezing with fear, I opt to go and study in the library until the class is finished, but Mr. C turns his head as I look away. I caught him in my peripheral vision, which means he saw me too. I take off down the hall, and hear his door open.

"Ms. Bennett," he calls after me.

My feet stop their forward motion at the mere sound of authority in his voice. I stay turned away from him, cringing for a few reasons. First, for being stupid enough to have been caught, and second the fact the hall is now completely isolated and I'm alone with Mr. C.

"Yes, Sir," I respond without turning to look at him.

"Going somewhere, are you? You have pressing matters elsewhere?" his voice is dripping with sarcasm.

"I was going to go to the bathroom." I'm getting way too good at lying and I hate myself for it.

"Then you need a pass. Back to class." I hear his heavy footsteps move away from me. I remain glued to the spot, not really wanting to go to class. "Ms. Bennett!" he calls with urgency.

"Coming, Mr. Collins." I turn and drag my feet. When I get to class, he follows me in and closes the door behind me. My usual seat has been taken by Levi with Lindsey draped over him kissing his neck.

Levi sees me walk in, clutching my books to my chest and curls his lip at me in disdain, then rolls his eyes and looks away. Thankfully, he ignores me, and I go to the opposite side of the classroom and take a seat.

The lesson really isn't a lesson. It's the class talking about what they're going to do on summer vacation, and who's going where. Mr. C is relaxed, just having fun with the rest of the class. I'm choosing to read because I have no interest in what everyone else is doing, and considering no one's asking, obviously no one wants to know what I'll be doing either.

I'm lost in my book, when I suddenly get hit in the head by a flying piece of scrunched up paper. I look up to see Levi sneering at me, of course it would be him. I ignore him and look back down at my book.

"Hey, Dakota," Lindsey calls me.

Steadying my breath I look up to see what she has to say. "What?" She points to the ball of paper next to my hand and indicates for me to pick it up. "No thanks." What I feel like doing is standing and leaving the class with my head lowered so they can't see me crying, but I refuse to give them that much power over me.

I glance over at Mr. C, who's now got his head down looking at something on his tablet, and turn back to Lindsey.

She encourages me to pick it up, but sneaks a look over to Mr. C to make sure he's not paying attention. I look at Levi to see him talking with Jason and ignoring us. Hesitantly I pick up the crumpled paper; I can see there's something written on it, but until I unfold it I won't know what it says. I hold my breath, *petrified.*

"Ms. Bennett, care to share what you have there?" Mr. C calls from the front of the class.

"Oh shit," Lindsey mumbles under her breath though still loud enough for me and the rest of the class to hear.

This tells me whatever is on the paper isn't nice. "I think this was meant for you, Mr. Collins," I say while standing to take the paper over to him. He rises from his relaxed position and meets me halfway. "Here you go." I hand him the ball of paper.

"Thank you, Dakota. You can sit down now."

He turns to walk away, and I can hear him unfolding the paper from its almost trash-like state. The huff of air which leaves him is a clear indicator the words were indeed, horrible.

"Mr. Matthews, I believe you'd like to spend the next two days in here with me."

Levi? I thought Lindsey wrote the note. I look over to Lindsey who's buried her head in her hands, then to Levi who has fire spitting from his eyes. "Ugh," Levi grumbles.

"You'd like to start off the new school year with an entire semester of being in here, then? Or should I call your parents to inform them of this piece of literature you've penned?" Mr. C pushes. "And Ms. Herbert, it appears you'd like to join Mr. Matthews."

"Yes, Sir," she mutters from behind her hands which are still planted over her face.

"What was that?" Mr. C challenges.

"Yes, Sir." She looks up with tears streaming down her face. Her eyes are puffy as Lindsey turns to shoot a vicious glare my way.

Damn it, what on earth is on the paper?

The class is completely silent. All chatter of summer vacation has ceased while everyone is watching Mr. C, Levi, Lindsey, and me. There's a crackling in the air, stifling and toxic, while everyone's eyes shift suspiciously between us.

Lowering my eyes I choose to not look at the already judgmental faces. I doubt anything I say will make any difference, from the way their gazes are trained on me. I suspect they've already come to their own conclusions. *It's my fault.*

Suddenly the heat of the naturally warm day drains from my body, a biting chill piercing straight through me. Shivering from the artic turn of my body temperature, I keep my eyes downcast to avoid all the hatred directed at me.

It seems like an eternity passes before the whirl of chatter starts up again. With a lump lodged in my throat, I continue to look at the words on the page of my book. I've read these words at least twenty times, and I still can't tell you what they say or mean.

The bell to the last class of the day sounds, and I stand as quickly as I can to get out of here. I clutch my book to my chest, and immediately I'm pushed into from behind, knocking my book out of my arms. It flies forward, and lands with a loud thud on the floor. I look beside me, I'm met with a pathetic smile from Lindsey. "What the hell's wrong with you?"

"You really need to keep those legs closed," she spits toward me, her eyes narrowing as one eyebrow lifts in defiance toward me.

The self-loathing I'd been feeling transforms into complete and utter hatred. Embarrassment is no longer relevant; I'm beyond that now. "You have no idea."

Scooping the paperback up from where Lindsey had knocked it out of my arms, I hang back and wait until everyone's gone before I leave class. Mr. C makes my skin crawl, he truly scares me and makes me want to run in the opposite direction. But in this case, I'd rather be in here with him then out there enduring whatever plan Levi and Lindsey are preparing for me.

I'm a coward, I know.

"Dakota, are you okay?" his deep, gruff voice asks as he stands behind his desk, leaning down on it. I nod and drag my feet to leave his class. "I'll walk you out." Terror blankets me as tension grips and tightens every part of me.

Damn it, I should have risked whatever was brewing outside the classroom; I have a better chance of survival with my peers at school. "S'okay." I quicken my steps until I'm near the door where Mr. C steps in front of me, blocking my exit.

A silent in-built alarm sounds in my body, and it puts me on high alert. *Fight or flight.* In this case, it's flight. Mr. C is solid, well-muscled, and a good head-and-a-half taller than I am. His broad shoulders scream there's dangerous power in his upper body. He can easily stop me, *hurt me.*

I push past his tall, imposing frame and run. The hallways still contain a few stragglers and I move fast, dodging their slow movements so I can get to the front of the school where Sam is waiting for me.

Harshly, I exhale all the while looking behind me in case Mr. C is following. "What's wrong? You look like you've seen a ghost." Sam asks the moment she sees me.

"Mr. C said he'd walk me out. Last class . . ." I'm breathing so hard, I have to bend at the waist and grasp my knees so I can get air in and calm down.

"What happened?" She rubs her hand on my back and stands protectively beside me.

"Levi and Lindsey . . ." Sam groans, interrupting me. I finally straighten and look at her. There's a whole heap of people walking around, some are standing by the curb waiting for the bus to arrive, some are going toward their cars and some are standing around talking. "Come on, let's walk and I'll tell you what happened."

Sam and I walk home, and I tell her what happened in class. By the time we get home, she's furious. "I swear to God, tomorrow I'm giving that bitch a piece of my mind." Her tenacious and protective manner puts a large smile on my face, and I seem to have calmed down quite a lot.

"Don't do that. Just don't worry about it. Only two more days of school left, then summer vacation. We have three months of things to do." An image of Calvin flashes in my mind, and instantly I'm swept away with guilt. "Sorry, Sam. You'll be spending your time with Calvin."

Sam's face breaks out in a huge smile. "Poor Taylor, will you ever get his name right? And besides, sure I'll be hanging out with him, but not every day and you can hang out with us too."

"Three's a crowd."

"Not when one is my best friend and the other is my boyfriend." She hums and looks up to the sky, pretending she didn't just drop that massive bombshell on me.

"No way!" I half-yell with excitement. I'm so happy for Sam. Calvin must've finally asked her to be his girlfriend. "When?"

"Before lunch today. He was so cute. He was shifting from foot to foot, looking like he was going to throw up. He blurted it out, then turned and left. I was standing outside the gym looking around because I had no idea what happened. He mumbled, "Will you be my girlfriend?" but didn't hang around to hear my answer, he just walked off. I had to track him down at lunch to say yes."

"Why did he leave?"

"He said he thought I was going to say no, so he got nervous and left. He was so cute." She smiles at me.

"What did you do?"

"Hell, Dakota. I made him suffer. Told him he was lucky he ran away because I was about to embarrass him."

I bring my hand up to cover my mouth, which is hanging open in shock. "You did not!"

"Yep, then I turned to walk away."

My eyes widen. "You did not!" I repeat.

"I so did. He ran up to me and told me he was sorry for leaving. I told him I accepted his apology and of course I'd love to be his girlfriend."

"Aw, that's so sweet." I smile as I drop my hands from my mouth and give her a big hug.

We walk inside and I have a great feeling this vacation is coming at the perfect time. I need to get away from school, and I need to be around my family.

CHAPTER 16

T HERE'S ONLY TODAY and tomorrow left of school, thank goodness. I'm not sure I could ignore the stares and whispers for much longer. Over the loudspeaker, one of the ladies in the office makes an announcement. "After lunch, female students from all grades will go to the gymnasium. All male students from all grades will go to the athletic field bleachers. I repeat; after lunch, all females from all grades need to go the gymnasium and all males from all grades need to go the athletic field bleachers."

I look over to Sophie, who's in my art class, and shrug my shoulders. These last few days of school are a real waste of time. But, school doesn't finish until tomorrow, and I think most parents are happy to have us out of the house for as long they possibly can.

When art finishes, Sophie and I head over to the cafeteria and grab a table as far away as we can from my former friends. "I wonder what's going to happen after lunch?" Sophie asks while she picks at her lunch.

"Who knows?"

"Maybe it's going to be the 'have a good summer, and when you come back you'll be young ladies and young gentlemen so we expect you to act the role,' speech like they did last year before we broke up for vacation."

Sophie squints and crinkles her nose. "I don't remember that."

"Yeah, but they didn't split us up, they had us all in the gymnasium."

Sophie shakes her head. "Nah, I don't remember. Anyway, who cares? It's probably only for their duty of care or some crap like that." She chuckles.

"Hey, why are you sitting over here?" Reece comes and sits beside me placing his tray down on the table. "You should come over. You too,

Sophie."

Sophie nearly spits out her drink and begins to cough as she quickly swallows the water she had in her mouth. "Whoa, you're so funny. Hi, I'm Sophie. I'm the black sheep no one wants to talk to or acknowledge," she says as she holds her hand out to him. Her words are sarcastic as she rolls her eyes at Reece.

"That's not true, you can come sit with us."

"Seriously, Reece. You really think they'll accept Sophie when Levi and Lindsey have made it very obvious how they don't even want me hanging around? Especially after their stunt yesterday."

"What stunt?" both Sophie and Reece ask.

Sophie looks at Reece, and smiles. Reece looks at Sophie and shakes his head, but his face is filled with an easy smile.

I spend the next few minutes telling them about the crumpled up note that was thrown at me, and what happened afterward. By the time I finish, leaving out Mr. C's actions at the end of class, both are looking at me with their mouths open in a perfect 'O.'

"Are you kidding me?" Sophie asks.

"You're just bullshitting, right?" Reece questions.

"I'm afraid not." I let out a humorless rumble deep from within my chest.

"I'm going to kick his ass." Reece stands abruptly and I register exactly how angry he is. The deafening sound of blood in my ears makes me leap to hold onto his shirt. "Let me go, Dakota." Reece's face is colored with fury. His cheeks are flushed red, but his eyes are narrowed in rage. His shoulders are back and he's standing at his full height, ready to fight—*ready to fight for me.*

"Please," I beg him. "Don't bother. I don't know what was on the paper, and truthfully, I don't want to know."

I watch as the determination to beat Levi slowly recedes from his body. "It's not right. He shouldn't be treating you like this."

There's something shifting inside me; a small candle that's been sitting idle since *that* night has sparked. The flame is tiny, but it's there.

"No, you're right, he shouldn't. He's being an absolute jerk, but honestly it's Lindsey who's hurt me the most."

His shoulders relax and he finally sits back down. "It's not right," he says again.

"Hmmm," Sophie huffs while her eyes flicker from to Reece and back again.

"What?" I ask.

She curves her mouth up into a half-smile and looks down at her food. "Nothing." Her features are relaxed and amused. "What would I know?" *Weird.*

Reece's gaze reaches Sophie and he offers her a shy smile. I'm sitting, looking at both of them and wondering what the hell I've missed. "Look," I start, interrupting the awkward silence amongst us. "You should go over there, and don't worry about me. Sophie and I are fine."

"Like hell. He's an ass and she's a bitch. I don't want shit like that in my life."

"Really, Reece, what are you going to do? Ignore them? Levi's your best friend, and well, now he's with Lindsey. You guys hang out all the time, and I'm not going to be the one to get between you two."

"*Ex*-best friend. If a guy can be such a dick to a girl he's broken up with, the girl he claimed to love, then I don't want to be around someone like him. As far as I'm concerned, they can hang out with each other as much as they want. I'm not like him, and I don't want him making me look bad by association." He points over to their table, and then back to himself. "I'm telling ya, Dakota, it's not right."

Taking a deep breath, I try and wrap my head around Reece's protective behavior. But the fact of the matter is, I still can't trust him. He was the one who got me the drink and handed it to me. He had ample opportunity to slip me the drug, and he had even more of a chance to do what *was* done.

Reece talks easily to Sophie and when the bell rings to signal the end of lunch, he stands and grabs our trash to throw out.

"I can do that," Sophie protests as she grabs her rubbish.

"So can I." He snatches it back from her and playfully runs in front of her to the trash can. "See," he teases her. "Easy."

I can't help but laugh at those two. Maybe, he's interested in her. That would be pretty cool, I think they'd make a nice couple. But still, I don't trust him completely, and until I do, I'm going to remain quiet.

"What do you think this is about?" Sam asks me as she, Sophie, and I sit on one of the front rows in the gymnasium bleachers.

"Have you met Sophie?" I whisper. Sam shakes her head. "Sam this is Sophie. Sophie this is my younger, though so much smarter sister, Sam."

Sam leans across me and extends her hand to Sophie. "Hi," she says.

Sophie smiles warmly at her and takes her hand. "Hi," she responds. "We were saying at lunch how we think this might be a 'have fun and don't do drugs' speech."

Sam laughs and leans her elbows on her knees. "Who knows?" She shrugs.

Quickly, everyone shuffles in and are now sitting and waiting. I look around the gymnasium and I spot Lindsey, Jordan and Mariah. Lindsey's looking straight at me but the other two are talking with someone sitting in front of them. Lindsey flicks her hair out of her face, then scratches her cheek with her middle finger. Clearly it's directed at me. "Whatever," I mouth to her and turn away.

"Want me to smack her one?" Sam asks following my line of sight to Lindsey. "'Cause I so will." She throws a punch into her palm, her chin is high with confidence and her shoulders are ready to fight.

"Neither you nor Reece are going to hit anyone."

"Reece? What did he do?"

I quickly tell her what happened at lunch. "He did? Really?"

"Yeah, really. Both of you are feisty and I don't want the argument. It's not worth it."

"They're not worth it." She points over to Lindsey. "But you are."

My heart bleeds and opens for the best sister and friend in the entire world. "Thank you." I lean in and give her a hug.

"Eeew, Dakota. That's embarrassing." She pushes me off her, but smiles.

"Ladies," Miss Johnson, the head of the sports department, yells out. A hush falls over the vast space, all eyes shift forward and we all await the reason for this gathering. I notice out of my peripheral vision three women, all dressed in smart pantsuits, walking out to join Miss Johnson. "Detectives Miller, Garcia and Young have joined us because they want to talk to you." She looks over at three police officers and smiles. "They're all yours." Miss Johnson moves to the side, and sits down at the front.

"Hello everyone. I'm Detective Garcia and my fellow officers and I are here to talk to you about your summer vacation." She walks back and forth, commanding our attention. She attracts it easily. Everyone is listening, looking between her and the other two detectives. "We want all you girls to have a great time over the next three months. We're sure you'll be going to the beach, going to the mall, maybe even attending a few parties. You may even have a few drinks, although we can't condone that." She smiles and half of us giggle. "Some may even have sex for the first time." *Cringeworthy*. But more laughs.

"We're not here to tell you you can't, although you really shouldn't. We're sure you're all aware of the legal drinking age. But again, that's not why we're here," Detective Miller cuts in and everyone's attention shifts to her. "We're here specifically because we want to bring to your attention something that's been happening for a few years now, and will unfortunately continue until we stamp it out. Date rape drugs."

Sam's hand discreetly moves to engulf mine. She gives me a small squeeze and shifts her body closer to mine. My body reacts to the words 'date rape,' every muscle in my stomach tightens painfully and I have to make a very conscious effort not to double over in pain.

Out of the corner of my eye I notice Sophie's shoulders tense, and the muscles in the side of her neck stiffen. I hear her inhale sharply and breathe out just as viciously. I'm fighting with myself to not look over at her. Slowly I move my right hand down to find Sophie's clammy one, gently clutching it with mine.

"Who here knows what RAINN stands for or who they are?" Detective Young now steps in and starts talking. We all look around the gym to see only a few hands have risen. "You there, what is RAINN?" she points to someone on the far end. I can't hear the answer, but I can see Detective Young nodding her head. "That's right. RAINN stands for; Rape, Abuse and Incest National Network. It's an Internet site set up to help survivors of sexual assault. There's no judgment and anyone who listens to you will believe you. RAINN—that's rain with an extra N on the end. Now I want to give you some statistics that have come directly from RAINN."

"But first, I want to ask a question," Detective Garcia steps forward, and in synchronized movement, Detective Young steps back. "How many sexual assaults do you think go unreported to the police every year? Here are your choices: thirty-two percent, forty-four percent or fifty-five percent?"

There's low murmuring among the girls, but Sam, Sophie and I remain quiet. I mean thirty-two percent is huge, so I'm hoping the figure isn't any higher than that. "Hands up. Who thinks it's thirty-two percent?" Detective Young waits and most of us put our hands up, including Sam and me. "Now who thinks it's forty-four percent?" A smaller number put their hands up. "And who thinks it's fifty-five percent." An even smaller number put their hands up. "Interesting."

"Okay, everyone put your hands down. Now I want this side of the room to stand up." She indicates my side of the gym. I look to Sam and

Sophie and give them both a smile as we stand, still holding hands. The three cops are circling each other, when one speaks the other two step back.

"Do you know the name of every girl who's standing?" Detective Garcia asks. "Just a yes or no."

Collectively we all shout out the answer. Most girls say 'yes,' with a few saying 'no.'

"All those girls have been sexually assaulted." She points to those of us who are standing. The hair on my arms stand straight and a feeling of nausea rises up. "Just over four out of ten people are sexually assaulted. Forty-four percent." She goes quiet and walks the length of the room. The three female police officers keep their eyes on us.

The room is chilly, the atmosphere thick from shock . . . or maybe terror. "Scary number, isn't it?" Detective Young says in a solemn, heavy voice. "But do you know what's worse than that number?"

Not a sound can be heard; it's eerily silent. Everyone's looking toward the cops, who have our complete attention. I can't help but sneak a look sideways to see how everyone's reacting to these horrific stats.

"Here's the scariest part: the first two rows standing, keep standing, the rest of you sit down." Sam, I, and Sophie all sit down along with most the other girls. There are only a few left standing down the front. "See these girls standing?" Detective Miller stands right in front a handful of girls. "These are the girls who go to the police and report it."

"Oh my God," I whisper tightening my grip on Sam.

"Sixty-eight per cent of you will not tell anyone. You'll hold that in you, and never say a word. Maybe you're too ashamed or maybe you think it was your fault. What you need to know is sexual assault is *never* the victims fault," Detective Garcia takes over. Her words are harsh, but her tone is soft. *Holy crap, she's describing me.*

The room breaks out in horrified gasps. "What's even worse than those figures is that four out five assaults are committed by someone the victim knows. Four out of five. Think about that for a moment, because it's not the creepy old man your parents have told you to avoid, it's not a random act someone commits because they see you walking home from school. Four times out of five the attacker is someone you know."

My hands tremble with fear. I'm trying to calm down, but my body is betraying me. "It's okay," Sam whispers, clutching my hand even tighter.

"No, it's not."

"Scary, right?" Detective Young says. "To think so many of you have been or will be sexually assaulted by the time you turn eighteen. Your friend, the one you're sitting next to, or the little sister you love, maybe she's already been assaulted, or maybe she's being groomed by someone she knows."

Spit gathers in my mouth, but I seem to have lost the ability to swallow. My jaw is tightly clenched and all I can think about is Sam. I'm praying she hasn't been touched. I sneak a look beside me, and catch her looking at me. There are tears in her eyes. My heart drops to my stomach and I can't help but cry. My greatest fear has now come to light. By her reaction I think maybe she's a victim, too.

"We're here because we need to educate you on the facts. Summer vacation is hours away. You'll be spending time at the beach, at parties, maybe even camping with your friends. But do you know the most common way these assaults take place?" she pauses and looks out over the sea of girls. "A drug is slipped into your drink."

Oh my God.

"Remember, four out five assaults are perpetrated by someone we know. It could be anyone—a friend, boyfriend, brother, uncle, father or even a friend of theirs."

The statistics are abhorrent, *vile*. My body's reaction is even worse. I'm hot and cold, and I'm shaking uncontrollably. My skin is covered in pebbly goose bumps while my breath is caught in my throat.

"There are ways to safeguard yourselves so you don't become statistics," Detective Miller says. "First of all, don't accept a drink from anyone. If you want a drink, go get it yourself. Don't take a drink from anyone, not even your friends. Why? Because someone could have slipped a drug in there and even your friend didn't see it. So it's best to eliminate that threat completely and get your own drinks."

"Second." Detective Garcia holds up two fingers and continues, "If you put your drink down for any reason whatsoever, do *not* pick it up and drink it. It doesn't matter if it's full or almost finished. The drugs they use are tasteless. Some will knock you out within minutes; some may take half an hour. Some will immobilize you but you'll still be awake and aware of everything being done to you."

"Third, keep your hand over the top of your drink. Or better still, take a bottle of water with you and keep it in your hand and capped the entire time. If you put it down . . . tip it out and recycle the bottle," Detective Young says.

"Remembering these actions may save you, but they're only tips to help prevent an assault from happening. We can't be everywhere at once, but we can give you the tools so you don't put yourself at any higher risk then you already are."

"We believe knowledge is power, and if you know these small life hacks, then maybe you won't become a statistic," Detective Miller says in a straight, no nonsense voice.

Nothing can be heard, not a word, not a whisper. Just the harsh reality of what almost half of us have already or will experience sinking in.

"And one of the most important things we will tell you is something you won't believe if you are assaulted. You need to know you are not responsible for an abuser's behavior. You are not at fault if this happens to you. You weren't asking for it, you weren't flirting, you weren't dressed slutty." Detective Young air quotes 'slutty.' Her piercing gaze captures each of us, but I feel like it lands and stays on me.

Shivering, I look away and focus on nothing. I heard what she said, I'm not responsible and it wasn't my fault. But I can't tell anyone now. *It's too late.*

By the time the three detectives finish talking, there are a lot of tears and an air of heaviness in the gymnasium. The atmosphere is thick with worry and dread, and there are many hushed whispers as we all file out. There's a distinct shift in all of us. The detectives went over everything with us. From the affects a drug can have on us, to what we should do if we suspect we've been drugged.

Too late for me.

CHAPTER 17

"**WE NEED TO** talk," I say to Sam the moment we're home. Grabbing her arm I drag her into my bedroom and close the door. "Tell me, Sam. Tell me it didn't happen to you." My heart stops as I wait for her to speak. "I saw the way you had tears in your eyes when the detective was talking about the statistics." I begin to pace in my room, terrified of the words about to spill from her mouth.

"I was crying because it happened to *you*. And if those stats are correct, it won't happen to me. You've taken something which could've made me the victim instead of you." Her eyes are brimming with tears as she tries to hold them back.

"You're the prettiest girl I know," I say to her, trying to coax her into a sense of normalcy. "You know, you look exactly like Mom. You have this beautiful, thick blonde hair." I gently reach out and brush my palm down her silky strands. "Your gorgeous, dark eyes."

Sam smiles weakly at me. "We both have Mom's eyes," she corrects.

Breathing deeply I try to convey to Sam how important she is to me. "I'd rather it be me than you."

Her shoulders fall and she buries her face in her hands. I try to hug her, but she shakes her head at me. "I know this is stupid, but I feel guilty because I would hate for it to have happened to me, and hate it even more that it happened to you."

"You weren't there, Sam. And even if you were, I'd never let it happen to you. Out of the two of us, I prefer this outcome."

"I wish people like these monsters didn't exist. And I'd prefer we didn't have to hold our drinks and guard them in order to avoid getting drugged." She looks up at me with the most deadly look in her eyes. The venom deep in her dark brown eyes can't be mistaken for anything but what it is—*hatred.* "And I wish for the fucker who did this to you to be dead." Her words are as calm as the ocean on the most serene of days. She means it, with every drop of blood in her body.

Lightning strikes my body with as much force as the eerily potency of Sam's sentence. "I want him dead too, but there's nothing I can do."

"There is, Dakota. You have to tell Mom and Dad."

"It's too late now. It's been almost two weeks. I should've told them when I got home, then maybe something could've been done. But I did everything the police said I shouldn't have done. I came home and had a shower, washing any evidence off me. I've kept it a secret for too long, and now it's too late."

"It's not. If you tell Mom and Dad they can do something."

I half chuckle at Sam, her positivity blinding my reality. "There's nothing anyone can do. Look, I need to get through tomorrow and then we're going for two full weeks to Canada to see Aunt Carol and Uncle Ben. We're going to spend time with Jamie and Alyssa and I'm going to work hard on putting this all behind me."

Now it's Sam who lets out a laugh. Though I know she's not happy, because the only thing I see in her eyes is anger and the agony of the entire situation. "Is that what you think is going to happen? You can't push it aside. You can bury it only for a while before it all erupts and comes to the surface."

I squint my eyes at her, and resolve to bury this awful event. Bury it so deep, push it so far into a darkened corner that I'll never be able to reach it.

"Girls, get ready for dinner." Mom opens the door and smiles at us. "I'm making tacos. Can one of you set the table please and the other take out the trash." The question is rhetorical, because she isn't expecting us to say no.

"I don't want to talk about this anymore," I say to Sam, already starting the process of banishing my secret to the furthest corner of my mind.

"Okay," she responds, transfixed by my words. "Okay." Sam nods her head and stands to leave my room. She puts her hand on the doorknob to open it, but she stills her hand and in a steely voice whispers, "For now."

Over the next hour, Sam and I set the table and then I take the trash outside. Dad gets home and has a quick shower before we sit for dinner.

"How was school today, girls?" Dad asks as we settle into dinner.

"They split the entire school up. The girls in the gym and the boys out on the back field, and they had three female detectives for us, and Taylor said there were three male detectives for the boys and they gave us a talk about staying safe."

"Is that right?" Dad asks. "That's a great idea, splitting the kids in girls and guys. If there are any questions, then there's less chance of embarrassment."

"It is a great idea," Mom adds. "How long did the talk go for?"

"It went from after lunch until the last bell," I say.

Dad picks his taco up and takes a huge bite out of it. Half the filling falls on his t-shirt, and some more lands on his plate. "Well that didn't work out so well." Dad smiles at us, and we all laugh.

"Your father and I have some bad news," Mom says. Questions about the talk the police officers gave at school are pushed aside.

"Oh, what?" both Sam and I chorus together.

"We can't go to Canada. Jamie got chicken pox about a week and a half ago and Alyssa has been showing signs of it, too."

"Oh man. Really? I was looking forward to it," I say. I can't tell Mom and Dad why. But I was hoping to use the time away from here to bury the past, and come back to a fresh new start.

"But, your mom and I have decided, considering I've already got those two weeks off from work, there's no need to waste them. I've cut it down to one week, and we're going camping." Dad's face lights up with an eager smile.

I look to Mom and she's just as happy as Dad. Looking to Sam, I widen my eyes and give her a small look. Mom and Dad look delighted they're taking us camping, the least we can do is pretend we are too. "Yay! That's awesome."

"It is?" Sam asks.

"Yes." I grit my teeth toward her and try to kick her under the table, but I miss her and get Mom instead.

Mom and Dad are trying, and I suppose camping might be fun. "Hey," Mom protests. "Kick your sister next time, not me."

Dad chuckles and rolls his eyes. "Did you kick Mom?" Sam snickers from behind her taco.

"I was trying to kick you."

"Well you missed and got me instead." Mom looks at me, and I can't help it, I burst into laughter. "Yeah laugh now, 'cause you're stacking the dishwasher," Mom says with mirth in her voice.

"Come on, it'll be fun. Just like when you girls were little," Dad says. He walks over into the kitchen and comes back with a fork. "It's not making it into my mouth any other way." He points to all the taco filling sitting on his plate. "Just think, we'll have s'mores, and share a tent, and go swimming in the lake."

"It'll be fun," Sam finally concedes. "I'm in."

"Yeah, me too," I add. "It'll be heaps of fun."

Dad and Mom smile triumphantly. Mom looks at Dad with so much love in her eyes. Dad works as an engineer for a steel company, working long hours and sometimes six days a week. This camping trip is more for Dad to unwind than anything else. I'm sure it'll bring us closer together as a family.

Lying on my bed, listening to the soft tunes on the radio, my eyes drift shut. I try not to fall asleep because it's still early, but the rhythm of the song currently playing is relaxing.

"Dakota!" Sam bursts into my room.

"Oh my God, what?" I startle out of my relaxed state.

Sam's phone is in her hand, her face is ghostly white, and her eyes are huge and round. I know, by her appearance, whatever it is, isn't good.

"Look at this. Taylor told me to go to his page and have a look. I opened the app, and I, along with a bunch of other people have been tagged in a photo. A photo of you, on the night of your prom, and you're . . ." She swallows so loudly I hear her as she down casts her eyes.

"I'm what?" I ask, dreading the answer.

"Look." She thrusts her phone toward me. Taking it out of her outstretched hand, I swipe at the screen to reveal a picture of me. I'm on the grass, like the other picture, with my eyes closed but I'm holding my dress up showing my panties to everyone.

"Shit," I whisper as tears start falling freely. "Who posted it?" I click on the picture and the name above it, but an error message comes up. "What is happening?" I yell at the phone. I go to the home page, and scroll the newsfeed trying to find the picture. "Where is it?" I keep looking. My shaking hands are making it difficult to touch the screen, and the whirling of my mind is making it even harder to focus.

"Let me." Sam grabs the phone out of my hand, and looks for the picture. "It's gone," she says after a few incredibly long and drawn out seconds.

I grab my phone, and open the same social media app. I've been avoiding going on social media since that night, afraid of what could be on there.

My nightmare becomes real.

Countless messages, over ninety-nine notifications and numerous friend requests all light the top of the screen in big, bold red numbers. I hastily look through my newsfeed, but I can't see any pictures anywhere. "I don't have anything," I say while I frantically keep scrolling.

Sam's on her phone desperately immersed in the seriousness of this moment. "I can't find it anywhere. It's in my notifications saying a Lauren White tagged me in it, but when I look for it it's disappeared, and so has this Lauren White's profile. I don't know what's happening here, Dakota," Sam's voice is frazzled, as is my brain.

We both sit on my bed and keep looking for the picture, thankfully after what seems like hours neither of us can find it. "What if someone other than Taylor saw it?" I ask. "Oh God." The beating of my heart hasn't stopped thrumming wildly inside my chest. My own pulse is hammering in my ears, and my breath seems to have stopped.

"It's not there," Sam whispers and puts her hand over mine, stopping me from searching for it.

"Someone posted it, which means people saw it."

"If it's a fake account, which I bet it is, then that means they wouldn't have had friends, only the people they could tag. And I think you can only tag a certain amount of people, meaning not everyone would be on at the same time." I flick a look to Sam. One that screams, 'are you kidding me.' "I know, what teenager isn't on their phones. But maybe just maybe not everyone saw it."

Trying to push the boulder-size lump in my throat down, I keep swallowing; but my mouth is dry and my stomach is knotting in nervous anticipation of what else I might come across.

Suddenly my phone vibrates in my hand and Reece's name comes up on the screen. I don't want to answer it, but I have this gut feeling that if I don't, he's going to continue calling.

"Hello," I answer in a shaky and frightened voice.

"What the hell is going on, Dakota? I just got tagged in a photo by some chick called Lauren White. The damn picture is of you. What the hell is going on?" Reece's voice is laden with worry and concern.

"I don't know," I admit in a sigh.

"What do you mean you don't know? I saw the damn thing with my own eyes. It was you, Dakota. In your prom dress, but this time you were lying in a different position. Explain this to me, please."

"I can't, Reece. I can't tell you anything. Please, don't call me again."

I press the end call button, and hang up on Reece. Looking at Sam, she's sitting on my bed, clearly distressed. Her hair is a mess from where she's been running her hands through it, and her eyes are red and puffy.

Worrying my lip between my teeth, I walk over to Sam and hand her my phone. She looks at it, then back at me, blankly.

"I can't deal with this, Sam. You keep it for a while." She nods her head then slowly extends her hand to take it. "I'm so sorry to put all this pressure on you. I should *never* have put you in this position."

"You'd do the same for me."

I nod my head, and collapse on my bed. Bringing my knees up, I lean my head down and hold on to the sliver of dignity I have. "Can you leave me, please?" I struggle to ask Sam through my strained voice.

"Okay," she concedes. I feel the bed shift, and she stands to leave.

When she's gone, I crawl into bed and cry.

And cry.

And cry.

My bedroom door opens, and in my shock, I try hold in my sobs. My bed cover gets pulled away from me, and the bed dips. "We're in this together," Sam whispers and lies down behind me.

Closing my eyes, I finally manage to stem the tears. My head is pounding and it doesn't feel like it's going to let up anytime soon. *If ever.*

Listening to Sam's breathing, I finally match my breath with hers and my tired eyes close as my body begins to drift.

"Shhh, I'll take care of you. I'll take care of you real good."

I startle out of my sleep and sit up in bed, trying to blink the blackness away. Sam's out of it, lying on her back with her mouth open and slightly snoring.

I climb over the top of her and go to the bathroom. Splashing water on my face, I look in the mirror and cringe at the revolting girl looking back at me. I'm not entirely sure if I'll ever be able to look at her again.

CHAPTER 18

THE LAST DAY of school has gone by without a hitch. It's the last class of the year, and it's English. Our teacher, Mrs. Walker, has brought some food and laid it out on her desk. When I walk in and see the spread, it immediately takes me back to when I was in elementary school. Our teachers would do this, bringing party foods for the last day of the school year.

And Mrs. Walker has done the same thing. She looks at us all eagerly as we enter the class. Everyone likes her. She's always got the clunkiest shoes and lipstick on her teeth. But she's nice.

"Hey, you getting excited for Canada?" Reece asks as he comes and sits beside me.

Suspiciously I cast a wary eye over him, taking in the cautious vibe he's giving. "We're not going anymore," I curtly reply. I don't want to be rude to Reece, but it's best I keep him as far away from me as possible. Last night he called, questioning the 'photo' he was tagged in, and I simply won't give him an answer.

"Dakota," he starts as he leans in to me.

Automatically I move back, not wanting him in my personal space.

Reece's shoulders slump down and he moves back, clearly noticing the obvious reaction I'm having to him. "Can we just talk?"

"There's nothing to talk about, Reece." I cut him off, and look away. The more I can isolate myself from him, from everyone, the better it will be. Because I won't run the risk of anyone finding out.

"You and I both know, that's a load of crap." I sneak a peek back at him, and his eyebrows lift in defiance. I turn my gaze away from his, not wanting to engage in conversation. I hear the scrape of a chair being moved and involuntarily look up. Reece drags the chair in front of me toward my desk, turned it around so it's backward, and sits. His arms are crossed on the back of the chair, and he looks at me with an eyebrow raised . . . waiting for me to say something.

"What do you want from me?" My jaw locks and my teeth grind together. Through my peripheral vision I notice I've caught the attention of Levi and Lindsey. He's whispering something in her ear and both sets of eyes are locked on me. "I can't tell you anything, so you can go ahead and form your own opinion and leave me the hell alone."

"I'm not going to form an opinion until you tell me what's going on." Breathing deeply, I close my eyes, trying to settle my body down, wishing Reece would leave me alone. "Does it have anything to do with all those photos?"

All those photos? What the fuck? I've only seen two. "What do you mean by that?"

"There's the one Levi was showing everyone; which was sent from an unknown number that's since been disconnected. And then there's the picture from last night, and the two from this afternoon."

"This afternoon? What are you talking about?" My body is exhausted, I've not slept properly and I feel as if I'm on DEFCON 1 at all times. One moment I have a glimpse of normalcy, and the next it's ripped away from me in realization of the truth. I'll never be me again, I'll never be popular Dakota. I'll never know how my life was supposed to turn out, because I now have a secret and I can't let anyone else find out.

"I got sent a text with two photo attachments. By the time I saw it and tried calling the number, it was disconnected."

I stare blankly at Reece, trying to make sense of the words he spoke. I think I heard him say he got two photos, but I'm not sure. "What?" I ask in a monotone.

"Dakota, are you okay?" He leans into me, and I can't make myself move away. I can see him, but I can't respond. It's almost as if the message isn't reaching my brain and I'm slowly losing the battle with myself. "Dakota." Reece grabs my shoulders and shakes them.

But I can't stop my drifting, I'm trying to pull myself back. The darkness is so beautiful, and there's the sweet smell of melted chocolate wafting through the air, encouraging me to let go.

"Dakota!" Reece yells.

Suddenly, I'm back in the classroom with Reece only a few inches from my face and a number of class members forming a circle around us. Some have their hands over their mouths whispering to one another. "What the hell happened?"

"You almost passed out. Again, Dakota."

"Dakota, I'm getting worried for you," Mrs. Walker says as Reece helps me up.

The bell sounds and I'm relieved that as of now, I'm free from all the stares and whispers.

"I'm sorry, Mrs. Walker. Not sure what happened," I honestly admit. One minute I was perfectly normal-ish, and the next, darkness had strangled my mind and forced me under its spell.

Reece helps me up from where I collapsed, grabs my backpack and starts walking with me. "How are you getting home?" he asks, concerned.

"Sam and I will walk. It's not far."

"If I had my license I'd take you. I'll be getting it in the next few weeks."

"Good for you. Look, thanks for helping me back there." I nervously tuck some hair behind my ear and look down once we're out in the hall. "I'm sorry, Reece, I didn't mean to snap at you it's just . . ." I pause talking and take a deep breath.

"Dakota." I hear Sam yelling my name. I look to see her standing right at the other end of the hallway. I hold up a finger, indicating I'm going to be another minute. "Come on." She waves me over impatiently.

"I don't know what to tell you, Reece."

"Just the truth."

I smile at his words. My small chuckle is humorless, and my smile doesn't reach my eyes. Looking down at my shoes, I look back to him. "I can't. Have a good summer." I turn and walk away as fast as I can.

"Dakota," he calls after me. But I ignore him. "Dakota," he yells again. But I can tell by his tone, he knows it's hopeless. *I'm hopeless.*

"What's going on?" Sam asks when I reach her, her eyes transfixed to where Reece is standing.

I grab onto her elbow and keep walking out, not turning to look behind me. "Nothing."

"Don't bullshit me, Dakota. What happened?"

"Keep walking and I'll tell you. Just don't look back." Sam turns to look over her shoulder the moment I tell her not to look. "I said, don't look at him."

"Tell me why." Our steps quicken as we head out the front, down the twenty-odd steps and start toward home. "Will you let go of my arm?"

I loosen my grip, eventually dropping my hand when we're half way down the block. I sneak a look over my shoulder, to make sure Reece isn't following us. "I almost passed out again."

"What?"

"Reece started questioning me and asking me what's going on. He told me he got a message with two new pictures and when he tried calling the number it had been disconnected. Now he wants to know what's happening."

"Oh shit," Sam whimpers.

"I know . . ." *Beep, beep.* I look to where the horn sounded and spot Sophie in the passenger seat of a car. "Hey," I say, putting on a smile and facade that everything is fine and I'm unaffected by all the pictures.

"Hey, want a lift? Mom said she can drop you home if you like."

Her mom leans over and waves to us. "Um." I look to Sam then back to Sophie. "Nah, it's all good, we'll walk." Sophie's face drops, and I can see the disappointment hit her straight away. Immediately she plasters a fake smile on her face, I can identify it as fake, because it looks a lot like mine has been ever since *that* night. "Hey, I don't have your number, Sophie and I don't think you have mine." By this stage both Sam and I are standing beside the stationary car.

"No, I don't have it," Sophie says.

"Have you got your phone on you?" I ask. She nods with enthusiasm, and I can tell she's happy to be getting my number. I rattle it off and she enters it in her phone. "Can I have yours?" I ask.

"Sure."

She waits for me to take my cell out so I can input her number. I search my pockets and remember I've given it to Sam. I turn to look at Sam, silently requesting her phone. Sam catches on quickly and hands me her phone. "Here, I know you forgot yours at home today," she adds, covering for me. I give Sam a smile, one only she and I understand. A discreet 'thank you' without actually saying the words.

"I'll call you," Sophie says when her mom taps her on the leg and says they've got somewhere to be.

"Bye." I wave to Sophie and to her mom.

"Now, what were you saying about Reece?"

"He got new pictures." I grab my stomach, feeling it tighten in response to the knowledge there are pictures out there of me doing things while I wasn't conscious. "I can't believe this shit. Whoever is doing this is probably taking great pleasure in torturing me by sending these pictures to people I know."

"It doesn't really make sense. Why would they risk getting caught by being so public?"

I shrug my shoulders and narrow my gaze on the sidewalk. "It was bad enough being humiliated and having my free will violated. Now though, to have it publicly thrown in my face and be further humiliated with photos of me looking like I'm there willingly . . ." I breathe out deeply. "No wonder Levi and Lindsey hate me so much."

"Then tell them and hopefully they'll understand and stop all those cruel things they're saying and doing to you."

I shake my head. "It's too late now."

"That's bull, Dakota. And you know it."

"I get why they are the way they are. Especially Levi. We broke up because I wasn't ready to have sex with him, then he sees pictures of me half-naked, in disgusting positions with someone else clearly taking the photos. Lindsey, she's just hurt for Levi."

"It doesn't give them the right to be assholes to you though," Sam says in a very assertive and serious tone. "The least they could do is leave it alone."

"I suppose to them I look like the bad guy; especially to Levi. He's probably hurt by it all. I know I would be."

"You wouldn't judge without knowing the full extent of the other person's side."

My eyebrows draw together and I can't help but think about what Sam's said. "Not now that this has happened to me, but I think I would've judged just as quick, if not quicker before . . . well you know."

Sam turns to me, her lips in a thin line and worry is etched on every inch of her face. "You have to say the word, Dakota."

I'm already shaking my head at her before she's even had a chance to finish the sentence. "I can't."

"Why?"

"Because then it's real and it actually happened to me. And I can't deal with that."

Sam's lips turn up in a sympathetic smile. I simply keep walking and keep trying to bury *that night* as deep as I can.

CHAPTER 19

"WHAT ARE YOU girls doing today?" Mom asks as I sit at the dining room table having some cereal.

It's been a few days since school finished, and Sam's been begging me to go out with her and Taylor. But all I want to do is lie in bed, read and listen to music. I don't want to go out, and I certainly don't want to socialize with anyone.

"I want to go to the fair, C'mon on, Dakota, let's go," Sam eagerly asks me with a huge encouraging smile brightening up her face.

"I don't know," I grumble.

"Please?" She flutters her ridiculously long eyelashes at me. "I'll be the best sister in the whole wide world." She brings her hands up to under her chin as she continues to give me a pleading look. She's giving me those big puppy dog eyes while she continues to bat her eyelashes at me. "Please?"

"You already are the best sister in the world, so yeah, let's go."

"Yippee!" Sam claps her hands together.

"What time do you two girls think you'll be ready to go? Unless of course, you don't mind me taking you in my very elegant attire." Mom steps out from behind the kitchen island and does a small spin for us. She's wearing her Batman pajamas, and her hair is all over the place exactly like every other morning.

"We can wait until you've changed, Mom," Sam says while eyeing Mom's wardrobe choice with a hint of disgust.

Mom looks down at her clothes and puts her hand on her hip. "Oh, I see. You don't think I'm trendy enough," she mocks us. Mom is Mom, always threatening to do something to embarrass us. She never would, but she jokes around about it all the time.

"Nah, not at all. You look way chic like that." Sam sweeps her hand up and down, indicating Mom's summer pajamas. "Maybe you can do your hair."

"I'll put them in two pig-tails and tease the ends."

"Oh God," I mumble and rake my hand over my face. "Here she goes."

"What about your gold sparkly tank top, Mom? You should totally wear that," Sam says.

"Don't encourage her, Sam. Because one day, she will *so* do these things."

"Oh yes, I know which top you're talking about. How about a pair of black hot pants teamed with my red boots."

"See?" I say, looking at Sam. "See what you're doing?"

Sam's smiling at me, and Mom's chuckling. "I can walk you girls in, and if we happen to see any of your friends, I'll make sure I'm nice and loud for you too."

I roll my eyes and shake my head. One day, I expect Mom to do something exactly like that. "You will not!"

"I'm hurt by your behavior, Dakota." Mom clutches at her heart pretending to be devastated. "Seriously hurt." She even fake cries. I look over to Sam and roll my eyes again. Both of us are laughing at Mom and her great, easy nature. "And to prove how hurt I am, I'll be sure to have lipstick all over my teeth and to beep for as long as I can so everyone looks at you while you get out of the car."

"Good idea, Mom," I say as I stand and take my bowl over to the sink. "I'll tell everyone you've been released from the hospital and you're really excited to be home."

Mom smacks me in the arm, then howls in laughter. "You girls," she says shaking her head. "I'll go get ready. Red or pink lipstick?" She looks at me then cracks a huge smile.

"C'mon," I say to Sam as she's downing her orange juice.

I head to my room to get changed, and Sam walks down the hallway toward her room.

"Just call me when you want me to pick you up," Mom says as we pull up to the parking area where the fair is set up. "Here you go girls." Mom takes out some money from her purse and hands it to us. "Have fun, and remember, don't go to the bathrooms on your own, go together.

Don't accept drinks from anyone. And most importantly, don't get in anyone's car. Call me if you need anything."

My heart palpates when Mom tells us not to accept drinks from anyone, but only because of *that night*. "Thanks, Mom," Sam and I chorus together.

We get out of the car and Mom yells out to us before she pulls away, "I love you."

"Love you," Sam says.

"Love you, too," I add.

Mom leaves and Sam and I walk over to the short line to pay the admission into the fair. "I hope I don't see anyone from school," I lean over and whisper to her. "I couldn't handle running into Levi or Lindsey, or really anyone." I want to have fun and enjoy myself with Sam. "Hey, how come you're not hanging with Calvin today?" We shuffle forward in the line, but there are still a few people ahead of us.

"Taylor." She rolls her eyes while teasingly pushing on my shoulder. "He's got to work."

"Has he got a job?" I ask and furrow my eyebrows together.

"Yeah, he's saving to buy a car. He works as a dishwasher in a restaurant downtown. He's working from one until eight tonight."

"Wow, really?"

"Yeah. I'm really proud of him."

"I didn't take him for a dishwasher."

"What's that supposed to mean?"

"He's tall and lanky and he wears those glasses, he's kinda a nerd."

"That's not nice." Sam holds back a smile. "True, but not nice."

"I gotta say, I think he's really sweet, Sam. You know how he came over for dinner the other night?"

"Yeah, and Dad kept looking at him like he wanted to kill him."

I laugh and know exactly what look she's talking about, because that's Dad being Dad. He did it to Levi the first few times he came over. "You know what I liked about him?" I look over to Sam and she shakes her head. "I like how when you sat at the table, he pushed your chair in. Like an old-fashioned guy. Like they used to do in the olden days, and like Dad does for Mom."

Sam smiles, and a pink hue creeps up to sit high on her cheeks. "I asked him about that when I walked him out. He said his Dad once told him, 'Son, we may not have a lot of money but we can show the important women in our lives how much we appreciate them by simple manners.' My heart melted when he told me that."

"Aw." My heart skips a beat too at hearing such a beautiful thing. "That's so cute," I say as we take a few more steps forward toward the entry.

"I know. You know what else?" I shake my head. "He opened the door for me and waited for me to go through before he came out."

"He sounds like Dad. He always holds the door open for Mom and us, and pushes her chair in, makes her a drink at night."

"I know."

"Just two?" the bored woman working the admission asks when we step up.

"Yes please," I say taking out some of the money Mom gave us.

When we've paid and entered, we head over to some of the rides first. "Which one do you want to go on?" I ask Sam.

Sam's eyes light up when she sees the Drop Tower. "That," she excitedly squeals as she sizes up the height.

"Ugh," I mumble and walk beside her. Sam loves anything with extreme height. "Alright." I don't really think it matters what I say, she'll be on that ride whether I join her or not.

"Come on, it'll be fun." She links her arm with mine and picks up speed to get to the already forming line. "I hope it goes really fast." She looks up and watches the slow ascent to the peak of the ride. "Watch, Dakota." She's looking up, shielding her eyes from the sun when we hear a lot of high pitched scream as the suspended seats free drop toward the ground. "Oh my God. That looks like so much fun."

"Yeah, fun," my voice is flat, showing no enthusiasm. Sam tilts her head to the side and her smile drops. I feel like such a spoil sport. "Sorry, Sam."

"S'okay, I know you hate heights. Maybe you can sit this one out and I'll go on my own?"

I slump my shoulders even further and feel like a crappy sister. Everything she's done for me, and I can't even go on a stupid ride with her. "No way," I perk up. "I declare today to be 'Dakota and Sam Day.' And if you want to go on a ride like that . . ." I say and point up to the ridiculously high ride, " . . . then we're going to go on it and any other ride you want to go on too."

Sam throws her arms around me and hugs me. "Thank you," she whispers. "I know this mustn't be easy for you." She gives me a kiss on the cheek and steps back to look up as the seats on one side start their trip back to the top with new victims . . . I mean passengers.

It doesn't take long before we're at the front of the line and it's our turn. My stomach knots and my pulse quickens as the fat, sweaty guy calls us up and directs us to two available seats. "You sure you'll be okay?" Sam asks while the guy checks our harnesses.

"Yeah," I lie. My heart's in my throat and my skin prickles as sweat forms small beads across my forehead. Sam's eyebrows lift and she tilts her head to the side. "I swear, I'll be fine."

"Just close your eyes and enjoy the ride."

Enjoy the ride, she says. Like that's going to happen.

"All ready," the controller calls.

My eyes are glued to him. "Last chance," Sam says close to my ear.

"Nah, I'm good." I don't take my eyes off the guy, instead I watch as we slowly ascend toward the clouds. Everyone below gets smaller and smaller, as my heart evens out and I find a kind of peace up here. "I like this," I say to Sam as we climb higher.

"See, it's not that bad."

I look over the breathtaking horizon. Green grass meets an alluring sapphire sky which creates an illusion of soft waves peaking in the distance. "Wow," I murmur as I marvel at the spectacular sight created free for everyone's pleasure.

"Beautiful, right?" Sam asks. I nod my head and keep watching the absolute perfect painting with the finest of brushstrokes.

"It's simply . . ." Suddenly it happens. The carriage drops, my stomach is still at the top, while we're hurtling toward the ground. I don't scream, I don't do anything. Sam's arms are flapping around in the air as she lets out an almighty scream.

We get to the ground in seconds although it took a few minutes to drag us to the top. "Oh my GOD!" Sam yells when we safely reach the bottom. "I want to go again."

"That was so much fun."

Sam's eyes are wide and bright and I can imagine I must look the same as her. We jump out of our seats and run down the few steps to line up again. "Hey, let's go on the Pendulum Swing first, then the Ferris Wheel, then we can come back and do this," Sam eagerly looks at me, her smile broad and encouraging.

"Hell yeah, let's go before I lose my nerve."

We go and line up at the Pendulum Swing and wait our turn. "Oh my God, Dakota, I never in a million years thought you'd do this." She bumps shoulders with me and smiles. "I'm so proud of you."

The day goes by in a blur, and we spend a lot of time up in the air, only to be thrown from side to side, upside down and round and round on various rides.

It's getting on in the afternoon and we decide to stop and have a bite to eat before we check out the side attractions.

"I feel like having a burger and a milk shake," Sam says to me as we walk toward the covered food area.

"Burger and lime lemonade," I say. "Oh my God, and a piece of key lime pie."

Sam's head whips around and she looks at me. Her mouth falls open and her eyes widen. "Oh yeah, key lime pie. How did I forget key lime pie?" She smacks her cheek playfully and quickly shakes her head. "What the hell is wrong with me? Maybe I can have dessert first."

We both chuckle and head directly over to one of the food vans selling what we want. When we get our food and drinks, we find a spot and head over to sit and eat. "You know, today's been fun," I say as I bite into my burger.

"It has."

"Hi, Dakota, Sam," I hear Reece's distinct, deep voice. I look to my left and he sits down beside me. On the opposite side is someone else who looks a lot like Reece. "You remember my brother Miles?"

"Hi," both Sam and I chorus together. Miles is almost exactly the spitting image of Reece, but much older. I bite into my burger and keep an eye on Miles.

"Wanna get some lunch?" Miles asks Reece.

"Yeah I'll have . . ." He turns his face to look at what I'm having and jerks his chin up to Miles. "Can I have a burger and a soda?"

"'Spose I gotta buy it?" Miles questions Reece.

"Jerk," Reece mumbles.

Miles stands and walks around the back of Reece, then darts his hand out and smacks Reece on the back of the head. Reece's head jerks forward and he turns to flip his brother the bird.

"Don't you have another brother?" I ask putting down my burger.

"I'm one of three. My younger brother, Luke, has recently turned five. Miles is twenty-one."

Mentally I'm doing the math in my head, but unconsciously my mouth opens and says, "That's gotta suck. Huge age gaps." I slap a hand to my mouth and look away. "Sorry, clearly I have a problem with saying what I think."

Reece laughs and shakes his head. "I think it's cute," he says shyly.

Sam kicks me under the table discreetly—which is actually really obvious to everyone—and tilts her head toward Reece. 'Stop it,' I mouth to her. "How come your older brother wants to hang out with you?" I ask. Suddenly I feel my entire face turn red, heat is rolling off me as I realize exactly what I said. "Crap, sorry, that sounded so bad. I didn't mean it like that."

Reece is chuckling as his eyes widen in surprise. "I can't believe you said that. Anything else you want to insult? You may as well get it out of the way now while you're still on a roll."

"She's got a case of foot in mouth syndrome," Sam interjects happily.

"Shut up," I playfully snap.

"Please, go on. Maybe she doesn't like the jeans I'm wearing today, or the t-shirt. Should I have styled my hair on the side?" Reece flips at his hair, teasing me further.

"Dude," Miles says walking back to the table with a tray full of food, having caught Reece playing with his hair.

Sam and I look at each other and burst into laughter. "Great, now you've given my brother ammunition for the next three months."

Miles picks up a fry and throws it at Reece. "They weren't the ones playing with their hair. And even if they were, they're chicks, it's what they're supposed to do."

"Sexist much?" Sam says.

"Nah, not like that. You misunderstood what I was saying."

"Dude, these two are a force to be reckoned with. Don't argue with them, you won't win," Reece points to us.

"I misunderstood what you were saying?" Sam turns her body toward Miles in order to continue this with him. He watches her and smirks to himself. "How can I misunderstand a sexist comment?"

Miles chuckles and I smile too. "You went and did it now, brother," Reece says in an 'oh shit' tone.

"I'm just saying, girls can do that kind of stuff all the time but guys really can't or don't. It's not typical guy behavior." He shoves a fry into his mouth and winks at me. He can obviously see Sam's trying to goad him, and clearly he's okay with it. "Reece, is this what you have to put up with at school? All this 'girl power' crap?"

I can't help but laugh. Miles has Sam worked out, and now he's giving it right back to her, making her work even harder.

"Crap?" Sam shrieks. "Seriously?"

"Next thing you know they're going to want equal pay too." Miles keeps eating his fries, one by one. Reece is shoveling his burger in his mouth and Sam realizes exactly what's going on. I finish my burger and watch the amusing sparring match between Sam and Miles.

"I'm tired of you," Sam says casually to Miles.

And that's all the four of us need to laugh. "Your brother's having a great time teasing Sam." I sip some of my soda.

"He likes to talk shit; he's harmless." Reece polishes off his burger then lifts his soda to finish that too. I look over to Sam and Miles and they're having an easy conversation with each other. I'm surprised because usually guys who are in their twenties aren't so easy to get on with. They'd usually think girls our age are beneath them and not really worth their time unless they're hoping to get laid.

Suddenly reality hits hard. The thought of Miles trying to chat up Sam for sex smacks me in the face like a bolt of lightning. "Your brother's not going to get laid," I say to Reece as I turn to face him.

Reece's face drops, and his eyebrows knit tightly together. "What?" I look to Miles and Sam, then back to Reece. It takes Reece a couple of seconds, before his eyes tell me he finally understands what I'm saying. "First, she's jail bait, second, he has a girlfriend he's been dating for like two years, and third, the only reason he's here is because I saw you and wanted to spend time with you."

I stare at Reece, trying to find words. But I'm afraid the only thing I can do is blink at him. "Huh," I puff. The words aren't forming, I don't actually comprehend what he's saying.

"Is 'huh' all you can say?"

My blinks increase, as does the white noise in my head. "Um." A barrage of questions surges through me; suddenly I'm tripping over my own tongue.

"Now it's 'um.' Maybe by the time the sun goes down, I might get a complete sentence," Reece teases me.

"You're right about one thing." Miles says to Reece. I look over to Miles. "She really is pretty, little bro, but not sure what you said to her to get her to go quiet." He winks at me and gives me a goofy smile.

Sam kicks me under the table again, and I look at her. "Stop kicking me or you'll give me a damn bruise," I snap at her.

"I'm going to get key lime pie, want a piece?" Sam offers as she looks at me.

"Hell yeah, I want a piece."

"Be back in a minute." She stands and Miles stands too. "Where are you going?" Sam casts a watchful eye over Miles.

"These places are filled with crazy people, I'm coming along to make sure you're safe."

"Hmm," Sam huffs. "Fine." She walks off and Miles walks alongside her. I watch them leave and I'm guessing he said something funny because she turns to him and smiles.

"I like your brother." I push my trash to the side and bring my soda closer to me. "He's nice. What does he do?"

"He recently enlisted. He's due to leave in a couple of weeks so he's been spending time with all of us before he goes."

"Why didn't you bring your little brother with you then, considering this is a fair and little kids love it here."

"Luke was supposed to come, but he was running a fever last night and this morning. So we came, and Miles said he'll take Luke somewhere when he gets better."

"That's gotta suck for Luke."

A moment of quiet falls over us, it's awkward and tense. I can feel Reece's eyes on mine, and I know he's desperate to talk to me about *those* photos. "Dakota, how are you holding up?" The question takes me by surprise, it's almost as if he knows about *that* night, and what happened to me.

"Wh-what?" I stutter, trying my hardest not to give anything away. "What do you mean?" There's a scratch to my voice, a clear caution and uncertainty.

"Levi and Lindsey," he breathes in a small restrained tone.

"They're a couple now, and I'm happy for them." I don't dare look over to Reece, because I know he'll see the hurt rolling off me.

"It sounds like you're real happy," he says sarcastically.

"Truthfully, I really don't care." I look at him, and notice his intense gaze locked on mine. "I wish they'd leave me alone."

"What are they doing?"

"More what they're saying than anything else. It doesn't matter, summer vacation is here and by the time school starts back up again, they'll be so immersed in each other that no one else will exist." I shrug my shoulders, pick the rubbish up and start toying with it attempting to distract myself from this conversation.

"What really happened? All I have is Levi's side of the story, and what he's saying isn't very nice."

My eyes flash to his and I see he genuinely wants to know, which makes me think, maybe it wasn't Reece who drugged then assaulted me. "It doesn't matter. It's all in the past now, where it deserves to stay."

Reece huffs and turns on the bench seat so his body is directly facing mine. "This pisses me off so much," he grunts. "Because I know something's happened. You've changed so much. You're quieter and more timid then before. You dress differently and you're entire personality is different." I look down at what I'm wearing, questioning my wardrobe choice of jeans and a t-shirt. "Something's happened, and it's so damn obvious to me."

"It's nothing," I try to say, but my throat constricts because I hate lying, and especially to someone who's fighting so hard to know the truth. "Just leave it all alone, Reece."

He drags his hands through his hair, then down over his face. Reece lets out a huff before focusing his gaze away from me. "One day, Dakota, I hope I can prove to you that you can trust me."

"Hey, here's your key lime pie," Sam interrupts, smiling at me. But her smile is tight and her brown eyes are suspicious of the conversation she walked in on. I give her a small nod, silently telling her I'm okay.

"What are we doing, little bro? Accompanying these two lovely ladies, or are we going to try to win Luke one of those giant stuffed dogs?" Miles asks Reece.

"Um. What are you two doing after you finish those?" Reece asks looking between Sam and myself.

"We're going to check out some of the sideshows too," Sam happily reveals, smiling. "We can all go together."

I roll my eyes as I shovel in forkfuls of the pie. "Then I might grab another soda, and when you're done, we'll head off." Miles claps a hand to Reece's back. "Want anything?"

Reece picks his soda up and notices he's finished it all. "I'll get a soda too. Hang on, I'll come with ya. Do you want anything?" he asks Sam and myself. Both of us shake our heads.

The moment Reece and Miles leave, Sam leans over and says, "Whatever was going on, it looked intense. You okay?"

"Yeah, I'm okay. He was asking about Levi and said he hopes one day I'll trust him enough to tell him."

"I gotta say, I think he's all right. I don't know, Dakota, I don't think he did *that* to you," she whispers as she tilts her head slightly so no one can hear us. "I've got a good feeling about him."

I shrug my shoulders and crinkle my nose. "I don't know anymore, Sam. You're the only person, other than Mom and Dad I trust."

"I'm not saying you should fully trust him, just cut him some slack. I really don't think he's the one who hurt you."

"I s'pose."

"Ladies, are you ready to head off?" Miles asks as he and Reece both come back to the table.

Reece looks at the half eaten key lime pie on my plate and says, "Not good?"

"It was, I'm just so stuffed."

"Then you're ready? Unless of course you've changed your mind?" Reece's voice is overshadowed by sadness. It seems as though he really wants us to continue on with them.

"You ready?" Sam asks looking at me. I nod and stand from the bench seat, grabbing my trash. "Let's go."

I grab her trash too and go to take it to the bin. "Here, let me." Reece holds out his hands to take them. A big, friendly grin easily sprawls across his face. We head off to the side shows. Reece spots a giant stuffed dog and heads straight for it. "We have to win this for Luke," he says as he turns to Miles.

It's a shooting game where there are ducks going across a makeshift pond, and you have to use a carnival gun to shoot at them.

"You need to shoot six ducks," the carny says as he takes Miles' money.

"Six, you can do this one," Reece says to Miles.

"Nah, not me." He holds his hands up in resignation and steps back chuckling. "C'mon, Dakota, give it a go."

I look to Reece who offers me the gun, then at Miles, whose gentle smile is encouraging me to have a go. "I've never been interested in this game before," I admit.

"Well it's not for you, it's for my brother, so you better get interested in it," Miles says and softly shoves me toward the game.

"You can do this, just pretend they're Levi and Lindsey," Sam says and laughs at her own joke.

I grab the gun, and look over my shoulder at Sam. Reece chuckles too, but he puts his hand up to his face to cover the snickering. "Come on, Dakota."

I take a breath in, line the gun up with a duck, and shoot. The first one falls over. "YAY!" I scream in excitement as I jump up and down on the spot. "Oh my God, I got it!"

"Five more to go," the carny guy says, in a bored monotone.

"How many shots do I have?"

"Ten in total."

Suddenly I get really nervous, because this is for Reece's brother, and if I don't get them, they've wasted their money. "Here, you better do it." I turn around and offer the gun to Miles and Reece who are standing next to each other.

"No way, you're having too much fun." Reece shakes his head.

"Here." I thrust the gun toward Miles and he takes a step back. I look to Sam who also shakes her head. "I won't get them. Someone take it, please."

Reece steps up to me, and turns me around so we're facing the stupid ducks. "Have faith in yourself, Dakota." He guides me so I've got aim on the ducks. "If you don't have faith in yourself, no one else ever will either."

I squint as I look down the barrel and take aim. Stopping for a second, I tilt my head toward Reece, trying to catch his attention. But he's not looking at me.

The next nine shots see me lose . . . spectacularly. But I had so much fun trying. "I'm sorry I lost," I say to Reece and Miles.

"Did you have fun doing it?" Reece asks. I nod and smile at him, because even though I didn't manage to shoot down six ducks, I still shot down four. And every time I got a duck, I screamed and surprised myself. "Good, because you looked like you were having a ball."

Miles comes up to the game, pays the attendant and shoots six ducks, all in a damn row. "Seriously?" I say as I flail my arms frustrated at myself.

"Hey, you did well." Reece moves so he's standing beside me to my right, as Sam's on my left.

Miles wins the stuffed toy for his brother, and we head on to the next game.

CHAPTER 20

"**DID YOU GIRLS** have fun?" Mom asks when she comes to pick us up. "Who's that?" Her keen eye goes to Miles who's standing by the curb.

"That's Miles Hendricks," I answer as I wave to him.

"Reece's brother? Boy, he's grown. I haven't seen him in years. Where's Reece?"

"He's gone to the bathroom," Sam answers.

"Oh right. Who's that stuffed dog for?" Mom pulls away and heads toward home.

"Luke. He's sick, so they won him a toy to make him feel better."

"They're good kids, those three. I remember when I first met his mother, I thought she was a new-age hippy type. As it turns out, I was right, she *is* a new age-hippy type, but so nice and generous. Anyway, I've spent the day packing everything we need for our camping trip and we still need a few things, so tomorrow I'm going to the mall to get them. Do you girls want to come too?"

I look behind me to Sam and she eagerly nods. "Sure thing," I say.

"Oh crap," Sam huffs. "Taylor's coming over tomorrow. We were going to hang and go for a swim."

Mom lets out a small sigh and takes her hand off the steering to rub her chin. "Right, well I'm not leaving you two on your own. What time is he coming over?"

"He said about ten. Is that okay with you, Mom?"

"No, ten's too early. Tell him to come over at lunchtime, that way we can go to the mall and be back in time for lunch. Tell Taylor to bring an appetite." Mom smiles at Sam through the rear-view mirror.

"I'll text him now."

We get home and I take a shower. The weather's been steadily getting hotter, and today is no exception. When I get out of the shower I go to Sam's room. "Hey, can you do me a favor?"

"Always," she replies as she sits up in bed. "What is it?"

"Can you check my phone, see if there's anything there." I scrunch up my nose, and draw my eyebrows together. "If there is, don't tell me." Grabbing the hair tie I have around my wrist, I gather my long hair and put it in a ponytail. "No actually, do tell me." I huff a deep breath. "No, don't tell me." God, I feel ill. My stomach contracts in anticipation of what Sam's going to find.

She's got my phone in her hands, and she's powering it up. We both wait, our breathing ragged. Sam's slim shoulders shake as she scrolls through whatever she's seeing on with my phone.

"Crap," I mumble. Frozen with terrified fear, I simply wait for Sam.

"There's nothing here." Her eyes are down, glued to the screen of my phone. "There are a few messages from Sophie saying she'd love to hang out. And one from Reece, he messaged this afternoon after we left the fair, here I'll read it.

'Hey Dakota, thanks for letting us hang out today. Maybe we can do it again.'

She looks up at me and her kind eyes find mine. "See," she says. "He's alright."

"I must admit, I'm kinda comfortable around him. But nowhere near enough to say he wasn't the one who . . ." my voice trails off, refusing to say the word. "You know." Sam nods as she looks at me. "Maybe, when we get back from camping, then we can all hang out. You know, me, you, Taylor and Reece."

"Yay," Sam happily exclaims while she drops my phone on her bed and claps her hands together. "You called him Taylor, not Calvin."

"Thank you, Sam. You've made this whole thing less stressful for me."

"I can't imagine it's a pleasant experience for anyone." She screws her nose and mouth up as she says the word 'pleasant.' "I'm sure there are people out there who don't have any support. You have me, and if and when you let them in, Mom and Dad too."

Shaking my head, I stand and start pacing in frustration. "You know I can't, it's too late. Weeks have passed and I've had loads of opportunities to tell them and haven't. Now, if I say something, I'm going to look like a liar. I should've told them the night it happened."

"Yes, you're right. You should've," Sam agrees. Her voice isn't harsh and scolding, more like sympathetic with understanding. "But I'm sure they'd prefer to hear it from you, rather than hearing it from someone else. Secrets always have a way of blowing up."

So many emotions hit me at once, Sam sings the same tune all the time and she's right, I know it. "Just stop it," I bark toward her. Annoyance is bubbling under my surface, I'm overwhelmed by everything.

"Dakota."

Running my hands through my hair, I tug on the ends while closing my eyes and kneeling to the floor. "I can't tell them," I cry out in frustration. "I just can't."

Sam gently lays her hand on my back. "I'm sorry, Dakota, I didn't mean to push you so hard," her voice is soft and wispy and, I can tell she's trying to appease me.

"I'm not mad at you." I look into her soft eyes and notice there's not one ounce of judgement. "I'm angry at myself." She expels a deep breath and slumps her shoulders. "I shouldn't have gone that night."

"You're still laying blame on the wrong person. You're a victim, not a villain." Her features are soft with love for me. Her eyes are gentle, her smile tender, and her body affectionate. She moves closer wrapping me in her love. "Please don't tear your hair out, I didn't mean to sound like I don't understand." When she envelops me close to her warm body, I accept it, desperately needing her hug.

Minutes drift past and when I finally let my body relax and I resolve to stop hating myself. I untangle from Sam. "Sorry, I freaked out." Standing, I head over to the bed to sit. "I shouldn't have yelled at you. I know you're only trying to help."

"You didn't yell at me. You panicked. I kinda freaked out when you fell to the floor. But I suppose, as much as I understand what you're going through, I'm not the one who's actually living it. I'm trying though. I'm scared for you, so damn terrified that whatever you're feeling will last a lifetime if you don't get help."

Breathing raggedly, I try and swallow the shame that's sitting in the back of my throat. "I love you." I stand and go hug Sam again. "Thank you, for everything," I whisper.

"I love you too." She tightens her arms around me in a gentle squeeze before letting go and walking over to her bed. "Here, take your phone and call Reece, tell him we should definitely go out when we get back from camping."

"You're too grown up, stop acting like you're eighteen instead of fourteen."

"Well." She rolls her eyes and smirks. "Someone has to be the smart one, and seeing as you missed out in the brains department, it has to be me." She shrugs her shoulders teasingly.

"Whatever." I walk toward her door and open it. "But seriously, thank you."

"Ah." She flips her hand at me dismissively. "It's what sisters do."

"Hello," Sophie answers her phone.

"Hey, it's Dakota."

"Hey, what's doing?"

I lay on my bed and turn to put some music on in the background. "Sam and I went to the fair today, and we saw Reece and his brother there. And we're getting ready to go camping."

"Camping? I haven't been camping in years, since . . ." she pauses for a few seconds. "Since before Dad was sent to jail."

"Do you wanna come?" I ask excitedly while sitting up on my bed. I'm about ready to run out to Mom to ask if Sophie can come too.

"Hell no. There's no way I'd go camping now. I'm much more aware of snakes, and bears and shit like that."

"There are no snakes where we go camping."

"Aha! You didn't say anything about bears."

I chuckle to myself before I add, "And no bears, either."

"Still no," she adamantly replies.

"Come on, it'll be fun. It's just my family, but it'll be so fun."

"Is there indoor plumbing?" she asks in a sassy pitch.

"Well, no not exactly. We'll go off track, and do the whole tents and digging a hole thing."

"Will there be a proper bed?"

"Again, no. More like sleeping bags and a campfire."

"Hang on a second. Back up right now, sister. There will be s'mores?" Her tone changes and perks slightly.

"Of course, you can't go camping without making s'mores."

"See," she huffs and half chuckles. "Given there'll be s'mores I'd have seriously considered coming. However, there's still a minor problem."

"Which is?" I'm already smiling because I can sense, by her easy tone, she's about to say something amusing.

"Snakes and no toilets. Not to mention big bears, and other wildlife who sometimes wander into tents and make themselves at home."

My face has a broad smile and I can't help but feel totally comfortable around Sophie. "Alright, alright. No camping, but what about if you come over when we get back? We've got a pool, Dad can do a cookout, and we can make s'mores, 'n stuff like that?" I become hopeful as I wait for her response.

"Yeah? You want me to come over? Really?" There's a wary hopefulness to her question, as if she doesn't believe me, or worse still; doesn't think we're really friends.

"Of course! We're friends, right?"

She lets out a sigh and a small groan. "I've found it hard to make friends since we moved here a few years ago. I'm more of a loner, preferring to spend my time in the library." My heart breaks for her because being isolated from people sucks. I should know, my barriers are getting higher and higher. My walls are becoming impenetrable and rock solid.

"Well, we're friends now, Sophie. Sorry, but there'll be no getting rid of me." I smile triumphantly into the phone. I must look like a crazy person, grinning to myself. But I know us being friends will make a world of difference to *both* of us.

"Good, 'cause I kinda like you and Sam."

"So, you'll come over?" I feel as if I'm eight years old again, asking her to be my friend. I hold my breath and wait for her reaction. I'll be cut if she says no, and giddy if she says yes.

"Hell yeah, and you better make good s'mores."

"Yay. I'll call you when we get back from camping."

"Okay. I've gotta go, Mom's taking me out for dinner so I gotta go get ready."

"Have fun. See ya soon," I say before hanging up.

I sit back on my bed and an air of calm washes over me. Today's been such an extreme day. I had heaps of fun at the fair, and I loved spending time with Sam. I even felt comfortable with Reece and Miles which surprises me because after *that* night, I never thought I'd have the confidence to feel okay around people again, especially boys.

I toy with my phone, and contemplate calling Reece. I'm not a hundred percent sure, but my gut is saying he's okay. But then again, I thought everyone was okay before the night I became a target, and then a victim.

Dialing his number, I wait for him to answer the call. "Dakota?" he says while puffing.

"Hi, how are you?" I slap my forehead because immediately I sound like an idiot.

"I'm good." His voice sounds cautious. "How are you?"

"Yeah good." Suddenly my stomach knots and my hands shake. "Um . . ."

"Thank you for letting us hang out today. I had a great time. Miles likes your sister, he said she'll make a good lawyer when she's older. He also said she'd be the type of little sister he could imagine having if he didn't have two brothers."

I laugh out loud. "Wait, does that mean Miles called you a girl?"

"Nah," he defensively says, quite loudly. I laugh again. "Well, yeah."

"You make me laugh."

"I'm so not a girl. I can guarantee that, Dakota. Miles likes to say shit like that to get under my skin. It used to irritate the crap out of me, but now I know it's just his sense of humor."

"You're gonna miss him when he leaves."

"Yeah, I know." He sighs. "So, I'm thinking, maybe we can go to the movies if you're not going anywhere for vacation." I furrow my eyebrows together and pull my phone away from my ear to stare at it. "Dakota?" I hear Reece call.

Putting the phone back to my ear, I sit there quiet for a few seconds. "Are you asking me out on a date?" Scrunching my nose I smack myself on the forehead. It's ridiculous to even think that's what Reece is asking.

"Yeah, I guess I kind of am."

Stunned I stare at the pale yellow wall ahead of me. "Um," my voice is heavily strained, and guarded.

"It's um . . . it's okay, don't worry about it. I thought maybe you'd like to hang out and watch a movie or something. No big deal." His tone isn't saying 'no big deal' it's saying he's embarrassed he's even asked.

"I'm nowhere near ready to date again, Reece."

"Yeah, of course." He lets out a breath, but I can still hear the unease in his voice.

"How about this? We're going on a camping trip, and when we get back I'm going to ask Mom and Dad if we can have a cook out here. Sophie will be here, and Sam's boyfriend." I should probably let Sam know. "Why don't you come over for that?"

It's safer in numbers, *although* . . .

"I'd love to. Thanks for the invite."

Just then there's a knock on the door. "Come in," I half shout. "Hang on a minute, Reece."

The door opens and Mom pops her head in. "I need help with dinner." She smiles at me and her eyes go to my phone. "When you're finished." She juts her chin toward my phone.

"Okay, I'll be out in a couple of minutes." Mom then closes the door and leaves me to my phone call. "You there?"

"Yeah, I heard. You have to go help your Mom with dinner. That's cool. Give me a call when you get back from your camping trip. How long are you going for?"

"I think just a few days. We were supposed to go to Canada to see my cousins, but a few of them ended up with chicken pox, so it's safer if we don't go. Dad had two weeks' vacation for it, but he's cut it back to just one."

"I remember you telling me about your cousins in Canada. Sorry you're not seeing them now. But, yeah, that sounds cool. I haven't been camping for about a year. We do it rough when we go though. You know, digging holes and stuff."

"Oh my God, us too. Dad always says if you're going to go into nature, it means we have to strip everything back to basics." Dad's like that, he's a guy's guy. "Dad loves camping so much, but Sam and I aren't really into it. So he's learnt to adapt with having daughters instead of sons." I draw my eyes over my bed and have an onset of guilt. "Sad really," I whisper.

"I don't think your dad is upset he has girls," Reece says, obviously picking up on my sadness.

"I didn't mean it like that. I meant, it's sad we don't do more of what Dad likes." Slumping my shoulders I make a mental promise to myself, to start doing more things with Dad—and making sure Sam and I appreciate him more.

"I know you've got to go, so give me a call when you get back from your camping trip."

"Okay, I will. By the way, thanks for today. I had fun." I smile.

"Me too."

I smile even broader. We hang up, and I head out to the kitchen to give Mom a hand with dinner.

CHAPTER 21

TODAY'S THE DAY before our camping trip and Mom's driving us crazy. She's stacked the car, twice and now she's going through everything and making sure we've got supplies in case of every possible weather situation.

"Mom, it'll be okay," I say as she repacks the car, again.

"I know. Have you seen the water bottles?" she asks as she looks around the ground in the garage.

"You've packed them. The first thing you put in."

"Did I?" She scratches her head, brings her eyebrows together then smiles. "Yes, you're right, I did."

"See? We'll be fine."

"What about the first aid kit?" She repeats the process, looks around her and goes into a mild panic attack.

"It's in the glove compartment, where it always is. Look." I walk around to the passenger side, open the glove department and pull out the kit she's assembled.

"Is everything we need in there? Just bring it to me so I can check it."

I huff out a small frustrated breath, but I know Mom wants to make sure this trip goes as seamless as possible. For us, and for dad. She opens the clear plastic box and rummages through it. She's muttering to herself while she checks its contents. "Yeah, it's good. Put it back please, Dakota." She hands me the container, and I put it where I found it. "Sleeping bags?"

"Check," I yell out from the passenger side.

"Tents?"

"Check, check."

"You sure? Where did I put them?" She peers in through the back of the car trying to locate the tents.

"They're here, look." I point to them and Mom smiles.

"Great. Snacks. Where are the snacks? I can't see the damn snacks. I don't want to run out of food."

"They're inside on the dining table, Mom, right where you left them."

Her face turns toward the house and she looks at the garage wall. Cocking her hip to one side, she places her hand on it and keeps staring at the wall, deep in thought. "I wonder, should we pack them now so we don't forget them? Or should we wait until morning when we head off. Hmm."

"I can go get them," I offer.

Mom looks over and beams at me. "Can you read minds? I was thinking maybe we should pack them now."

"You were thinking out loud. I heard you."

"Oh gosh, I'm losing my damn mind." She closes her eyes and runs her hand over her face. "If you can get the food, I'd appreciate it."

I run inside and see the boxes set on the dining table. I'd usually call Sam to come help, but she's out with Taylor at the mall. They've gone down to get frozen yogurt and hang out for a while considering they're not going to see each other for a few days.

Taking the first of the two boxes out, I place it by Mom's feet. She looks at the box and scrunches her mouth. Then I run in to get the smaller of the two boxes. When I come out, Mom's got half the car unpacked again.

"It's like a jigsaw puzzle," I say to her.

"It is. We've also got the camping fridge to go in and the cold food too. But, I'm determined to get it done before your father gets home."

"Or, you could leave it for Dad and let him do it. I remember when we used to go camping, he'd pack it so easily."

"No," Mom snaps at me. "I want to do it, so he can relax tonight before we leave early in the morning. He's been working so many hours that I really want to do this for him so he doesn't have to worry."

I go over to Mom and throw my arms around her. "You're a good person, Mom," I say to her and kiss her.

"Thank you, sweetheart. Now, let's play this game of Tetris and hopefully get everything in the car."

We spend the next hour and a half arranging, re-arranging, and re-arranging yet again. When we get everything in, we end up with lots of room left over. It's the convenience of Mom's car being a large SUV—

it has an abundance of space.

When we finish, we head inside and start dinner, because we plan on having an early night since we're leaving for our trip at four in the morning. The campground is only a few hours away, but off-loading and setting everything up will take time.

"I'm really excited for this trip. I think it'll do everyone a world of good," Mom says as she prepares the meat for dinner. "Can you peel some potatoes please?"

"Sure." I take the potatoes out of the bottom of the fridge and start peeling them. There's something about Mom's tone which says she's worried. "What do you mean it'll do everyone a world of good?"

"Your father's been working so hard, you've been different lately, a lot quieter than normal, and Sam, well she's now got a boyfriend. It's just, everything's changing and I think this trip has come at the best of times."

Silently, I peel the potatoes and avoid looking over at Mom. Once the potatoes are done, I grab a pan so I can boil them. "Mashed, right?"

"Yeah, mashed." Mom's voice is whisper quiet. "Dakota?"

My hands tighten around the pot and I steady my breathing. "Yeah."

"Are you okay?"

A spark of dread surges inside me. Quivering with fear I look over my shoulder to Mom, not fully facing her. "I'm great," I lie. Worst still, I lie convincingly.

"You sure?" *Obviously not convincingly enough.*

"I'm positive, Mom. I'm good. I've just come to realize how the people I thought were my friends ended up not really being friends. I'm okay with that, because truthfully they've shown their true colors."

"Are you talking about Levi?"

"And Lindsey."

"Lindsey? What's happened with Lindsey?"

"Levi and her are together now. Not even a minute after we split up. And she's been ignoring me." *To say the least.* "It's okay, I'm kind of over it."

"Over it? You've been best friends for years."

"Yeah, we were. Clearly, she decided to take sides, and she chose Levi over her friendship with me."

"It's okay, sweetheart." She rubs her hand over my back in comforting circles. "She'll be back."

"Honestly, I don't think I want to be friends with her again. She's hurt me much more than Levi did by breaking up with me. She's been mean, to say the least."

"Mean?" Mom's voice crackles with concern. It's a deep seated worry engrained in the fundamental foundation of a mother's core. "How has she been mean?"

"She's just not the person I thought she was. It's okay, Mom, I'm not interested in what she says or does any more. I thought we were friends, but clearly our friendship means absolutely nothing to her. So now, she means absolutely nothing to me."

"I'm so sad to hear that. You girls have been friends for so long, but if she's wronged you then I suppose there's not much anyone can do about that." She pauses for a moment then adds, "Is there no going back to how it was?"

"I don't think so. It's pretty much gone."

"Hmm," she huffs. "I'm sorry."

"It's not your fault, you've got nothing to be sorry about." I put the potatoes on the stove and lean up against the kitchen counter.

"I'm sorry you've had to go through whatever it is that happened." She offers me a weak smile, and I can tell she wants to know exactly what has been said and done. "Unfortunately, it's part of growing up. People will always find a way to disappoint us. However there are a rare few who'd rather lift us up than tear us down."

The words jumble around in my head then fall into place. It makes sense, and I'll have to be a lot more careful as to who I allow to be part of my life. "It sucks, hey?"

"It happens all the time. And don't think it's just when you're a teenager. You have to be careful even as an adult. Even more vigilant when you have kids of your own. There are so many bad people out there, Dakota. You have to keep your eyes open all the time."

I groan with frustration. "It must be exhausting having to protect us all the time."

"You have no idea. Trying to keep you safe from not only obvious dangers, things like drugs, and sex. But also from lurking hazards too. How many times do your father and I turn on the news, or read the on-line paper to see teachers, doctors, people with power who are pedophiles or have been arrested for rape? There's been a spate of assaults in the area and around the neighboring suburbs over the last about eight months or so. It's terrifying for us to know we have two beautiful girls who could become victims. We just pray, every day, we've done enough to teach you and Sam how not to become targets."

My stomach tightens and a fine sheen of sweat starts to form on the back of my neck. The moisture trickles down my back. I'm fully aware *I am* a victim, I've been targeted and I'll never be able to tell Mom the truth. "You and Dad have done a great job with us." I lean over and give Mom a kiss on the cheek. "Sam's super responsible, and I'm seeing my future for how it really is."

"Sam's like an old lady in a fourteen-year-old body." Mom laughs and I can't help but laugh with her. She's right, Sam's wise beyond her years and she always has been. "Now she has a boyfriend, I have to make sure she's not influenced into doing anything she's not ready for."

"I don't think you have to worry about that, Mom. Sam's pretty smart. She won't let Taylor pull any of that 'if you love me' crap."

"Oh God, I remember when I was in high school. I had a boyfriend, who I dumped, might I add, because of this crap. First it was, 'if you love me you'll let me touch you.' Then it progressed to, 'all the girls are doing it, you should too.' Then it went to, 'you must be frigid if you don't want to have sex with me.' When he called me 'ice queen' I dumped his ass. Told him I wasn't going to let some guy pressure me into doing something I wasn't ready for."

"You go, Mom. Good for you." Mom had some serious balls to be able to do that. A couple of years ago I wouldn't even want to have this conversation with her, but hearing it now, I know Mom's tough and so strong.

"Sex is great, Dakota, when it's with someone you love."

The feeling in my face suddenly turns into an inferno. "Ahh, okay. This is now officially awkward."

Mom chuckles and rolls her eyes at me. "Good, I've successfully embarrassed you. I wouldn't be doing my job as a mother if I can't manage that every so often." I laugh and hug Mom again. "Dad will be home soon. Do you want to give your sister a call and tell her to get her butt home, then have a quick shower?"

"Sure." I head over to the house phone, and dial Sam's number. When she picks up I can hear classical music playing in the background, and I pull the phone away to check the number, "Sam?"

"If you're calling me to tell me to get home, Taylor's mom is about to pull into our street."

"What are you listening to?"

"Okay, I'll see you soon," she says, deflecting my question.

"Bye." I turn to Mom and tell her Sam's only a few minutes away and go get in the shower. When I get out, I wrap a towel around my body and another around my hair and head straight to my room to get dressed. When I go out to the family room, Dad has his arms around Mom's waist and is kissing her. "Sorry," I mumble. I look down at the floor and back away. I hear Mom giggle like a schoolgirl and Dad chuckle.

Knocking on Sam's door, she yells for me to come in and when I enter her room I find her on her stomach with her legs up and entwined at the ankles while she flirts—I mean chats—on her phone. "I gotta go, Dakota's here." She listens for a moment and her face flames a brilliant crimson shade. "Yeah, me too." She looks at me, and I smile at her. "I'll see you when I get back. Bye." She hangs up flips onto her back. "Oh my God, Dakota. I think I really, *really* like Taylor." She hugs her pillow and squeals.

"I'm so happy for you." I go and sit on her bed. "Now tell me why you were listening to classical music."

"Taylor's Mom is into classical and opera music. He told me she plays it all day and night, and everywhere they go."

"Wow. Intense."

"You should meet her. She is really intense, and so proper. She's nothing like Mom. Mom will have a joke and try to make us laugh, his Mom doesn't even crack a smile."

"Lucky Taylor's normal."

"*Kinda* normal. He likes classical musical too. Should've seen him in the car. He actually closed his eyes and was swaying his head back and forth as if he was in the orchestra." She mimics what he was doing in the car. "At least he's into music and not smoking and drinking. That would suck."

"Yeah, I hear ya. Mom wants you to take your shower."

"Okay." She stands and gets her pajamas out of her drawer.

"Hey, let's try and make this trip extra special, okay?"

Sam frowns and stops walking toward her door. "Why, is everything okay? Are Mom and Dad okay? What do you know? Are they alright?" She quickly becomes agitated.

"Stop stressing; they're fine. It's just today when I was helping Mom with the car and dinner, I got the feeling she's been stressing out about all of us. It's like she was sad we're growing up, and this might be one of the last camping trips we'll ever go on all together. And you know how much Dad loves camping."

"Remember how he'd make us go fishing with him, and we'd end up soaking wet? Or how he'd make us collect sticks so we could start a fire and he'd try for an hour to rub two sticks together, only to end up using matches to finally start it? Or how we'd go with him to collect fruits and berries which we never ate because we never knew which were poisonous and which weren't?"

I nod my head and laugh, "Yeah, I think Mom wants to hold on to those kinds of memories for both her and Dad's sakes. Maybe this camping trip, we can give that to them."

An easy smile graces Sam's face and her eyes light up as she nods her head. "We're getting older, and it'll only be a matter of time before we've both left for college. You're right, let's have fun and give Mom and Dad their best camping trip yet."

"Dinner's ready," Mom calls out from the kitchen.

Both Sam and I leave her room and head into the dining room where Mom asks us to set the table as she brings everything out.

Dad's sitting at the head of the table scanning through his tablet while Sam and I set up. "Do you need help?" he asks not taking his eyes off the tablet.

"Um, no, we've got it," I say when I peek over the tablet and see he's researching weather conditions for the duration of our camping trip.

Once we set up, Mom sits beside Dad and Sam and I are opposite each other. Sam next to Mom and me on my own. "How's the weather looking?" I ask Dad once he's gotten his dinner.

"We might get rain one day, but the rest will be good." He takes a forkful of his mash potato. "Hmm, good," he says while shoveling more.

"Dakota made it," Mom replies with a sly wink to me.

"Not really, I just peeled the potatoes, Mom did the rest."

"Hey Dad, can we go fishing?" Sam asks enthusiastically.

Dads' face lights up, a sparkle shines bright in his eyes while a wide, beaming smile lights up his handsome features. "You want to go fishing? You're not toying with your old man's heart here?"

"Seriously. Dakota and I were discussing it. We even packed clothes and shoes that won't matter if they get damaged. We want to go fishing with you, Dad."

Mom's fork is frozen in mid-air as she flicks her eyes between Sam and myself. It takes a few seconds of staring at us before she finally finds her voice. "I haven't packed the fishing gear." She continues to stare at us disbelievingly.

"I'll pack it straight after dinner," Dad happily chimes.

It's so obvious to me, and to Sam because she taps me under the table, how happy Dad is. And not only Dad, but Mom too.

We eat dinner in a stream of excited chatter, mostly coming from our parents. But I can tell their enthusiasm comes from a place deep inside them. As we eat I cast my eyes over my family and know everything will work out okay.

CHAPTER 22

WE'VE BEEN AT the campground for three days, and it's been fun and easy. As the days pass, I'm almost my normal self, as if *that night* had never happened. I had forgotten how much I enjoyed being in the woods.

The first morning I smelled the dew on the large, overgrown leaves hanging low like a canopy over the tents and heard the sounds of the nearby creek, running softly along the water's edge. I felt a rush of my childhood memories.

The native sounds of the woods have had such a calming effect not only on me, but all of us. We've all woken early today, and Sam and I are dressed and ready to go fishing with Dad. Mom's sitting on a large log by the small campfire which still has red embers burning, sipping on a cup of coffee.

"Are you coming, Mom?" Sam asks.

Mom shakes her head and then lets out a small yawn. "I'm a bit tired, I'm going to stay back and have a nap. Your father was snoring so loud last night I thought he'd attract every form of wildlife to our tents. It's got to be the mating call of something dangerous." I laugh and Mom looks at me. "I'm serious. Maybe a bear, or a coyote, or even a boar."

"I don't think we'll encounter any of those around here," Dad says to Mom. His left hand is holding three fishing rods, and his right hand is holding a bucket with tackle. "Your Mom has always hated fishing. She'll make any excuse possible not to come with us."

"I'll cook them," Mom adds with a smile. "After your dad cleans them."

I shiver at the thought of Dad having to descale and rip the poor fishes' guts out. My face must show what I'm thinking because Mom laughs at me, and Dad looks at Mom then follows her gaze. He leans down, plants a kiss on Mom's forehead then indicates for Sam and me to follow him. "Come on, girls," he says, starting through the clearing. "We've got some fish to catch."

Sam and I both stand and look at each other. We're silently telling each other this is what Dad wants, and we're happy to do it if it makes him happy. Just these few days we've been out here has seen a positive shift in Dad. He's shoulders aren't as tense as they normally are, and he's been laughing a lot too.

"Come on," I say to Sam as I bump my shoulder into hers playfully.

"Watch it, or I'll tell Dad you want to scale the fish."

I screw my nose and take a huge step away from her. Sam laughs at me while Dad looks over his shoulder at us. "Hurry up, you two," he enthusiastically calls toward us.

We walk about half a mile to where the stream is running fairly rapidly, and Dad sets the rods down, along with the bait. "Do you want me to bait the hook for you, or do you remember how to do it?" he asks opening the bait container and picking up a worm.

Sam gags and shudders. I look at the plump worm wiggling around between Dad's thumb and forefinger. "Yuck," I moan giving Dad a look of pure disgust.

"I'll do it then." Dad chuckles and shakes his head.

No way. As revolting as it is to have worm guts on my hands, I'm going to prove to Dad that I can do it. "Hand it over, Mister," I say assertively as I take the few steps to Dad.

I stand over the worms, and the smell coming up from them makes me almost throw up in my mouth. "You look like you're going to barf," Sam laughs from a safe distance.

"At least I'm not afraid of a little worm." I lean down toward the bucket, dip my hand into the slimy mass of worms and grab one. Holding back the vomit, I look at Sam whose horrified features are frozen with complete disgust. "Just grab one," I say as I take a step toward her. She recoils and shakes her head almost violently. "Go on."

Sam dry retches again and moves behind one of the large trees lining the river. "Go away," she yells at me from behind the tree.

"Come out, come out wherever you are," I taunt as I creep toward her hiding spot.

"Dakota, go away." I can hear the mirth in her voice and see her head poke out from behind the wide tree. But I've managed to sneak up her, holding the squirming worm out in front of me. She pokes her head out again, and this time I'm so close I can almost touch her with the worm. She sees me, screams, then shoots off running from behind the tree.

I give chase, the stupid worm wiggling around as I try and land it on her back. "It's just a worm," I laugh while chasing her.

"Ewwww, go away." She looks over her shoulder as she runs behind Dad and uses him as a shield. "Save me from the crazy person. I think an alien's invaded her mind."

Dad's chuckling as he threads the worm onto his hook. He looks at me, trying to get Sam with the worm, then turns and looks at Sam who's bouncing from foot to foot attempting to avoid me. "Let's catch some fish." Dad stands and Sam leaps back, out of my reach.

"Yuck," she says as she eyeballs me and what I'm holding between my fingers. Cautiously she casts her gaze down to my feet, then up my body.

I'm laughing so hard, I don't think I can chase after her anymore. "I won't get you."

She eyes me suspiciously, but decides to move toward me. "You sure?"

This makes me laugh even harder, to the point I double over and grab my knee with my worm-free hand to balance. "I'm sure," I manage to get out between gales of laughter.

"Good." Sam walks past me, narrows her eyes and taps the side of her nose. "I've got my eyes on you, Bennett."

"I'm going fishing, who needs their hook baited?" Dad offers one last time. He's got those plastic pants on, and his fisherman's hat. It looks a cross between a beanie and a large bucket hat. It's bright and swirly with many colors and lots of lures hooked into it.

"Nice hat," I say to him heading over to the rods. He gives me a smile which quickly turns into a snarl when he realizes I was being sarcastic. "Here, I'll do Sam's rod." I pick up the hook, and spear the worm. Its guts come out and the worm instantly dies. I look to Sam, whose nose is scrunched up while she's watching me.

"Thanks," she says when I give her the rod. Sam goes and stands at the water's edge, careful not to get too close.

I place my rod down once I've got the hook ready, take my shoes and socks off then pick my rod up and go stand in the water. I wade until I'm almost knee-deep. Dad's walked even further, the water coming to below his waist. Looking back at Sam, she's standing on the coarse sand, looking bored. She's cast her line, but considering how shallow the water is there, she'll be lucky to catch a tadpole let alone a fish. And Dad has always been a responsible fisherman, if the fish aren't of a certain length, then he tosses them back in.

"Hey," I call out to Sam. Looking forward, I notice Dad turn to see what's happening. Then I turn to look over in Sam's direction again. "Hey!" This time she looks over to me and gives me a half-wave. "Come out." I beckon her over.

"Shoes." She points to her feet.

"I have some too, they're over there." Directing her to where my shoes are.

Sam scrubs her free hand over her face, and from this distance I see her smile. "Hang on." She walks over to where my shoes are, and takes hers off then starts toward me. It takes her a few seconds to come out, and when she does she stands about ten feet from me. "This better?"

I cast my gaze over to Dad who's in his element. He's waded further down the river and he looks like a man who's at peace with his surroundings. "This trip isn't about us remember, it's about him." I pointedly look over to Dad. "And Mom."

"I know." She rolls her eyes. "It's just fishing is so boring. I haven't been a buzz kill at all for the past three days, but fishing . . ." She shudders and screws her mouth up. "Ugh." She casts her line and cocks it against her hip. "I'm trying not to think about this." She wiggles her rod.

We stand in the water for what seems like forever with our rods remaining sturdy in our hands. "Just a nibble," Sam huffs. "Anything."

Smiling at her I listen to the sound of the water running down stream. It's serene out here, nothing but the flapping of birds wings while some of them fly in flocks overhead. Everything is calm, *peaceful.*

"Oh my God!" Sam yells. I look over to her and see her rod is bent while she tries to pull it back with both her hands. "Holy crap. This thing is huge." The rod arches even further, and if it keeps going it looks as if it's going to snap while she's holding it.

Out of the corner of my eye, Dad starts making his way toward her, but he's too far out to help her. "I'm on it," I call as I wade through the knee-deep water to get to her. "I didn't think we'd catch anything this close to the water's edge."

"You haven't caught anything," she growls toward me. "I have."

I laugh while helping her with the rod. The fish is desperately attempting to get away, and we're both just as desperate to pull it back. "Dad," I call as I one-handedly help Sam. Dad's still wading toward us, but the water is causing resistance around him, slowing him down.

It takes what seems like forever for Dad to get to us, and when he finally reaches us, the line snaps. Both Sam and I fall back in the water, losing our footing from the loss of the pull on the rod.

My head goes under water as my back finds the shallow pebbles and sand on the floor of the river. Sitting up, I come up out of the water in absolute hysterics, laughing so hard I almost pee myself. Sam sits up in the water, looking like a drowned rat, and wipes her sticky hair from her face. "What?" she challenges when she sees me laughing.

"You . . . look . . . hilarious." I try to stand, but my foot slips from under me, and I'm dunked straight back in the water. The water floods my mouth because I'm laughing so hard, and I end up swallowing some. Spluttering and trying to spit out the water while still submerged is quite a feat.

Dad reaches in and grabs me, but like me, he's got tears in his eyes from laughing so hard at our misfortune.

I'm guessing by the scowl on her face, and the lack-luster attempt to pull at the soaking clothes clinging to her body, Sam's obviously irritated. Her eyebrows are knitted together and if I look hard enough, I'm sure she's breathing fire from her anger.

Her gaze follows my body, and suddenly she bursts into laughter. "You look so bad," she says while doubling over and trying to grab at her knees. "Oh my God. I like to bathe without sharing it with the fish."

"You girls are making this trip the best one I've ever been on," Dad says while scooping up both my and Sam's rods which are now floating nearby. "The best!" Chuckling, Dad makes his way back to us, shaking his head he goes toward the river's bank. "You coming?" he calls to both of us.

Sam turns to me, and rolls her eyes. "You're gonna be laughing for a while, right?"

"Sure am."

She shoves at my shoulder, making me step back, lose balance . . . again, and fall back into the water. But before I go down, I grab onto her t-shirt, and bring her with me. "Ugh," she grumbles while trying to push back from me.

I lose it. Really lose it. Sam's features are too funny not to laugh as hard as I do. "I have to pee." I shoot up and start wading as fast as I can back toward the edge.

"Go ahead and pee. The fish do it, you can too," Dad calls out as loud as he can.

Suddenly an image of fishing peeing makes me laugh even harder.

"Yuck. I swallowed the water too."

"You swallowed fish pee," Sam chuckles. "Dakota swallowed fish pee. Dakota swallowed fish pee," she sings while stomping up behind me and points at me, just like little kids do.

My laughing hasn't stopped, and I try to run away from her but my sides are hurting badly. As I get out of the water, I run toward camp so I can pee, but my rolled-up shorts manage to slip from around my waist and bunch around my knees, making me collide with the ground. Face first.

At this stage I no longer need to pee. My face is covered in sand and dirt, I'm completely filthy and everyone, meaning an older gentleman who was walking down to the water, my Dad and my sister are all laughing at me.

"That has to be the funniest thing I've ever seen, lass," the old man says to me in a rich Australian accent. He holds his hand out to help me up.

Waving it away, I merely sit on the damp ground, laughing my butt off. "Thank you, but I'll get you dirty," I say to him.

"Suit yourself. I thank you for providing my day's entertainment." He shrugs and keeps walking toward the water.

"You're so funny." Sam leans down, and tries to help me up. "Did you wet yourself?" She looks at me and slaps her hand to her head.

"Shotgun for the shower."

When we get back to the campsite, Mom's sitting on a folding chair, reading on her Kindle. She looks up and sees me, looks down then immediately looks back to me, doing a double-take. Her eyes are wide and her mouth pops open when she lifts her nose at me. "What happened to you?" Sam follows behind me and Mom's gaze goes to Sam. "What on earth happened?" She then looks at Dad who's got the bait bucket and the fishing rods minus the dinner we managed to lose. "I'll get some towels." Mom hesitantly steps away, but she turns over her shoulder to catch one last glimpse at us before going to get towels.

Sam and I spend the next hour trying to wash off all the muck of the river. Where we camped is further away from the campground's utilities, more isolated, although there are other people who still camp here. At the campground's center, there are communal showers where Sam and I wash our hair and the fishy smell off ourselves.

Going back to where we've set up camp, Mom's prepared some lunch and has set up our small fold-away table. "Where's Dad?" I'm half-expecting he'll come out from behind a bush to try and scare us.

"He's gone to have a shower, too," Mom says. Sam and I sit at the small fold away bench seat and Mom hands us our plates. "No fish for dinner then."

I can't help the smile tugging at the corners of my mouth. "Sorry, Mom."

"Yeah, sorry," Sam adds while she fixes herself a sandwich from the ingredients Mom's set up on the table.

"I heard you had fun. And I saw *how much* fun you had when you returned. Looks like the fish didn't want to be made into dinner." Mom chuckles as she makes a sandwich for herself.

While we're eating our lunch, Dad returns and saunters over to the table. He sits beside Mom, and leans over to kiss her temple. I watch their intimate exchange and it absolutely makes my heart sing. When Dad's lips connect with Mom's skin, she smiles and gives Dad a loving gaze. I honestly don't think he's even noticed what he's done, but that delicate touch makes Mom so happy.

"This looks good," Dad announces as he sits beside Mom and starts making himself a plate.

"Let me." Mom takes the plate out of his hand and begins stacking an assortment of food on the dish.

Watching Dad's shoulders vibrate from a huge sigh, I notice the look on his face. His eyes admire Mom and it's so obvious to everyone how much love he has for her. There's so much appreciation and tenderness radiating off him. It's the most relaxed I've seen him in a long time. His affectionate beaming gaze takes Mom in. His respect for her shines as bright as the sun at noon in midsummer.

Dad looks over at me and smiles, then winks. He then looks to Sam who's in her own little world as she reads a book while holding half her forgotten sandwich mid-air.

"Here you go," Mom says and sets the plate in front of Dad.

"Thank you, darling." He leans over and kisses her again. She turns to look at Dad and gives him a smile that I can only describe as magical. I can see raw emotion they have for each other, the deep and soul consuming connection they have.

Looking down at my food, my heart stutters as I realize I'll never be lucky enough to share a connection as profound as the one my parents have.

Trying to push the sadness aside, I finish my food in silence and tune out the talking between Mom and Dad.

My faith was shattered the morning I awoke behind the bleachers with my dress torn and the knowledge something awful had happened to me.

I've been trying to hold on to my confidence that I'll be able to overcome the darkness. But it's moments like these that make me think that I'll never be myself again. I am, and always will be, a broken version of the girl I once was.

CHAPTER 23

T HE SOUND OF raindrops splashing rhythmically on the tent nudges me
from my sleep. Sam's got her arm thrown over her face and her
mouth open as she softly snores. I rub my eyes to wake me, but the
warmth of my sleeping bag keeps me from getting up. Lying on my side,
I carefully shift so I'm on my back. Looking up at the almost translucent
tent, I watch the raindrops hit then roll down the steeple and to the
ground.

There's a beautiful peace in listening to rain fall. It's natural and
organic and although it's usually depicted as cumbersome and draining,
I find it rejuvenating and lively. There's nothing more natural than
smelling rain which has fallen on lush green grass. Together they create
a scent which is distinctive and wholesome. *I love it.*

"Is that rain?" Sam's voice is gravelly and hoarse.

"It is. Isn't it just gorgeous?"

"Nothing gorgeous about being in a tent with rain falling around us.
Means we're going to be stuck in here and can't do much."

"We can read." I watch the life span of a drop. It falls at the top of
the pitch, then rolls too quickly toward the edge, before disappearing
over the rim. Smiling, I watch for more rain. "I love the sound of rain.
How the drops all patter together and make a perfect sound."

Out of the corner of my eye, I notice Sam turn her head and give me
a questionable look. "You on drugs? It makes me want to pee."

"Only you, Sam. Only you."

I catch her smiling broadly at me before she wiggles her arms out of
the top of the sleeping bag. She unzips her bag and gets to her knees.
"Seriously, I need to pee. And I'm hungry." She unzips the tent and pops
her head out. "Mom! Dad!" she hollers.

"I've checked the weather forecast. You girls will have to pack up your tent. It looks like it's here to stay, and it isn't going to shift," Dad says. There's a crack in the tent from where Sam's stuck her head out, and Dad's made a makeshift covering over the entrance of our tent so we can get out and not be rained on.

"Dad, I gotta go to the bathroom," Sam whines while crossing her legs and moving her butt from side to side.

"Here you go, I've got a couple of umbrellas."

Sam tiptoes out and squeals when the water that was gathering on the lip of the tent falls on her head and runs down her back. Smiling at her 'girliness,' I get up and start packing.

"Here," Dad says handing me an extra umbrella once I've packed the inside of the tent.

"I already have one." I hold the umbrella out to show him, clearly confused because the umbrella is large.

"For your sister."

I take the umbrella and stand to the side waiting for Sam to return as Dad continues taking things to the car with Mom. "Great trip," Mom mumbles on her return to the campsite. Sam comes back, holding her tiny umbrella over her head. "Your father got you a bigger umbrella." Mom indicates to the one I'm holding.

"Thank you." Sam takes it, opens it, and stands beside me. Mom and Dad make a few more trips to the car, packing up the last of our belongings. "Let's go." Sam and I walk toward the car and move to get in. Sam rounds the back of the car and stops before she enters. "Crap," she says.

"What?" I call out from the dry and cozy interior of the car.

"Dad?" Sam calls as he gets into the driver's side.

"What is it?"

"You might want to see this."

Dad gets out of the car, without an umbrella and rounds the car. "Oh, for God's sake," he yells, exasperated.

Sam looks at me through the open door, her eyes widen and she moves away from Dad. I shake my head at her and wave her to get in. She slides in and closes the door. "What is it?" I ask and Mom turns in her seat to see what's happening.

"We have a flat tire."

"Of course we do," Mom responds by rolling her eyes and huffing. "Our relaxing trip is turning into a nightmare." She gets out of the car and goes to stand by Dad.

"What should we do?" Sam asks.

"We can't stay in here while Dad jacks the car up, so we gotta get out."

We both get out, taking our umbrellas with us, and go stand behind our soaking wet parents. "Great," Dad groans. "The spare is in the back." *Oh no.* "Under all of our things." *Double oh no.* "And we're on mud, so jacking the car up here will be almost impossible." *Triple oh no.* Mom looks at us and shakes her head. Then she calms Dad by placing her hand on his back. We all remain silent, not really saying anything. No one wants to make the situation any worse than it is. "Well, I better get this done. Though I'll have to get it on a firmer surface first." He looks over at Mom.

"Back in the car," Mom calls.

We all get in the car, and Dad starts driving very slowly toward the closest paved surface, which turns out to be a painfully quiet ten minutes. The windshield wipers are going crazy, and the rain keeps pelting down. As we carefully pull onto a flat surface, Dad turns the car off and takes a deep breath before turning to address us all. "Sorry, ladies, but you're all going to have to get out and help."

Sam nudges me and clenches her jaw tightly together. "What?" I mouth to her. She eyes the packed trunk and juts her chin toward the back. "Huh?" I mouth again.

She rolls her eyes at me and steps toward the open rear door. "We'll offload everything, Dad." She turns and motions for me to come over.

"That's what you meant. You should've just said." We start offloading everything, while Mom holds one of the large umbrellas over everything we're stacking. Dad helps too, making it even quicker.

"Sorry, ladies. I know how crappy it's been for you," Dad apologizes and suddenly my heart rips into two.

"I've had fun," I say. "Especially when we went fishing."

"That was not fun," Sam huffs. "Except when you wet yourself. I wish I'd taken a photo of that," she chuckles and goes to stand under the protection of the umbrella.

"You're already wet, Sam, why bother?" I point to the umbrella and roll my eyes.

Dad's getting the tire and the jack out and then starts changing the flat. I go to stand behind him and watch as he gets on his back, and carefully places the jack under the car. "Why are you being so precise?" I ask.

"There are certain spots you need to put the jack so it holds the car up and doesn't damage anything. Look here." He points.

I squat down and look to see at what Dad's pointing to. "Oh yeah, I see it." It's a small flat surface about half way under the back passenger door. "Now what are you doing?" Dad's moved and has started loosening the bolts on the rims. "Why don't you do that when the car's up?"

"Here, come help." He moves to the side so I can get in there. "What you want to do is loosen them. Don't take the bolts off completely. You need the friction of the ground to keep the tire steady so you can loosen the bolts. But it's slippery so you may not be able to do it."

Pushing down on the tire iron I try and get the bolts to move. But they're not budging. "Man, these are on tight."

"They're usually put on with a machine, which means they're tighter than if done by hand. Stand and try to put your knee into it, use all your weight to get it done."

Standing I do what Dad says, but I can't make them budge at all. "I can't," I say in frustration.

Dad stands and gently grabs me by the shoulders. "Yes, Dakota, you can. These are pretty shit conditions to learn in, but when you get a car of your own and you're out and you get a flat tire, at least I'll be confident in knowing you can change the damn thing." He smiles at me and lets go of my shoulders. "Now, use your entire weight and push down on it. Remember to keep a strong grip on the tire iron."

Swallowing hard I wipe the rain from my face, and I try again. The conditions are really bad, making everything slippery. But I keep trying, and as the moments pass on, I become more exasperated with myself because I can't get the darn thing to shift. "I'm not giving up," I mumble to myself. With my knee hurting from the cold, hard steel and my shoulder suffering, I grumble out loud.

I look to Dad who's kneeling back on his hunches, water dripping down his face, his entire body soaking wet. He's got his eyebrows lifted as he watches me struggle to get this damn thing done. He doesn't move to help me, instead he asks, "Want me to do it?"

I look at his posture and scrub my hand over my face again. Mom and Sam are huddled together under the large umbrella, and although I know if Dad does it we'll be out of here sooner, I also resolve in myself that I'm not a damn weakling and I can do this.

"No, I've got it," I say looking back at the stupid flat tire.

"You've tried getting your knee into it, now you'll need to stand on it." I look to Dad, puzzled by what he's said. How do I stand on it, without losing my balance and hurting myself? Dad can clearly see that I'm considering this. Obviously he wants me to work it out.

"Help her," Mom calls.

"No, I can do this, Mom." Puzzling the problem, I come up with what I think is a solution. I open the back passenger door, and find somewhere I can grip so I don't slip off the tire iron. Then I stand on the firm steel bar, and push down with all my weight. The bar shifts, and I jump off with so much pride. "Yes," I shout to myself.

Looking over at my Dad, he has his arms crossed in front of his chest, smiling at me. "Just loosen them, don't take them off completely," he instructs me.

"Okay." It seems like forever, like hours have passed before I finish with the nuts. Some of them I can get my knee and back into it and they're loose. Others, I need to stand on the iron to get them to budge.

"Now that they're loose, we need to jack it up further. This way, when the tire is clear of the ground, you can undo the bolts the rest of the way by hand and then take the tire off. Be careful though, the tire is heavy."

"Heavy-schmevy. I can do this." I flippantly flick my hand in Dad's direction.

Dad puts his hands up in surrender and steps back. "Off you go, you're strong."

Smiling, I start jacking the car up. Oh my goodness, my shoulders are protesting in pain, I'm breathing heavily as I'm jacking the car up, and every time I think I'm getting somewhere I look at the car and it feels as if the car hasn't budged. "Damn it," I grumble, but I don't give up. I keep going, because I need to prove to myself that I'm strong and I can do this.

I stand and straighten my back and stretch my arms out in front of me, trying to relieve the burn in them so I can motivate myself further. "Keep going, Dakota," Sam calls from behind me and claps. This spurs me on, because I also know my sister's encouraging me to do this. She's not protesting at the fact that I'm taking forever and Dad would've had this done an hour ago.

Grinning, I keep going, proud of myself. I notice how the tire is off the ground. "Yes!" I jump up and down like a little kid, proud at what I've managed to do with the guidance from Dad.

"Yay! You go, girl," Sam calls from the shelter of the umbrella.

"Well done, Dakota," Mom echoes in.

"Now what?" I turn to Dad who's got the proudest look on his face. He's beaming with happiness and I can see he wants to let me do this on my own, but it must be killing him to stand back and watch.

"Now you need to take the nuts off, and keep them safe." I lean down and remove them fairly easily, considering I've already loosened them, and place them inside the hubcap for safekeeping. I look back to Dad for further instructions. "Now you have to take the tire off. Careful, 'cause it's heavy."

I flick my hand again. I'm Wonder Woman. *I* did this, *I* managed this entire thing all on my own. I'm not letting something like a 'heavy tire' get in my way now. I squat down in front of the tire and try to pull it off. I'm met with resistance and find the darn thing *is* heavy. "Damn it," I half sigh as I prepare to really tug at it. "Right, let's try this again." Squatting in front of it, I get a good grip on it, and heave back.

What happens next makes all of us gasp, Mom cries out, Sam yells, and Dad leaps forward. I pull on the tire with so much force, the tire comes off, I go flying backward, land on my butt in a huge muddy puddle, and the tire rolls away. It's heading straight for Sam and passes her while flicking mud up in its wake.

Dad lunges forward to chase the tire. Sam screams because as it's rolled by her, it's flicked mud into her face and in her eyes, and Mom's shocked because she doesn't know who to go to first.

Mom turns to Sam who's angrily groaning and says, "Are you okay? Here let me help you." She lifts her soaking wet t-shirt and tries to clear the mud from Sam's face.

"I'll be fine." Sam shoos Mom away and rubs at her eyes. "I think I've got it all." She blinks wildly as she tries to focus on me. When she sees me sprawled out in the biggest and muddiest puddle she loses it. She laughs so hard, her eyes become red and tears freely fall. "Oh my God. You're covered in mud."

Mom's taking steps toward Dad who's retrieved the tire and is rolling it up toward us, but she stops and turns to look at me. "You really are a sight, Dakota." She laughs too before heading over to help Dad.

I manage to stand, with thick oozy mud dripping off my butt and try to flick all the big gunky parts off me. "Ah," I groan in resignation. "No use." I stomp toward Dad and wheel the tire the rest of the way. "You're right, it's heavy. But I'm going to do this."

Dad stands with amusement beaming off his face. The heavy wrinkles around his eyes are more prominent as he smiles at me. "Atta, girl. Now get the spare out." He points to the back of the car and I follow where he's indicating.

"Right," I say with determination. I'm going to change this darn tire even if it takes me all night.

Analyzing how the tire is fastened into the cavity, I undo the one bolt holding it in, and lift it out. This time I don't underestimate its weight and use my back and legs to get it out. Lifting the muddy flat tire, I put it in its place. Taking a step back, I smile triumphantly at myself. I'm so proud I managed to get as far as I have, although I'm filthy and making my family wait in the rain. Thankfully, the rain isn't cold, instead it's humid and incredibly sticky.

The next part goes fairly easily because it's working in reverse to what I've already done. By the time I fasten the nuts on the tire, Mom and Sam are already packing the car . . . again.

Dad instructs me on the final steps and when I lower the car I smile with so much pride. "I did it!" I say while turning to Dad. I tighten the bolts and stand to admire my work.

He holds his hand up, and I jump to give him a high-five. "Yes, you did. I'm really proud of you, Dakota. Well done. Now let's get home."

Still on cloud nine, I help Mom and Sam with the last couple of things, then get in the car. We're all wet, dirty, and tired on the way home. Everyone's quiet while Dad drives, only the soft tunes of the radio are on, lulling Sam and me into a calm and relaxing state. The rumble of the tires against the road is so rhythmic and gentle it acts like a sedative for me. My blinks become longer as I feel my breath start to ease into the relaxed rhythm.

Turning my head, I pretend to look out the window so no one sees me with closed eyes. The car smoothly rocks, making my environment so much more comfortable. My mind forms a perfect, carefree void. Nothing can disturb the relaxed state coursing through me.

A man appears and smiles at me. His face is blurry, but I can see the shine of his teeth when he smiles. He lifts his hand to me, and beckons me over to him. Cautiously I take a step toward him, but something doesn't feel right. My stomach is buzzing nervously at an unfamiliar, yet known, hazard. "Come with me," he tempts as he smiles again.

I try to focus on his face, squinting harder I attempt to make the color of his eyes. However, the closer I look the less I see.

"Who are you?" I ask as I lift my foot to shuffle closer to him.

"You know who I am."

A gush of cold wind touches my skin, and when I look to see where the gust has come from Sam's standing beside the faceless man. "Sam, no!" I yell, trying to run after her. My feet become weighted and I look down to find them covered in heavy concrete with water rapidly rising around me. When I look up to Sam, she's no longer there, and the faceless man has disappeared too.

"Sam!" I yell startling awake. Blinking rapidly, my terrified body is vibrating from shaking. "Sam!"

"Hey, I'm here," Sam answers. Looking over to her, she sits up in her seat and scrubs her hand over her eyes.

"Are you okay, Dakota? You were mumbling in your sleep," Mom says, shifting in her seat to have a better look at me.

Sam places her hand on her thigh, and I lean over to grasp it. She tightens her fingers around mine, and gives me a reassuring smile. My gaze follows her, just to make she's actually here and not with the man from my dream. "Yeah, I'm okay. I had a weird dream." Shaking my head, I run my free hand over my eyes to try and help wake me. "Like really weird."

"What happened?' Mom asks, her brows crease while her eyes intently stare.

"It was really strange." I blink rapidly trying to recall the dream, but just as it came, it's managed to disappear. "I don't remember it all." Mom's face becomes warm as she relaxes all her features. Shrugging my shoulders, I say, "I don't remember."

"It was only a dream, dear."

Looking out the window, I notice we're nearly home and I sigh with relief. Home is my safe place, my haven where I know everything will be okay.

We pull into our driveway, and Dad presses the button so the garage door rolls up. When I get out, I look at the back bench seat and notice all the mud and dirty water from where Sam and I were sitting. Dad comes and stands beside me, enveloping me in a hug. "Sorry, Dad." Heaviness sits inside me, we dirtied Mom and Dad's car.

"We'll clean it tomorrow. Go have a hot shower, and get into your pajamas. Your mother and I can unload the car."

"I'll help," I offer.

Sam pipes up at the same time and offers to help, too.

Dad lets out a large puff of air and runs his hand through his hair. "Alright, then let's get this done. One thing I've learned is never stand in the way of a woman. And since there are three of you standing here looking at me, I'm no fool." He throws his hands up in resignation then goes to the car to begin unloading.

It doesn't take us long to finish and then Mom sends Sam and me to have a shower. She said we've done enough for today. She also said we'll be ordering pizza for dinner because she hadn't prepared anything.

Taking myself to the shower in Mom and Dad's room, I adjust the temperature to the hottest I can handle and lean against the wall. The water flowing over my body instantly relaxes all my muscles and I'm made aware of the heaviness and aching in my entire body.

My insides feel as if they've been put through a very intense obstacle course. Changing the tire has created pain in every muscle, even ones I never knew existed.

I let my head roll forward, my chin touches the top of my chest as the pounding, hot water brings every strain to light, before lulling them back into comfort. My mind drifts as I begin to soap my body, slowly massaging the ache burning through me.

With my eyes closed, I mewl softly when I knead a knot in my calf. The heavenly feeling of the warm water and my tender fingers, releases the knot and sends me into a blissful state of relaxation.

My body is slowly responding to the heat of the water and my hands as I brush over the tired muscles. A beautiful memory of Sam and me high on the Ferris Wheel pops into my mind.

Opening my eyes, I smile because it's been a while since I've felt normal. And even longer since I've been carefree and happy.

There's a knock on the door, and Sam shouts, "Hey, dinner's here. Hurry up." *Bang, bang, bang.*

"I'll be out in a few."

"Good, 'cause I'm hungry."

Bang, bang.

Quickly finishing washing myself and rinse hair, I get out of the shower, towel dry and get changed into my pajamas. Wrapping a towel around my head, I find my family sitting around eating dinner.

Mom's laughing, and Dad's chuckling while he helps himself to another piece of pizza although he's already holding one.

"Hey, slow down or there'll be nothing left for me," I say as I pull the chair out, fold one leg up under me, and sit.

"Quick, don't let Dakota get any." Dad lunges forward to pick up the pizza box, quickly smashing the lid shut and dragging the box over to him.

"Very funny, ha ha." I fold my arms in front of my chest and stare at Dad, giving him my best ever death stare. "Come on, I'm hungry."

"Gotta pay the piper." Dad looks at me with raised eyebrows and holds the pizza box closer to his chest.

"And the price would be what?"

I slowly unfold my hands, and place them on the table getting ready to leap over and grab the box. Just as Dad shoves the rest of the piece he's holding into his mouth, I lunge, and he moves the pizza box, resulting in me not getting the damn pizza.

"Ha, you'll have to try harder, kiddo." He chuckles. "Told ya there's a fee if you want to eat."

I look over to my sister, who's smiling while she's eating, and Mom, who's getting glasses and a bottle of soda for us all. I'm darn hungry, so I sigh and sit back down. "What's the price?" I grumble.

Dad sticks his cheek out, points to it, and closes his eyes.

He wants a kiss.

Standing, I wet my lips so they're saturated, and plant a huge, sloppy kiss on his cheek. The moment my wet lips make contact, Dad lets out an "Ewww," but doesn't move away. I reach out, quickly grab the box and move to sit. "See, it wasn't that bad."

Smiling, I open the box and grab a piece of pizza.

Mom returns and places the glasses down in front of us, and pours us all a drink. "I was thinking, is it okay if next week sometime we have a cookout with a couple of my friends?" I ask while devouring the pizza.

"Who'll be coming over?" Mom asks.

"Sophie, and Reece, and Sam can ask Taylor."

"Yeah, Mom, can we?" Sam's eyes pop wide open as she sits forward on her chair, eagerly looking at Mom.

"Why don't you ask them to come over during the week, that way I'll still be home and I can cook while you kids use the pool?"

Smiling at Dad I look over to Sam, who's so excited she's almost bouncing out of her seat. I nod to her, and wait for her to agree; but I don't think I'm going to get too much out of her, she's way too excited to say anything. "Thanks, Dad. That'll be great."

"Who did you say you're inviting?" Mom sits back down and relaxes back into her chair.

"Sophie and Reece. And I'm pretty sure Sam will want Taylor here." I look to Sam who's nodding like one of those cartoon characters.

"I see no problem with that. Do you?" Mom asks Dad.

"Nope. Get 'em over and enjoy the pool while the weather's nice."

Sam jumps up off the chair and hugs Mom, then Dad. "Thank you," she says and gives Dad a kiss before turning to give one to Mom. "What food can we have?"

"S'mores," Dad pipes up and adds. "We brought the graham crackers and marshmallows camping with us, and we didn't get to have any. We have to have s'mores."

"Not too many for you, darling," Mom says as she reaches out and squeezes Dad's hand.

Dad's chest deflates as his shoulders slump. Mom's the best caregiver in the world, she really looks out for Dad and his health. "Maybe, I'll have just three or four."

"More like two."

Dad groans and rolls his eyes. "Urgh," he mumbles again. "Fine, I'll have two."

Mom smiles triumphantly to herself and Dad catches my eye. He nods his head as his eyes widen, he's silently asking me to help by sneaking more s'mores to him.

"Hey, after dinner can we play the whisper challenge?" Sam asks.

"Oh gosh. Last time we played that, my nose was running because I was laughing so hard," Mom says.

"That was so much fun. Hell yeah we can play it," Dad adds. "I'm going to try and make your mother pee herself laughing this time." Dad looks so pleased with himself.

We finish dinner quickly and get ready for the whisper challenge. Dad has his turn with the headphones first, and I blast a real chick song through my iPod making Dad wince when he hears the music. He yells, "Can't you pick a better song? Chick music hurts my head."

We're all laughing, because we know how much Dad hates modern music, but even more so at the fact he's yelling. I shake my head at him.

Tonight's theme is movies and movie characters. Dad has to guess my movie character first. "Scooby Doo," I say.

Dad's watching my mouth intently and squints at me. "Again," he yells.

"Scooby Doo."

"Scabby."

I laugh. "Scooby Doo."

"I did a poo."

Sam loses it, laughs so much she half rolls off the sofa. "Scooby Doo."

"I am blue."

"Your father's a Smurf," Mom says and laughs.

"Scooby Doo." Dad shakes his head. His eyes following my mouth with so much concentration. "Scooby Doo."

"The man flew."

"Scooby Doo." Tears are springing to my eyes, and I'm finding it so hard to contain the laughter which is bubbling away inside me.

"Soccer balls curfew."

I look to Sam and smack my hand on my forehead. None of what he's guessed are movies or characters. "Scooby Doo."

"007."

"Scooby Doo."

"Adele rules."

"Scooby Doo." I can feel myself becoming more frustrated with every time I repeat the character.

Dad puckers his lips while I'm saying 'Scooby Doo' and the way his lips form an almost perfect O, makes me burst into laughter. "Oh I think I've got it," he yells over the music. "Chewbacca." That's all it takes from Dad and we're all in hysterics. "Judging by all the laughing, I don't think Chewbacca is right," he hollers even louder.

Mom shoots up off the sofa and runs down the hallway. Sam is doubled over, clutching her stomach with tears of laughter rolling down her cheeks, and I'm laughing so hard my cheeks are hurting and I can't say anything.

The song finishes and Dad takes off the headphones. Our rules are if it hasn't been guessed in the length of a song, you lose the round. "What the hell were you saying?" he asks me in seriousness.

"Scooby Doo," I say clutching my side because I'm laughing so much I now have a stitch.

"Really?" Dad's face has no emotion. "Scooby Doo?" I nod at him. Mom comes back, her face flushed from laughing so much. "Hmmm." Dad stands and gives the headphones over to Mom, who's still laughing.

The remainder of the night is spent with us laughing hysterically. By the time I head to bed, my cheeks are sore, my sides are aching, and I can't help but still laugh at *all* the wrong answers . . . and the shouting.

Closing my eyes, I'm taken away to dreamland. Thank goodness, dreamland warmly accepts me and shows me images of pure happiness.

CHAPTER 24

"**CAN I HELP?**" I ask Mom while she prepares the food for the cookout. We planned it for two nights after we got back from our camping trip-slash-disaster.

"Sure, want to make the salad?"

"Yep." I slide in behind the large island bench in the kitchen, and start working around Mom who's peeling potatoes. "What are we eating?" I look around the food on the kitchen counter, hoping it'll give me some hints as to what's for dinner.

"Salad." She pointedly looks down at the ingredients I'm getting out of the fridge. I roll my eyes, but smile. "Hamburgers, potato salad."

"Yum," I interrupt her to say.

"Hot dogs, steak, and watermelon."

"Mom, there's only seven of us, why so much?"

"There's no such thing as too much, Dakota. We can head down to the local church and give them what's left over. They run a homeless kitchen, so I'm sure they'll appreciate it."

I shrug my shoulders. I suppose she has a point. Mom has always said, better for us to give food away than not have enough. She's thrown a few parties, and there's always way too much food left over, so she packs it up and takes it to the local church.

"We should make extra anyway, so we can take them some food." I chop the lettuce for the salad, and out of my peripheral vision I notice Mom stop what she's doing.

"That's really thoughtful, honey. I'm proud of you for thinking of others." She leans over and kisses my cheek. "Then we're also having chicken and corn on the cob." She heads over to the fridge and takes the chicken and corn out.

Mom and I work together in the kitchen, seamlessly helping each other while chopping, and cooking. "There's so much food," I sigh while looking at everything we've prepared.

"How about we halve everything? Package half in containers and put it in the fridge and if we run out, all we have to do is grab it from the fridge. Then if there's anything left at the end of the night I can take it down to the church."

"Good idea, Mom." We spend the next ten minutes separating all the food. Once it's all done, we store it all in the fridge. "Do you need any more help?"

"Nope, everything's done."

"Okay." Leaving Mom I go out the back where Dad and Sam are cleaning the grill. "It's been a hot day today, I'm sure you all will be in the pool."

"I'm going to put my swimsuit on and jump in," Sam yells over her shoulder as she runs inside.

"What about you, sweetheart. You going to put your suit on?" Dad asks while cleaning the grill.

Suddenly I shudder with the thought of exposing my body so much. I've been living in shorts and t-shirts, not wanting to put on anything that's too revealing. Instantly my body tortures me by churning my stomach as fine goosebumps pebble my skin. "Ah . . . yeah," I say, my voice crackling.

Dad stops cleaning the grill, and walks over to where I'm standing at the large outdoor table. He hugs me without even knowing why my voice broke. "You okay?" he asks. He kisses the top of my head and tightens his hug. He moves back his arm now draping over my shoulder. "You seem down, is everything okay?"

"Yeah, it's all good," I reply immediately. The sadness in my voice is obvious. I look to Dad who squints at me. "Really, I'm great," I add eagerly. *Shut up, Dakota.*

The panic intensifies, and sweat beads on my neck. Dad's holding me in his regard and he's got hard 'Dad eyes' happening. Those are the ones where you're sure he can read your mind, but he doesn't want to say anything in case he's mistaken and it turns out to be 'time-of-the-month' business.

"Okay then. Well I'll get back to cleaning the grill." He lets go of me, kisses my hair once more and heads back to the grill.

I go to find Sam, because she has one-piece swimsuits, whereas I only have bikinis. Knocking on the door, I can hear her giggling in her room. "Hang on," she says. She comes to the door and opens it. Her eyes take me in, she frowns and takes a step back. "I gotta go, I'll see you when you get here." She hangs up and tosses her phone on her bed. "What's wrong? I know that look. You're stressing about something."

"Am I really so obvious?" Cold fingers of dread pinch my throat, because if Sam can see it, then that means Dad was able to, too. Sam tilts her head and lifts her eyebrows at me. "Right." I close the door behind me. "You know me the best out of everyone."

"Ah-ha. So what's wrong?"

"I've got a problem."

"Well, duh. You're clearly not as pretty as me. I'd say that's a huge problem." I laugh at her, because I know she's only trying to lift the intensity I brought in with me. "Huge problem." She extends her arms to show me in size how big the problem is.

"Other than that glaringly obvious fact." I roll my eyes, but smile. She calms me. She has a special gift of knowing when I'm about to freak out, so she adjusts her tone to soothe and calm me. "You should get into counseling," I randomly say.

"What? That's your problem?" Sam screws her nose up and looks at me as if I've grown three extra heads.

Chuckling I become sidetracked by my thoughts. "Hang on." I put my hand up to halt her saying anything else. "First, I need a one-piece and I was hoping I can borrow one of yours?" I put my hands together like I'm praying and I batt my eye lids at her. "Pretty please?" Then I give her the hugest cheesiest grin I can.

"Yeah, cool. Here." She walks over to her chest of drawers, opens the fourth drawer and throws me a one-piece. "Why?" She turns and looks at me.

"I only have bikinis, and I don't want to . . ." my voice trembles with fear. "Wear it," I almost whisper. "Because . . ." Knotting my hands together I look down to my toes, too ashamed to hold Sam's gaze.

"It's cool. It'll suit you better anyway." Looking up to Sam, her features have softened and I can see by how wide her eyes are, she's sympathetic toward me, but doesn't want to say anything.

"Thank you." I take a deep breath, giving me enough time to gather myself and step out of the prison my mind's been caught in. "I think you should go to college and learn to be a counselor. You're so strong, Sam. And you have a way about you that makes me feel like I'm not so lost."

"Lost?" Sam squints her eyes and rubs her hand over her face. "What do you mean?"

"Since, *that* night." I pause for a moment, again gathering strength. "Since *that* night, you make me want to try to push past it so I can maybe be normal again one day."

"I've done that?" Sam puts her hand to her chest, covering at her heart.

"You have. It's like you know what I'm feeling, and you can adapt to it, make me take a moment and step back, keep me from spiraling out of control." I may have the strength to tell her this, but I'm also nervous about how she'll react. "You're so mature, and so level-headed."

Sam's face breaks out in a broad smile, her eyes sparkle with so much joy. "Thank you," she timidly says.

We stand in her room for a few seconds, and it turns uncomfortable. Sam's not really into compliments. She shuffles on the spot, avoiding me. "Well, I better go get ready before everyone gets here."

"'K."

I walk out and into my room to get changed while thinking about Sam and everything she means to me. She's my stability, my rock, keeping me sane when I start to drift toward the edge of darkness.

Taylor and Sophie are here already, and we're all in the pool hanging out. "Your sister is so sweet," Sophie says as we sit on one of the steps in the shallow end.

"Yeah, she's cool."

"Tell me about you and Levi. I heard a few rumors the last few days of school, but I think they're all a load of shit." Sophie's dark gray eyes hold their own secrets. She looks to the left, breaking our connection. "Not like it's any of my business." She looks up to the sky and squints.

"What did you hear?" I may as well know everything people are saying, it'll tell me how many untruths Levi is sprouting.

"He's angry at you because you've been sleeping around behind his back. And, that you kept saying no to him, but you're happy to open your legs to anyone else." I cringe when she relays all the crappy gossip she's heard. "I don't think that's true. Actually, I know it's not."

I shrug although my stomach is all bunched up, and my pulse is racing crazily through my veins. "Then why did you ask?"

"I wanted to see your reaction, and hear your response."

She now turns to look at me. "You weren't even looking at me. You had your eyes glued to anywhere but me."

A smile pulls at one end of her mouth. "I can see it in your eyes, Dakota. What's being said is either an exaggeration of the truth, or they're being horrible and just saying shit. Either way, I can see you're nervous *and* upset about what people are saying."

Swallowing hard, I slump my shoulders and look down at my legs which are floating aimlessly in front of me in the water. "I don't know what to say."

"You don't have to defend yourself to me. Matter-of-fact, I don't think you should have to defend yourself to anyone. Whatever you do has nothing to do with anyone else."

"Problem is, I haven't done anything." My blood pumps quickly through me, while my vision clouds with angry red spots.

"According to all those pictures floating around, you *did* do someone."

"That's bullshit," I angrily retort. "I didn't know what was . . ." I clap both my hands to my mouth realizing I'd said way too much. I drop my hands and close my eyes, putting up an instant barrier and closing Sophie out. It takes me a few minutes, but when I finally open my eyes Sophie's looking at me with a calm and soft expression. "I . . ."

"It's okay, Dakota, I get it." The hair on my arms stands as I watch Sophie's eyelids flutter before her face pales, and her slender shoulders shudder. "I get it." A tear escapes from her eye and she quickly moves to wipe it away.

"Shit," I mumble and move to hug her. Sophie purses her lips together and shakes her head. "Please, don't," she begs. "I don't want to relive it. I need to forget."

"Does anyone else know?" Her head moves in small shakes. "Not even your mom?"

Her head snaps up to me, and her eyes beg and plead for me to stop asking her questions. "Does yours?" Our conversation may not have been verbalized, but we both understand the other's been through something traumatic.

Deflated, I simply shake my head too. "Sam does though." I look over to Sam flicking water at Taylor, who retaliates by swimming over and dunking her under before picking her up and throwing her a few feet away from him.

"Did she see something?"

"Kinda. She got a picture messaged to her cell and she showed me. I panicked and ran down to the park a few blocks over, she followed and found me in a crumpled mess."

"You're lucky, Dakota. You have someone to talk to about this."

There's so much pain in her voice. She's trying really hard to hide the heartache. "When did it happen?" I have no doubt, not one single shred of uncertainty that she's making this up. I can see how hurt she is, how her raw emotions are a reflection of mine.

"About a year ago." The sadness in her eyes tells me she's struggling to talk, to open up. I don't want to push her, but I also want her to know she can talk to me anytime. I don't blame her; it's humiliating. "It was at a party. We'd won a home game, someone had a party . . . you know how it goes." Her voice is wispy, soft, and incredibly controlled.

My hands tremble as I become restless, a sudden shooting pain tears through my spine right into my head. Cringing, I rub the spot on my temple, hoping I can ease the tension that's hit me unexpectedly. "Do you know who?" my voice cracks on the last word. I move my head to the side, hoping the crick in my neck cracks. It wasn't there earlier, it's only just happened.

Sophie's gray eyes fill with tears. One lonely tear escapes and she swiftly moves her hand so she can wipe it away. "I don't know who did it." Another tear falls and she wipes that one away too.

Furrowing my brows together I take a deep breath and watch her as reality settles over me. *Please don't say you were drugged. Please don't say you were drugged.* "What do you mean?" *Please don't say you were drugged. Please don't say you were drugged.* "I don't get it."

She blinks rapidly while the tears are coming stronger and faster than before. "I just . . ." her body quivers as she tries to breathe. I find my own breath has stilled, suspended while I wait to hear what she has to say. "I don't remember."

All the blood drains from my body, shards of ice stab into me as my body temperature drops. "You don't remember?" My eyes try to stay connected to hers, however my vision is filled with dense black stars. Wildly I close and open my eyes, then screw them shut allowing her words to register. In defense I wrap my arms around my torso, all my barriers fly up as my body begins to twitch.

"Dakota?" I hear Sam call my name. The darkness is keeping me from responding. "Dakota, you're trembling." Her words are a jumbled mess, I'm not even sure if she's talking to me. "What happened?" There's a panicked desperation in her quiet voice.

"I'm okay," I finally find the strength to answer Sam. "I'm okay," I repeat.

Sam grabs onto my knees and leans into me. Her face is within inches of mine as she keeps her focus on me and how I'm reacting. "What happened?" Sam then looks over to Sophie who's still crying.

"Nothing, please let it go," I beg of her. Reaching out, I grab Sophie's hand, reassuring her I'll never tell her secret to a living soul. "I promise, I'm okay."

Sam keeps her eyes trained on me, occasionally looking back to Sophie. Her expression remains suspicious, her dark brown eyes are pensive yet soft. She leans in and hugs me, then widens her embrace to include Sophie. "Okay," she says in a small voice.

We remain in each other's arms for a long time, letting go only when Taylor clears his throat. "Um, everything okay?" he asks.

Taylor's in the pool, near us but still at a distance as if he knows we're all emotional and doesn't know how to deal with it. *Typical boy.* "We're okay," I answer on behalf of the three of us.

Taylor's eyes are wide with fright. Not scary like he's seen a ghost, more like *'these chicks are crazy.'* I can't help but chuckle when I see how his eyes are darting between us before he swims backward in the pool.

"We're good," Sophie says wiping her tears away.

"Yeah, you know, we're girls."

Taylor's face lifts in a surprised expression. "I'm kinda already aware. I just didn't realize how um . . . ahhh, *different* you all are." He pinches the bridge of his nose with his thumb and forefinger, and moves even further away from us.

Sophie, Sam, and I look at each other, and can't help but laugh. "Who you calling different, buster?" Sam swims toward him and he moves to the opposite end. "Hey." She stops swimming and brings her hand back down with force, scooping the water—and splashing Taylor.

Just like that, the intensity has been shattered by the playfulness and easiness of Taylor being clueless toward women. I watch as they play, and Taylor turns to catch my eye. He smiles at me, winks, and gives me a slight nod.

Dragging the side of my mouth up in a half smile, I know Taylor isn't so clueless. He defused a potentially ugly scene, and it makes me wonder how much he's seen in order to know when to do that.

CHAPTER 25

"I'M GOING TO get the grill started," Dad calls to the four of us.

"I don't know where Reece is," I say looking to the other three.

Taylor shrugs his shoulders, Sam doesn't even flinch and Sophie smiles at me. "I don't know," Sophie ends up replying. "I don't have his number."

The intensity from earlier is now forgotten, and for the past hour the four of us have been talking and swimming in the pool. "What do you all think of Mr. Collins?" Taylor asks as he stands beside the lounges along the edge of the pool. We've all been sunbathing, having had enough of swimming. My skin is starting to get too much color, so I lean over and grab the sunscreen.

"He's a bit intense," Sam says. "He seems like he's everywhere."

"Yeah I thought that too. The first day of vacation, Mom and I went to the mall to buy some stuff, and I ran into him three times while we were there. First time I didn't think much of it, but when we saw him the third time, I made a joke asking if he's stalking us," Sophie says, squirting some lotion on her hand and rubbing it into her shoulders. "He smiled and said we must be stalking him."

Looking over to Sam, I catch her puzzled expression. She lifts an eyebrow to me, her body language is subtle but it's telling me she thinks how weird he is.

"I don't know, I've never really noticed," Sam adds looking away from me before anyone catches on.

"I think he's weird and all, but I haven't noticed either." I offer a smile to back up my lie.

"Anyway, I'm going back in the pool. Watch out." Taylor backs up, runs and jumps in the pool right near where we all are. He jumps high, holding onto his knees as he bombs in the water, splashing the rest of us.

"I'm in there too." Sophie stands and goes to sit on the edge, water droplets hanging on her hair from Taylor's splash.

"Sorry I'm late," I hear Reece saying while he comes through the sliding door.

Smiling, I wave him over to where Sam and I are. Reece's face lights up when he sees me, a broad smile brightens his features as his eyes sparkle. He walks over to my dad first, shakes his hand, says a few things then heads over to us. "Not swimming?" he asks as he slips his shoes off and sits beside me.

"Sam was gonna put some sunscreen on my back before I headed back in."

Wiggling the sunscreen in Sam's face, she arches an eyebrow at me. "I am? I'm going back in the pool." She stands and jumps in, close to where Sophie and Taylor are swimming.

"Hey, brother." Taylor swims over to the edge of the pool and holds his fist out to Reece to fist bump.

Reece smirks and gets up, returning Taylor's fist bump and saying hello to Sophie. He then comes back over to me and sits down. "I'll do your sunscreen. Just on your back?" He squirts some in his hand and looks at me, waiting for me to turn around. "Well?"

"Well what?" My pulse spikes and I become extremely nervous at the thought of having Reece's hands on me.

"Do you want sunscreen or not?" He keeps watching me, waiting.

Sam glances back at us, her lips pulled up into a gleeful smile. Sophie swims over to Sam and both are having fun lying across a noodle each while sneaking small looks over to Reece and myself.

It takes every ounce of strength I have to turn around so Reece can rub sunscreen into my back. Closing my eyes I mentally and physically prepare to have his hands on me. I try to swallow past the rock lodged in my throat. Holding my hands together, I will them to stop shaking and trembling from fear of contact.

"Are you sick? You're whole body is shaking," Reece asks.

"I'm okay. Just tired." Again the lie comes so easily. *I hate myself.*

Keeping my eyes screwed tightly shut, I take a deep breath in, and hold it. Waiting for the moment he touches me, my shoulders come up in anticipation and edginess washes over me. The moment his big, warm hands gently touch me, I exhale loudly. Easiness bathes me and the anxiety my body was freaking out over, just disappears.

Reece lightly rubs his hands all over my back, massaging the thick, slightly oily lotion into my skin. "Hold your hair up," his voice croaks. I lift my ponytail, and with tenderness he continues to apply lotion all the way up my neck and on my shoulders.

His strokes become more delicate, longer and softer. I hear his breath catch while his hands run down my arms and back up again. My own heartbeat picks up in pace and I feel my cheeks flush with a warm tingling feeling I've not felt in a while.

"Um," I say, terrified at my body's reaction to Reece's touch. "Thank you." I move away, to sit opposite him putting, distance between us.

"Yeah, no problem." His own face has a slight red tinge to it, and he quickly takes his t-shirt off and leaves it in his lap before applying sunscreen to his own body. "So, what's been happening?" he asks awkwardly.

Averting my gaze from his toned stomach and broad shoulders, I look over to where Dad's standing in front of the grill. He's waving his hand over it, checking the heat, while pretending he's not watching all of us.

"Not much. Mom and I got everything ready earlier, and Dad cleaned the grill before anyone got here. We've all been swimming. Hope you're hungry; there's a ton of food."

"Yeah? We're going to have s'mores tonight, right?"

"Is it not an American teenager's rite of passage to have s'mores at a family cookout?" I lift my brows at him and smirk.

"Well, of course." He slaps his forehead. "How stupid for me to even ask. Well, bring on the food." He rubs his defined abs, "'Cause I'm hungry."

"You coming in?" I ask as I get to my feet and head over to the pool.

"Ah, yeah in a minute or so," his voice croaks as he looks away. There's a look of shame running through him. He's avoiding my eyes, his voice is scratchy and he shifts uncomfortably.

Oh . . . crap. It seems I caused a reaction to his body, like he did mine.

"Okay, well I'm jumping in. If you want a drink or something, there's a cooler beside the barbeque. There's soda, juice and water in it." I point to beside Dad.

"Yeah, thanks. I might just sit here and let the sunscreen soak in." He's trying to conceal a smirk, but the tips of his red ears are giving away exactly *why* he's not getting in the pool or going to get a drink.

"I'll be in the pool." I turn, run, and jump in right near Taylor who has his back to me. The weight of me lands under water, my head completely immersed and I push up off the floor of the pool toward the surface.

"Good one, Dakota," Taylor grumbles and splashes water on my face. I have my mouth open, laughing at my spectacular entrance into the pool. Taylor's aim isn't deliberate, but I end up swallowing some of the pool water and begin to cough. "Sorry." He swims over to me, remorseful at his actions. "I'm so sorry," he adds, his face long and stressed.

I'm laughing, but thanks to the water I've swallowed I continue to choke-slash-laugh. "I'm good." I take a few breaths, calming myself before looking at Taylor. He's pale, and looks horrified. A few more seconds pass and I manage a smile. "Seriously, I'm fine."

"Phew." He breathes and swims toward Sam.

Laughing, I look back to Reece. "Come on," I encourage him. He stands and runs toward the pool. "Crap." I can tell this splash is going to be huge. Swimming as quickly as possible, I head over toward Sophie. Reece throws himself in the pool, landing on his stomach. The splash is so huge, I look over to Dad who's putting the burgers on the grill, and he shakes his head with drops of water flicking off him.

"Man, that freaking hurt," Reece says when he comes up from under the water. His torso is dark red from the belly-flop, and he's rubbing his hand over it. "I won't be doing that again." I wince at his words, because his chest *looks* painful.

Swimming over to me, he smiles. "Good one. You even got Dad."

He looks over to my father who's watching us all closely in the pool. "Sorry, Mr. Bennett," Reece calls over to my Dad.

"It's just water, Reece. But I must admit, by the look of your very red chest, I'll be hedging my bet to say you won't be doing that again." Dad rubs his chin with his hand, and chuckles to himself.

"You're right about that. I won't be," Reece calls back.

"Good idea, son."

Reece turns to me, his face as red as a fire truck. "I'm so embarrassed. I shouldn't have done that in front of your father."

"Dad's cool. He would've told you if it made him angry, but he's just cool about it." Reece starts laughing, shaking his head as he runs his right hand over his eyes. "What's so funny?"

When he stops laughing, his smile is huge. "One time, last summer, we were over at my cousins' place. They've got a pool like this, but deeper. They've got a springboard at the deepest end. Anyway, my brothers and my cousins were all making bets to see who'd make the biggest splash." He starts laughing again, and this makes me smile widely too. "When it was my turn . . . well, I was wearing a pair of my cousin's trunks. He's much bigger than me." His laughing continues and I have a sneaking suspicion where this is heading. "Anyway, let's just say when I came up from my dive, I went one way and the trunks went another."

"Oh my God." I clasp a hand to my mouth, laughing from behind it.

"Yeah, but that's not the worst part."

"Seriously, there's more?"

"Yeah. Miles grabbed them before I got to them, and took off out of the pool."

Dropping my hands from my face, my mouth falls open and I'm completely speechless. It takes me a few seconds before I can find any words. "What did you do?"

"Well you'd think your parents would have your back, right?" *Oh my gosh.* "Not in my family." He laughs again. "I asked Mom to grab me a towel." He moves his head sideways, and laughingly screws his mouth up. "She grabbed a towel alright."

"Oh no." Why do I suspect he's going to say something to make me laugh?

"Yeah, matter-of-fact she grabbed *all* the towels. And took off inside. With the towels . . . and a newspaper they had sitting out on the table where my uncle was reading."

"Oh my God." I can't help it. I laugh so hard everyone turns to look at me. "Are you serious?"

"I'm very serious. But of course, it doesn't end there."

"What?" I'm laughing so much I have tears rolling down my cheeks. The entire thing is so freaking funny. The priceless look on Reece's face, his resignation to the fact it actually happened, the tone in which he's telling the story . . . everything is hilarious.

"They locked me out. Do you know how hard it is to try and open a slider while holding your . . . you know?" He looks down at the water and I lose it even more. "The only thing I could do was get in the pool and hope to God someone would feel sorry for me. That didn't happen. Miles came out recording it on his phone, while Mom kept taunting me from the pool's edge with a towel."

I lose it. I'm laughing so hard I have to grasp the pool's side and hold on. "You can't be serious!" I gasp through the bursts of insistent laughter.

"Deadly." He huffs. "They uploaded it to show everyone too. Thank God you couldn't see . . ." he clears his throat. "Anything."

"Your family is nuts," I say wiping the tears away. "Like seriously crazy."

"Taught me a damn lesson. Don't go swimming if your trunks are too big."

Once we've gotten over our laughter, the five of us have a race to see who can swim the fastest laps. We race four times, Sam won two, Reece one, and Taylor one. Sophie and I didn't win a race, but we had the most fun trying to slow the others down.

It's not long before the sun starts to descend behind the mountains and the sky turns a beautiful burnt orange. "Wow, look at that," Sam points to the huge full sun as it falls rapidly.

"Have you ever seen a sunset so perfect?" Sophie says in awe.

"I'm hungry," Taylor adds. And I hear a slap, obviously from Sam. "What? I am."

The back slider opens and Mom comes out carrying some plates. I quickly get out of the pool, foregoing the majestic sunset to help Mom. "I'll help." I dry myself off in record time and go into the kitchen. The island counter has a huge spread on it, so I start bringing everything out.

When I place the first two bowls down, I look over to the pool to see everyone coming out and drying themselves. Reece is already out and helping Dad with the hot food on the grill.

When the table's set, we all sit down in peaceful harmony to eat dinner. Today, I've had a glimpse into the world I once knew, and it gives me hope that everything will be okay.

I'm not hating myself. *For now.*

CHAPTER 26

M OM AND DAD are inside washing up, and the five of us are sitting around the fire pit making s'mores and talking.

Reece has gotten on really well with everyone, even Sophie seems to like him. She makes a s'more and starts eating it. "You know, Reece, you're nothing like the others." She looks over to him and smiles. The smile is soft and apologetic.

"What do you mean?" He turns the marshmallow over the fire, crisping it up further. The outside catches on fire and you can hear the sizzle of the small blue flame coating the exterior. The sugars quickly burn and the fire goes out on its own.

"I mean, most of the guys on the team are jerks, Levi being the leader of the jerks."

"I'm not denying that. It's only been recently I've seen exactly how much of a dick he is." He sandwiches the marshmallow with a piece of chocolate and two graham crackers and starts eating it.

The whole process is quite hypnotic. Watching the marshmallow burn, then watching the assembly procedure.

"He's not very nice," I manage to say in a small voice.

"Neither are a lot of the girls who hang off you guys like you're some kind of rock stars. You're not rock stars," Sam says. "I gotta tell you, it's sickening! They have no self-respect."

"I have to agree. I watch the way they act around the team, and how they throw themselves at the guys." Sophie shakes her head, disgusted.

I crinkle my forehead and scrunch my brows together. "Was I like that?" I ask, looking at everyone.

Sophie averts her eyes and so does Sam. My own sister is implicitly saying I'm the girl she was describing. "Not as bad as Lindsey and

Jordan, but you weren't great either."

Slumping my shoulders I sink into the chair and look to the ground. "Really?" I ask with a small sigh. Man, how blind was I? Does this mean I was asking for what happened to me? Did I lead someone on? Could I have avoided it if I was a nicer person?

My stomach knots in agitation and my heart starts pounding heavily in my chest. Tangling my fingers together I try not to look at anything but the grass beneath the chair.

Chatter continues in the background. I can't make out the words they're saying, but I know they're still on the same subject. "Sorry," I whisper to everyone. The talking stops, and I feel four pairs of eyes turn to me. I keep my head down, ashamed and embarrassed at how I once was. "I'm really disgusted by my old behavior. I wish someone would've told me earlier." Looking up I'm met with them all looking at me with different expressions.

Taylor's confused.

Sophie's concerned.

Sam's sympathetic.

And Reece's proud. "You know now, and you're a better person for it,' he says. "You can't let the past dictate your future."

"But I was a bitch."

"That's right. You were a bitch. Now you're pretty cool." Reece winks at me and smiles.

"I'm sorry, guys. I really am." I meet all their eyes so they know I'm actually remorseful for everything I may have done to them. "I won't give you an excuse, because truthfully I don't have one. I'm sorry for anything I've said or done."

Sophie jumps up and hugs me. "Now you know you weren't the nicest person, but you're making up for it all." She pulls out of the hug and her face softens. "You're alright now."

"Wow, this has become a downer," Sam adds. "I wanted to bitch about those bitches Jordan and Mariah, and more importantly, Lindsey and suddenly everyone's on the edge of crying."

"I'm not a huge fan of those girls." Reece shivers and down turns his mouth. "None of them are nice. I'm kinda glad you got away from them. You were definitely the nicest one out of them all." He shivers again. "That Jordan." He shakes his head in revulsion.

"What? Why?" I ask.

"She and Aaron had a fight at one of the parties someone threw after a game we won. She made a beeline straight for me. She literally draped her arms over me, and leaned in for a kiss. She was drunk, but let me say, she knew what she was doing."

Against my will, I feel my face betray how I *shouldn't* be feeling. I shouldn't care, but something inside me begins to boil and snaps in frustration how she'd throw herself at Reece. I shouldn't care, but my churning stomach, my rising anger, and my thumping heart all say I *do* care. "What did you do?" My voice is so small, the question barely reaching my ears. Reece looks at me, and tilts his head to the side. "What did you do?" I say much louder, and more forcefully.

"That particular time, I held her hand, led her outside and called her a cab. I took her back to her house and made sure she got in okay."

"How many times has she thrown herself at you?" Sophie asks the question burning on my lips.

"Only one other time. Remember when she and Aaron broke up for like two days just after the New Year?" His gaze turns to us all individually. I sneak a look at everyone to see Sophie shrugging her shoulders, like she doesn't know *or* care. Sam's holding Taylor's hand, nodding her head. I smile to myself when I look at Taylor leaning forward desperate to hear more. He looks like a gossip queen.

"Yeah, I remember," I say.

"Yeah, well that time she was even worse."

"How so?" Taylor asks, wide eyes and desperate for more.

"She came over to my house, and flirted with Miles. Even told him she'd be glad to share herself with him and me. She didn't say it in front of me, but Miles pulled me aside and told me about ten minutes after she got there. She kept asking me if I wanted to go to my room, and I kept her out in the family room. Mom would walk in, give her stink eye and walk out again."

"Stink-eye?" I ask, laughing.

"Yeah, Mom's not real keen on her. Or too many of the girls I know."

"Great," I mumble and look away. That dreadful feeling creeps inside me, as if I already know she won't like me. *Not that it really matters.* I'm never going to date again. Ever.

"Needless to say, when Miles told me she threw herself at him, I told her to leave 'cause we had a family party we were going to."

"She's a real skank," Sam announces loudly. "I didn't think she was like that. I thought Jordan was nice." She huffs out a breath while her leg bounces in agitation. "Christ." I can tell by Sam's reaction she's taken aback by what she's hearing.

"Yeah, she's not as nice as what you think she is. And trust me when

I say, she has *never* had your back." Reece pointedly looks at me.

This causes a nauseating feeling to sit in the pit of my stomach. I almost don't want to ask, but at the same time the sucker in me needs to know what she's said. "I don't think I want to know." *But I do . . . no I don't.*

"She's nasty, as bad as, if not worse than Lindsey. Mariah's okay though." Reece shrugs his left shoulder. "By okay, I mean she's better than those other two. She's never said anything bad about you, but she never stood up for you either."

Sam gets up and sits in the vacant chair beside me. She leans over and whispers, "Lucky you're no longer hanging out with them." Sam moves back, and gives me a smile.

"Yeah."

"They're all bitches." Sophie declares as she stands and stretches. "I need a soda, who wants a drink?"

Everyone says they want a drink and Sophie walks over to the fridge outside, grabbing an assortment.

"Darling," Mom says coming out of the slider, her eyes travel the entire backyard, checking on everyone.

"Yeah, Mom."

She walks over and lays a kiss on Sam's forehead, then mine. She's holding five fleecy throws in her hands, giving one to each of us. "I thought you might want these if you get chilly." She smiles at us as she passes them out.

"Thank you, Mrs. B," Reece says and takes the dark red throw Mom holds out for him.

"Thank you, Mrs. Bennett," Sophie replies when she comes back with the drinks. "You can put mine on that chair, please." She nods her head to where she'd been sitting, while she juggles the five drinks she's holding.

"Your father and I are ducking down to the church to give them the food," Mom says to me when she reaches me last.

"I'll come too." I stand.

"You stay here, darling. You can come with us next time. We won't be long, about twenty minutes. Here's the house phone in case you need to call us." Mom hands me the cordless phone and leaves. She quickly turns and points her finger at me with a smirk on her face. "No wild parties."

"I'm so putting the call out," Sam teases. "Wild night at the Bennetts.' Hard core drugs, lots of unprotected sex, loud, obnoxious music. You know, all the things us teenagers get up to." Sam smiles at Mom while Mom stands with her hands on her hips, giving Sam the 'death stare.'

"Just don't disturb the neighbors, we don't want to piss them off," Mom retorts sarcastically.

I look to Sophie who's laughing, and Reece whose mouth is gaping wide while Taylor's trying to shrink away. "We'll keep the loud music down then," I say cheekily smiling at Mom.

Mom rolls her eyes and walks away. I think I hear her mumble something, but I can't be sure. It sounded like, *I've got the best kids in the world.'* If only she knew. "We won't be long," she calls over her shoulder then disappears through the slider.

"Your parents are so cool," Taylor says. He sits back in his seat and has a long, wistful look on his face.

"Your Mom's really nice too," Sam responds. "She's kind of different. Like she likes all that opera music and stuff. But she's nice." Taylor's eyes land on Sam and I can see the love he has for her. He worships her, absolutely adores her. It's there for everyone to see, and he has no shame in showing it.

We all sit around the pit fire, talking. Reece and Taylor gossip like two old women about the guys from school while Sam, Sophie and I keep quiet and listen.

"I thought girls were bad," Sophie whispers behind her hand to me.

"I know. I didn't think guys were this bad. Levi never bitched the way they are." I point between Reece and Taylor.

Reece stops talking about some party that's going to happen in two weeks and looks over at us. "What are you two talking about?" He tilts his head and narrows his eyes.

"Us? Nothing." Sophie laughs. "Except you two can gossip like nothing we've ever seen." Sophie points between herself and me.

"Hey." I stand and stretch. "Don't involve me."

"Great, you're gonna let me take the fall?" Sophie teases.

"Hell yeah."

Reece smiles at us, and Sophie stands too. "Hey, I'm getting tired, I might have a shower and go crash."

"Sure thing, I'll show you where everything is." Sophie's mom is letting her stay here tonight.

"I better call my Mom, ask her to pick me up." Taylor reaches into his pocket and grabs his cell.

Sam hugs Taylor around the neck, and gives him a peck on his cheek. My heart melts when I see that. It makes me so happy they're into each other. Taylor's a cool guy, and although he likes classical music, he's still pretty fun.

Leading Sophie into my room, I give her a clean towel and show her to the bathroom so she can shower. Then I head back out. Taylor and Sam are near the slider, hugging each other. Reece is still sitting on the lounge chair, looking out over the clear, rippling water of the pool. I leave Sam and Taylor and head over to sit opposite Reece.

"I hope it's okay if I stay a while longer?" he asks.

"Yeah it's cool with me."

"I like him." Reece points to Taylor. "For a junior, he's alright."

I look over to Taylor and Sam. They're entwined tightly together. One of Taylor's hands is resting on the top of Sam's butt, and the other on her opposite hip. Their foreheads are touching as they talk quietly together. They're cute, and sweet, and it makes my heart sing to see them like this.

Mom's figure appears from inside, and she comes through the slider, her eyes landing straight on Sam and Taylor. I start to laugh at Taylor's reaction. Reece sees my amused face, and he turns in time to see Taylor pull away from Sam and look at Mom with pure horror. "Oh my God, Mrs. Bennett, I swear I wasn't doing anything," he stumbles over the words.

Even in the dim light, I can see the red tinge on Taylor's cheeks. They seriously weren't doing anything, but it amuses me to watch him squirm.

Mom cocks her hip and looks at Taylor. "Is that right? You weren't doing anything?"

"No, ma'am, nothing. We were just saying goodnight because I called my Mom to come pick me up."

Mom looks over to me, and I'm trying to hold in my cynical laugh. Getting up I walk over to Mom, who's seething, Taylor, who's crapping himself and Sam, who's very quiet. "Seriously, Mom we've all been sitting out here talking. Taylor called his Mom to pick him up, and when I got back from showing Sophie where the bathroom is, they were here cuddling."

Mom arches an eyebrow while still looking between Taylor and Sam. She brings her index and middle fingers up to tap them on her mouth, then points them to Taylor and says in a low tone, "I'll be watching you."

Poor Taylor looks like he's about to lose his dinner.

"Mom," Sam whines. "We really weren't doing anything."

"Okay, I believe you. But how about you two come in the family room and wait for your mom to pick you up, Taylor?" I chuckle, because

Mom's not too subtle.

Taylor's gaze goes straight to me and Reece, and we both wave to him.

Reece and I fall into an easy conversation, and before long we're joined by Sophie. She sits for a few minutes before she curls up on the lounger, and her eyes begin to drift shut. "I might head off to bed," she says while yawning.

"Goodnight." Reece looks up at her to smile, before crossing his arms and snuggling further into his chair.

"Night," she yawns again and heads inside.

We have already made up the pull-out sofa. "Goodnight," I add.

Sophie takes herself inside, and goes to sleep. Sam's probably having a shower and then she'll crash soon too.

"Just us left," Reece says.

"Not for long, I'm tired too. I'll be throwing you out soon." I give him a cheeky smile.

"Yeah, it's probably for the best. I've got so many things I have to do tomorrow. But this was fun, I enjoyed it."

"Me too."

"I was thinking, maybe we can go to the movies or something. There's a new Marvel movie coming out, want to go?"

"Um." I run my hand over the back of my neck, suddenly nervous he's asking me out on a date.

"It's okay," he quickly adds. "I get it, you're not into me like I'm into you."

Blinking, I stare at him. He thinks I don't like him. "It's not that," I say in a small voice. "I'm not ready to get into anything." I want to tell him why, but I can't. *I can't tell anyone.*

"Yeah, it's cool." He fidgets in his seat before he stands to his feet. "Anyway, I should go."

He turns and takes huge steps to get away from me. "Reece," I call, following him. But he ignores me and speeds up. "Reece." My voice sounds flustered and edgy. "It's not like that."

"Really. It's cool, no pressure."

"Reece!" I shout loudly causing him to stop walking. Slowly he turns around to look at me. His cheeks are red, and I can see the embarrassment from me rejecting him. "How about we go." His eyes light up and a small smile starts tugging at his mouth. "And we can invite Sam and Taylor." The smile quickly drops.

He visibly gulps, his Adams apple vibrates with the every breath he takes. "Sure, like a double date." I nod, hoping he's okay with this. He focusses on his shoes, then lifts his face. I see his lips brighten in a smile. "Yeah, that sounds cool."

"Great."

"Great," he says straight after me. "Well, I gotta get going too. Can I call you so we can plan going to the movies?"

Crap, my phone. Sam still has it. The idea of getting it back terrifies me, I simply don't want to see any messages or even log into social media. This is my bubble. My happy place. No one can reach me here in my happy, safe, bubble. "Yeah, that's cool. If I don't answer just text me. I've kind of being staying away from social media and . . ." I pause and scrunch my mouth not really wanting to say anything else.

"People, right? Especially people who've not been so nice."

"Yeah, them."

"That's cool. Just call me when you get my messages."

We walk through the house, where Mom and Dad are sitting in the family room watching TV. Sophie's tucked in a nook where we have a sofa bed for when we have guests stay.

"Good night, Mr. and Mrs. Bennett. Thank you for dinner."

"You're welcome, Reece." Mom smiles up at Reece while she's safely tucked under Dad's arm. Dad gives Reece a nod.

We walk out front and sit on the sidewalk, waiting for someone to come pick him up. "I need to ask you something," Reece says in a gentle voice.

"What is it?" I sweep my hand through some leaves that have fallen and gathered in the gutter.

"Did something bad happen with Levi?" My shoulders tense and my breath hitches. Turning my head away, I avoid his penetrating stare. "Something happened, right?" Shaking my head, I bring my knees up and lean my head on my bent legs. "Dakota, you can tell me."

I take a deep breath and try to steady my shaky voice. "He didn't do anything. But I hate how he and Lindsey are treating me. I've done nothing to either of them to justify how they're handling this whole situation. He broke up with me, and then goes straight to her. It hurts like hell, you know?"

"I'm sorry he's treating you like this."

Offering him a weak smile I nod. "He's not your responsibility."

A car pulls up, and Miles rolls down the window, leans over and whistles at Reece. "Come on, Cinderella. I've got your glass slipper."

Reece rolls his eyes, stands and dusts off his butt. "Thanks for tonight. Talk to you soon."

"Hurry up, Queen Elsa, I've got somewhere I have to be. Let me get you back to your ice castle."

Laughing, I stand from where we're sitting. I walk over to the car and lean down on the edge of the window. "It scares me how you know all about these female princesses considering you only have brothers. If I didn't know better, I'd think you were into Disney movies."

Miles winks at me, turns, and punches Reece in the arm. "Who says I'm not?"

Laughing, I say goodnight to both before stepping back from the curb and heading inside. I go straight to my room, grab my pajamas and have a shower.

Today's been crazy. Sophie told me what happened to her. That heaviness she bared is now shared with me. It's got to be hard on her, I at least have Sam, where she has no one. Washing myself, I keep thinking about Sophie's situation and how she was ra . . . ra . . . *assaulted.* I still can't say the word.

It's dirty.

Not the word, the word holds its own stigma. The act, the thought and even the reputation given to a victim once it's out in the open. I've heard what was said about others who were r . . . attacked.

It's disgusting and dirty.

A tear runs down my cheek as I stand under the hot stream of the shower.

I'm disgusting and dirty.

I will forever carry this damage with me.

CHAPTER 27

W HEN I WALK into the kitchen, Sam and Sophie are already sitting at the dining table while Mom cooks up bacon and eggs for breakfast.

"Good morning," I say. Looking down the hallway I search for Dad. "Where's Dad?"

"Dad had to go to the store. He needs some new business shirts and ties for work, so he's gone shopping." Mom prods an egg and checks the bacon in the oven. "Maple bacon and eggs sunny side up," she proudly announces.

"Can I help, Mrs. B?"

"You can get the orange juice from the fridge and get the glasses from that cupboard over there." Mom nods her head to the side, pointing.

Sophie grabs the glasses and juice. Sam gets some plates and cutlery.

"I'll make some toast," I offer walking over to the toaster while grabbing the loaf of bread off the counter.

Breakfast is ready quickly and Mom sets a plate for Dad and leaves it under the heating lamp for him. "Enjoy, girls." We all dive in.

"Guess what I heard last night?" Sam shoves a piece of buttered toast in her mouth. We all look and wait for her to tell us. "Taylor said he heard from one of his friends, that a girl in my year let a boy . . ." She looks at Mom warily. "You know?"

"What? They had sex?" Mom asks in the most disgusted tone.

"No!" Sam eagerly responds. "She let him put his hand down her pants."

"How old are they?"

"My age."

I shake my head, stunned at what I'm hearing. Sophie gasps but keeps eating her breakfast in silence.

"Hold up a second," Mom says placing her cutlery down on the plate. "Are you telling me two fourteen year olds were messing around?" Sam nods her head. "Wow, what a girl," Mom mumbles while arching her brows, clearly disgusted.

I look at Mom, shocked at her reaction. "What do you mean?" I question.

"What kind of girl would do that?" Mom asks.

"Hang on, Mom." I become defensive and irritated. "You've just heard two fourteen-year-olds are doing things to each other, and you automatically blame the girl, shaming her and not him?"

Mom leans back in her chair, and tilts her head to the side considering what I've said. "Well, she's not a very nice young lady if she lets the boys do things like that to her."

"Did you hear what you just said? In that one sentence you excuse him because he's a 'boy' and blaming her because she's a 'young lady.' She's being shamed, but he's not getting any of the blame or responsibility. That's not right, Mom."

"It's not like that," Mom protests.

"It *is* like that. Because you've got an image of her being easy and letting boys do this to her. But says who she *is* easy, and why hasn't the boy been labelled? Who according to what Sam said, stuck *his* hand down *her* pants. Why is he allowed to do that, but only the girl is blamed for it?"

Mom blinks a few times and nods. "You have a valid point. I suppose I didn't think of it that way."

My heart's beating wildly because this tells me all I need to know. I should've told my parents when it first happened, but if this is how my Mom—who's normally really open-minded and easy to talk to—sees things, then I know I'd be blamed. There was never any chance for me.

"It's how we've been conditioned," Sophie says. We all turn to look at her. "We have; from a young age, we've been taught to question women if they cry for help. Maybe because we're supposed to be stronger, maybe because we're not supposed to point fingers or speak up when something happens to us." Sophie shivers. I feel like she's indirectly telling us what happened to her, and as I look at Sam and Mom, I think they can see it too.

"It's not that," Mom says.

"Then what else can it be, Mrs. Bennett? Your automatic response was to judge the girl. To make it her responsibility to keep her legs closed and if anything happens to her, well then it's her fault. But we don't know the full story, what if he forced her? Or what if she forced him?"

"Forced him?" Sam exhales a laugh. "Forced him, like really?"

"You can't trust anyone, Sam." Sophie looks down to her plate. Her hair veils her face, and after a moment her shoulders shake telling us she's trying to contain her tears.

"Oh, sweetheart." Mom gets up and goes to her.

She wraps her arms around Sophie and kisses her hair. "I'm sorry, there are so many bad people in our world and I hate to think of anyone hurting my girls, or even you." Mom hugs her tighter and Sophie lets out a low, pain-filled breath.

Sophie shifts in her seat, and Mom lets her go, moving back to her chair. She lifts her head and gives us a quick, weak smile. "It's something I'm fairly passionate about. There are always two sides, and they both need to be heard. Somewhere in between is the truth."

"You're completely right. I jumped in and judged, and I shouldn't have. I would hate it if my girls were as judgmental as I showed myself to be a few minutes ago."

"It's not judgment. It's lack of awareness. We need to see the whole picture, not just the preconceived one put in our minds." Sophie looks down at her plate. "Thank you for breakfast, it looks great." Her tone says she no longer wants to talk about this. She's friendly and sweet, but essentially she's saying, without the words, 'end of conversation.'

Mom keeps her eyes on Sophie, understanding the subtleness of her words and nods slightly. "So, what are you girls doing today?" Mom salts her egg before beginning to eat it, letting go of the tension bouncing around the room.

"Want to go to the mall?" I ask both Sam and Sophie.

"I have to ask my Mom first," Sophie says.

"Yeah I want to go," Sam excitedly squeals, jumping up and down on her chair. "I want a new skirt. Oh!" she cries, making me jump. "And a new pair of shoes."

Sophie looks at Sam as if she's suddenly grown two heads and shakes her head. "She's enthusiastic," I say with a grin.

"Dakota was the same when she was Sam's age. She'd always be so excited to get out of the house and go to the mall with her friends. It was always Lindsey, Mariah, Jordan and Dakota. The four of them were virtually inseparable at that age. Now . . . nothing." Mom shrugs her shoulders, clueless to what's been happening. "Anyway, Sophie, if you want to call your Mom, go ahead. Let her know I can take you girls, and drop you off at home when you're all ready to be picked up."

"I'll be a minute, I'll give Mom a call now." Sophie stands and excuses herself.

"Go in my room," I yell to her as she goes down the hallway.

Mom sits, quietly staring down at her food. "I hope I didn't upset her. She's a nice girl. I really don't want her to think I was judging anyone."

"You were, Mom. But it's okay. Once we pointed it out, you realized what you were doing and stopped. I suppose it's got to be hard for old people," Sam says.

"Old eh?" Mom frowns at Sam for calling her 'old' but chuckles.

"Yeah, heaps old." Now Sam's being sarcastic and trying to cause trouble in her usual friendly way.

"Keep calling me old and see what type of skirt and shoes five dollars buys you." Sam's eyes widen as she tries to hold onto her smile. Her fork's frozen in midair, while she blinks slowly. "Yeah. *Now* call me old," Mom challenges her.

"What I meant to say, but stupidly jumbled up the words, was my incredible hip, cool, youthful mother. Did I mention gorgeous? Like seriously beautiful?"

"Now you're sucking up."

"Has the five dollars increased?"

"Only to ten."

"Then I better keep going because I need to give you at least sixty dollars' worth of compliments."

"You'll be here all day."

"Can I get an advance and continue with them when we get back?" She flutters her eyelids at Mom. "After I get my skirt and shoes?" Sam brings her hands together as if in to prayer.

"We'll see. But for now, you can pick up where you left off."

I finish my breakfast and take my plate to the sink. Laughing to myself, I leave the kitchen and head to my room. Sam is still throwing around sentences like 'best Mom on the planet,' and Mom is telling her to make them good because at this stage, she's only secured the sole of one shoe.

Sophie's sitting on my bed and finishing the call to her Mom. She hangs up and looks at me, her eyes wide with worry. Immediately I rush to her. "Are you okay?"

"My Dad's found out where Mom works. He somehow had a bunch of flowers delivered to her and now Mom's scared he'll come after us when he gets released from prison."

"How did he find out?" I ask, sitting beside her on my bed. She shrugs her shoulders. "When's he due to be released?"

"Not for a few more years. But there was a note on the flowers."

"What did it say?"

"It said he wants me to go and see him in prison, and if I do that, he'll never bother us again."

"Are you going to go?"

"Mom said no way, but I don't know." Her hands relax against her thighs while her shoulders drop. "I want to know why he treated us like he did, and this may be my only chance to get a real answer."

"He's been in for three years?" I try and recall what she's told me in the past.

"Just over. Maybe he wants to seek redemption." She lifts her shoulders.

"Redemption," I sigh. It would be nice to hold onto that dream. But there's no happily ever after in real life. If there was, I wouldn't have been *r . . . r . . .* assaulted.

"Yeah, I doubt it too."

I huff and shake my head. "Isn't it horrible how we're only sixteen years old and we view the world as toxic already?"

"We look at it realistically. I know if anyone found out about my Dad, they'd automatically assume I'm like him and my Mom's a no-hope loser too. Mom works two cleaning jobs so I don't go without. I mean we don't have the best clothes or anything, but we get by. So, can you, you know, not tell anyone about my Dad?"

I cross my heart. "I swear I'll never say a thing to anyone. It's not my story to tell. But what if Mom asks me? She was worried to think she may have made you upset at breakfast."

"You can tell your parents, but not Sam. It's not like I don't trust her, but it's better if fewer people know. She may accidently tell Taylor, then if they break up he may tell someone, and so it starts."

"I promise you, I'll only tell Mom if she asks. Your secret is safe with me."

She leans in and hugs me. "Thank you, Dakota. It's nice to know I actually have someone I can talk with."

"Hey, what did your Mom say about coming to the mall?"

"She said it was okay. She's going to come over to drop off some money for me, but she only has thirty dollars spare this week. I know I can't really do much with that, but at least I can come along."

"Yeah, that's cool. I like hanging out with you."

"Hey, there's something else." She winces, and I can tell she's uncomfortable about something.

"What's wrong?" Worried I watch her face contort with discomfort.

"I don't want your mom to see where I live. She may think badly about me. Is it okay if I tell your mom my mom will come and pick me up after we're done at the mall?"

My heart snaps with sadness. I lean in and hug her tightly. How horrible, to feel as if people will judge you based on where you live instead of the person you are. "My Mom won't judge you."

"We live in an apartment over a store. It's nothing as beautiful as this. The man who owns it gives us real cheap rent if Mom cleans the store below it. She has to mop and clean the toilets, and the windows three times a week. When she's really busy, I help her. I told Mom I wanted to get a job through summer to help with everything, and she started crying saying there's no way she wants me cleaning toilets like her. She told me I'm better than she ever was. She hates it when I help with the store downstairs, but sometimes, Mom gets home so exhausted she can barely keep her eyes open."

"Sophie, never be ashamed of where you live or where you've come from. Your mom sounds like an amazing, beautiful person, just like you."

Sophie smiles but the happiness doesn't reach her stormy eyes. I hate to think what she's seen, where she's been and what she's had to do in order to live. Both Sophie and her mom sound like people who are the backbone of this world. Getting through each day, and trying to make their world better.

"Thanks." She nonchalantly shrugs her shoulders. "But I still don't want your Mom to see where I live."

A huge lump forms in my throat, and I want to shout at her how Mom won't judge her, she'll only have respect for her and her Mom for trying to better their lives. "Okay, but one day I'm hoping you'll trust my Mom."

"One day. Anyway, we'd better get changed, and then go help clean up."

We stand and Sophie goes to her bag, grabbing her clothes before going to the bathroom to get changed.

CHAPTER 28

"**M**AKE SURE YOU call me when you're done," Mom calls as we all get out of the car.

"Bye, Mom," both Sam and I say in chorus.

"Thank you for having me, Mrs. Bennett. And thank you so much for driving us to the mall," Sophie says to Mom.

"Don't be a stranger, okay?"

Mom pulls out of the parking lot and drives off down the street. The three of us head into the mall and Sam decides she wants to go to Forever 21 to try on a skirt she's been eyeballing.

Sam tries on the skirt she's seen, and as it turns out, it looks horrible on her. "What do you think?" She comes out of the fitting room and twirls in front of Sophie and me.

I look at Sophie sideways and catch the horrified look on her face. "Um," Sophie stumbles, not really wanting to tell Sam what she honestly thinks. "Do you like it?"

"It looks terrible," I finally say. She's my sister, so there's no way in hell I'm going to let her leave the house with that skirt on. It's too short, and the pattern on the material makes her look as if her hips are huge.

"What?" Sam looks down at the skirt and runs her hand over the fabric, straightening it. "I think it looks nice." She pouts.

Shaking my head I crease my mouth into a thin line. "It's not nice at all, Sam. It doesn't sit on you well. It makes your hips look too big and beside that, I know you; you won't wear it."

"Hmmm." Sam slumps her shoulders and looks down. "I guess you're kind of right. I think it's a bit too short. Okay, I won't buy it." Sam ducks back into the changing room and comes out a few minutes later.

The three of us head out to American Eagle and Sam starts looking through the racks while Sophie and I hang back looking at some t-shirts. "What do you think?" I ask holding up a plain gray t-shirt. Sophie scrunches her nose. "So that's a no." I chuckle.

We spend about twenty minutes in here, and Sam ends up purchasing a more modest skirt, something much more flattering to her long, slim body type.

"I'm hungry. Can we go get something to eat?" Sam asks when she comes out of the store.

"Where do you put it? You're so thin and all I see you do is eat." Sophie playfully pushes Sam.

"I'm a growing child. I need my energy." Sam raises her arms and flexes her muscles. Or I should say she flexes her non-existent muscles.

"Here comes slut one and slut two."

I turn to look at Sophie and I see in the background, Lindsey, Mariah and Jordan all walking in our direction. "Great," I mumble and roll my eyes. They're walking in formation, like you see on those trashy movies where they portray high-school hierarchy. Lindsey's front and center, with Jordan and Mariah flanking her. "Let's go." I keep going toward Starbucks where we've decided to have lunch.

As we keep walking, Sophie goes tumbling forward and falls to her knees. "Hey," I say as I turn to face Lindsey and her bitchy face. "What the hell do you think you're doing?" I stand up to her, and step right into her personal space. "You don't put your hands on other people, Lindsey. What the hell is wrong with you?"

"She's just trash." She rolls her eyes and Jordan sniggers from behind her. Both of them put their hands on their hips trying to intimidate us. But I notice Mariah step back and hang her head in shame. "She opens her legs to anyone who wants her." Lindsey arches an eyebrow and triumphantly smirks at her own hurtful words.

"Wow, you just described yourself," I say as I take another step closer to her. "Does Levi even feel the sides?" Mariah grins but keeps her head down and Lindsey shoots her an evil stare before turning back to me.

Lindsey's eyelashes keep fluttering as her small mind tries to think of something clever to say. Clearly, she has nothing.

"Come on, let's go," I say to Sam and Sophie. Sophie's hurt by the shit Lindsey spat about her, and Sam looks as if she's ready to jump in and smack Lindsey.

The three of us walk away, and Lindsey yells out, "Go on little sluts, go and have your little slutty meeting."

We stop walking and I turn to face Lindsey. "How does it feel,

Lindsey?"

"What?" She puts her hand on her hip while her jaw tightens. I look around to see we've got a small crowd gathering, mostly teenagers who have their phones out and are recording it. They're probably hoping for a confrontation they can post on social media.

"How does it feel to know you're not his first choice? And probably not even his second?" I start walking backwards and flip her the bird. Mariah claps a hand to her mouth, but not before a rumbling laugh sneaks out.

"Shut up, Mariah!" Lindsey screams at her.

Jordan's standing like a statue, mouth wide open, gawking. "Oh my God, she's such a bitch, I can't believe she said that to you."

We walk away, and we hear Lindsey screaming at Mariah and Jordan because they didn't defend her.

"Man, I was about to smack that bitch for what she said," Sam excitedly says.

"I wouldn't let you, they're not worth getting banned from the mall."

Sam smiles and so does Sophie. "Thanks, Dakota, I'm so embarrassed they pushed me and said what they said. What did I ever do to them?"

"Don't be embarrassed. It shows how ugly they are, not you."

"Did you see the look on Mariah's face? That was priceless," Sam says, still bouncing high from adrenaline.

"I gotta say, I'm really surprised by her."

"How so?" Sophie asks.

"I didn't think she'd stand around and let them act like that. Jordan, well after what we learned last night, nothing really surprises me, but Mariah . . ." I shrug my shoulders. "She hung her head in shame when Lindsey was being bitchy and laughed when I told her she's nothing more than sloppy thirds."

"Still, Mariah's mom wouldn't be happy with her," Sam says. "She's such a nice lady and I know she'd be upset with Mariah if anyone ever told her what happened." Her eyes light up and she smiles in a devious kind of way.

"No," I say looking at Sam and shaking my head. "You're not going to do anything, Sam."

We get to Starbucks and Sam goes first to get something to eat while Sophie and I grab a table. "You don't think she'll say anything to Mariah's mom?" Sophie shifts her eyes to look at Sam.

"She won't. She was just hyped up, and her brain is probably going a million miles an hour."

I get tapped on the shoulder and look up to see a woman standing beside me. I catch a glimpse of her teenage daughter sheltered behind her. "Are you the young lady who told that other girl she's some guy's third choice?" she looks at me with a scowl on her face, and I'm beginning to think what I said may have repercussions.

I sneak a look at Sam who's still in the line then turn my eyes back at the lady who's beside me. "Yes, ma'am I am." I wait for the well-deserved lecture. I should've just ignored what Lindsey did, but putting her hands on someone is not only wrong, it's immoral too. *Not cool, Lindsey, not cool.*

"I'm really proud of you for standing up for your friend. I didn't see it all, but my daughter Josephine, did, and she told me exactly what happened. I only saw the tail end of it, and I was about to intervene but my daughter stopped me. If I was your mom, I'd be extremely proud of you." Josephine steps to the side and hugs her mom. "She gets picked on all the time, and if there were more girls like you around, I'd know she'd be safe at school."

"Thank you, ma'am." I look at Josephine, and the first thing I notice is how much depth her incredible eyes hold. She's young, maybe Sam's age, but she's so beautiful, yet really sad. She also has Downs' Syndrome and it makes my heart burst with compassion. "You're very beautiful, Josephine."

She smiles at me and shyly ducks behind her mom again. "She's very timid." Her mom tries to get her to move from behind her, but she doesn't want to. "I'll leave you girls to have your lunch. But like I say to Josephine, many people have ugly hearts, and sometimes we come across people who have golden hearts." She smiles and leaves.

"Who was that?" Sam asks as she plonks down and takes a drink.

"A lady who thanked us for what happened back there with Lindsey."

Sam frowns. "She thanked you? She didn't rip it into you?"

"Her daughter who has Downs' Syndrome told her what happened. She wants people to stand up for their friends."

"Cool." Sam starts her lunch.

"My treat, Sophie. What do you want?"

Sophie has been deep in thought, not really commenting or saying too much since the lady came over with her daughter. She looks as if she's really bothered by something, but at the same time, who wouldn't be, considering what Lindsey said about her. "You know, I'm not a slut," she says to Sam, as if her approval is necessary.

Sam flicks her hand at Sophie and rolls her eyes. "I know that." She sips on her drink again before going back to her lunch.

"I need to make sure you know I'm not a slut." She looks at Sam, then me, waiting for us to say something.

"You don't need our validation, Sophie. We don't believe a word Lindsey says. And even if you were a slut, which you're not, it has nothing to do with us," I say pointing to Sam then me. Sam's too busy stuffing food into her mouth to do much more than nod her head in agreement.

Sophie looks down at her hands, twisting in her lap beneath the table, and she nods her head. Her cheeks grow pink and I see her visibly gulp. "Thank you," she whispers.

"C'mon. Let's get lunch."

CHAPTER 29

WHEN WE FINISH lunch, we decide to get some frozen yogurt. It's something Sam and I love, and we introduce Sophie to all our favorite flavors.

"I like this flavor," Sophie says as she samples the salted caramel. "It's really good."

"I want to buy a bath bomb for Mom," I say as I eat my vanilla yogurt.

"That's sweet. I should get something for my mom too, she works so hard."

"There's a Lush store downstairs, it sells all kinds of natural bath products. We'll go after we've finished," Sam says to Sophie. "I think Mom would like a bath bomb."

"We don't have a bath, only a shower. Maybe I can find a nice body wash for Mom."

As we walk down stairs heading toward Lush, Sam gets a text a message. "Mom's messaging." She stops to see what Mom wants. I keep walking but I've got my head turned as I watch Sam and I walk straight into someone else.

"Sorry," I mumble as I fall over the person I walked into. A masculine hand shoots out to help me up and I grab on to it. Slowly my gaze draws up jean clad legs and I meet the eyes of my math teacher, Mr. C. "Oh, Mr. Collins, I'm sorry."

He hoists me up, and immediately I take a step back while dusting off my butt. "It's okay, Dakota. Are you hurt?"

He steps closer to assess me, and I step back again. "I'm fine."

Mr. C smiles at me and continues to look me over. "How's your vacation?" he asks. Sophie and Sam step up beside me. I turn to look at them and they both edge closer to me. "Hello, girls. I was just asking

Dakota how her vacation has been. How have you all been?" he asks my sister and Sophie.

"Good, thank you," Sam replies in a cold tone. "We have to go. Mom will be meeting us soon."

"Take care, girls," he says as we go to step away.

"Bye," I reply in a strained voice. When we're a safe distance away from Mr. C, I discretely look over my shoulder, to see he's actually following behind us. "What?" I whisper. "Don't turn around, but Mr. C is following us."

"Huh?" Sophie huffs in annoyance and turns to look. "No he's not." She stops and turns around.

Both Sam and I stop too, and when I turn, he's disappeared. "I swear he was right behind us."

"Maybe he was heading into a store around here," Sophie tries to justify what I saw.

Unease flutters in my stomach and my pulse doubles as a dreadful niggling sensation settles within. "Something's off with him," I say, fear overtaking me.

"What's wrong?" Sam asks.

My hands ball into fists and my jaw tightens in anticipation that something horrible is lurking nearby. "Let's go." The three of us quickly walk to the other end of the mall, and stop only when Sam sees a t-shirt she likes at Charlotte Russe. "What are you doing?"

"What? He's not here. And I like this, what do you think?" She holds the t-shirt up against her and though I'm extremely cautious of my surroundings, I still take a second to admire it.

"It looks good," I answer. "I like it."

Our attention is quickly drawn to the store next to where we've stopped when we hear a deep, burly voice say, "Girls, store security. Show me your bags."

We all look to our left, and see Lindsey and her stuck-up posse leaving the store, while an older guy in a security uniform quickly approaches Lindsey.

"Now this is interesting. Hang on a second." Sam grabs her phone, and starts recording what's happening.

When Lindsey sees us, her face turns tomato red and she turns her back to us. "What?" she half yells at the security guy. He may be older, but he looks like he's been doing this for a long time and can take anyone down who'd attempt to cross him.

"This is so amusing. Can't wait to upload it to social media," Sam says loudly so Lindsey can hear it. "I wonder how many shares I can get on this considering Lindsey's been stopped for shoplifting." Sam chuckles as she now moves to sit at a bench close by while she continues to record.

"We believe you've got some items you haven't paid for and I'll need to see inside your bag," the security guard says, loudly.

Ding, ding, ding. Sam's right. Lindsey's been stopped for shoplifting.

"I can afford anything I want in here, why would I shoplift?" Lindsey defensively scoffs at the guard, who's now crossed his arms and looks unimpressed. He's probably heard every excuse under the sun.

Lindsey looks back at us and snarls, while Jordan and Mariah slide as far away from her as possible. "Look, we've got you on surveillance. I was watching you and your two little friends who refused to put anything in their bags when you asked them to."

Sophie, Sam and I look over to Mariah and Jordan, and their faces turn the same shade of tomato red as Lindsey's. We turn back to watch Lindsey. She sneaks a look over her shoulder and uncomfortably shifts. The guard's eyes travel the length of her body and he catches how she tightens the grip on the bags she's holding. He straightens his body and shakes his head. "I wouldn't run if I were you," he warns her.

Lindsey looks like she's a wounded animal backed into a corner. Her eyes are wild as her shoulders shake uncontrollably from the adrenaline and fear pumping through her body. "She's going to run," Sophie whispers.

"Not in those shoes," Sam says loudly.

And she takes off. She turns and runs toward the exit. But the security guard, although old, is agile and fit and he catches her before she's made it three stores away. He grabs her arm and escorts her back.

"Why did you run? I told you not to," he says while marching her back to the store. "Now I gotta call the police, and I didn't want to do that. I was going to give you a warning."

Lindsey's face is covered in tears. Her bottom lip is quivering as she's pleading with the guard to let her go. "I'm so sorry, I promise I won't do it again," she says between sobs.

"It's too late for that now, girl. Should've thought about it before you decided to run."

Jordan and Mariah leave her and start walking away. "Oh my God," Sophie bursts as she springs to her feet. Both Jordan and Mariah turn to look back at Sophie. "You two are going to leave her to deal with this on her own?"

"We didn't steal anything," Jordan bitchily replies.

"But she's your best friend. You both stood there and backed her up when she pushed me to the ground and tried humiliating me, but you're walking away when she gets caught for shoplifting? Great friends you are."

"We didn't shoplift," Mariah finally speaks. "And we told her not to."

"Thank God you're not my friends. You don't know what he's going to say or do to her in there and you're walking away. Wow, great friends." Sophie shakes her head and huffs in disgust at them both.

"Whatever, slut girl," Jordan spits toward Sophie.

"You did not." Sophie runs for her, and Jordan lets out a high-pitched squeal as she tries to run from Sophie. Sophie grabs her by the ponytail, yanking her head back before turning her around and backing her up against the nearest wall. Jordan squints and cowers from Sophie.

"Sophie, she ain't worth the hassle," I call, trying to calm her.

"I'm so sorry," Jordan profusely snivels. "I'm sorry, I promise I won't do it again. Please, Sophie, please! Let me go!"

"There's only so much bullying a person can take before they snap and teach the bully a lesson," Sophie spits in Jordan's face while heaving her from the scruff of her incredibly teeny tiny shirt. "You're a damn coward. Look at you." Sophie lets her go and steps back from her. "You think you have power in numbers yet all you are is a worthless bully. Karma will kick your ass, exactly like Lindsey got hers." She points to Sam who's still recording. "I just hope I'm around to see you get yours, bitch."

Sophie turns her back, and walks away. Jordan, the quivering bully she is, runs away shouting over her shoulder, "You're all nothing. Losers!"

Sophie takes a few steps toward Jordan who squeals in a high-pitched voice, and picks up speed to run away.

When it all settles, the nervous energy makes me laugh. "Wow," I say. "That was interesting. Lindsey got caught shoplifting and Jordan almost peed herself with fright when Sophie cornered her."

"Typical bullies. The moment they're confronted they buckle. Anyway, if they want to cause us any problems, I've got a nice little film I can post to social media. I'll even tag them —and everyone we know— to give them maximum exposure," Sam says happy with herself to have captured it all.

We sit on the bench together and let our hearts calm down from those intense few moments. "Um." A pair of pretty shoes stop in front of me. I look up to see Mariah.

"Mariah," I say through my clenched jaw.

"I'm sorry for everything." She looks down timidly and slouches her shoulders.

"You're just as bad as those two," Sophie says. "Because even though you've never said anything to us, you continue to hang out with them and back them up when they do and say horrible things."

"I know." She blinks repeatedly and her mouth turns down in a frown. "I just want to say I'm sorry." She slowly turns and starts to walk away. "You're right, We don't know what's happening to Lindsey in there, so I'm going to go wait."

"What about Jordan?" Sam calls after her.

"She's probably already found Aaron. They came together but Aaron and Levi went in one direction and we went in the other."

Suddenly my heart rate spikes and I shiver while I suspiciously look around me, it feels like watchful eyes are burning into me.

"Don't be like them, Mariah," Sophie says.

Mariah puts her head down and walks into the store while the three of us gather together and decide what we're going to do.

"Truthfully, I've had enough excitement to last me a lifetime," Sophie says. "I think I'm going to call my Mom to come pick me up."

Sam looks at me and nods her head. "Yeah, me too. Anyway, I miss Taylor and want to call him when we get home."

Sophie calls her mom, and Sam calls ours. We decide to meet our moms at the same place so we don't have to split up. Knowing Jordan is here with Aaron and Levi means they may try to harrass us if we're on our own. And this scares the shit out of me. We all head into Lush, selecting a few things before we need to meet our moms out near the frozen yogurt store.

"Mom's going to love this moisturizer I got her," Sophie says. "It's mango and vanilla, it smells good enough to eat."

"I got Mom a bath bomb, strawberry and chia seed," I say.

"Chia seed?" Sam screws her nose up. "Was that the pink colored one at the front of the store?" I nod my head. "I didn't like that one."

"Lucky it's not for you then; it's for Mom."

"Whatever." She rolls her eyes and grabs her phone out of her pocket. "I'm seeing if Taylor's home or at work." She turns her back and walks a few steps away.

"Do you think anything will be said about today?" I shrug my shoulders. "I'd be so humiliated if that confrontation was caught on anyone's phone and uploaded."

I squint at her and shake my head. "Why? You told her off."

"Not that one. The one where Lindsey pushed me."

"If anything is said, it just shows what a bitch she is for doing that to you. We were walking away from her, we didn't even know she was there, so it'll make *her* look like a bully."

"She said some horrible stuff."

"Which isn't true."

"She's popular, Dakota, I'm not. Everyone will believe her, not me."

"I wouldn't worry about it. Besides, it's still summer vacation. By the time we're back at school, everyone will be talking about something else. And we have something she doesn't want anyone to see."

Sophie's face breaks out into a huge smile. "I'm positive she wouldn't want anyone seeing that." She bumps into my shoulder, still smiling.

She leans against the railing outside of the mall, near where the cab stand is. "You know, you're pretty cool, Dakota."

"You're only figuring that out now?" I say sarcastically.

She shrugs a shoulder, her long blonde hair slightly swaying as a small gust of wind picks it up. "Yeah, you'll do."

Both her mom and our Mom pull up behind each other. "Thanks for today. I had a lot of fun." She walks backward to her car.

I wave to her mom then go and tap on Sam's back to tell her Mom's here. She's still got her phone to ear and quietly says goodbye to Taylor telling him she'll call him later on.

Sophie's mom beeps her horn as she leaves, and we jump in our car. "How was the mall?"

"Good fun," Sam replies before I get a chance to say anything. "Lindsey got caught shoplifting."

"What!" Mom shouts slamming the brakes on. Luckily, both Sam and I have our seatbelts on because the abrupt way Mom stops makes us both lurch forward. "What were you doing hanging out with her? And what do you mean 'shoplifting'?"

"We weren't hanging out with her. Actually we had no idea she was going to be there. But, I saw a cute top in Charlotte Russe, and while we were there Lindsey, Mariah, and Jordan came out of the store next to us. The security guard followed them out and stopped Lindsey from leaving. Anyway, Mom, she tried to run and he grabbed her and dragged her back to the store. And guess what else? Jordan left her there. She left her there! Can you believe it? She walked away. What type of friend would do that? But anyway, she got dragged back into the store. The guy said he was going to let her off with a warning but because she ran he had to to call the cops." Sam's only taken one breath the entire time, telling the story in an animated way.

Mom's listening intently, and when Sam finishes talking she quickly glances over at me. "Is she serious?"

"I even got it on my phone. Do you want to watch it when we get home?"

"You recorded it?" Mom sounds cross, and frankly disappointed.

"I did," Sam happily responds. "She's been really horrible to Sophie and when this happened, I thought it was a good opportunity to record it. If she wants to be a bitch, I can always threaten her with it."

Mom's mouth gapes open as she looks at Sam in the rear-view mirror. "You can't be serious?"

"I am."

"Sam, that's not right. You're going to delete it off your phone."

"No, I'm not."

Mom's hands tighten around the steering wheel, her knuckles turning white. Taking in her appearance, she looks so mad. "You *will* be deleting it from your phone, young lady," she almost growls at Sam. Her jaw is tight, and her shoulders are high.

"No, I'm not," Sam stubbornly replies. "You don't get what a nasty piece of work she is, Mom. I'm keeping this as backup, you can even call it insurance. But I'm not deleting it."

"This isn't open for negotiations Samantha Kristen Bennett. You *will* delete it."

Oh shit, Mom is using Sam's full name. This isn't a good sign. "No, Mom, I won't. She's horrible and if this is the only way I can assure she stops being a bitch to everyone, then so be it. It's called karma with a capital K. I promise you though, I won't post it and if I think about posting it, I'll talk to you first."

There's silence in the car for a few moments while Mom calms down from her anger. "If you post it, then you're no better than her."

"I told you, I won't post it."

"You can ruin her life if you post it for no other reason than simply posting it." I smirk and chuckle to myself. "What?" Mom asks while she pulls into our driveway.

We get out of the car and start walking up to the house. "I'll be surprised if she hasn't already ruined it for herself. The things I'm finding out." I shake my head while we head into the kitchen. I grab three water bottles, handing one each to Sam and Mom.

"Don't go looking for trouble, Dakota. Your friendship is over, respect it and leave it at that."

"Hey." I hold my hands up in resignation. "Believe me, I'm not looking for anything to do with her, Jordan, Mariah, Levi . . . any of them. They aren't who I thought they were." With my water bottle in my hands, I freeze in midair. No, they're not nice at all and what's even worse, I used to be one of them.

Filled with shame, I tilt my head down and look at my shoes. I was horrible.

CHAPTER 30

J UST OVER TWO weeks have gone by since the whole 'Lindsey is a felon,' incident. Sam and Sophie have been keeping an eye on social media in case any footage is posted.

Funnily enough, Lindsey and Jordan have remained really quiet on social media. Nothing has been posted, which is incredible considering there were quite a few people milling around when Lindsey pushed Sophie.

It's probably only a matter of time.

I'm in my room, listening to the radio when I hear a knock at my door. "Come in."

Sam opens the door and slides in before closing the door behind her. "Thought you might want your phone back," she says with a smile.

Sitting up in bed, I cross my legs and take my phone when she holds it out. "Why?" I ask suspiciously. "Has something happened?"

"No." She happily jumps on my bed. She's got a huge smile spreading across her face, her eyes following me as I slide to unlock the screen.

The first thing I see is a text message. The name at the top of the box tells me it's from Reece. It reads:

> Hoping we can get together and watch a movie soon. What do
> you think? Double date? ☺.

The time stamp is a few minutes ago. "Huh," I blow out a breath while re-reading the message.

"So?" Sam asks while leaning into me. "Can we go?" I'd told her all about the conversation Reece and I had by the pool the night of the cook-out. "Can we?" She bounces on the bed enthusiastically.

The thought of going on a date with Reece scares me to death. "I don't know," I whisper while looking down at my phone. My hands begin to shake while my pulse frantically races through my veins. "Um."

"What's wrong, Dakota?" Sam moves closer to me, gently laying her hand on my thigh.

Tears sting my eyes as every harbored feeling pushes to the surface. "I'm so scared," I manage to whisper through a strangled breath.

"Hey." She wraps her arms around me. "Why are you so worried?"

Trying to contain myself, I manage to curb the tears and look into Sam's concerned eyes. "What if he tries to . . . do something with me?"

"You don't have to do anything you don't want. And besides, he doesn't come across like the type of guy who would force you."

I nod my head, because logically I think I know that of Reece, but then my mind goes back to prom. Waking up out in the field with my dress hitched with no memory of anything occurring. Shuddering with just the memory, I nod my head again. "I won't be able to survive if *that* happens again."

"You can't live your life frightened of what *might* happen."

"I know." Sam sighs a long breath as she lets me go and sits back on my bed. "I'm getting better, really I am. I'm not as terrified as I was and I know I'm smiling more."

"I think it's time to tell Mom and Dad."

"No!" I shout, almost lunging at her. "We can't say a word. It's been way too long, and besides." I shrug as I tilt my head and focus on my phone. "I have no proof. I don't want them to know."

"I promised you I wouldn't say anything, and I won't. But maybe you need help to figure out how to deal with these emotions you're having."

Looking at Sam, her face is encouraging and loving. However the depths of her eyes show pity and sorrow. "We all have a war to fight and conquer. This is mine."

"But you don't need to fight it alone."

"I'm not fighting it alone. I have you."

Sam's shoulders slump, and her face falls. "You'll always have me, no matter what."

The air in the room thickens as I kick myself for bringing Sam down from her high. "Hey, let's go on that double date," I say attempting to lift the mood again. Sam smiles at me, but the happiness is a façade only. She's still concerned for me.

"Yeah?" she asks.

"Yeah. Do you want to call Taylor, see when he's free?"

"I'm all over it." She jumps off my bed and runs out of my room. Within seconds she's back with her phone.

I send Reece a message saying:

Hey. Movies sound G8. When?

Immediately I get a text back:

WUD 2NITE?

"He says he can come any night this week, but not during the days," Sam says while her head is down, still texting Taylor.

"Reece asked what I'm doing tonight."

Sam looks up at me with a smile. The glimmer in her eyes makes me happy, I like seeing her excited to hang out with me. "Mom," she calls and runs out of my room. She's gone to ask Mom, so I send a text back to Reece:

NM, Sam asking mom abt movies.

Sam returns with an even bigger smile. "Mom will drop us off and pick us up. I'll just call Taylor." She hurries out of my room and I hear her talking in a hushed voice to Taylor.

I send a text to Reece:

Mom dropping us off. What time?

There's no reply from Reece and I frown while looking at my phone. Sam comes back into my room, and sits on my bed. "We'll just meet there and see what's playing. You okay with that?" I nod my head. "And then maybe we can go get pizza?" she asks hopeful I'll say yes. I nod again. "And then maybe Taylor can come over."

"Did you ask Mom?"

She scrunches her mouth and shakes her head. "Not yet. See, if Reece comes over too, then it won't be so bad for me to ask if Taylor can come."

Sneaky. "I'll ask Mom and Reece."

"Yay!"

My phone rings in my hand and I look down to see Reece's name flashing on the screen. "Hello?" I answer perplexed as to why he's not texting me.

"So much easier for me to call rather than text."

"Oh, okay."

Sam enthusiastically grabs onto my thigh and squeezes while watching me talking with Reece. 'Come on' she mouths to me.

"We're good for tonight. Sam's already checked with Taylor and he's okay with it. Mom said she can drop us off and pick us up, but Sam asked if you'd be into grabbing a pizza or something after the movie for dinner. And if you want to hang out here afterwards?"

"Grab a pizza and take it back to your place?"

"Well, I suppose we can do that."

"Do what?" Sam whispers. I flick her with my hand to be quiet so I can hear what Reece is saying.

"I got my license last week, I can bring us all back to your place."

"Um," I stumble. "I gotta check with Mom, but it should be okay."

"What time do you want to meet? And what movie are we watching?"

"I'm not sure about the movie. I don't even know what's out. How 'bout we meet there at around six, and we can decide when we all get there?"

I look to Sam who's already texting Taylor the time to meet us there. She looks up and gives me a thumbs-up.

"Yeah, six works for me. See you then."

We hang up and I look to Sam who's got a goofy grin stretching across her beautiful face. "What? You look worried."

"Reece got his license last week, and offered to bring us back home. He suggested grabbing a pizza and come back here."

"Hell, yeah. But you better ask Mom if it's okay for him to drive us."

I tee it up with Mom, and she says if we text her when we get the pizza and come straight home, then she's okay with Reece driving us and for Taylor and Reece to hang with us for a few hours.

Sam flutters around the house in an excited and happy state all day. By five o'clock she's ready to go and trying to get me to hurry up. Rolling my eyes at her enthusiasm, I get ready too.

CHAPTER 31

M OM DROPS US off at the movies with about ten minutes to spare, but Taylor's already there, pacing outside while he waits for Sam.

The minute he sees our car, his face lights up and he comes over to open Sam's door. "Hi!" she squeals and throws herself into his arms for a hug.

"Hi, Mrs. B," Taylor says once Sam's untangles herself from him.

"Hello, Taylor. I'll see you back home soon."

Taylor waves, Mom beeps and leaves. Reece isn't here yet, so we wait until we see Reece's brother's car pull into a spot.

Reece gets out, locks the car and starts walking toward us. Dressed in an AC/DC t-shirt and jeans, I can't help but look at the way the jeans hug his body. My cheeks flush as I continue staring at him walking toward us. I shouldn't be looking at him, and I definitely shouldn't be feeling anything at all toward him, but I can't help the way my body is reacting to him.

The small flutter in my stomach gets a little wilder when he spots me and smiles hugely. He runs his hand through his hair and when he makes his way over to us, he leans down, gives me a sweet kiss on the cheek. He holds his hand out for Taylor to shake, and leans in to give Sam a kiss on the cheek.

"Only old people shake hands," Taylor teases Reece.

Reece throws his head back and laughs in a carefree way. "Well I'm not going to give you a kiss. Besides we're gentlemen, Taylor. Don't you forget it." He looks at me and winks.

Crap, more fluttering.

"Touché," Taylor responds. "Alright, let's see what movie is playing." Taylor slings his arm around Sam's shoulders and brings her in close to him. They go ahead of us, up the stairs and into the cinema.

Reece hangs back, and waits for me to go first. "You look very pretty, Dakota."

I look down to what I'm wearing, and try to hold in my smile. "Thank you." Reece sticks his hands in his pockets once we're in the lobby and takes a step away from me. Suddenly I feel self-conscious and discreetly sniff the space around me to make sure I haven't forgotten to use deodorant.

Taylor and Reece want to see the new horror movie, Sam wants to see the new Disney movie, and I want to watch a new comedy.

"Majority rules," Taylor proudly announces.

"I hate horror. I'll end up watching the movie from behind my hand, which means I won't watch the movie," I plead my case.

"I hate horror too. I won't watch a horror movie. You two can go sit in there together and watch it, and Dakota and I will go watch something else."

Taylor's nose wrinkles, and Reece takes a big step away from Taylor. "Sorry, dude. I'm not homophobic or anything, but no way do I want to watch a movie with you. You're not the reason I'm here," Reece tells Taylor, but not before turning and winking at me.

Double crap, another flutter.

"Right, so no horror." Taylor lets out a frustrated breath. "That leaves either Sam's Disney movie, or Dakota's comedy."

"Comedy," Reece immediately replies.

"Yeah, sorry, Sam, but I'd rather see a comedy than a Disney flick." Taylor shudders and shakes his head.

"Fine." Sam pretends to be peeved, although the smile breaking out on her face belies her words.

We stand in line to get our tickets, and true to his claim of being a gentleman, the moment it was our turn to buy the tickets, Reece pays for both mine and his.

"Here you go." I pull some money out of my pocket and hand it to Reece. Looking down, he smiles and shakes his head. "Reece, you didn't have to pay for my ticket." I try to shove the money at him, but he steps back.

"I didn't ask you out so you could pay for yourself. Do you want popcorn or a drink?" He turns and heads to the candy bar, lining up behind Taylor and Sam.

"Let me buy the popcorn."

"Do you want popcorn?"

"Well, yeah. It's sacrilege to come to the movies and not get popcorn."

"And a soda?"

"A bottle of water for me."

We get to the front of the line, and once Reece gives our order, I take my money out of my pocket and try to pay. Reece gently smacks my hand away and hands his own money to the the guy serving us. "You can't keep doing that," I say, frustrated with him.

"Yeah I can." He chuckles. Handing me my water, he carries the jumbo popcorn and his soda and leads the way into the movie.

"Where are you guys sitting?" I ask Sam and Taylor who've been waiting for us at the candy bar.

"In front of you guys."

"Let's go in, it's about to start," Taylor says.

Reece and I go in and find our seats. The lights are still on and people are shuffling in, finding their allocated seats. We sit in the second to last row, with Sam and Taylor directly in front of us.

"I hear this movie is really good," Reece says while he sits and places his soda in the cup holder next to him.

"Yeah, me too. I'm looking forward to it."

"Look," he whispers as he leans over to me, jutting his chin toward Sam and Taylor.

They're both sitting low in their seats and Taylor has his arm around Sam. Both their heads are together, and they're giggling and whispering to each other.

"Aw." It makes my heart swell, seeing them like this. They're so cute together.

The lights dim and darkness engulfs us before the huge screen comes to life. The movie starts, and I sit back in my seat, relaxed and completely oblivious to everything around me.

I'm getting lost in the movie, laughing at all the funny lines and the over the top, ridiculously hilarious storyline.

I reach into the popcorn and vow to myself to not have anymore, because I've been eating so much of it. Dusting the copious salt from my hands, I rest them on my thighs and keep watching the movie.

Reece takes his phone out of his pocket and hides the screen as he reads what I assume is a text message. Frowning, he looks over his shoulder to our right, then puts the phone away. Shifting in the seat beside me he finds a comfortable spot and just as he settles, he shifts again. For the next few minutes I'm distracted by Reece and his restlessness. He mumbles something to himself, and I turn to look at him. "Are you okay?" I whisper.

He nods at me and crosses his arms in front of his chest. Minutes later he huffs and moves again. His edginess keeps me from paying full attention to the movie. I keep an eye on Reece. Maybe he's getting sick, or something could be wrong.

Abruptly, he stands and leaves the cinema without saying a word. Sam turns around just in time to see Reece leaving. She looks at me and her shoulders come up in question. 'I don't know,' I mouth while my hands rise, palm side up to match my whispered words.

I begin to worry something has happened to Reece. Maybe the text message he received is bothering him and he has to reply to it. Maybe, it's got something to do with his brother Miles and enlisting. Or maybe, something's wrong at his house with his little brother. Panic swiftly rises as I keep looking over my shoulder toward the door, just waiting for him to return.

Tapping Sam on the shoulder, I lean in and whisper, "I'm going to go find Reece."

"Do you want me to come with you?"

"Nah, it's okay. I need to go to the bathroom anyway. Just watch our stuff and here, hold my water."

"Okay." Sam turns forward again, and tells Taylor what's going on.

Quietly, I get up and head outside to find Reece.

He's over in the furthest corner, his head is down and he's on his phone. I walk over to him and he doesn't realize I'm out here until I stand right in front of him. "Hey, is everything okay?"

Reece startles when he hears me. "Yeah, everything's okay, let's go back inside." His face is red and his body is vibrating. Reece's shoulders are pulled back tight but his eyes are everywhere, looking around us but avoiding me.

"Reece, what's going on? Do you need to go home?" I'm beyond worried now, I know something's going on, but he's not telling me.

"No!" he says way too loud. "Nothing's wrong, let's go back in." He sticks his phone and hands in his pockets and waits for me to go first. *I wonder what has him so agitated?*

"I need to go to the bathroom, I'll meet you in there."

"So do I," he responds way too quickly. His eyes keep darting back to the door of the cinema we came out of, and he looks distracted and worried.

Unsure of what the hell is going on, I go to the bathroom. When I come out, Reece is leaning up against the wall opposite the bathroom where he has the best view of people coming and going. He's still looking stressed though and something's not adding up. "Have you been waiting for me the entire time?"

Reece looks down the corridor, as if he's on guard detail. "No."

I stand in front of him and put my hands on my hips, tilting my head to the side in question. "Really?"

He huffs a breath, but not before looking down the hallway again. "Okay, yes. Can we go back into the movie, please?"

"What's going on? Something's wrong and you're not telling me."

"I promise, it's nothing." Nothing my ass. He wouldn't be so protective if it was 'nothing.'

"Fine," I respond sharply and start walking back into the cinema. "If you say so."

"Thank you."

We open the door to the dark cinema, and Reece leads me back to our seats. The moment I'm comfortable, Sam turns and looks at me. Her eyebrows are drawn together and she quickly lifts her shoulders. I lean down to her and whisper, "I'll tell you later." Though really, I have nothing to tell her, because Reece won't tell me shit.

By now Reece and I have missed a chunk of the movie, but luckily it's an easy film to catch up on. As I'm watching the movie, I feel a foreign warmth on my hand. Instantly I pull away tucking my hands under my opposite arms, while panic begins to consume me. My breathing increases as I tense and tremble.

Looking to Reece, he quickly steals the offending object back, and I notice he tried holding my hand. "I'm sorry," he whispers.

"It's okay." A rock sits in the pit of my stomach, and I feel terrible for reacting so badly toward him.

With the film now forgotten, I keep a watchful eye on Reece and notice how he's shifted as far away from me as possible.

I can't lead him on; it's not fair to him. But at the same time, he does something to me. He makes my heart spike with happiness when I see him, my pulse races and those butterflies flutter like crazy. But it's not fair to him, to give him false hope that he can have a relationship with me. It's obvious that's what he wants, or what he wants to try for. If he wanted just sex, he wouldn't be going to all the effort he is. He wouldn't want my sister and her boyfriend around, and he wouldn't be happy to simply spend time with me.

Am I being selfish? I really enjoy hanging out with him, but I can't give him what he wants. He's a guy, and I'm sure if he wants a relationship from me, then there's no way I can offer him sex. I just can't. I'm not ready for that step, and I'm not sure if I'll ever be ready for it.

The damn emotional part of my brain is screaming how worthless I am to him. How I have nothing to offer him because I'm damaged goods. Damn it! Stop thinking about it. He wouldn't want a relationship with me. He just wants sex.

"Are you okay?" It's now my turn to be restless and shift in my seat.

"I'm fine," I snap at Reece. Closing my eyes I tilt my head so he can't see me and take a few deep breaths to get back in control of my stupid emotions. Once I've managed to calm myself down, I lean toward Reece and whisper, "I'm sorry."

If Reece wanted nothing more than sex, he would've hit on me ages ago. He wouldn't have gone to all this effort. He would've tried the night he beat Levi at the charity basketball game. He wouldn't have waited.

And I *do* like him. He's shown himself to be caring and sweet. He's kept his hands to himself and not tried to force anything on me. I'm so torn. I like him, I do, but I don't think I could ever be enough for him. If we do take a step toward a relationship, how long will he be willing to wait for it to become physical?

Levi made it perfectly clear to me, he didn't have the patience to wait. And I really have to be fair to Reece.

Reece smiles at me then shifts again in his seat, sitting squarely instead of moving as far away from me as he can. He turns his head to watch the big screen, and puts his hand on the arm rest between us. He looks uncomfortable like this, but at the same time I know what he's doing.

He's giving me the option to hold his hand if I want to. Reece is leaving it to me to decide, without putting any pressure on me. His big hand is on the arm rest, between us; he's making no more effort to touch me, probably because of my initial bad reaction.

Moving my hands, I place them back on my lap. My head is turned forward, pretending to watch the movie, while I try to sneakily look at Reece's reaction. I inch my hand over, only enough for it to be resting on my outer thigh.

I can't do it. I can't bring myself to touch him and to give him false hope. Pulling my hand back, I knit them both together in my lap and hold them there. Reece's hand doesn't falter, he doesn't move away.

Damn it, why does he have to be so understanding?

Slowly I unravel my hands, and shaking, I begin to move one toward his. My throat becomes dry as I nervously draw closer to his. I can feel he's looking at me, and watching for me to take his hand.

Swallowing down the dryness in my mouth, I inch my hand closer to his. Gradually I extend my shaky pinky, only just reaching his. He too stretches his pinky out. Deliberately slow, our pinkies meet, barely touching.

My body reacts by shivering and cold goosebumps pebble my skin while I try to breathe normally through this monumental obstacle I've overcome. Relaxing into his touch I move my hand closer to his, the length of our pinkies touching together.

Reece moves his finger on top of mine, hooking them together.

Watching the screen, I breathe through the intense anguish bubbling away beneath my pebbled skin. I don't want to pull away; I like the warmth of his touch. I even like how he's curved his little finger over mine.

It feels comfortable, it feels *right*.

There's not much left of the movie, but suddenly I find myself paying attention to it. Reece's finger entwined with mine isn't stressing me out as much as I had built up in my mind. I had stressed myself out, completely making a huge deal out of something which has turned out to be nice.

When the lights in the cinema turn on, Reece's body becomes rigid as he looks around the huge room. There's a steady line of people already shuffling out. Sam stands and turns around, her eyes going straight to where Reece and I are holding hands, or I should say, holding pinkies. Her face brightens with a giant smile when her eyes lock on our hands.

"Huh, look what we have here, my former best friend, and the slut I was dating. Two love birds by the looks of things." The voice pierces me and makes me cringe. *And to think, I thought I was in love with him.*

"Levi," Reece declares as he stands and steps in front of me.

Trying to look out from behind Reece, I catch a glimpse of Levi peering at me, his eyes narrow and his mouth is pressed into a thin line. I stand and move so I'm beside Reece, however he angles his body so he's still shielding me.

"What do you want?" Reece asks.

"That slut isn't worth our time," Lindsey calls out from beside Levi. I hadn't noticed her until she spoke. She has a hand on her jutted hip, with an eyebrow cocked high.

"How are you Lindsey?" Sam asks while waving her phone in her hand.

Lindsey's face flushes a flaming shade of red, and Sam cheekily smiles at her. Lindsey steps back behind Levi, trying to disappear behind him.

Levi's face morphs into a snarl while his beady eyes roam my body. "Fucked her yet?" he spits toward Reece.

A low hiss rumbles through Reece and he grabs my hand and holds it tight. "Do *not* speak about her like that," Reece warns in a dangerously low voice.

Levi's jaw tenses as he stands to his full height. "What happened to you, man? You used to be cool, now you're chasing after damaged goods." His eyes stay focused on me, his entire demeanor trying to intimidate me.

"You happened. You became a dick who thinks it's okay to treat girls like shit."

The side of Levi's mouth tugs up in a condescending smile. "Not all girls." He leans out and swings his arm over Lindsey. "Just her." He pointedly looks at me.

Reece's hand softens as he lets mine go. He steps forward about to do or say something he may end up regretting. I maneuver my body in front of Reece's and say to Levi, "I know you're hurt because I wouldn't have sex with you. But I promise you, Levi, I never betrayed you."

Levi snarls at me, turns and leaves with no further words. This leaves me even more convinced he's hurting because of what he's seen in *those* photos.

"You okay?" Reece asks.

"I'm fine. Sorry you had to be part of it, and I'm even sorrier you and Levi aren't friends anymore. I know it's because of me."

He reaches for my hand to hold, and while it's different, it's also okay. "You're not the reason we're not friends. *He's* the reason." He tightens his fingers around mine while he leads me out of the cinema.

"That was intense." Sam chuckles from behind me.

"Did you see the look on Lindsey's face when you held up the phone?" Taylor says with a laugh.

"What have you got on her?" Reece asks.

"Oh yeah, you don't know. We were at the mall, and she was caught shoplifting," I answer his question.

"When we get home, I'll show you what I recorded," Sam proudly announces.

"I'm intrigued. Let's go get pizza and get back to your place where you can show me the video you took."

CHAPTER 32

W HEN WE GET home, Mom and Dad are in the family room watching
TV. Mom's feet are up on Dad's lap and he's massaging them. Mom
says we can have our dinner out back near the pool and offers to get
us plates and sodas. Sam beats me to it, and tells Mom to stay where she
is, we can look after ourselves.

"Your parents are pretty cool," Reece says once we've settled out
back.

"Yeah, I got to agree. They are." I grab a slice of pizza.

"Show me this video you have." Reece holds his hand out for Sam's
phone.

"It's so funny. She kind of gets tackled by the security guard, look."
She brings it up on her phone, and although I can't see it because Reece
is watching it, I can hear everything going on.

From Lindsey shrieking like a banshee to the clicking sound of her
heels as tries to get away from the security guard. "Shit." Reece gasps,
then chuckles. When Lindsey gets dragged back into the store, Sam
stops playing the mini movie.

Looking over at Reece, I watch his face as he smiles and shakes his
head. "I stole a little toy car when I was a kid. I asked Mom for it, but
she said no, she couldn't afford it, so I shoved it in my pocket when she
wasn't looking because I really wanted it. When we got to the car, Mom
packed all the groceries away while I sat in my seat and took the car out
of the packaging."

"You did not," I say clasping a hand over my mouth in shock.

"Trust me, I did. Anyway, Mom got in the car, and she looked behind
her to reverse . . . aaaaand she saw the car I was playing with." He looks
bashful as he reminisces.

"Oh no," I mumble. I look to Sam and Taylor and they're both listening intently while devouring their pizza.

"I remember it like it was yesterday. She asked me in this scary, quiet voice, 'Reece, where did that car come from?' I shrugged and said it must've fallen into my pocket. God, the look on her face. She parked the car again, opened the back door, pulled me out and dragged me by my ear straight back into the store."

"By your ear?" I squeak, horrified, yet strangely amused.

"By. My. Ear." Reece shakes his head and rubs his palm over his ear. "Damn well hurt too."

"What happened?" Taylor asks.

"She marched me into the store, made the girl call the manager over the loud speaker, the manager came down and Mom made me tell her what I did. By this stage I was a mess, bawling my eyes out and promising I'll never steal again."

"What did the manager say?" I ask completely intrigued.

"The manager said my apology was enough."

"That's good."

"Yeah, but not good enough for Mom." Reece shudders then swallows hard. I have a feeling, there's a lot more of the story to be told. "Mom decided I hadn't learned my lesson, so she asked the manager if I could use the loud speaker. She made me tell the entire store how old I was, and how I stole a toy car. Then she made me go to every person working on the registers and apologize to them for making their job difficult."

"Oh my God," I whisper, desperately trying to hold in the laughter.

"Far out, man. That's so damn funny," Sam says and laughs.

"Man, your mom is hardcore," Taylor agrees.

"That wasn't the end of it. To humiliate me even further, she asked the manager, if I could pay off the debt by tidying the shelves where the cars were. And then, to top it all off, she bought the car I stole and, made me pick my next favorite which she also bought. Then she had me go hand them in to the local church and tell them the cars were for a little boy who didn't have toys."

"Are you serious?" I ask. Reece's mom sounds like she's incredible.

"But, you know what? I've never stolen a thing again. Miles thought it was hilarious, and didn't let me live it down for a long time. Still every now and then he hassles me about it. So I will say, if Mom was Lindsey's mom, that video would've already been shown to every relative every friend, and shared all over social media too."

"Our Mom would never do that," Sam says looking at me.

"I don't know about that. I think I can take on Reece's mom," Mom says from behind us. We all turn to stare at her, Reece has the most shocked look on his face, with his mouth gaping open and his eyes wide with surprise. "Us moms can get quite creative when we need to teach our kids a valuable lesson."

"I don't doubt it," Sam mumbles under her breath.

"What was that, sweetheart? You want me to start working at the school so I can come sit with you at lunch every day and tell you how much I love you?" Mom envelops Sam in a huge hug, overly emphasizing how she certainly can embarrass us.

"I said, I think you're great." Sam's face is squished against Mom's stomach. Her mouth is distorted while Mom folds her into a bear hug to make a point.

Mom steps back and we can't help but laugh when Sam flexes her jaw. "I came out here to see if you kids need anything."

"You were checking up on us." I call Mom out.

Mom looks at me with a straight face. "There's that too. Let's say a combination of both. Does anyone need anything? A drink? A throw? A toy car?"

That's all it takes for us all to burst into laughter, even Reece. We all tell Mom we're okay. Mom says she's going back in to put on a movie so she can watch it with Dad.

Once we finish eating, Sam and Taylor decide to go in and watch the movie with Mom and Dad too, leaving Reece and myself outside.

We throw away the pizza box and grab a drink before sitting down to look out at the sparkling water of the pool. I settle in my lounge chair, and look up at the small sliver of the moon. "It's a shame the moon isn't bigger."

Reece leans back and looks up, crossing his arms in front of chest while his left foot bounces on the lounger. "Look at the sky. It's weird. Although most of the moon is in hiding, there are still a few stars shining quite brightly."

"It's pretty."

"It is."

Looking down at the drink in my hands, my mind goes to what happened at the movies. "Will you tell me what had you so jumpy at the movies?" I don't dare look at Reece.

"Well, um, it's kind of difficult. But I do have a question for you."

"What is it?"

"I tried to hold your hand, and you freaked out." *Crap.* "Did you freak out because you don't have any feelings for me beyond a friendship?"

Shit. "It's not that."

"Then what is it?"

I keep my eyes firmly focused away from Reece. Now I don't want him to see the secret I'm hiding. I've had it hidden for so long and from virtually everyone, to tell him—or my parents—after all this time, is unfathomable. "I can't really say," I whisper in the smallest of voices.

"You've changed, Dakota."

"No I haven't," I reply forcefully.

"Yes, you have. Something's changed you, and it happened a while back, like around two or three months. I can't quite pinpoint the exact time." I shiver when he announces the time frame, because, *he's right.*

"I'm not different." I look down to my toes, I'd rather focus on them than acknowledge the intense look Reece is giving me.

Reece clears his throat and shifts beside me in his seat. "Remember when they split us at school just before vacation started? They talked to us about all those statistics and stuff." *Oh God, please no.* Pursing my lips together so I don't spill any secrets, I nod my head. "Does your dad touch you, Dakota?"

My eyes fly to him while I violently shake my head. "My God, no way! What the hell, Reece?"

Reece stares at me, squinting his eyes while his mouth keeps opening as if to say something, but he stops before any sound comes out. He closes his eyes and lightly shakes his head before snapping them open to look straight at me. "Then tell me what's happening, Dakota. If it's not your dad, then who has you so scared? Because this shit, the way you react to me, the way you tense whenever you're close to me, even the way you've been talking . . ." He stops speaking to shake his head and pinch the bridge of his nose. "At any time, I'm afraid you're going to curl up in a ball out of fright. What the hell is going on?" He sits up, swinging his legs over the side and leaning his elbows on his knees. He stares at me, intently. Waiting for me to speak.

"Nothing." I look away, not wanting to meet his eyes. But my voice contradicts the façade I'm trying to master around Reece.

"Bullshit!" He stands abruptly, causing me to flinch back. Immediately I regret my sudden movement, although I couldn't control it. He moves away from me, taking a step backward as he holds his hands up in surrender. That simple gesture makes my eyes sting with fat tears. Reece starts to pace back and forth. "You were never like this with Levi.

You'd hold his hand, kiss him, you were never scared of him."

My throat starts to close as my heart pounds rapidly against my chest. "It's different now," I manage to croak in a strangled voice.

Reece stops pacing at the end of the lounger. There's a lot of distance between us, and it's obvious to me he's moved far away so I don't feel threatened by him. "Why is it different? Do I intimidate or scare you?"

"No." I shake my head. "Not at all."

"Have I done something to you to make you think I'll hurt you?" I shake my head and close my eyes. I feel the seat dip beside me, and I know Reece is sitting here, watching me, and waiting to hear why I can barely hold his hand without fighting with my mind. "Tell me, please."

"I can't." Though my eyes are closed, a tear escapes and I tilt my head to the side so I can wipe it before he notices.

"I hate seeing you cry." *Too late.* "And I hate seeing you so . . ." he pauses. "So . . . it's like you're . . ."

Before he has a chance to finish the sentence, I say exactly what he must be thinking. "Broken." Burying my head in my hands I cry. The tears streak through my fingers and run down my hands. It's not only my eyes that's weeping, it's also my soul.

Someone's figured it out, or at least they've noticed the fragile wall I've been hiding behind and now they're making me step out and face them.

"It's okay, I promise you, Dakota, it's okay. You can tell me anything," he whispers. His face is close to me and I can feel the warmth of his breath touch the back of my hand.

"You'll think I'm disgusting."

"No, I won't."

"I'm humiliated, and so ashamed."

I can hear the deep breaths he's taking from beside me, they're hard and intense. Exactly how he is right now. "Please, Dakota, you can trust me." He lays his warm hand on my back. I can feel the hesitation as he slightly lifts it before placing it firmly down. "Is this okay?" It takes me a few seconds, but I eventually nod my head. Trying to soothe me, he begins to move his hand, rubbing my back in gentle circles.

It takes forever for me to stop crying and even longer before I drop my hands from my face. I turn to look at Reece and give him a weak smile. "I have to look like a mess. I bet my eyes are puffy, and my face is red and streaked with tears." I wipe under my eyes.

Reece stands, walks over to the table, picks up a clean napkin and brings it over to me. "I'd go get you a tissue, but for some reason I doubt you'd want your parents seeing you like this. Here you go." He sits beside me again and hands me a napkin.

Taking a moment, I compose myself and wipe my eyes and nose. "Thank you." I smile.

"Hey, there's the Dakota I know." He points to my smile. "That's a real smile, like the one I saw earlier when I was telling you what my Mom did." I smile again and this time a small chuckle follows. Reece lets out a huge breath while still rubbing my back. "Will you please tell me what's going on?"

My body reacts to his words. Small goosebumps cover my exposed skin as the breath hitches in the back of my throat. My hands ball into fists and I shudder. "Can't you understand, it's impossible?" Standing I walk away from Reece and straight toward the pool.

I stop on the edge of the pool, the water below gently moving as it softly hits the sides. Wrapping my arms around my waist, I keep my focus on the soothing water as it moves around the pool.

"Please." Suddenly he's beside me. I didn't hear him moving, I was too entranced by the gentleness of the water.

Pulling my shoulders back, I close my eyes and tighten my arms around my waist. "I was . . ."

Don't do it, Dakota.

Tell him, he'll understand.

"What?"

Don't say anything.

"I was . . ." The word I need to say is stuck. Wedged deep inside my throat. There's no way I can say it and not vomit. I'm shaking, and sweating and this is just at the *thought* of telling him.

"What happened?"

God, no I can't do it.

"I-" *Yes, do it. Take back your strength.*

"Please."

My pulse is racing, my hands are shaking violently as my throat constricts even further. "I was raped."

I don't look at Reece. I can't. His sharp intake of breath tells me everything I need to know. *He's disgusted,* exactly what I thought was going to happen.

"Fuck," he says on the smallest sigh.

Tightening my arms around me, I can't help but let the tears fall freely.

It's not a word I want to ever say again. It's not something I ever want to talk about.

"You can leave now," I whisper through my sobs.

He swings me around by my shoulders and smashes my body to his in the tightest hug I've ever had.

Laying my head on his chest, I let him hold me while I cry into his t-shirt. Grasping the soft fabric of his shirt in my hands and lay my head on his heart. His arms are wrapped around me and he's gently drawing lazy shapes on my back. "I'm not going anywhere," he says.

I cry even more. "I'm sorry."

In no more than a hushed tone he says, "You haven't done anything wrong. I'm so grateful you've opened up to me."

I catch my breath, finally stemming the tears, yet I don't want to leave the comfort and security of his embrace. "You must think I'm . . ."

"You're a victim, Dakota. I don't think anything else other than that. When did it happen?"

"Prom," I answer slowly, still not really wanting to tell him anymore than I already have.

"Who?"

"I don't know," I respond.

He moves his arms so he's gripping the top of mine; it's not hard or uncomfortable or even scary. "What do you mean you don't know?"

"It was a drink I had."

He moves me back to examine my face. "A drink?" I nod my head and look down, still way too scared to meet his eyes. He places his finger under my chin and lightly lifts my head so he can see all of my face. But I shake my head and lower my chin again. "How many drinks did you have?"

"Two. The soda you got me, and then another drink I got for myself from where the sodas were."

Quiet overtakes us, and he moves to hug me again. Breathing deeply I can smell the subtle sweetness of his aftershave. It's a cross between mountains and rain and the smell reminds me of the early mornings on our camping trip.

"I gave you one of the sodas." I nod my head. "I didn't do that, I swear, Dakota."

Deep down, I know he didn't. Although initially I was suspicious, over time I've grown to understand he's not capable of this. No one I know is. "I know it's not you."

"Do you have an idea of who it might be?"

"Yeah, but it's going to seem crazy when I say it."

"Tell me."

I may as well tell him everything now. "I think it may have something to do with Mr. C."

"Mr. Collins? Our math teacher?" I nod against his chest. "Why him?"

I take a few more minutes to get my emotions back under control then I step back and sit down on my lounger. Reece sits opposite me and waits as I take a huge breath and tell him everything.

By the time I finish telling Reece the story, he hasn't moved. Not an inch. He's remained silent the entire time, not asking any questions or making any type of sound. He's motionless, the only thing moving are his shoulders as he breathes and his eye lids as they blink.

For a moment, fear runs through my body. I'm petrified that now he's heard everything, he'll think I *am* disgusting. I'm terrified of the words that must be jumbling around in his mind.

Maybe he doesn't believe me.

Or worse, maybe he thinks I deserve what happened to me.

"Say something," I whisper. I'm on the brink of losing the little control I've regained. He's not speaking and I'm teetering on the edge of reality and a gory, tragic nightmare. "Please, say something."

Reece is sitting quietly, he's not stirring and it's really worrying to me. I hate to think what thoughts are going through his mind. "I . . ." My eyelashes flutter while I hang on every word he has to say. "I don't know what to say."

I let out a breath, and my throat constricts. My hands shake from the sheer nervousness coursing through me. "Oh."

Suddenly something happens within Reece. An obvious change takes over his body. His eyes snap up to mine, his shoulders straighten and his jaw tightens.

I swallow, hard.

"You were raped," he says. It's not a question; it's a statement.

"Yes."

"Someone hurt you." My eyebrows knit together as he makes yet another definitive statement. "Someone put their filthy fucking hands on you." My heart falls into the pit of my stomach. "Someone fucking took you without your consent." My hands shake.

Without saying a word, I nod my head.

"Fuck." I've never heard Reece swear so much in my entire life. "And it happened at *our* prom?" I nod again. "So it's someone we know." His dark brown eyes darken even further. Something snaps inside him. He looks around the backyard, as if he's waiting for a threat to jump out and attack us. "When we go back to school, you stay close to me."

Blinking rapidly, I stare at Reece. "What?"

My eyes go to his hands, now balled into fists. He's angry, and for a split second I can't help but worry his anger is directed at me. I lean back in anticipation of whatever he's about to say or do. I can't help the reaction. It's a natural reaction. "I'm not going to hurt you, Dakota."

"I know," I reply instantly. "I can't help my instincts though."

"I need a drink." Reece makes his way over to the outside fridge and grabs two bottles of water. He brings them over, hands me one and sits down opposite me. Once he's finished half the bottle of water he puts the cap on and places it down beside him on the ground. "I need to ask you a few questions."

I look to the side, close my eyes and nod my head. I don't want to be looking at him when he asks. I hate to see any judgment from him. "Okay. I'll answer what I can."

"First of all, the most important question is; how are you doing?" He reaches his hand out to touch my leg, but stops midway and retracts it.

"I'm doing okay."

"Okay?" he questions and raises his brows at me.

"I mean, at first it was really difficult. And I still can't look at myself in a mirror and like what I see. It's tough, you know?"

"And now?"

"Now, I get through the day. But when things like today happen, it makes me become introverted."

"I didn't notice that today."

"That's because I had Sam, and you around me. Sam always knows how to get me through the difficult stuff."

"So she knows?"

"She found out soon after it happened. Someone sent a disgusting photo to her phone. I had to tell her." I bury my head in my hands again.

"Don't do that, Dakota. Don't hide. You have no reason to be ashamed."

"But I am," I whisper. "I didn't want anyone to know. It's bad enough three people know. Four if you include whoever did this to me. And with all those pictures he's posting, more and more people will know. There's been whispering at school."

"Don't worry about them. Who gives a shit what they think?"

"People know, and what if someone tells my parents?"

"You haven't told them?" I shake my head. "You need to, Dakota. They're the best people to protect you and get you the help you need."

I sit up straight when he says that. "Get me the help I need? What's that supposed to mean? I'm not crazy, Reece!"

"Dakota." He lets out a frustrated breath. "I didn't say you were crazy. But this is huge, you can't keep this a secret; or it'll rip you apart from the inside. You'll never be able to heal." He looks down at his knotted hands, as if he knows exactly what I'm going through.

"How do you know?"

"Everyone has a story to tell." He shrugs one shoulder while keeping his eyes down.

A huge knot forms in the pit of my stomach as an icy cold shiver runs up my spine and lands at the base of my head. I bring my hand up to rub at the pain and wince when my fingers land on the sensitive area. "Have you got a story to tell too?" I ask, feeling sick in my stomach at the mere thought of Reece going through anything similar to what I have.

"Not me, but my aunt."

"Your aunt?"

"My Mom's father was a prick."

"Your grandfather?"

"I've never called him by that name, he doesn't deserve it. Or I should say, he didn't deserve it." Reece's face contorts with fury. I shouldn't ask, but I think he wants to tell me.

"What happened?" I don't really want to know.

"He thought my aunt was pretty. He also thought he should groom her, get her ready for him to sexually assault her."

My stomach churns and my heart breaks. I cringe while I look away. "She was nine when it first started. The only reason he never did that to my Mom was because he said she was too ugly to love." I let out a pained and agonized breath.

"I don't know what to say. I'm thankful it didn't happen to your Mom, but I'm so sorry it happened to your aunt."

"My mom and aunt have never hidden it from us, because they've always said you can't trust anyone. Unfortunately, that's why I asked if your dad's . . . you know."

"There's too much of this crap going on. Why can't people just not do this?" I run my hands over my hair and try to distract myself.

"I'm sorry this happened to you." The edges of my mouth pull up in a small smile, and I try to find solace in his words. "I think it's important for you to tell your parents, they can get you help. And besides all this, you need to tell the police."

"No! I can't. If the police get involved they'll probably interview everyone who was at the prom, which means everyone will know. And it's way too embarrassing for me."

"What if this isn't an isolated incident? What if you weren't his first victim, and he's planning on doing it again, if he hasn't already?"

I grip the sides of my head, covering my ears with my hands to block out what he's saying. However, his words are echoing deep inside me. "I can't."

"You have to, Dakota. You have to be a survivor, not be a victim. And the only way you can survive is by speaking out about it and getting help."

"I'm not crazy," I say again.

"I didn't say you were. But you can't do this on your own."

"I'm not on my own. Sam knows and she's helping me."

"She's how old? Thirteen?"

"Fourteen," I correct him. I know where he's going with it, and I've struggled with it every day.

"Do you think she's properly equipped to help you? And whoever did this to you needs to be caught before he can do it again. Not to mention, what if the next time, the girl doesn't live to tell what happens."

Oh God. Bile is snaking its way up my throat. I feel ill; I'm going to be sick. "Please," I plead with Reece. "Stop." I can't take it anymore. Grabbing the side of my head I knot my fists through my hair.

Reece moves so he can hug me again. His touch isn't unwelcome, and I'm surprised to find I don't freak out. It's warm and comforting and so right. "I'm not saying these things to put pressure on you, Dakota. But I do think you have a social responsibility, and a personal one too."

"Whoever did this to me has a damn responsibility to stop."

"And who's going to make him? How many people has he slipped a drug to so he can take advantage of them? And how many people will report it?"

"Can we please not talk about this anymore tonight? My head's about to explode and I don't think I can deal with it anymore."

Reece steps away from me, his hands rubbing up and down my arms. "You're right, I'm sorry. Tonight's been intense. You really should go to bed."

Suddenly my eyes feel overwhelmingly tired. They're heavy and droopy while my entire body slumps with exhaustion. I honestly didn't realize how tired I was until Reece said it.

"I think I agree with you, but I don't want you to go."

"I don't want to go either, but I have to. How about we do something next week? Mom needs some help around the house and now with Miles gone, I'm helping with my little brother. I'm taking him to the park one day next week, want to come?"

"Oh, um . . ." I'm not sure. I know I can trust Reece, but I'm not entirely ready to go back out in public yet, especially considering the way Levi and Lindsey behaved earlier. If by chance we see them, I don't want Reece to react like he did, in front of his little brother. "You know." I flinch. "After the movies, dealing with Levi and Lindsey . . ." I hope he knows where I'm going with this. But he continues standing in front of me, rubbing his hands up and down my arms. "I don't really want to encounter them again."

His face falls with disappointment. "Sure, I get it." But his tone defies his words.

"Thank you," I answer, though I know he wants me to hang out with him.

"Before I leave, you need to know something about me, Dakota."

Crap. "What?"

"I won't force you to do anything. I won't demand anything from you. If it takes you months, or years to just kiss me, I'll wait for you to be ready."

Suddenly a flash back to prom flicks through my mind. "At the prom, you said the person you like didn't even know you existed. Who were you talking about?"

His cheeks get a slight tinge of color to them as he smiles at me. "It's always been you."

My stomach flips, and warmth takes over my entire body.

"Well, I better go before I say anything else super sappy." He steps back, dropping his warm hands from my heated skin. "I'll call you, okay?" he asks while fishing his keys out of his pocket.

"I'd like that."

He flashes me a sweet smile and heads toward the house so he can leave. I follow him and once he says goodnight to everyone, I head into the bathroom for a shower.

When I'm done, I fall on to my bed in an exhausted heap. Completely drained, my eyes close on their own as my body relaxes in my soft sheets.

"Can you take me home?" Did I speak or am I thinking it?

"Shhh, I'll take care of you. I'll take care of you real good."

"My house is over there." I point behind me.

"We're going to a party, a special party."

"I want to go home. Please just take me home." He places his arm under my arms, and walks me out the backfield. "There's no party here."

"Yeah there is. And you're the main attraction."

Startled I sit up in bed. Sweat's pouring off me while I blink like crazy trying to adjust my eyes to the darkness. I run my hand through my hair, and even my scalp is wet from my sweat. My heart is beating so fast I feel sick and my entire body is violently trembling.

I get up out of bed, and write down what I remember from the flashback.

His face though, it's blurry and I can never see it. But his voice, it's one I'm familiar with. The more I try and focus on the tone, the less I recognize it. The drug he gave me that night makes the details fuzzy and confusing.

Sitting at my desk I try my hardest to remember everything and write it down. I only wish the fuzzy, crackly tone of his voice was clearer, so I could finally know who the hell did this to me. And then, I could set everything in motion to get him taken off the streets.

If only I knew who *he* was.

CHAPTER 33

I'S BEEN A week since Reece came over and I told him what happened. He's been calling every day, checking in to see how I am.

He hasn't brought up what happened to me again. Instead, he asks me how I'm feeling. He hasn't called me today yet, but I think it's only a matter of time.

We're half way through summer vacation, and Sam's been spending as much time with Taylor as she can. Sophie and I have hung out a lot too.

Sam and I are in the pool and the sun is beating down on us. We're right in the middle of a heat wave and the only way we can stay cool is by either being inside with the air conditioning blasting, or in the pool.

Mom comes out, runs toward us and jumps in the pool. "It's so hot," she moans. "Even the water is warm."

"I know. It's crazy how hot it actually is."

"You two should invite your friends over."

"Is it okay if Sophie comes over?"

"Sure, I like her. She's got very nice manners." Mom smiles.

I get out of the pool and call Sophie. As it turns out, she's at home reading and asked her Mom if she can come over. She said she'll be here in about half an hour. I go back to the pool and jump in. "She coming over?" Mom asks.

"Yeah, she said she'll be here soon. I told her to bring her swimsuit and to come around the side gate."

Dad's come home from work. "How are my girls?" he asks shrugging out of his tie and shirt.

"It's too hot today, Dad," Sam replies.

"I know." Dad toes off his shoes then starts unbuckling his belt, pushes his pants down and kicks them off.

"Dad!" I shout covering my eyes.

"I'm in my boxer briefs, no need to yell." He takes his watch off, then his socks.

"Are you coming in?" Mom asks.

Dad's down to his boxers and he comes right to the edge of the pool. He sticks one foot out, and falls face first in the pool. He comes up taking a deep breath. Mom swims over to him, and gives him a kiss.

Dad closes his eyes, puts his hand over them and says, "Marco."

"We're not five years old anymore, Dad," Sam half-whines but quietly swims away from him.

"Polo," I say and duck under water to swim away.

I get to the far end of the pool and make myself as small as possible. Dad's at the other end, headed straight toward Sam. She's smiling and trying to hold in a laugh. She splashes to one side, but Dad knows what she's doing and lunges straight at her.

Mom starts laughing because Sam ducks under water and swims away only just getting out of the way in the nick of time. "Damn it." Dad hits the top of the water and a huge splash gets Mom in the face. "Marco."

"Polo," I whisper.

"I hear your breathing." He swims in my direction, and I move as quietly as I can. But Dad has stealth-like tendencies, as I move left, Dad comes at me and moves right.

"Ah!" I squeal.

"Gotcha," Dad says engulfing me. Mom jumps on his back and gives him a huge kiss.

Dad uncovers his eyes and swings around to give Mom a kiss. "You're gonna be the death of me, woman," he happily crows before giving Mom another kiss.

"Eww, you have impressionable young children here." Sam screws up her face in mock disgust.

"Is that right?" Dad lets go of Mom and heads straight to Sam who shrieks and tries to run away. An impossible feat considering she's surrounded by water. Dad easily catches Sam, picks her up and throws her back in the pool.

A mess of flapping arms and legs splash into the water along with loud laughter. "My turn," I call as I head over to Dad so he can throw me the way he just threw Sam.

Dad grabs me around the waist and says, "Ready?" I don't even get a chance to reply before I'm flying out of the pool and land with the biggest splash ever known to man.

When I come to the surface, Sam, Mom and I are laughing. Dad swims over to me and sticks his arms out. "What?" I ask looking at him.

"My turn."

"Your turn what?"

"You're gonna throw me."

My mouth falls open and I stare blankly at him. "I can't lift you; you're heavy."

"I see, but you want me to chuck you around?" I see Mom and Sam sneak up on Dad quietly. Both of them jump on Dad, one on each arm. Dad falls backward into the pool, laughing so much.

"Hey, what's going on?" Sophie asks from the side of the pool.

"Jump in," I say. "Dad's getting smashed by Sam and Mom."

Sophie strips down to her one-piece and jumps in the pool. "Hello, Sophie," Dad says with Mom and Sam still hanging off him.

"Hi, Mr. Bennett. Mrs. Bennett." Sophie smiles.

"Well, time for me to get out and go wash up," Dad announces.

"I'll get a start on dinner. We're having chicken and salad. Sophie will you be staying?" Mom asks.

Both Mom and Dad are now on the steps and about to leave the pool.

"If it's okay?" Sophie looks to me, I nod. Mom and Dad nod too. "Awesome, thank you."

"We'll leave you girls to do whatever girls do." Dad and Mom link fingers and walk into the house, both drenched.

"Your parents are so cool."

"I'm going in, too. See you guys in a bit," Sam says, climbing out.

Sophie looks at me with a worried gaze on her face. "Do I smell?" She sniffs at her armpits for dramatic effect.

"I guess they wanted to leave us alone. Mom and Dad don't hang around, they're cool."

"Yeah, they are."

Sophie dunks under the water and comes up with her long blonde hair completely wet. "Man, it's nice in here."

"Yeah." I swim over and go sit on the steps leading into the pool. "Reece has been calling me every day."

"Since you told him?" I had filled Sophie in on what happened the night we went to the movies.

"Yeah." I take a deep breath. "Is it wrong for me to like him?"

"No way. He's nice. And he knows and he's not judging you. That has to mean something. To me, it speaks volumes."

"It feels weird. Like I shouldn't like him. I mean, I'm nowhere near ready to do anything with him, but I have this gut feeling he wouldn't push me for anything."

"Why shouldn't you like him?" She swims over to me and sits beside me on the step. "What happened can't define you."

"But, isn't too soon?"

"Are you going to have sex with him?"

"Oh God, no way. I'm not sure if I'll ever be ready for that."

"You will be, one day. But for now, just go with it. If you don't think he'll pressure you, or try anything on you, or tell anyone, why not hang out with him? There's nothing wrong with wanting to have a normal life."

"What if it comes out and people think I am a slut because suddenly I like Reece?"

Sophie's mouth pulls up into a weak smile. "You're worried about what others might think? Is it important to you what they think of you? Besides, you yourself have said you're not going to have sex with him in a hurry."

I shrug and kick my feet in the water. "I suppose."

"Look, he knows what happened, and he still wants to hang out with you. Has he tried forcing you to do anything?"

"Of course not."

"So if you like him, and he likes you, go with the flow. Who knows, you may not like the way he is in a couple of months. You can say 'see you later.'"

I shake my head at Sophie. "Like the way he is? I doubt that. He's already said I have to stick by him when we go back to school."

"See? Cool guy right there. Honestly, Dakota, give it a shot and see where things lead."

"He asked me to go the park with him and his little brother, but I don't know."

"Go, see how he is with his brother. It's not marriage. It's him wanting to get to know you better while doing it in a safe environment *for you*. He hasn't asked to be alone with you, or put you in a position where you would feel unsafe. And he's with his little brother."

I think of Sam and the lack of filter she had when she was younger.

"Yeah, you're right. Kids do have a tendency to say what they hear and see. Okay, I'll text him later and tell him I'll go to the park with him and his brother."

Sophie smiles, but her eyes drop and so does her mood. "I wish I knew who hurt me the night of the party. I'd like to hurt him."

A shiver rips up my back and even though the heat is inching toward a hundred, coolness automatically overtakes me. Nodding my head I whisper, "I know how you feel."

"Whoever he is, I hope when they find him they also find what he took from me."

"What do you mean?"

"Whoever . . . *you know* . . ." her voice drops when she says 'you know.' "He took my panties. When I woke, they were gone."

Thinking back to the morning I woke on the back field and lifting my dress to find mine were missing too. "Oh my God." I clasp a hand to my mouth and look at Sophie in sheer shock.

"What?" She moves her body, ready to jump up and run to get help.

"Mine were gone too."

"What?" she gasps softly. "Yours were missing too?"

I nod my head, startled by this revelation. Both Sophie and I sit on the step, stunned and horrified by what we've discovered. "Are you saying . . . ?"

"We were raped by the same person?" she finishes my thought, and my sentence.

"Oh my God," we both say synchronized. We sit in the pool, completely speechless and horrified by what we've just worked out. This can't be happening, can it? We can't both have been victims of the same person. Things like that don't happen in the real world, do they? It seems like hours pass, because neither of us are talking, silent while thinking about the situation. "That means, if your panties were missing, and mine were missing, then it's likely he took them as trophies."

"More horrifying than that is the fact he's a serial rapist."

"But . . . but . . . but . . ." I try saying, clutching at nothing. "It happened to you about a year ago?" I question. Sophie nods her head, confirming my words. "Then that also means, logically, if he got away with it with you, then it's probably happened to someone else in between you and me." I point to Sophie, then point to myself. Sophie nods again. "Shit," I whisper.

A serial rapist. Someone who takes our panties and keeps trophies. "Shit," Sophie says.

"Do you realize what this means?"

I look at her. Her face is pale white, her dark gray eyes hooded with fear. Her skin has small prickly bumps all over it. "I'm trying not to think of what it means, Dakota. I'm not sure I'm strong enough to survive this again."

"I'm sorry. I'll be quiet."

"No, you have to tell me what you're thinking."

Swallowing, I try and calm my rapid pulse. "You went to a party and were assaulted. Then, a year later, it happens to me at the prom. Both times, our panties were missing. It means those aren't coincidences. It means it's most likely the same person. And if it's the same person, then it's someone who lives here and knows us. And it probably means they've done it again and since. And hopefully soon, they'll be caught."

"Fuck, what a mess." She drops her chin to her chest and cries.

And I'm left wondering what the hell is going on.

If I'm a victim and Sophie's a victim, how many more girls have fallen prey to this monster?

But more importantly, who the hell is he?

CHAPTER 34

"I 'LL PICK YOU up in about an hour?" Reece asks. We'd been messaging back and forth and I told him I'd love to go to the park with him and Luke. He's called so we can organize a time and a park to meet at.

Although I'm comfortable with him, I'm still not ready to take the next step and be in a position where I have to say no if he asks for anything more than holding my hand. "You know the park a few blocks over from my place?"

"Yeah, down on Brown Street."

"Yeah, that's the one. Can we meet there? There's a swing set, a slippery slide, and some other things for Luke to play on."

"Sure." I can hear the disappointment in his voice. In a roundabout way I've said I don't trust him to ride in his car alone. I do, but I don't want to put either one of us in an awkward position.

"Okay, see you in about an hour." I hang up and go into my bedroom to put a pair of shorts and a t-shirt on. Then I head out to Mom to tell her I'm going to the park to meet up with Reece and his little brother Luke.

The hour flies by. When I get to the park, Reece and his brother are already playing on the swings. I walk over to them, and when Reece sees me, his eyes light up and a huge smile spreads over his face. He stops pushing Luke on the swings and walks straight to me. "Hi," he says stopping only a foot away from me.

Looking up into his dark brown eyes, I smile. "Hi."

He reaches out to touch me, but quickly changes his mind and drops his hand. "Hi," he says again.

A bigger smile pulls at the corners of my mouth. "Hi."

"Is it wrong for me to say how much I've missed you? Does it sound corny?"

Aw, my heart fills with happiness. "Not at all. I've missed you too."

He takes a step closer and extends his hand, offering it to me. He's waiting for me to take it, and he's not trying to make me hold it. Slowly, I extend my hand until our fingers are linked together. The warmth of his hand calms me.

Something inside me beats wildly while we walk toward Luke who's swinging his legs high on the swing. "Are you the girl Reece thinks is pretty?" he asks while looking up and squinting from the sun behind me.

My cheeks instantly glow pink and I look to Reece, who's looking down at the dirt while smiling. "Come on, bud. We talked about this," Reece says to Luke.

"Oh, yeah, that's right." He scrunches his mouth and nose, and keeps pumping his legs faster on the swing. "Will you push me?" he asks Reece.

"I'll push you," I offer.

"But you're a girl."

"Nice of you to notice," I reply dryly.

"Girls don't know how to push kids on swings," he pauses. "Unless you're a mommy. And you don't look like a mommy. Are you?"

"No way. But I have a little sister who I used to push when she was your age."

"Is she pretty too, like you?"

I walk around behind him, and start pushing him. "I think she's beautiful."

"Does she look like you?"

"Nah, she looks like my Mom. And my Mom is really pretty."

Luke turns around and looks at me from over his shoulder. "You push like a mommy. Reece pushes better than you."

This kid is funny. He's got a lot of charisma for someone so young. So, I give him what he wants. I push him higher, and he squeals and yells in excitement. "Is that better, Luke?"

"Yeah. Higher, higher, higher!" he chants.

This makes me laugh. Reece is sitting over on a small ledge watching us, and smiling at our antics.

"You know, I think you can push yourself for a while. I want to talk to Reece."

"Yeah, I can. But I like it better when someone else is doing it for me."

I stop pushing, and walk over to Reece, who's now looking down at his phone. When he hears me approach, he puts his phone back in his pocket and watches as I sit beside him. "How have you been, Dakota?"

"You know." I nonchalantly shrug. "I'm okay."

"Well no, I don't know. That's why I'm asking." He chuckles.

"Each day gets easier. Sometimes I wake up to horrible dreams and sometimes I don't."

"Dreams? As in from that night." I nod my head and look up to Luke who's still happily playing on the swings. "Have you remembered anything?"

"It's all kind of muffled. You know, it's like I'm underwater when I see these dreams. The voice belongs to someone I know, but it's almost like it's disguised. It's hard for me to pinpoint who it is."

"I can't tell you how sick this makes me feel."

"Yeah, I know. It makes my stomach churn every time I think about it. Not only that, but to think he's more than likely done it to someone else before me, and probably to others since, too." I can't tell him what Sophie and I discovered the other day when she came over. Her story is not mine to tell, and she may not want me to say anything. I know I'd hate it if she told anyone about me.

"Whoever this person is, if he *has* done it again, then it'll only be a matter of time before he gets caught."

I shrug again. "Who knows? There are so many cold cases. I was doing some research on the website those police officers talked to us about, RAINN. Did you know four out of five assaults are committed by someone the victim knows? This means it's pretty likely I know the guy." I know I know him, because it's way too coincidental for Sophie and me to have been attacked, and for both of us to have the same thing stolen.

"Sick fuckers," he mumbles.

"There's something else, too."

"What?" His head snaps to the side so he can watch me intently.

"He took my underwear. I didn't have them on me when I woke up. I was missing a shoe too, but I don't think he took that. But then again he might have."

"What a sick son of a bitch. Who the hell does shit like that?" He runs his hand through his hair then looks at me. "You think he took them as some kind of prize?"

I shrug my shoulders. My breath catches in my throat as I try to not think about this. "I don't know," I say, feeling defeated by everything.

"I'm sorry this ever happened. I should've come looking for you when you disappeared."

"It's not your fault."

"I should've stayed beside you the entire night. I shouldn't have left you." He stands and walks away, angry.

"Hey," I call to him as I look between him and Luke who's now moved to the slippery slide. There are a couple of other boys playing and they're all talking together. "Reece." The hard and rigid lines of his body tell me how angry he is, at himself more than anyone. "Reece."

He looks up and I see his shoulders visibly rise as he takes a deep breath. He heads back and comes directly to me. "I'm sorry, Dakota. I should've protected you, I should've tried to find you. I shouldn't have let this happen to you. If I had just gone out looking for you, then maybe . . ." His eyes go to the ground, and he bites the inside of his cheek.

"You can't say these things. How were you to know? You couldn't have. No one could've, except for the person who did this."

"He's not a person. He's a damned animal. Dakota, I need to hug you," he whispers. "I know how you are, and that you're still not sure of me, but I need to hold you. Please."

He makes no attempt to move, he simply holds my gaze. Silently begging for me to allow him. A rush of energy surges inside of me. It's more like a nervous fire bubbling inside, ready to explode. A strength I never knew I had. One that was once stolen, and slowly, Reece is giving back to me. He's shown me over and over again that I have the power to move forward by not pushing me or making unrealistic demands.

Stepping forward I go straight into his welcome embrace. "Thank you," he whispers against my hair.

I tighten my hands around his waist and bury my head into his strong chest. His arms wind around me as he binds me to him. At this moment in time, everything feels right. He feels right. *We* feel right.

"Reece, is Dakota your girlfriend?" Luke asks. Opening my eyes, I notice he's standing right beside us.

"Yes, she is," Reece replies. "Now scoot and go play."

"She's got girl germs. You're gonna have yucky girl germs if you kiss her. Ewww, are you going to kiss her? That's gross."

"Go away," Reece playfully barks at Luke.

"Reece has got girl germs. Reece has got girl germs. Reece has got girl germs," Luke happily sings as he skips back to the swing.

"Sorry about him," Reece says. "He can be a bit much."

"I'm not your girlfriend, Reece. Why would you tell him I was?"

"You may not be my girlfriend now, but you will be."

I let go and step back, shaking my head with worry. "You'd be better off finding someone who can give you the things I can't." I hope he gets what I'm trying to say.

He frowns and steps closer to me again. "It's not all about sex, Dakota. Jesus, what do you take me for?"

"I didn't mean it like that. But let's be perfectly clear. We . . ." I point to him and then back to myself. "I don't know if I'll ever be able to be intimate with you the way you'd want."

He shakes his head like I've slapped him across the face. "What?"

"You're going to want our relationship to progress further, and there's no way I can tell you when or even, if, I'll ever be ready for that. Please, do us both a favor and pick someone else who can give you everything you need."

"What we have isn't based on sex. And truthfully I don't want someone if the basis of our relationship is sex."

"I can't give you what you want," I almost yell at him, but look around and make sure no one can hear us. "I'm barely breathing as it is. I struggle to get through every day without thinking about that night. That night changed my life, the night that took everything good I knew and dirtied it. I'm broken. I'm disgusting for fuck's sake. It's brought me to my damn knees; it's ruined me."

"I know. I can see it in the way you behave now. You're only a shadow of the girl I knew before. But she's still in there. She may be frightened, and she may even feel as if she's drowning. But I'm here for her."

"Stop," I say with my eyes stinging and my breath caught in my chest.

"You know why I'm here for her?" I shake my head, not wanting to use my voice because I know it'll crack and I'll cry. "Because that girl is here." He steps forward, lifts my hand and places it over his heart. "She's been there since the first time I saw her. Do you know when that was?"

"No," I whisper, looking down and using my shoes as a focal point rather than looking at the beautiful boy standing in front of me.

"The day I moved to this town and started school. You walked into class—grade four—wearing a yellow sundress with your hair in a high ponytail. You looked at me, smiled and asked me if I was new to the school."

"I don't remember," I admit, more than a little ashamed. Embarrassed, because Reece remembers everything, and I remember nothing.

"I do. I remember every word you said, even the way you smiled at me. My heart knows you, Dakota, it belongs to you."

"Don't make this any harder than it has to be. Please, forget me, Reece. I can't give you what you need."

"Feel the way my heart beats." He presses my hand further to his chest. "It only beats for you. No one else holds it in their hand the way you do."

"Reece."

"Don't! Don't tell me you don't feel anything for me because I know you do. I also know it may take you years to feel free with me, but I'm willing to wait because of this." He taps his hand on mine. "This will never belong to anyone else. Ever." I look into his intense brown eyes. They hold a promise, an abundance of hope that everything will work out. "Have enough faith in me to get you through this until you find your strength again."

I can't believe it, but more damn tears spill as I step into Reece's space and hug him. "I'll try," I say, finally admitting how I feel about him.

His lips brush against my forehead and he whispers, "You, Dakota, put a spell on me when I was nine years old. Now, you damn well own me."

"I never knew you felt like this about me."

"You're the girl every guy wants. And when you started dating Levi, I was never going to say anything because he was my best friend and I thought you two were happy. I'd never come between you and your happiness. You mean way too much to me for that."

"Reece, you have a very high opinion of me. You shouldn't."

"And you have to stop this. What happened to you is not who you are. What happened is a major hurdle, one we have to overcome. But it doesn't define you unless you let it."

"How can you still want me after everything I've told you? Someone forced themselves inside me, he took something that I can never give to anyone again; he stole it. But you're standing here, holding me and telling me I've been in your heart since we were kids."

"Because, Dakota, you've captured my heart. No one else has ever been able to do that, and no one has ever kept it captive for as long as you have. It's been seven years, and I still l . . ." he stops, catching himself before he says something he may regret, or isn't ready to say. He regroups and says, "It's always been you."

"I don't know what to say. Where do we go from here?"

"From here? We go and play with my brother, who will say things that will embarrass me and may even be awkward enough to make you cringe."

I can't help but chuckle. "Oh no, what else is he going to say?"

"No one knows with Luke. He says what he thinks."

I take a few seconds to regroup. "You know what I mean, Reece. Where do *we* go from here?"

"We take one day at a time, be completely honest with each other, and talk about everything."

Normal teenage guys don't want to talk, or take one day at a time. They'd be ready and happy to make me Miss Right Now, but Reece is so different from anyone else I know. "I really like this, and I'm pretty sure I really like you," I tease him.

"Pretty sure?" He moves his hand down to my waist and applies gentle pressure while snaking his other hand down my lower back and gripping onto me. "Do you want to change that?" He playfully digs his fingers into my side, tickling while supporting me.

"No, I think I'll stick to 'pretty sure.'"

"Tsk, tsk, tsk. I gave you a chance, Dakota." His moves his fingers, tickling me in earnest now. Giggling, I wriggle around in his grip, but he has a firm hold on me so I won't fall, or get away.

"Stop, stop," I beg through laughter.

"Not until you say you like me." He digs in further, and I can't help but double over and try to curl into a ball so he stops tickling me.

"You're alright," I push him, teasing further.

"What? This is going backward, not in the direction it's supposed to." He mercilessly jabs my side with his long fingers.

"Alright, alright. Stop tickling me."

Reece lets up enough for me to catch my breath and stand straight. My cheeks are hurting from laughing so much, and a few tears fall out of my eyes from all the laughter. "So, tell me you like me."

"Ilikeyou," I mumble in a low voice all in one long word.

"Oh no, that's so not good enough." He brings me in tight to him, and his fingers move quickly to start tickling me again.

"Okay, okay. I like you." God, he's a pain in the butt. *A fun pain in the butt.*

His hands loosen around my waist and he smiles at me. "See, that wasn't too bad, was it?'

"'Spose not." I scrunch my nose and look away, pretending I'm disgusted with him.

"Do I need to tickle you again?"

"No!" I shriek. "Yeah, I like you."

Reece's face lights up as he proudly smiles at me. "Let's make it official. I want you to be my girlfriend."

"Are you asking me? Because that doesn't sound like a question, more like a statement."

He shrugs, links our fingers and starts walking over to Luke. "Whatever."

"You have to ask me then wait for my answer before you can make it a statement."

He flicks his wrist dismissively at me. "Semantics, that's all it is. If you say no today, you'll say yes next time." He's playing with me, hiding his fear of a negative response.

"Huh, interesting." My lips turn down and I nod my head. "And here I thought I had a choice."

"You'll always have a choice, Dakota. If your answer is no, then I'll keep asking until it's a yes. See, choice. I'm a very giving guy." He squeezes my hand.

"Giving, huh?"

"Yeah, really giving. You say no, and I'll give you another chance to say yes. Keep saying no, I'll keep giving you chances to say yes."

"What if I never say yes?"

"Pfft, that's crazy people talk. There's no reason for you to not say yes. I'm great boyfriend material." I start laughing so hard, I begin to cough. He pats me on the back, helping me settle my coughing fit. "See, I can make you laugh. One tick for excellent boyfriend material."

We reach Luke, who's talking to one of his new friends and Reece offers to push him on the swing. Luke happily leaves the conversation he was having, and hops up on the swing waiting for Reece to push him again.

"See? Good boyfriend material."

"What's happening?" Luke asks.

"I'm trying to convince Dakota to be my girlfriend. Can you help me out, buddy?"

"Sure. Reece told Mommy he thinks he loves you."

My eyes widen and my mouth gapes open while I stare at Reece. His face is exactly a reflection of mine. "Buddy, that's not really helping. What did we talk about?" Reece's face changes to a very red hue.

"Hey, we're not supposed to lie."

"No we're not, but we don't have to repeat everything we hear, either."

"Oh. Um, sorry." Luke looks at me and adds, "He thinks you're really pretty. And he *didn't* tell Mommy he thinks he loves you. He also *didn't* tell Miles how he thinks you're the girl for him."

"Buddy, stop talking now."

I crack up. I start laughing hard. Reece's face is beyond humiliated, and Luke truly has no idea what he's said.

A few minutes pass and the only one who's having fun is Luke, being pushed higher and higher on the swing. When I stop laughing, and Reece can look me in the eyes again, I walk around to where he's pushing Luke. "I like you too," I whisper.

His face is still a pretty shade of horrified pink, but at least he smiles when I tell him.

Smiling to myself, a tiny part of me feels like a normal sixteen-year-old teenaged girl. Some might even say, happy.

CHAPTER 35

THE LAST FEW weeks have flown by. It's the second to last week before the new school year starts, and panic has begun to set in.

I told Mom and Dad about Reece and me, and surprisingly, they're both really cool about it. Mom launched into the 'sex' talk, but after convincing her I'm nowhere near ready for that, she dropped the whole subject. She did say for me to come to her when I'm ready. I felt guilty when she was being so understanding, because really, I don't know how long it'll be before that will happen. *If ever.*

Sam told me Mom gave her the same talk, considering Taylor's been hanging around here at home with her. Sam said she cringed when Mom brought up sex, which in turn, made me laugh at Sam.

Today we're all here. We've had lunch and we're hanging in the pool. Reece is here with Luke, Taylor's here and so is Sophie.

"Your parent's are the best to let us all hang out here," Reece says while he keeps an eye on Luke, who's paddling around like a champion.

"Mom and Dad put the pool in because they said they'd rather have all our friends hanging here, than us being somewhere where we may not be so safe." I cringe at those words, because all their efforts have been in vain. Even *they* couldn't protect me.

Reece notices my shift in moods and swims over to me, embracing me in a hug. We haven't kissed yet, unless you count Reece giving me a peck on the cheek, or on the forehead. I'm nowhere near being ready to become that intimate with him. Suddenly the mood shifts even lower, and now I feel horrible for not being able to give Reece a kiss *and* for Mom and Dad not being able to protect me. "Stop it, Dakota," Reece responds to my plummeting mood.

"I can't help it." I look up into his eyes and he gives me the sweetest smile. "I can't even kiss you yet."

"Remember." He taps me on the nose. "My heart is yours. And it can wait until you're ready."

Suddenly, I get hit in the back of the head with something soft and wet. "What twas that?" I shriek, turning around to see Sam laughing hard, and the evidence of what was a water bomb. "You did not!"

"I so did." She wobbles her head from side to side, and lifts her finger to make a sassy 'Z' before snapping her fingers together.

"That's it."

"Come on, buddy. Let's go get the girls," Reece says to Luke.

"Yeah, water booooommmmbs," Luke eagerly replies.

Sam and Taylor have been busy, because there are literally hundreds of small water bombs in a huge bucket on the patio. "You're so gonna get it," I say to my sister and her devious boyfriend, who are using the side of the house as a shield.

I look over to the pool where Sophie is sitting on the steps, laughing and shaking her head. "I'll sit this one out," she yells at us.

"Party pooper." I poke my tongue out at her in jest.

Picking up some water bombs, I sneak quietly around and lob three at my sister, who ducks down, dodging every single one I throw. Instead I get Taylor, who then chases me, throwing his bombs at my back. Laughing I try to get away, but I'm met with Reece and Luke, who are both armed and ready to attack.

"Hey, Luke?"

Luke throws one bomb from hand to hand, standing tall with a huge smile on his face. "Yeah," he responds.

Sneaking a look over my shoulder, both Sam and Taylor are hiding while Reece and Luke are ganging up against me. "You like my pool?"

Reece's mouth drops open and he playfully glares at me. "Don't listen to her, buddy. She's going to try to get me, and she's going to use you to do it."

"Nah, she won't. She's nice."

"If you like using my pool, you can come over every day and use it if you help me get your brother and my sister."

Luke's little eyes smile mischievously and I know he's on my side now.

"Don't listen to her, buddy," Reece reiterates, desperate to hold onto his little brother.

I give him a small nod, and with both of my hands fully loaded with water bombs, and Luke's little hands holding a bomb each, we attack

Reece.

Reece starts laughing, and makes a beeline straight for me. He grabs me around the waist, and calls to his brother, "Now, buddy."

Luke pelts me with water bombs. I'm laughing so hard I have happy tears streaming down my face. "Let me go," I try to say between the laughter.

Reece leans in and whispers, "Let's go get your sister." He then lightly pecks me on the cheek. I nod my head enthusiastically and stop struggling. "Luke, come here." Luke comes over and Reece leans down to whisper to Luke how we're going to get my sister and Taylor.

"Ready," Luke announces proudly, sticking his little chest out.

The three of us sneak around the side of the house, however we don't find Sam or Taylor. As we turn back, we're ambushed by them. "It's a trap!" I yell and start throwing with my eyes closed, hoping I hit either of them and not Reece or Luke.

There's a lot of yelling, laughing and water flying around.

Reece, Luke, and I start taking charge and keep moving forward, making Sam and Taylor retreat toward the back slider. We're encroaching and they're looking around, trying to find something to shield themselves.

"Right," I say while throwing a water bomb up and catching it, taunting them.

"Right," Luke's little voice echoes mine.

"Right. This is war," Reece announces.

Sam's eyes are frantically moving, searching for something she can use as cover while Taylor's gaze is focusing on our three water bombs versus their two.

"Ready?" I ask my two soldiers.

"Ready," they respond, synchronized.

"Set."

They both take aim, and Sam bursts into laughter before the water balloons even leave our hands.

Then, the absolute worst thing that could happen does, just as I scream out, "Fire!"

Sam and Taylor duck at the same time that Mom comes through the slider carrying a pitcher of lemonade, and all three water balloons miss Taylor and Sam and get Mom. One in the face, one in the head, and one knocks the pitcher off the serving tray.

It's so quiet, all I can hear is everyone breathing. Mom gasps and looks down at her completely drenched sundress. Her hair is all wet, and stuck to her face. Water is hanging on her cheek, big droplets falling to land on her chest.

"Did I just get hit by three water balloons?" she asks in an eerily quiet voice.

I look to Reece and then Sam. We've all got our lips pursed as tightly as possible, holding in gales of laughter, bursting to rip out of our mouths.

Taylor looks like he's going to be sick. And although Luke has his little hand over his mouth, the giggles are escaping.

"Even you, Luke?" Mom asks when she lifts her head to look at us all.

"I'm sorry." Luke answers, though his tone really says 'this is the funniest thing ever, Mrs. B.'

"That was fresh homemade lemonade," Mom says looking at the huge puddle at her feet in dismay.

"Or pee," Luke cheekily says.

"Damn," Sophie mumbles from over at the pool, then claps her hand over her mouth to hide her laughter.

Mom turns her head slowly, her eyes narrow and a menacing smile tugs at her lips. She looks sideways, seeing exactly where we're all positioned and then at the bucket which has only a few water balloons left down the bottom.

We're all watching her, ready to have her rip us a new one because we made her spill her lemonade.

Oh crap.

Mom dives to the bucket and grabs the last few water bombs, attacking us while laughing hard.

We all duck for cover, but not before she pitches some pretty decent throws at us. She gets us all, at least once.

"Right. I'm going inside to get cleaned up, and to have the last little bit of the lemonade I made. You can all have water," she calls from over her shoulder.

We're all laughing, tears streaming down our faces. Reece picks Luke up, and throws him in the pool then jumps in to join him. "Come on, it's so nice in here," he calls to us when he comes up from under the water.

Sam's already running toward the pool, and I head over to get the hose so I can clean the patio where Mom dropped the pitcher of lemonade.

Once I've cleaned up, I go and join the rest of them in the pool.

"I can do a handstand, wanna see?" Luke asks me as I sit on the step of the pool.

"No you can't."

"I so can. Look." He's in the shallow end and ducks under the water. He barely makes it down to touch the bottom before he swims up with a huge smile on his face. "See?"

"Did you even touch the bottom?" I ask.

"Yeah, look!" He dives back in and no quicker than he's gone under, he's back up again.

"Luke is such a confident swimmer," I say to Reece.

"He's a water baby. Mom had him in lessons from when he was six months old. He loves it."

The back slider door slams open and we all look to the commotion of what's happening. Dad's home from work early and he has the angriest look I've ever seen on his face. He steps through, his hands on his hips, his back straight and his chest puffed out. His wild eyes look everywhere, taking in everyone who's out here in the pool.

Mom stumbles out behind him, with a dry dress on and a towel in her hands as she wrings the water out of her hair.

"Honey, what's going on?" she asks, placing a calming hand on Dad's shoulder.

Dad looks at Mom, his jaw tight and body stiff from sheer rage. He looks back to us, where we're all still from the attention he acquired with his overwhelmingly angry presence. "Unless you're either of my two daughters, get out."

Double crap.

"Um." Reece looks over to me, his face etched with worry.

"It's okay. Just go, I'll call you later."

"Come on, buddy, we gotta get home to help Mom with some chores."

Luke swims over to Reece and the two get out of the pool. "Hey, Reece can you give me a lift home please?" Sophie asks.

"Sure. Do you need a lift too, Taylor?"

"Yeah, thanks."

We all get out of the pool, and they all leave with a promise to call us later on tonight.

I grab a towel and wrap it around my body, and Sam does the same thing.

Dad's standing incredibly still, his face is furious and everything inside of me is saying he's angry at me. I must've done something to make him this mad.

"What's going on, Owen?" Mom asks, her voice dropping.

"Go and dry off, then get your asses into the family room."

"Owen, why are you being so rough with the kids?"

As I walk past Dad, his eyes narrow further and his brows draw in together. "We need to talk," Dad says to me.

My stomach flips and drops. His tone screams, 'I know.'

I take myself to my bedroom, close the door and lose every ounce of control I have.

CHAPTER 36

C HANGING OUT OF my one-piece, I put on a pair of jeans and long sleeved, light sweater. Shudders of ice tear through me, cooling my body . . . *terrifying me.*

Opening my door slowly, I try and listen to the hushed whispers coming from the family room. I can't hear anything definitive, only small murmurs. I stick my head out of my door and see Sam's leaning against the hallway wall, listening intently.

"What's going on?" I mouth to her and lift my shoulders in question.

"I don't know," she mouths back. Then she puts a finger to her mouth and shushes me.

Stealthily, I move to stand beside Sam, hoping to get some insight as to why Dad's home early, why he threw everyone out and why he wants to talk to me specifically.

My stomach drops.

Deep down inside, I know why. But I'm hoping it's not that, it's humiliating enough that it happened, it's vulgar for my parents to know. A shudder rips through me at the thought.

"Girls, get in here," Dad calls. My shoulders stiffen and I'm abruptly hit with the inability to respond or move. My legs feel like a ton of concrete has been poured over them, making them immobile.

"Let's face this together." Sam links our fingers encouragingly.

But I can't move. Fear is rising rapidly inside me, causing all of my senses to shut down. I can't hear anything, it's all muffled and strained. Black spots float in front of my eyes. I can't do this. I can't look into their eyes and lie any more. "I can't, Sam," I whisper and squeeze her hand tighter.

"We have to. I'll be with you. I promise, I won't leave." Her words should ease the guilt and shame pounding in my veins, but all they do is reinforce the severity of what's about to happen.

"Girls," Dad calls again, his tone is deadly low and holds an air of command.

Sam stands in front of me, looking me square in the eyes. "You can do this," she says. "I'll be there with you."

I nod my head, and slowly shuffle in to the family room, with Sam beside me. Mom and Dad are sitting on the sofa next to each other, and Dad has his cell phone out on the table in front of him. I look at Mom, who's been crying. Her face is pink and splotchy, her eyes are red-rimmed and she's clutching a tissue in her hand. The tissue box has been moved, and sits beside her on the sofa. *Crap.*

Sam and I head for the opposite sofa, and sit, huddled together. In this explosive moment, she's my rock, my strength. There's nothing I'll ever do in my life that will even come close to repaying her for everything she's done for me.

Dad's eyes focus on us. He takes in exactly how close we're sitting, and how we're holding onto each other. He takes a deep breath and looks down to his phone. Picking it up, he silently swipes at the screen, and brings something up. He places it on the small wooden table between us. He pushes it over to me, his eyes glued to the phone's screen.

Closing my eyes for a moment, I regroup and take a deep, pained breath, gathering all my courage to pick the phone up and look at whatever is on the screen.

Deep down, though, I know. A picture has gotten back to him.

Mom's sob makes me open my eyes and stare at the innocent phone waiting for me to pick it up. Opening my mouth I take a deep breath in, hold it for a few seconds before releasing it. Untangling from Sam, I lean over and pick up Dad's phone. The picture on it is the one Sam received shortly after *that* night.

"Care to explain?" Dad asks in a tone I've never heard him use before. There's definite anger, heavily tinged with disappointment, possibly even shame.

"I can't," I croak with the scratchiest voice. The words I speak are tiny, almost breathless.

Looking over at Mom, her chin quivers as she holds in a cry.

"Then care to explain how they ended up on social media this morning?" I place the phone back on the table, and don't look at the sickening photo taunting me . . . *haunting me.*

He said, *they*. I look to Sam and she lifts her shoulders to me, silently telling me she has no idea what on earth is going on.

"They?" my voice breaks.

"Yes, they." Mom hasn't moved, but Dad takes the phone and brings up another offensive image before placing it back on the table. Both are sitting, waiting for me to explain.

I hesitantly reach out to take the phone, my fingers are icy cold and trembling from dread as I reach for the phone again. My anxiety level is sky high while my chest hurts from the way my heart is wildly beating against it. I retract my hand quickly and grab onto Sam's hand.

It's so quiet in here. Other than Mom's small wail, nothing else can be heard. "I can't," I repeat, terrified and ashamed.

"You need to start talking." Dad pushes the phone in my direction.

My eyes land on the screen, and I take in another large breath. It's a picture of me, at prom, but not one I've seen before. It's explicit and revolting. I look up at Dad, and don't dare look at Mom. Dad's eyes show a new level of disgust.

"It's not what you think," I say.

"Dad," Sam starts saying. But the moment Dad shoots her a 'don't you dare' look, she doesn't say anything else.

This is on me, not her. She shouldn't have to fight my battle.

Dad's intense stare comes straight back to me. I have to be brave. I have to tell my parents what happened, regardless of the consequences.

They won't believe me, not now. It's been too long, far too long.

"You better start talking, Dakota."

I swallow, and try to get everything sorted in my head. A part of me knew this day would come, I just never thought it would be here so quickly. Maybe twenty years, not weeks. "It happened at prom," I begin.

"Oh God," Mom sighs and clasps her hand to her mouth.

"Why didn't you tell us, or at the very least your mother, that you were considering having sex? And why on earth would you let someone take photos of you while you were having sex? Have you learned nothing about social media? Don't you know the dangers and risks involved in letting someone have pictures like these of you?" Dad says. His voice is eerily calm, however the tension in his tone is enough to tell me he's hanging on to his control by the thinnest thread.

Vomit quickly rises and my body shudders from the hell breaking out inside my body. They think I willingly did this, which makes it even worse.

"It's not what you think," I yell, losing all my control. I abruptly stand

and move away from the sofa, pacing back and forth. I bring my hands up to my hair, and tug on the ends in frustration and angst.

"If it's not what we think, then explain it to me," Dad counters, standing as well and following my pace from in between the facing sofas.

"Help us understand, darling. We won't judge you," Mom sweetly says.

Judging is exactly what they're doing.

"Dad, if I can say something," Sam interrupts.

"No, Samantha, you cannot say anything. You're here because you're part of this family, so just sit and listen."

Sam winces away at Dad's angry words, and she looks at me sympathetically. I shake my head at her and smile, telling her without words how it's okay and not to feel hurt with Dad.

"Dad," I start saying. Tears sting my eyes while my heart shatters into millions of tiny pieces. Once the words are out, I know I'll be unloved, I know they'll look at me with nothing but disgust and contempt.

"Tell me it wasn't Levi? Did he create the group on social media and upload all these photos of you, *like this?*" He spits the last words out, *repulsed.*

"What?! No! I don't know who did this." I point to the phone. "I don't know who took the photos." I let more tears slip as I huddle into myself. "I don't even know what happened," I finally admit.

Dad takes a stumbling step back.

"What are you saying, Dakota?" Mom whispers.

"She's saying she was raped," Sam announces as she too stands and holds me tight.

Oh my God. My heart is beyond repair now, I can't believe Sam told them. They shouldn't know, they're going to hate me. I already hate me, and knowing they'll despise me too, makes me sick.

"What did you say, Sam?" Dad whispers in a small broken voice.

I look over to our parents and Mom is sitting with her mouth open, tears now freely running down her face. Dad's collapsed back to the sofa, his body is stiff and rigid.

"She had her drink spiked, and she was raped."

"Jesus, Sam! What the hell?" I yell at her. Her face drops because I've yelled at her. "I'm sorry," I whisper.

"Dakota, sit down," Dad instructs. He leans forward on the sofa and balances his elbows on his knees. Sam and I go and sit. Dad looks to us both, his jaw tight and his shoulders squared back. I won't look at Mom.

I can hear her crying and I don't want to see the absolute humiliation on her face because I've disappointed her.

Dad runs his hand through his hair and lands his palm on the back of his neck. There's a vein that protrudes from Dad's temple whenever he's really angry, and right now it's throbbing.

He regains himself, and looks straight at me.

"You were raped," he says flatly.

I nod my head.

"At your prom?"

I nod again.

"Your drink was spiked?"

I look down at my feet, but nod.

"Tell me exactly what happened. And don't leave a single thing out."

Tears fall from my eyes, landing on the floor boards. There's a tiny puddle of tears quickly growing. I close my eyes, take a deep breath, and pull my shoulders back.

I'm strong, I can do this. *I can tell them.*

Looking up at Mom and Dad, I open my mouth and tell them everything that's been happening, from the night of the prom until now.

Mom and Dad sit opposite me, quietly listening. The more I tell them the more their shoulders drop and the more I see the shame flitter across their faces.

But I have to do this. It's toxic to hold something so monumental inside. It was bound to kill me, to send me over the edge of reality and straight into the depths of hell.

I can do this. I can be strong. I *will* be strong.

It takes me no less than an hour to relay everything that's happened. I don't hold back on anything. *Nothing.* As I finish talking, I notice a huge sense of relief flood me. It's as if a giant load has been lifted off my shoulders, and now, although I still need to deal with the aftermath of what's happened, I can finally move on with my head held high.

Mom and Dad sit opposite us, processing everything I've told them. They blink slowly, look at each other, and back to me.

"We need to get the police involved," Dad says breaking the tense air in the family room.

"I'm going to find you a counselor, Dakota. We need help dealing with this. Neither your father or I are educated in helping you through this." Mom stands and makes her way to me, she sits beside me and wraps her arms around me. "I'm sorry, sweetheart. I'm sorry I didn't know. I'm sorry I didn't see it. I thought you were just going through normal teenage stuff, not this. I'm so sorry," she keeps repeating. She brings me into her body, hugging me tightly and kissing my temple.

"You believe me?" I ask, stunned. I look at Sam who gives me a warm smile.

"Why wouldn't we?" Dad adds.

"I just thought . . ."

"No, Dakota. Don't ever think we won't believe or trust you," Dad says. "For now, go have a shower and clean up. I'm going to make a couple of phone calls, one of which will be to the police."

I break out of Mom's tight hug. Shaking my head, I look at Dad. "No, you can't. What if it gets out and everyone knows?"

Dad picks his phone up and shakes it at me. "That ship has sailed. These pictures have been uploaded to a group and hundreds of people were added to it. Everyone is going to know, regardless of whether you want them to or not. The next step is getting the police involved. Quietly though, because we don't want everyone knowing they're involved. It might compromise any investigation they conduct."

"I can't, Dad."

Mom squeezes me harder, and Dad moves to crouch before me, his hands embracing mine. "You have to. This is the only way we can move forward. The. Only. Way."

It feels like an eternity passes, but I know it's only been a few seconds when I finally realize, this is the natural progression of healing. Of moving forward and standing tall. I didn't choose this. *He,* whoever *he* is, did this to me. "Okay," I whisper. I'm stronger today than I was yesterday, because I'm no longer burying a horrible secret so far down it has the potential to turn septic.

"Go have a shower, and lie down for a little while. But no one, and I repeat no one is to be told about the police. I want them to catch this bastard and put him behind bars, and if the rapist knows the police are involved and gets wind of it, then he may destroy any evidence he has. We need to be smart." Dad points to me, then Sam.

"I promise, Dad I won't say a thing." Sam crosses her heart for extra measure. "Because I want him caught more than anything."

"I promise, I won't say a word."

"Okay, both of you, go. Your mother and I need to talk."

Sam and I stand and head into our rooms.

She whispers as we walk down the hall, "How do you feel?"

"Truthfully, I'm relieved, but this is only the start. I think this is going to get much worse before it gets better."

"Mom and Dad won't let anyone hurt you."

"I know," I say, ashamed of myself for thinking they'd see me differently because of the assault.

Sam stops walking when we reach my room. She hugs me and says, "I'll always be here for you. No matter how tough things get."

"I love you," I tell her.

"I love you too."

She lets go of me and walks to her room at the end of the hall. "Sammy," I call.

She turns around with a huge smile on her face. "That's the first time you've called me that since, *that night.*"

Huh, so it is. "Thank you for being my sister."

She smiles wide again, and goes to her room. I head into mine, and wait for whatever is about to happen.

Something's bubbling away, the calm before the storm. It's not yet turbulent, but soon I'm about to weather the worst storm of my life.

Regardless of what lies ahead, I smile, because I have the support and love of my family.

The numbness inside me eases.

Finally.

CHAPTER 37

I'VE BEEN LYING on my bed, listening to music and trying to relax. I heard the front door open about ten minutes ago, then Mom and Dad and some other voices, talking. I assume they called the police and they came to the house to interview me.

Although I know this has to happen, it doesn't make it any easier on me. My nerves are thrumming and my heart's been beating at a constant fast speed. I haven't been able to stop shaking either. I've got blankets piled high on me but I can't stop shivering.

"Dakota," I hear Dad's gruff voice beckon.

I take a few deep breaths before throwing all the covers off and heading out to the family room, where everyone is congregated.

I round the wall, and come in to see Detectives Miller and Young standing in the family room, talking with Mom and Dad.

"Hello, Dakota," Detective Young says to me. "I'm Detective Tracey Young, and this is Detective Andrea Miller." She holds her hand out to shake. I take it and smile.

"You both came to my school. You two and Detective Garcia talked to us about vacation, and the possibility of things going wrong. Including statistics on sexual assault and what we should look out for."

"Yes, we did. We were trying to educate as many students as we could on the potential dangers you could be faced with. I'm glad you remember us. Is it okay if we sit?" she asks me.

I look to Mom and Dad, seeking their approval.

"Don't look at your parents, focus on me and Andrea, okay?" she asks gently.

"Sure," I say casting my eyes downward. I try to flick them to the side to look at Mom and Dad surreptitiously, but I can't see them.

"Your mom and dad have told us a few things, but if it's okay, we'd like to hear from you?"

"Um." Oh God, embarrassment floods me. Having to tell a complete stranger.

Andrea can see the hesitation in me, she can tell I'm ambivalent about tell them anything. "Mr. and Mrs. Bennett, can you get us a drink please?"

"Of course," Dad answers.

They leave the room, and I look at both police officers. "Shouldn't they be here?" I ask pointing my thumb in the direction of the kitchen.

"They can be, if it makes you more comfortable. We've already talked, and they've said they'll do whatever you need them to. But how about we talk for now, maybe you can tell me what happened, and if it's okay with you, we'll record it so we don't forget anything. Is that okay, Dakota?" Andrea is so gentle and sweet. She's not talking *at* me, or trying to force me to say anything at all. She's simply waiting for me to open up to them.

"I can do that."

She takes a small recorder out of her pocket and shows it to me. I squint at the old thing. "I know, it's dark ages old. But it's still accurate."

"In TV shows I've seen, the police usually make the person go to the police station, and they sit in a room while the interview gets recorded."

"We can do that, but in these types of cases, we try to make things as comfortable for the victim as possible. Under stress, you may forget something and in our experience, we've found having the support of your family works best."

"What type of detectives are you?"

"There's a whole team of us who specialize in trauma victims."

"Trauma?" I question.

"We look into a lot of situations similar to yours."

"Oh," I answer. My shoulders tighten and I begin to think how many situations there are similar to mine. My mind goes to the statistics they were giving us at school. Forty-four percent of girls under the age of eighteen are sexually assaulted. I shiver. That number is so high it's nothing short of horrible.

"I'm going to start the recorder and we can begin. Okay?" Tracey asks. She presses a button on the recorder, places it between us, and smiles. "What we have to do is identify you. Your name, age, what school you go to, things like that before we continue with the events of that night. Is that okay with you?" I nod my head. "You need to speak, so we can get it all on this." She taps the recorder.

"Oh, sorry. Okay."

Andrea and Tracey both ask me questions, and they have an incredibly soothing quality about them. They ask me questions in their simplest form, without trying to trick me or make me stumble.

They're very easy to talk to, and they don't trivialize anything I tell them. They're listening to me, and I'm overcome by the most amazing feeling of validation.

"Can you tell me what you did with the dress you were wearing?"

I shudder and slump over, curling in on myself. "I hid it," I say.

"Where did you hide it?" Andrea asks.

"I was waiting to put it in the trash, but it's in my closet, in a box right at the back."

Andrea and Tracey both smile at me. "Mr. and Mrs. Bennett, can you come in here please?" Tracey calls. Mom and Dad appear in the hallway, Dad with his arm around Mom, and Mom still clutching a tissue. "Is it okay with you if I go to Dakota's room with her and one of you please? Dakota's kept the dress she wore that night."

I look between them all, trying to understand what she wants. "Do you want the dress?" I ask.

"Yes, we do."

"I can go get it." I stand and start heading to my room.

"Dakota, we need to be in there with you, just to make sure we handle this right. But we need your parents' permission, and we need them to witness what happens."

"Oh," I respond.

"Of course, please." Dad sweeps his hand out, indicating the direction of my room.

Dad, Tracey, and I all go into my room, where I uncover the box and start to open it. "We'll wait until we get back in the family room." Tracey smiles. I hand her the box, but she shakes her head at me.

I find it strange, but we all head back out, me carrying the box. Andrea is standing beside the coffee table, pulling gloves on. "Come over here, Dakota." She points beside her. I go to her, with the box still in my hands.

"Before you open it, tell us what you've put in the box." She points to the box but keeps her intense gaze on me.

"My prom dress."

"Did you wash it before you put it in here?"

"No. I took it off when I got home and shoved it in there. It makes me sick even thinking about it and how it looked."

"Okay, can you put the box on the coffee table, and open it up please?" I do as they ask, and then place the lid on the table. Tracey picks up the recorder, describing every detail of the dress, from its color to how it looks. When she finishes describing the dress, she looks at Andrea who takes the dress out of the box and lifts it so it's completely visible.

"Oh God," I mumble, horrified at the state of it. I feel two sets of hands on me; Mom to my right, Dad to my left. Both of them embrace me while they watch what I'm seeing.

The dress is ripped, torn, with grass and blood stains on it. "I'm so sorry, sweetheart," Mom whispers. "I should've been there for you."

I shake my head at her. My emotions are colliding inside me. Sickness, shame, disgust . . . everything is dancing off each other.

Tracey describes everything on the dress. Every tear, every stain, every discoloration. Andrea turns the dress inside out and there are huge patches of dried blood. "Oh God." I bury my head in my hands, unable to look at or listen to anything else they'll point out.

Suddenly my heart tugs in one direction, my stomach roils in another and all the contents of my stomach are on their way up. "I can't." I grab my mouth to stop the vomit coming out and run for the toilet.

Barely making it, I flip the lid and lose everything I had in my stomach. Numerous sets of footsteps follow me in. Mom and Dad are both apologizing as they fall to their knees beside me. They grab me, sheltering me while crying.

Dad keeps repeating the same words, "We're so sorry."

I pull back, and look at my parents. Dad's a strong man, but even he's broken by the state of my dress and what it means.

"I can't imagine how difficult this has been for you. How much you've had to hide. I'm so sorry, Dakota. I wish I'd been there for you that night. No fucker would've put his hands on you. Done *that* to you." He points toward the family room, indicating my dress.

"We'll get through this, as a family. We'll get through it." Mom's now the strong one and Dad's a mess.

It takes a lot for my Dad to cry. The dress was the final straw to break his strong personality.

We stand together and once I've washed my mouth and brushed my teeth, we all head back out to the police officers. The dress is back in the box, and the box itself is sealed with yellow tape proclaiming

'EVIDENCE.'

"Are you okay, Dakota?" Andrea asks as she approaches me and rubs my back.

"I am." I smile weakly at her, although the tears are on the verge of falling.

"As you can see, I've placed the dress back in the box and sealed it. We need to take it to run DNA tests on it. We also need DNA from you. There are a number of ways we can do that. A blood test, or a few strands of hair. But with consent from you and your parents, we'd like to do one right now called a buccal smear."

"What's that?" I ask, now I'm even more nervous than before. It sounds so invasive.

"It's a small cotton swab, and we use it to collect a sample of cells from the inside of your cheek. All you need to do is open your mouth, and we do the rest. It doesn't hurt; it's completely pain-free," Andrea says.

"Here's the swab," Tracey says, holding up something that looks like an extra-long Q-tip.

"If you want to do this, we're okay with it," Dad says, looking to Mom who nods her head in agreement.

"Okay."

"Come sit beside me, Dakota," Tracey says. She takes another pair of latex gloves out, and once they're snugly fitted she takes one of those swab things out. Andrea has another bag, and is writing my name and date of birth on it. Nervously, my eyes flicker between them, trying to watch them both at the same time.

"What I'm doing is putting all your information on it, so it doesn't get mixed up when it gets to the lab," Andrea says.

"Okay."

"Now if you can turn this way for me, and open your mouth as wide as you can, I'll swab the inside of your cheek." I follow her instructions and before I know it, it's over. "See, that wasn't scary, was it?" I shake my head.

"Mr. and Mrs. Bennett, could you take a seat please."

Mom and Dad sit beside me, one on either side.

"Have you been sexually active since that night?" Andrea asks me.

"What? No. I . . . yuck. Oh my God, *no way.*" I shudder.

"You'll need to get a blood test, to make sure you're clean and safe."

Clean and safe? What the hell? "Huh?" My brows draw together and my mouth drops open. "What does that mean?" There's a stillness inside my mind. It's blank and calm, no thoughts processing. "Huh?" I say again.

"Dakota, you need make sure you don't have a sexually transmitted disease," Andrea says as gently as she can to not to freak me out.

But freaking out is exactly what's happening. "Sexually transmitted disease?" I repeat. "Like AIDS?"

"Any type of disease," she says, trying to get me to look beyond the terrifying fact I may have AIDS.

"I might have AIDS," I say slowly, my breath matching my words. "Fuck," I whisper, stunned by the enormity of everything into uttering that curse while sitting between my parents.

"It's routine, and you should get yourself checked to make sure you're all clear. If nothing else, for your own piece of mind." Andrea places her hand on my thigh and gives me a comforting squeeze.

The next while is spent with me in a state of non-comprehension. I can hear them talking, they're discussing what's going to happen next and what we should do. Dad tells them about the pictures on social media, how the son of his work colleague was added to a group and he recognized me from a company picnic we'd both attended. He'd shown his dad, who in turn showed my dad.

I can barely think about anything beyond the possibility of me having a sexually transmitted disease. My entire future hangs in the balance of a blood test.

The calm inside me slowly recedes, hot lava replacing the control I had. He took my virginity, ripping it away before I could give it to someone of my choosing, and experience that special moment for myself. Now he continues to humiliate me by sharing personal photos that were taken when I was unconscious on social media. And today, I learn I may have a life sentence with a deadly disease.

My anger is starting to reach a boiling point. Inside me, something snaps. I want to shout, scream, yell at whoever did this. I want to kill them, to have them hurt as much as they've hurt me.

Abruptly I stand and head out the back door toward our pool. I fall to my knees and tear at my hair. Pain flares through me, making me feel alive. But I don't want to be alive. I want to die. I ball my hands into fists and start punching my leg, my other arm, anywhere I can so I stop breathing.

"Dakota!" Dad yells to me.

Hot tears fall down my cheeks. I can barely breathe while I continue to beat myself. I can't handle this, the pressure the humiliation, all of it.

"Dakota!" Dad's arms are around me as he pulls me up to stand and crushes me to his body. "Stop, stop," he whispers in my ear.

I fight him with whatever I can, my legs are kicking and I'm doing anything to cause physical pain, I need to make myself hurt. "I'm not worthy," I cry as Dad tries to hold my arms down. "I'm not worth anything."

"Stop it, darling, please stop." He kisses my cheek and holds me to him.

My tears don't stop, but I'm losing all my energy. I collapse against Dad and he holds me solidly. "Let me go," I cry in the smallest of voices.

"Never, darling. Never." In a split second he spins me around, and nestles my head to his chest. My tears don't stop. They have no cut-off mechanism. *Will I ever stop crying?* Dad kisses my forehead and weaves a hand up to cradle the back of my head. He holds me firm, letting me use his strength.

"Will the pain ever stop?" I ask.

Dad's arms are like a vise, not letting me go. "One day it will," his voice sounds strangled, like he's crying.

We stay out in the garden for a long time. Finally, I give up. A massive ache pounds inside my head. There's a stabbing pain behind my eyes, while at the base of my skull, a pulsing, splitting throb jabs away insistently.

"I'm tired," I whisper. Tired of everything.

Dad picks me up, swinging my legs over his arms and carries me into my room. He places me on the bed, tucks me in and kisses my cheek. My eyes close on their own. My brain turns off. And my body rejects this horrible thing called life.

"Shhh, I'll take care of you. I'll take care of you real good."

"GET AWAY FROM ME!" I yell as I sit up in bed, kicking the blankets off me.

"Dakota?" Dad turns on the lamp and sits up in his chair. He looks at me and jumps up, rubbing his eyes, and comes straight to me.

"What's happening?" I ask, looking around the slightly illuminated room, dazed and confused.

"You were having a nightmare." He hugs me, and soothes my hair while gently kissing my forehead.

"What are you doing in here?"

"It's best I stay with you, especially tonight, when you've relived everything and your emotions are so high. I need to make sure you're okay, sweetheart."

"You don't have to stay, Dad. I'll be okay."

I feel him smile against my forehead. "I know you'll be okay, but I want to."

My head's still spinning and thumping away. "My head hurts," I say as my eyes close and I relax against Dad.

"Go to sleep, I'll be here all night."

My eyes close. A warm black curtain shrouds me, whispering a soft lullaby, and encouraging me to let go and sleep.

I do, welcoming the void with open arms.

CHAPTER 38

MY EYES BLINK open and I feel like death. My entire body vibrates with a dull ache, from my head right down to my toes. It feels like death's hand has reached inside me, and squeezed the life out of my heart. Anguish and misery run deep through my blood.

Turning over I look around my room. Dad's fallen asleep in the chair he dragged in here. His head is hanging to the side, and his legs are spread wide while his arms hang to his sides.

Abruptly, I throw the covers off and Dad springs awake, wiping his chin in case he's drooled. "Sweetheart," he says in a deep, grumbly voice. He blinks rapidly, yawns then scrubs his hand over his face. "How are you feeling?" He stands to stretch then sits again, focusing his attention on me.

"Like I've been dragged for ten miles by a fast train." I swing my legs over the side of the bed and sit up.

"You look like it," Dad sympathetically says.

"I hate to say it, but so do you." The corner of my mouth pulls up in a tiny smirk.

"Let's go have breakfast." Last thing I want to do is eat.

When I stand, Dad comes to me and hugs me, kissing me on the top of my head. "I've got to go to the bathroom," I say.

"I'll get your breakfast ready."

Once I've finished in the bathroom, I drag my heavy limbs out to the kitchen, where Sam, Mom, and Dad are all talking quietly. The moment Sam sees me, she stands and envelops me in a hug. "I'm here for you, you know that, right?"

"I know. And if it wasn't for you, I don't think I could've survived this."

Dad brings over a coffee for himself and an orange juice for me. "I'll make some breakfast," Mom says, coming over to hug me, then Sam.

It doesn't take long for the conversation to turn to the events of last night. Once Mom places cereal, milk, toast and butter on the table, she comes to sit with the rest of us.

Nausea hits me.

"I have to ask you something, Dakota," she says biting on her lip. I can see this is making her uncomfortable, but after everything they heard and saw last night, there's nothing left they don't know.

"Can I ask something first?"

"What is it?"

"The police didn't ask about the underwear I was wearing that night."

"We told them what you told us," Dad responds. "They also said last night, if they need anything more from you, they'll be in touch."

"Okay." I sip on my orange juice, although really, I'm not hungry or thirsty. "What did you want to ask, Mom?"

"Oh God, I don't know how to ask this, but we need to know what we're dealing with and how we're going to handle the situation." I frown and my mind immediately dreads whatever question she's going to ask. "Have you had your period?"

My mind snaps.

Oh my God. My heart shatters.

I look down to my glass of orange juice, broken and humiliated even further. "We need to know, Dakota so we can decide what the next step is *if* you are." My hands go to my stomach, resting on it protectively. I don't know what I'd do if I was faced with having to deal with yet another obstacle. I simply don't know.

I shake my head. "I've had my period twice since that night," I whisper while still looking at the inoffensive glass of orange juice. There's a collective sigh around the table. I look up to find Mom weeping quietly, and Dad gives me a weak, broken smile. I can tell he's trying to show me unwavering strength. But when you think your daughter could either have contracted a disease, or become pregnant as a result of an assault, I'm sure that's enough to break even the mightiest of heroes.

"Okay," Mom says, nodding her head. "Okay."

Sam's hand finds mine and she links our fingers, squeezing me. "Dad, why aren't you at work?" I ask curiously.

"Because without this," he makes a circular movement around the table, "My life is not worth living. My family is the most important thing in the world to me. Your welfare, all of yours, comes before work."

"Dad, what if they fire you?" Sam asks with deep concern in her voice.

"I called my boss and told him I need some time off for my family. I've got some time up my sleeve, and I told him I need to take some of it."

"Phew," I breathe. "I'm sorry to make you use your leave, Dad."

"Don't be. I'm not."

"I did some research last night and again early this morning. I've managed to get you an appointment with a counselor today. She's a woman, her name is Tara, and she specializes in traumas like yours. I called her this morning, hoping to get her early and she said she had a cancellation late last night and can fit you in at four this afternoon."

"Already? It's too soon." I don't want to go. I don't want to be on display and prodded by everyone. I already feel like I'm a caged animal, slowly creeping back and forth waiting for the door to open so I can run for freedom.

"It's not too soon, Dakota. We need to get you help so we can all— especially you—start processing and dealing with it. Most importantly, you need to heal. This is the only way to move forward."

"I don't need it. You can all help me. I don't need a damn shrink!" I protest angrily.

Mom takes a deep breath and looks me straight in the eyes. "Okay, I want to ask you something."

"What is it?" I try and calm down.

"Remember with the last car we had and it broke down? It was that really hot day, I had groceries in the back and it wouldn't start. We had to get it towed to the mechanic."

"I remember that," I say.

"Did Dad or I try to fix it?"

"Well, no. You don't know anything about cars."

"That's right. We don't know anything about cars, which is why we leave these things to people who've studied and do have the knowledge. It's exactly the same with the counselor, Dakota. She's studied, and knows how to help you move forward. All we can do . . ." Mom points to herself, Sam, and Dad, " . . . is support you and be here for you when you need to cry, when you need to scream, and when you simply need us."

I nod my head in understanding. When Mom breaks it down like that, she's right. If I don't get the proper help now, I may not be able to move on with my future. I might get stuck in the past, always full of resentment and hate that may end up ruining my life.

"I get it," I say. "And I'll go wherever you need me to go."

Mom leans over and offers me her hand. Letting go of Sam, I reach across and take it. "We need to go to the doctor first, Dakota. And that appointment is at two."

I turn to look at the clock and see it's nearing midday. "Okay. I might go lie down for a while before we go. I'm feeling flat." *Weak*.

"Okay, darling. I'll come wake you up in about an hour."

I head into my room, and grab my phone from my table. Opening it up I see there are numerous messages and phone calls from Reece. They all have the same general theme of, 'is everything okay?.' Each message gets more desperate, and every voicemail has the same urgency as his messages.

I dial his number and he picks up on the fourth ring. "Dakota, are you okay?" he asks in a panic.

"Yeah," I sigh as I lie back on my bed.

"What's happened? Are you safe? Are you okay? Your dad looked really angry yesterday and I was calling because I wanted to make sure you're okay."

"Yeah, I'm okay." My voice is flat and lifeless. "They know."

I wait for Reece to take in what I said. It takes him an entire minute before he finally comprehends my comment. "Shit. How? What happened?"

"Someone at Dad's work told him." I have to be careful what I say, because the police are investigating it and I can't say much in case I slip up and hinder the process. "Anyway, I can't say much, but I'm safe, and I'm okay."

"Well." He clicks his tongue to the roof his mouth, and then grumbles something inaudible. "As long as you're okay. Can I see you today?"

"I can't today, Reece. I really don't feel like I have the energy for company, and besides there are some things going on here."

"What? Maybe I can help."

"Trust me, if I could tell you, I would, but I can't."

"Dakota, please."

"Don't ask me to do something I can't. I promise you, Reece, I'm okay and my family is looking after me. Maybe on the weekend you can come over if you still want to."

"Of course I want to," he replies with frustration in his voice.

"Can we talk tomorrow? Seriously my head is pounding and I need to have a rest before I go to my first appointment."

"What's the appointment for?"

Crap. I don't want to tell him. "Just a thing."

Frustrated he mumbles more into the phone. "One day, will you tell me?"

"When I can, then yes. Of course I will."

"Okay. Can you do me a favor?"

"What would you like?"

"I'm worried about you, Dakota. I know you said your parents are looking after you and of course I trust you, but can you message me later on? It makes me smile when I see your number, and it settles me down too."

Aw, how damn sweet. "Sure, I'll message you later."

"Bye."

"Bye." Looking up at my ceiling, I watch as the ceiling fan goes slowly around and around. I give myself over to the exhaustion clinging to my body. The blades of the fan make a soothing sound as they cut through the air. My eyes drift shut, and I fall asleep.

CHAPTER 39

"YOU'LL FEEL A small sting and the needle will be in," our Doctor says as he's inserting the needle.

"I hate needles," I say to Mom, who's sitting beside me watching our doctor take blood.

"I don't know of many people who enjoy them," he says with a chuckle. "My daughter, she's twenty-three, and still she hates them. But you'd never know, because she's got tattoos everywhere. I once asked her why those needles are okay, but these aren't. You know what she said, Dakota?"

"No," I answer while breathing through this stupid blood test. "What did she say?"

"She said, at least with tattoo machines, they end up giving you something pretty on your skin. These needles do nothing to make you feel nice."

"That can be argued. Because sometimes you need an antibiotic and the only way you can get it is through a needle, which in turn, eventually makes you feel nice . . . well normal."

"You should have this argument with my daughter, Dakota. Right, I'm done. That didn't hurt did it?"

I look over and he applies pressure with a cotton ball, and puts a Band-Aid over it. "That was painless." I smile, rolling down the sleeve of my lightweight sweater.

"Now, about the HIV test. It's slightly different to the tests for other sexually transmitted diseases. HIV has a longer incubation period, and it can take up to six months for it to show up in a test, which means you'll need to be tested again in two months, then two months later, and again two months after that."

"Six months?" I sigh. "Really? That long?"

"It's a long process, and unfortunately there are no shortcuts. I suggest you refrain from any sexual activity." I cringe and look away. "The blood system tries to fight any disease by making antibodies to it. The test looks for those antibodies and that process can take anywhere from two weeks to six months to get results. In the meantime, try to remain positive, Dakota."

With the hand I've been dealt, I don't know if I'm going to die an early death, or if I'm going to live to a ripe old age. He's telling me to remain positive. How am I supposed to stay positive when I have to live the next six months worrying I may have a disease that could kill me?

"If I do have it, can I infect someone else?" I ask, afraid to hear the answer.

"The only way HIV can be spread is by the exchange of body fluids, most likely through sex. And Dakota, even if you do have HIV, the drugs these days are so much more advanced than what they were twenty years ago. People are living a lot longer and healthier." I snarl at his word 'healthier.' "Trust me, we'll get through this."

I've got my head down, feeling self-pity and sorrow. I think I'm allowed to; this situation is horrendous. No one should ever go through this.

"Because the rape happened over two months ago, I won't do a rape kit on you since all the evidence has been washed away now. But have you had any itching, or burning when you go to the bathroom?" I cringe when he says the 'R' word.

"No, nothing."

"Any discharge or odor?"

"Nothing." *Yuck.*

"And you've done a pregnancy test?"

"No, but I've had my period twice since."

"That's great. We'll still do the blood test to confirm you're not."

"But I've had my period," I protest. "I can't be pregnant. I've had it twice."

"Usually, we'd say you're fine and that's okay. We'll just make sure."

"So I could be pregnant?" God help me, I can't cope.

"Very unlikely. But there have been rare times where the woman will continue having a light period throughout her pregnancy."

"You have to be kidding me. How long do I have to wait for those results?"

"I'll get the results for the pregnancy test back tomorrow."

"Thank you," I say with a deep sigh. "At least I'll know something quickly."

"Do either of you have any questions for me?" I shake my head, and look over to Mom. She shakes her head too.

"Thank you for seeing us today. Shall we make an appointment for tomorrow on the way out?" Mom asks.

"Yes, make it for later in the day though. I'm not sure what time I'll have the results back and I don't want you to have to sit here, waiting. It's only a matter of them sending it through electronically, but it depends on the backlog of work they have."

"Okay, well we'll see you tomorrow. Bye." I stand and press the button on the bottom of my phone. It flicks to life and the time brightens up the screen. We have about twenty minutes before my appointment with the counselor.

We leave the doctor's office and I'm suddenly overcome with anxiety. Mom drives to the counselor's office. She's chatting, but I can tell she's just trying to distract me. She laughs nervously over something she's said, and I look over to her, not really having heard a word she's spoken.

She smiles at me, and reaches across the center console to hold my hand. She gives it a small squeeze and lets go, returning her hand to the steering wheel. We head to the opposite side of town, and Mom easily finds the street thanks to her navigation unit.

We pull up outside an older-style home in a residential neighborhood. It has clean, crisp, white stucco on the outside with ocean blue window shutters. The house is well maintained with a lush green garden running along the length of the house, only interrupted by the five steps leading up to the porch.

"We're here," Mom needlessly points out as she turns and watches my reaction.

"It's cute," I answer, unbuckling my seatbelt.

Mom rubs her hands together, then tucks some hair behind her ear. She's nervous; this is obvious. But I'm not sure if she's anxious for me, or for another reason.

Hesitating, I open the car door, taking a minute to look at the cute, inviting house. Mom moves first toward the steps, and I follow close behind. As we approach I notice the gold plaque on the side wall near the door. It's small and not intimidating, but it lists Tara's full name, and what she specializes in. There's a lot of letters in her title separated by a lot of commas, so I can only imagine the amount of training she's had.

Mom stands to the side and waits for me to open the door. I reach out and grab the handle, turning it and walking through to a welcoming, light blue waiting room. There are a couple of sofas and four single chairs lining the L-shaped waiting room. To the left is a small, yet organized white desk with an older lady sitting behind it.

"Hello, dear," she says with a nice, warm smile on her face.

"Um, hi. My mom and I are here to see Tara. We have an appointment. My name's Dakota Bennett."

"Oh, yes. Now Mrs. Bennett, there's some paperwork for you to fill in. Here you go." She hands Mom a folder and a pen and indicates she can sit anywhere and fill it out. "Tara won't be long."

"Thank you," Mom and I reply in unison.

We sit down and I can't help but look around the waiting room nervously. My entire body is tense, nerves thrumming while I try to distract myself in the waiting room, I can't help but feel anxious. Nausea makes an appearance and I concentrate on my breathing to push the sick feeling aside.

I pick up an old, dated magazine and flick through it but nothing holds my attention for long.

"Dakota?" An older lady stands in front of me and smiles warmly. She has blonde hair, thick –black rimmed- glasses and a gentle, caring smile. "I'm Tara, would you like to come in?" I look to Mom, petrified. Tara catches my panicked gaze and adds, "Would you like your mom to come in too?"

"Yes please. Is that okay, Mom?"

"Of course, honey. Anything you need." Mom hands the completed paperwork to the lady at the front desk, and we all follow Tara into a room.

"Please, sit wherever you'll be most comfortable." She sweeps her hand across the room indicating any of the seating available.

Mom and I sit in two side-by-side armchairs. I take in Tara's appearance. She's older but dressed quite casually, in a t-shirt, jeans and black slip-on shoes.

"Your mom called me late yesterday and explained the reason you're here." I nod my head. "Do you want to be here, Dakota?"

What an odd and strange question. But I take the time to really think about it, I stare out the window and see a large tree shading us from the late afternoon sun. "At first, no," I answer honestly. "I didn't want anyone to know, and I didn't think I needed help."

"You didn't think you needed help?"

"Let me correct myself. I mean, I didn't think I needed help beyond what my family can provide."

"But now?"

"Now I think it's dangerous for me *not* to get help."

"Can you explain that to me?" She picks up a notebook and begins to scribble. "Why do you think it would be dangerous?"

"I've held this secret for months, and forced my younger sister to keep it too. I figured I'd eventually bury it so deep inside that I'd forget about it. But I suppose you can never forget something like that. I'm afraid it'll affect any relationship I may have in the future."

"How old is your sister?"

"Sam's fourteen."

"And how do you feel now knowing this is no longer a secret, particularly from your parents?"

"A little relieved. When it first happened, I did everything possible so no one would find out. Then I convinced myself that it was too late to say anything. And I also convinced myself that no one would believe me, or they'd think I'd been drinking and deserved it."

"Before you were raped." Every hair on my body stands to attention when she says it so bluntly. My breath gets caught and I shiver with revulsion at myself. "Is that what you thought when you heard of anyone being raped? They'd been drinking and deserved it?"

"I've never considered it before. I don't think I ever paid attention." I cross my legs on the chair and lean back so I'm comfortable.

"So this happened at your prom, right?" I nod my head. "And your parents found out yesterday?" I nod my head again. "What happened when they found out?"

"I don't understand the question."

She places the book on her lap and steeples her fingers together, placing the tips to her mouth. "Tell me how your parents found out."

"Someone at his work showed my Dad a photo from social media. His son was added to a group yesterday that shared photos of me." I gulp. "Explicit photos of me from that night. His son recognized me from a company picnic, he showed his dad, who showed my dad."

"Were you frightened, relieved, or indifferent? There was probably something running through your mind. Can you remember?"

"I was definitely scared, because I was worried that Mom and Dad wouldn't believe me." Mom reaches out and rubs her hand up and down my back. "At first they thought I'd had sex and let the other person take pictures, but when I told them the truth, they were both as horrified to hear it as I was to say it."

"Then what happened?" She picks up her pen and notebook and continues jotting down notes.

"There were a lot of tears, explanations, and then there was the police."

"The police are firmly involved?" I nod my head. "Okay, we'll get back to that, but right now, I want to know how you're feeling."

I look down at my fingers and begin picking at my nails. I push the cuticles back on every finger, while my leg twitches beneath my body. Eventually I find the courage to answer her. "I don't know how I feel. Maybe the best way to describe me is numb. I'm numb to what happened that night, I'm numb to the blood test I had an hour ago to see if I have a sexually transmitted disease or if I'm pregnant. I'm even numb to you. I'm numb to sitting in here, and numb to talking. My body is aching, my heart has been ripped out, stomped on and shoved back in while it's only partially working. I don't think I have any more tears left, and my head is splitting in two from a headache I've had ever since it all came out. I can't say anything else but I'm numb."

"I think your explanation is quite beautiful." She jots down more notes.

I stare out the window, and listen to everything Tara has to say.

We're only skimming over everything, and when she asks me to tell her what I remember of that night, I break down. I thought I had no more tears left, but as it turns out, I have plenty. The session seems to go on forever and toward the end of it, she has me looking at the situation differently, analyzing it.

We leave the office after making another appointment on Monday, three days away. Tara wants me to try some meditation techniques to help me relax when everything gets to be too much. She also said this weekend will probably be the worst for me because everything's coming back up to the surface.

We walk out of her office and I'm a mess. My tears won't stop, my head is banging loudly and my body is aching. All I want to do is go home, crawl into bed and forget about the world.

Forget about this entire chaotic situation and forget how one degrading night changed my entire life.

CHAPTER 40

THESE LAST FEW days have been a blur. Night and day blend into each other, with no clear distinction separating the two. My appetite has been lost, and it seems all I do is cry.

Today is Sunday, and tomorrow is my next appointment with Tara. She pushed me on Friday. She made me look at the severity of the situation, and dragged parts of me out that I had managed to bury deep. It feels as if I've run a marathon with no training. My body is aching, it's sore and it holds so much tension.

We went back to the doctor's office late yesterday, and he confirmed I wasn't pregnant. I breathed a big sigh of relief. Now begins the long, drawn-out, and incredibly painful process of waiting to find out if my HIV tests come back negative.

"Sweetheart, you need to get out of bed and eat something," Mom says gently as she sits on the edge of my bed and rubs circles on my back.

"I'm not hungry," I reply, my back to her as I stare at the blank, pale yellow wall.

She sighs, and I can tell she's frustrated with me. Truthfully, *I'm* frustrated with me. I simply can't help it. Something inside of me is broken. It's collapsed the carefully built wall that kept me from having to face things, and now I can't seem to rebuild it.

"I don't care," her tone changes into something more assertive. "You're going to get up and come out to the kitchen where I'll make you an omelet. Then you're going to call Sophie and have her come over so you can talk with her. She's been calling every day, and she sounds worried. Have you talked to her?"

"I sent her a text and told her I was okay."

"But you're not okay, Dakota. You're far from it. It's going to be hard to overcome this, and it's something you're never going to forget. But we're here for you, all of us. Reece called this morning and asked if he can come and see you because he said you're brushing him off. Sophie's worried. We're all worried. Right now, this is the eye of the storm and it may last another year before you can feel the sunlight. Don't shut everyone out, sweetheart, because we need you as much as you need us." Mom stops rubbing my back, leans over and kisses my forehead, then leaves me to my own thoughts.

I wipe the tears away, and swallow down the lump that's been sitting in my throat for the last few days. Right now, it all feels so hopeless. I feel worthless, as if I don't belong. Not because of the people around me, but because *he's* made me feel this way. Whoever *he* is. Does he even think about the devastation he's caused me? I doubt it.

I throw back my covers, and force myself out of bed. I don't even look at my reflection because I know I won't like what I see. Walking over to my bedroom window, I roll the blinds up and let the sun filter into my room. I can't continue to live in darkness, even though that's exactly what I want to do.

Opening my door, I head out to the kitchen where the delicious aroma of fresh cooked eggs fills the entire room. Sitting down at the breakfast bar, I lean my elbows on the counter and watch Mom flutter around the kitchen. She hasn't realized I'm here yet, and she's quietly humming a sad tune to herself.

Sam comes in, sees me and a big smile spreads across her face. She sits beside me and looks at me. "I'm happy to have you back," she says.

Mom startles and turns around with the spatula in her hands. She looks at me, then at Sam and smiles. She doesn't need to say anything. Seeing us together makes her proud. It's obvious by the way she pulls her shoulders back and continues cooking. "I'm making omelets," she announces and turns back to continue.

Sam leans in and throws her arms around me. She embraces me tightly. She sniffs and declares, "You need a shower."

I push her away, rolling my eyes and shaking my head. "You did not just say that."

"Hey, you're a little heavy on the nose. Seriously, I'd suggest a shower." She waves her hand in front of her nose dramatizing my odor, but she's smiling at the same time.

"Alright, smart-ass, I'll go after I have something to eat."

"Phew, save us all having to follow you around with perfume." She giggles to herself.

Mom chuckles quietly from where she's standing in front of the oven. "Hey, not you too," I say to Mom.

She throws her hands up and chuckles again. "What can I say, your sister has a point, you're a bit wafty." She too fans her nose with her hand.

"Alright, alright. I'll get in the shower after my omelet. I'm thinking, I might ask Reece and Sophie to come over today, if that's okay?"

"If what's okay?" Dad comes in carrying his tablet.

"For me to ask Reece and Sophie to come over."

"Can I ask Taylor?" Sam asks.

"Yes to both of you," Dad answers as he sits on the other side of Sam. He leans in, gives her a kiss then picks his tablet up.

When we finish eating, Sam helps Mom in the kitchen and I go into my room to call Sophie. "Hi, how are you?" she asks.

"I've been better."

"How are your parents? Are they okay?"

"Yeah. I started counseling and it's really knocked me around. I had my first session on Friday. It's just hard, you know?"

"You're lucky, Dakota, your parents support you," she says wistfully.

"I know your mom would too if you told her."

"Too late for that now. It's been over a year, I've learnt to deal with it."

"Like I was dealing with it? Just push it down and hope it never surfaces again?"

"Yes," she agrees with me. "As far down as I can push it."

Man, I feel sorry for Sophie. She hasn't told anyone, except for me. I know how hard it is to open up. And although I feel like death now, I'm still grateful Mom and Dad know. "Hey, want to come over today? We only have a week of vacation left before we head back to school. And before we know it it'll be fall and we won't be able to use the pool."

"Oh man, I really want to say yes, but Mom needs some help around here today. She's been at work since five this morning, so I want to clean up, and put on a nice dinner for her, you know? It's the least I can do considering she works so hard."

"Hey, yeah, I get it. Okay, well how about later this week?"

"Yeah, I'll ask Mom what day she can bring me over."

"Cool, let me know. I'm gonna call Reece and see if he wants to come over."

"Okay, have fun," she happily chirps.

"See ya." I dial Reece's number and he answers the phone yelling at Luke. "Dakota, I'm so glad you called," he huffs. "I've been worried about you. Are you okay?"

"Yeah, I'm okay. I've been trying to get my head around everything, you know?"

"Yeah, I hear ya. I've been tempted to come over every day since your dad kicked us out. Even drove past a few times hoping you would be out front." *Aw.* "I'm really worried about you," he whispers into the phone, *and it melts my heart.*

"Do you want to come over today?"

I don't even finish the sentence before he replies, "Yes! Can I come now?"

"Give me half an hour, I still have to have a shower and stuff."

"Okay, I'll be there in half an hour." I smile because he sounds so enthusiastic. "Dakota?" he calls before we hang up.

"Yeah?"

"I've missed you." He hangs up quickly, not letting me respond. I'm not even sure now if that's what he said. He spoke so fast that I could be mistaking it for something else.

I put my phone down, and head into the shower.

I'm sitting out in the back garden, soaking up some sun. Reece hasn't come yet, but that's okay. It gives me a minute to appreciate the glory of the sun's warm rays, beaming down on me. Taylor and Sam are inside watching a movie with Mom and Dad while I sit out here, enjoying the solitude.

The shower certainly helped, because it lifted my mood from deep and wounded to a realization that I'm going to be okay.

"Hi there, beautiful," Reece says as he comes into the backyard from inside the house.

I turn to see him walking toward me in jeans and a t-shirt. His broad shoulders stretch the t-shirt, and make him look as if he's only gotten back from bench pressing at the gym. My eyes take him in, and I can't help but think how beautiful he actually is.

"Hi," I say about to stand to greet him.

"Don't get up. I'll come to you." He leans down and kisses my forehead then sits on the lounge beside me. "How have you been?" he casually asks.

"I'm okay. The counseling session really kicked me in the ass. Ever heard the saying, feeling like you've been put through the emotional wringer?" He nods. "That's how I've been feeling."

"It's got to be tough having to face it all again."

"You have no idea, Reece. But I can't help but wonder how *he* does it. Whoever did this to me did it without a conscience. I mean, how can he live with himself? I'm struggling, really I am. Most of the time I feel ashamed and humiliated, then other times I feel worthless. Like I wasn't even worth asking permission to have sex with me. And then there are times I start thinking 'how dare he?.' How dare he do this to me and not give a shit about how I'm affected! He's ruined my life, ruined me, and he gets away with it? That's not fair. He shouldn't be able to do this and walk away with no repercussions."

"You're right. And clearly he's not a man, not even an animal. He's a predator."

"I'm really nervous about going to school next week and having to face everyone. I'm not sure I can handle the whispers or the stares or even the shaming they're going to put me through."

"Why would they shame you?"

I flick Reece a look of disbelief, my brows scrunched together as I shake my head. "You can't be serious. Everyone will have seen the pictures from that group. He's not only humiliated me by doing what he did, he's continuing to embarrass me by posting photos of me everywhere on social media. How degrading for my Dad to have a co-worker approach him and say his son has been added to a group that's showing explicit pictures of me."

"Who's the admin of the group?"

"Apparently someone who has no profile information."

"How were they not taken down? There are rules and administrators who looks after these sorts of things on social media. I posted a picture last year of me flipping someone the bird and it got reported as soon I posted it. So how is it possible this group hasn't been reported or taken down?"

"I don't know if it has, and I don't want to look. But Dad's co-worker said he went online and took screen shots to show Dad. He also said there were hundreds of members added by the admin.

"The point is, he ruined me, Reece. He took something which wasn't offered to him. Even now I have to wait for six months to find out if I'll have a life sentence with a disease I'll never be able to get rid of. Not only that, he continues to make my world crumble by uploading photos *he* took. I'm tired, Reece. Tired of hiding, but also tired of having to face the rumors, the stares, and whatever else is going to happen when we get back to school."

Reece huffs and pinches the bridge of his nose. "I can't imagine how you must be feeling."

"It's a rollercoaster. One moment I think I'm going to be okay, then something pushes me back into isolation and and makes me want to hide myself away from everyone. The next minute I'm okay again. I'm so grateful for my family, and you, and Sophie. Without you guys I don't know where I'd be."

"Can I hold you, Dakota?" he asks shyly. It's the first time I've seen him hesitant. I nod and sit up on the lounger. He moves and sits beside me, then brings me in nice and close to him. "I'm sorry you have to deal with this. But you've got me to help you through it. You can always count on me. All you need to do is call me and I'll be here in a heartbeat."

"Thank you." I close my eyes and get lost in his comfort. "For now, all I need is for you to hold me."

"I'm never letting you go." He tightens his arms around me. I feel his warmth, and how protective he is of me. I love the feel of his arms around me. It's comforting and soothing.

"Thank you," I whisper.

"Who do you want for math this year?" he asks after a few minutes.

"I can tell you who I don't want—Mr. C. He gives me the creeps, just the way he pops up all the time and watches us. There's something so wrong about him. The night of the prom, when I started feeling light-headed, I went to the bathroom to splash water on my face and as soon as I came out he was there waiting for me. It's almost like he knew what was happening to me."

"You've never liked him. Do you think it could be him?"

"At this stage, I have no idea who it is. It could be him, I mean he's in the perfect position to do something like that. He's always around, and he's got beady eyes that look at everyone. It feels like he's always checking me out."

"Have you told anyone how he makes you feel or that it could be him who drugged you?"

Crap, I promised I wouldn't tell anyone about the police, Reece included. "I told my parents," I lie. I need to protect myself and I also need to protect the work the police are doing. If Mr. C did do this to me, and they have a lead, and if he gets wind of it, he may disappear and he'll never be caught. I just have to pretend like everything is normal.

"As long as someone knows, maybe they can do something with that information. Please do me a favor. Whatever you remember just promise me you'll tell someone. Even if it's only me."

"I promise. But nothing more is coming to me. I've had a few dreams, but nothing new."

His arms around me reassure me and tell me how everything will be okay. It's not the words he speaks, but his actions that give me comfort. My life feels different . . . fuller, enriched from the moment we took our friendship to something deeper.

CHAPTER 41

"DAKOTA, TRACEY CALLED and she and Andrea are on their way over," Mom says.

It's Wednesday afternoon, only a few days before school starts again. I've been having intense counseling sessions with Tara and they seem just as difficult as when we started. The only difference is I don't feel quite as overwhelmed and hopeless when I leave her office. I have another session with her later today. Friday was difficult. It hit me hard and had me questioning everything about myself, but more specifically everything I believed about the world.

I've lost faith in my self-worth and my ability to judge people. If someone I know can slip something in my drink, in a public place, use me so badly—and get away with it—then what chance do I have? *David versus Goliath*. More like an ant versus the universe.

Mom announces that the detectives are on their way and it causes a negative reaction within me. A huge part of me doesn't want to know what they have to say. I'm anticipating them saying something like, 'Sorry, Dakota. We've done all we can, and we're closing the case.' That would be the worst possible scenario. But with the statistics I've been researching, it's also the most likely. If that does happen, what was the point of me stepping up and telling the world what happened to me? No good would come of it, only pain and heartache for all involved.

Of course, the best possible outcome would be for them to tell me they know who sexually assaulted me and they've arrested him. They may ask me to testify when it goes to trial.

But that brings another deluge of emotions. Great, they caught him . . . shit, I have to testify and relive the whole ordeal. Not only relive it, but tell twelve strangers what he did to me, dredge up a painful and humiliating event all so they can decide what will happen to him.

Then there's the *other* worst possible scenario. Me going through an emotional trial, losing days or maybe even weeks of school, *of my life*, because he's screwed me so badly on an emotional level that I'll have no choice but to hide at home in humiliation and hope the world swallows me whole.

"Oh God," I whisper to Mom.

We're in the kitchen, staring blankly at each other, anticipating the arrival of the police officers. At every sound, we look toward the door. Everything in my body is wound tight, and it's hard to keep from breaking down, falling apart and losing hope.

"They're here," Dad says coming into the kitchen.

"No matter what they say, stay strong. We're here for you. You know that, right?" Mom affirms, gripping my hands in hers. I nod. I can't say anything because I've lost the ability to comprehend and reply.

Anxiety is ripping through me. It has put its tap shoes on and is dancing all over my heart. My muscles tense, all of them bunching around my shoulders and the back of my neck. A splitting pain relentlessly stabs at the base of my head.

"Sweetheart," Dad says dropping his arm around my shoulders and looks at me with a kind smile.

I turn to him, tears a threatening to spill. But I work my ass off to keep them at bay. *I will not crack, I will not crack, I. Will. Not. Crack.*

There's a knock on the door. I look at Mom, whose own demons are just barely controlled. Dad's jaw is tight and his eyes are hard as steel. He lets go of me and walks over to open the door.

Be brave, Dakota.

"Detective Young, Detective Miller," he greets them as they come into the house.

"Tracey and Andrea will do," Tracey says, smiling at Dad.

She comes further into the house and her eyes land on mine. It's true what they say. Police have a certain way about them. Their eyes are suspicious of everything around them. Andrea gives me a warm smile, but I notice exactly how watchful her eyes are too.

"How are you, Dakota?" Andrea asks as she makes her way over to me.

I weakly smile, because at this moment I can barely think let alone speak.

Be brave, I repeat to myself.

"We're doing okay," Mom thankfully answers for me while her hands rest on my shoulders.

"May we have a seat?" Tracey asks.

You can do this, Dakota. No matter what the result is, I have to be strong. I have to accept whatever they're going to say. I have to push hard and deal with it.

"Please do," Dad says and sits opposite Tracey and Andrea. "Dakota," he calls and indicates for me to sit beside him.

Timidly, I make my way over to the sofa, and sit beside Dad. I'm so close, there's almost no distance between us. Dad swings his arm over my shoulder, and brings me into his comfort.

"How've things been?" Tracey asks looking straight at me.

Mom opens her mouth to answer for me, but I hold my hand up for her to stop. "It's been hard. There's a struggle inside my head every minute of the day."

"Okay. Maybe what I have to say may help you deal with it a little better." She smiles and looks to Andrea who gives her a small nod. "We came here today because we want you to know we have a solid lead."

The room remains quiet, giving me a few seconds to let the words resonate and actually sink in.

Oh God. They have a lead.

"Sweetheart, are you okay?" Dad asks looking at me, his face rapidly draining of color. Blinking, I stare at Dad. *Did he speak?* "Sweetheart." A searing pain rips behind my left eye and I cringe away. "Get some tissues!" Dad calls to Mom.

Tissues? Who needs tissues? I jump off the sofa to run into the kitchen for tissues, but Dad yanks me back down to the sofa.

The two detectives are staring at me, and Mom springs to her feet in a panic, running to the kitchen.

"What's going on?" I ask while looking around the room, trying to see who's hurt. The intense pain behind my eye almost cripples me, sending me crashing into the back of the sofa. "Oh God," I cry, clutching at my eye.

"What's going on?" Mom cries while shoving a tissue box in Dad's lap and tilting my head forward. She holds tissues to my nose, and it's then I notice the deep, crimson liquid pouring out of my nose.

"What's happening?" I whisper, unsure as to why my head's being so relentless in its blistering pain, and why my nose is bleeding so profusely.

"Look at her hands and neck. Her hands are shaking, and a rash has broken out on her neck," Andrea says.

I'm looking around me, trying to see who they're talking about, but all eyes are on me.

"She's having a panic attack," Tracey states as if she sees them often. *Maybe she does.*

"It's okay, sweetheart, we're right here." Dad wraps his strong arms around, crushes my head to his chest and starts rocking us. Suddenly all the blinds are drawn, and the ceiling fan is cranked up to high. I can hear the familiar whir of the blades cutting through the air.

"Get her some water. Let's calm her down," Andrea says.

Dad's shushing me while rocking back and forth.

Without warning, my shoulders give, my hands unclench and I relax into Dad and his supportive frame.

"It's okay, sweetheart, I've got you." He keeps pressing kisses on my head; light, soothing kisses. The sound of his calming heartbeat acts as a sedative. "Shhh, it's okay, I've got you." My arms wrap around Dad and I hold onto him as tightly as he's holding me.

It takes a while, but everyone settles down. Mom, Tracey and Andrea all sit and turn their gazes to me. "How are you feeling now?" Mom asks.

Peeking out from behind Dad's arm, my eyes travel to all three pairs of eyes. "Embarrassed. I'm not sure what happened."

"Have some water, Dakota, it'll help," Andrea offers.

Dad slightly pushes me, holding onto my shoulders. "Are you okay?" I nod my head and smile. He leans over, grabs the glass of water and hands it to me.

Gulping it down I finally place the glass on the table. "I'm sorry, I can't explain it. I felt okay, but you all went into panic and I didn't know what was happening."

"Your body went into shock, and your mind probably couldn't deal with it, so it stopped processing. That's the likely reason for your reaction and also explains why your nose was bleeding, your neck broke out into a rash and you were trembling," Andrea explains.

"I also had the most bizarre pain in my head. It literally felt as if someone drove an ice pick into it."

"We can come back another day and explain to you what's happening," Tracey offers.

"No! No, I need to hear what it is you've come here to say," I tell them. I *am* strong. I *can* do this.

Find courage, Dakota.

Tracey smiles and nods her head. "You're such a strong girl, Dakota. I'm proud of you." She winks at me. "We came here to tell you how we have a lead. We can't say too much about the investigation, however we're very close in making an arrest."

"Do you think you know who it is? Could this go wrong? Have you got it wrong?" I ask a barrage of questions.

"Go wrong? How so?" Andrea asks singling out only one of my questions.

"Is it possible you've made a mistake, and you'll come back to me and say, 'Sorry, Dakota, but we were wrong and we're actually nowhere near close to catching him.'? Is that a possibility?" I press my hands together nervously.

"We wouldn't be here if we didn't feel confident that we're close to catching the perpetrator. We wouldn't give you false hope, or even tell you unless we were quite sure."

"So you're saying this lead is solid and will most likely lead to an arrest?" I look at them, begging for a yes.

And my hope is answered. "Yes, that's exactly what we're saying," Tracey says.

"Okay." I don't know how to deal with this information, or even how to process it. I take a deep breath and let it out slowly.

I'm not feeling anything. I'm not happy, I'm not sad. I'm indifferent. *Numb*.

"We wanted to stop by and let you know what we can so far. We'll let you get back to your family now, and we'll be in touch when we have more information." Both the detectives leave, and I'm sitting on the sofa, my jeans and t-shirt completely blood soaked and I'm completely immobilized.

"Are you okay?" Dad asks sitting beside me, and Mom opposite.

"I don't feel anything, at all. Nothing. I'm trying to listen to my brain, but there are no thoughts going around. Everything inside me is quiet."

"Quiet?" Mom asks confused by my words.

"Yeah, like I'm detached from what Tracey and Andrea said, kind of like dazed. I don't think their words have sunk in. At least, not yet."

"Maybe that's why you looked so stunned with us when we panicked because of that nose bleed."

"I didn't know my nose was bleeding. And still, even with that." I look down at the red on my hands and on my clothes, and I don't freak out. "Even that . . . I don't have any reaction to it."

"Okay, well let's go get you changed. We have an appointment with Tara in an hour."

"Alright," I answer standing from the sofa. "I'm not sure how I'll do today."

This has been my life since I started with counseling. One moment I'm okay and functioning, and the next I'm a complete and utter mess. Before Friday, I was learning to hide all the hurt, and it was so much easier. Now though, my mind is unsure of what to do or how to respond, so it remains quiet and doesn't respond at all. Instead my body breaks and shows obvious signs of stress.

I go into my room and sit on the bed. I forgot why I'm in here. I look out my window and watch as a bird sits on the sill and looks into my room. It chirps at me, and the happy sound makes me smile.

"Dakota, we have to go," Mom says. "Get changed."

Vacantly I stare at Mom. "Where are we going?" I ask Mom.

"We're going to see Tara, remember?" she smiles but her tone is strained and filled with worry.

"Oh yeah, Tara." I stand and head toward my door.

"Dakota, you need to get changed." Mom's words are slow, and her tone is soft.

"Oh yeah, that's right." I pull out clothes and change, not really sure why I need to. Mom stands at my door, watching me with a careful scrutinizing eye.

"You need to wash your hands and face. Come on. Let's go, clean up."

"Right." Emotionless, I follow Mom. She keeps looking at me over her shoulder, her eyes intently watching me as I numbly follow.

We head into the bathroom, where Mom washes my face and hands then leads me out to the family room. "Are you okay?" she asks.

"Yeah, I guess." *I don't know, I think so.*

Mom takes my hand and leads me out to the car. She helps me put my seatbelt on and then gets in the driver's seat and reverses out of the driveway. "Where are we going?"

"To see Tara."

"That's right."

We get to her office, and I robotically unclick my seatbelt and head inside. Before I know it, I'm sitting on her sofa in her room. I look around me, staring at the beautiful colors. "Are you okay, Dakota?" Tara asks.

I shake my head and close my eyes tight, then reopen them. "What am I doing here?" I ask.

"You've come for your appointment."

"Have I?" She nods her head and jots crazily in her book. "I don't remember how I got here."

"Your mom brought you."

"I know that. But I don't remember actually driving here or even how I got in your office."

"You've suffered a major trauma today, Dakota. These past few days have pushed you beyond what you can handle. This is your mind's way of protecting itself."

"You sound like Andrea. She said the same thing."

"Tell me what's happened today? What did you have for breakfast?"

I stare at her, not really knowing how to respond.

Mom starts talking, running through the events of the day. I listen intently, because I can't recall any of the events Mom's recounting, except when she gets to Tracey and Andrea's visit.

Everything else is hazy, unclear and jumbled. Tara listens to Mom, her head nodding, and her hand furiously writing.

Tara turns to me and asks, "How are you feeling about the visit from the police?" I shrug my shoulders. "About the information they gave you?" Again, I shrug. "Okay, this is what I think is happening, and in my opinion the best way to handle it. You're in auto-pilot mode. Your mind doesn't want to cooperate with you because it's received information that it doesn't know how to deal with. At some stage over the next few hours, I suspect you're going to break down."

Did she say break down? As in cry? I can't cry anymore, I don't *want* to cry anymore.

She turns to Mom and talks to her, I try to listen, but I'm struggling with comprehending everything.

Before I know it, Mom's leading me to our car, strapping me in, and we drive home. The roads look different, but kind of similar too. Mom pulls into the driveway, and helps me out. I feel like a zombie, walking because I'm lead to do so. Breathing because I have to.

"Dakota, how are you, sweetheart?" Dad asks when I come into the family room.

"Good," I answer in a monotone.

Dad's eyes go to Mom, and he looks surprised by whatever she's saying to him.

Sam comes in and throws an arm over my shoulder. "Hey, big sis."

"Hey," I respond in the same dead voice.

Sam slowly removes her hand as she steps away from me. "Mom?" she questions. "What's going on?"

"Pick a movie, Sam, then come in the kitchen and help me with dinner. Dakota, here you go." She hooks our arms together and leads me to the sofa. "We'll put a movie on for you and Dad."

"Okay." I feel nothing. Empty. *Dead.* Sitting on the sofa my back is rigid, my hands are in my lap and my feet firmly planted on the ground.

"Lean back, enjoy the movie," Dad says encouraging me to be more comfortable.

"Okay." I stay in the same position.

The movie starts, and although I'm watching it, I'm not really watching it. It's playing; I can hear music, people talking, names appearing on the screen, but I have no clue as to what's happening. "I liked that part," Dad says and taps me on the shoulder.

"Okay," I respond.

There's chatter going on in the house, I can hear Mom and Sam talking in the kitchen. I try to focus in on what they're saying, but all I hear is white noise. I *know* they're talking, but there's no way I can concentrate enough for the noise to make sense.

I keep watching the movie, trying to understand what's happening. It's not like I'm trying to be removed from everything and everyone, I'm simply struggling to finding an edge to hold on to.

I'm lost.

The screen goes black and Dad stands, turning it off.

Did something happen? Have we had a blackout? I stare at Dad, waiting for him to tell me what's happening. "Dinner, Dakota. Did you like that movie?"

Crinkling my forehead I try and remember what film was even playing. "Yeah," I answer though truthfully, I have no idea what's happening.

"Come on." Dad holds his hand out to me, and I look at it, trying to figure out what his gesture means. "Dakota," he says in a low voice.

"Yeah, Dad?"

"Take my hand."

"Oh, right."

He pulls me up and we walk to the dining table where bowls with food have been set. I sit down and stare at the food. *It's so beige.* I can't even identify what it is. "What is it?" I ask.

"It's spicy chicken and rice, one of your favorites," Mom answers.

"Right," I respond. I can't see the rice or the chicken. It looks like nothing, like mush. Picking my fork up, I get some food on it and lift it to my mouth. It tastes like beige would. Bland, tasteless, dull. I go back for another bite, and experience the same lack of flavor.

"Whoa, this is hot," Dad complains and reaches for his glass of water.

I keep eating, but still can't taste anything. Nothing's being absorbed into my mind.

I lift my fork and my hand stills on its own. Dropping the cutlery, it bangs against the bowl. "Oh my God," I whisper.

And it hits me.

Hard.

"They have a solid lead," I say looking at Mom, Dad and Sam.

Dad puts his fork down, and clasps my shaking hand. "Yes, honey. They have a solid lead," he confirms.

"They have a solid lead," I repeat.

Visions of me on the witness stand, telling everyone what happened to me play on a continuous loop in my mind. Every detail being described for the world to hear. Details even I don't know, while the perpetrator tells the world what he did to others, to *me.*

"Oh my God." My mouth falls open and my body shivers while ice creeps through my veins. "It's going to get worse before it gets better."

I look to Mom, hoping she'll say no, but instead she's nodding her head. "I'm afraid it will," she confirms my nightmare.

"But we're all here to support you," Dad adds.

"All of us," Sam says. "We're all here."

The right side of my head starts pounding. It's making the connection to everything all at once, and it's hurting because of the overload of emotions and information. Standing I say, "I need to lie down." I head in the direction of my room, pull back the covers and collapse into bed. I have no more tears to shed, no more fight inside me. I just need to close my eyes and sleep.

Maybe I'll be lucky, and never wake.

CHAPTER 42

"DAKOTA?" I HEAR someone calling me. "Dakota." Someone puts their hand on my shoulder and gently nudges at me, waking me from my sleep.

"Yeah?" I answer, my voice is croaky and tight.

"Come on, you have to get up," he says. But *he* doesn't sound like Dad.

I turn my head, looking to see who's in my room, and it's Reece. "What are you doing here?" I ask.

"I've come to see how you are."

I turn my body so I'm facing him, and bury myself further inside my blanket. I know my breath must smell, and my hair is a mess. I don't want Reece to see me like this. He tilts his head so he's looking at me, and slowly moves his hand to smooth my hair back. "You look comfortable, I almost feel guilty for waking you."

"So you should, because I'm *very* comfortable."

"I said 'almost,' which means I don't feel guilty at all. Come on, you need to get up and changed."

"I'm not going anywhere, Reece. I don't feel like doing anything."

"Huh, well you're all out of luck. Up you get." He stands and puts his hands on his waist. "I'm giving you ten minutes to get up and changed, after that I can't guarantee my actions."

"What's that supposed to mean?"

"It means, I could come in here and tickle you, or get your mom to tip water over your head. Or better yet, I could ask Sam to sit on your head."

"Alright, alright I'll get up."

"Nine minutes and fifty-five seconds."

"Get out and I'll get ready."

He leaves my room and closes the door, but I hear him loudly counting down. I quickly get dressed and swing the door open. He's looking at the timer on his phone while leaning against the wall opposite my room. "Good, you're ready. You were down to a minute." He cheekily grins.

"Can I go to the bathroom?"

"You have fifty-six seconds." He looks back to his phone.

Rolling my eyes at him, I go to the bathroom and freshen up.

When I come out, he's talking to Mom and Dad who are sitting at the dining table playing a board game with Sam. I look outside and notice it's dark. "What time is it?" I wonder out loud.

"Nearly nine," Mom answers.

"I'm not going anywhere, Reece. It's dark and late and I'm tired."

"Do I have to get your parents to push you out the door? Because I'm positive they will."

"Go, sweetheart," Dad encourages me.

Mom's smiling and nodding slightly, she's clearly supporting this expedition Reece wants to take.

"Ugh," I grumble to myself. Seems they're all ganging up against me. "Fine, I'll go. But under protest." I know I won't make good company. There's no way I'll be able to focus on anything other than the words Andrea and Tracey hit me with earlier. *We have a solid lead.'* And I can't tell Reece, not because I don't want to, but because I literally can't.

"Duly noted, and disregarded," Reece sarcastically replies.

"Ugh," I moan again. "I'll go put a pair of shoes on."

"Sport shoes!" he yells at me as I head into my room.

"Okay, let's go." I drag my feet, trying to take my time and make Reece regret his plans.

As we head out, Reece turns to my parents and calls, "We won't be long, maybe an hour or so."

He closes the door and we walk down the path toward his awaiting car. "If you're taking me to a party, I'm going to sit in the car."

"We're not taking my car." He swings the small gate open and waits for me to go first before closing it.

I look around for any other mode of transportation, but I don't see anything. "If you tell me you're Superman and can fly, I'm going to be impressed."

Reece throws his head back and laughs. "I'm not Superman, but I could be Batman. Ever seen us in the same room together?"

"Ha, ha, ha," I emphasize the fake laugh.

"Well, have you?"

"Where are we going, Reece? And how are we getting there?" I stand and put a hand to my hip, frustrated with the lack of information.

"Come on. We're going for a walk."

"A walk?"

"Yeah, you know. Put one leg in front of the other, it's called walking. Hang on, I'll spell it for you."

"Stop trying to be funny." Although, to be fair, he's managed to put a smile on my face.

"Aw, are you saying I'm funny?"

"No. But in case you thought you were, you should quit while you're ahead."

"Come on." He laughs again. We turn to the right and start walking down the street. I live in a really quiet area, where everyone is friendly but keeps to themselves. There are never any loud parties, and when there is one, all the neighbors are usually invited. We all know each other, and wave when we see someone. "It's such a quiet street, there's no one yelling at their kids." He chuckles. "You can always hear Mom yelling at either Luke or me. Mostly it used to be Miles, but now that he's gone to the army, she yells at us."

"What does she yell at you for?"

"Usually it's to clean our room. Put the toilet seat down." He smiles broadly. "You know, guy stuff."

"Mrs. Nelson lives in that house." I point to a grand, double-storey house we're slowly approaching. "Her husband died years ago. She's pretty old, but she still comes out every day and gardens. She spends hours out here and that's why her garden is so beautiful. But we all keep an eye out for her. She's out here every day, and she's always here when Sam and I get home from school. One day she wasn't, and when Sam told Mom, Mom came over and found she'd fallen in the shower and couldn't get up. She's really independent and hates people helping her, but the neighborhood does."

"And she lives on her own?"

"Yes she does. Her oldest daughter, Irene, tried to get her to move in with her family, but Mrs. Nelson is as stubborn as she is independent." Reece chuckles again. "Are we headed in any particular direction?" I look around noticing we're nearing the park.

"Wherever the road leads us." He gently grabs my hand and links our fingers together. I freeze momentarily, and he stops walking. I look down to where our hands are joined together. "Is this okay?" He lifts our hands.

Everything inside me is yelling *yes*. It is okay; it feels right. My heartbeat takes off at crazy fast speeds, and my pulse quickens. Marveling at the effect he has on my body, I lean up and rake my hand through his hair. "It's okay," I answer.

Reece's eyes widen in surprise, because other than hugging him, I've never touched him in any other way without having a small meltdown first.

A hot flood of emotions overtakes me. My throat closes and my eyes blur when I realize exactly how intimate the touch I gave him was. "I'm sorry, I didn't mean to tease you." I curse myself for my own stupidity. *Stupid, stupid, stupid.*

"You're not teasing me, Dakota. And I'd never see it as anything other than a gentle, loving touch." He leans forward, and places a sweet, slow kiss on my cheek, lifting his hand to delicately brush it down my cheek.

My shoulders stiffen, but I still close my eyes to enjoy his light touch. Just as quickly, the tension eases and I lean into his caress.

Reece's face is close to mine and I can feel the warmth of his breath on my cheek. I open my eyes, look up into his tender brown eyes and give him a genuine smile.

"You're so beautiful," he whispers.

And for the first time since *that* night, I feel beautiful, thanks to Reece. A playful grin pulls at his lips, but the secrets behind his eyes hint at so much more. "Come on." He steps back putting space between us, breaking the connection we had.

We start back in the direction of the park and after a few steps Reece takes hold of my hand again. The feeling between us is gentle and easy. There's no pressure, nothing spoken. We walk slowly, more like a lazy stroll, taking in the darkness and enjoying each other's company.

"What happened today?" Reece asks as if he knows more than he's letting on.

"I had a bad day."

"How so?"

"I kinda had a meltdown."

"Because of Tara?" He knows everything about the counselor, and has even offered to take me when I need to go.

"No, she's good. She explains things to me as simply as she can. You ever hear doctors talking and they're using words so huge you need a dictionary to understand them?"

"Yeah, it's not only doctors who talk like that. Some people are like that, thinking if they use big words, they're smarter than you. I sometimes wonder if they know they sound like idiots." He laughs.

"Yeah, well she's nothing like them. I have no doubt in my mind she *could* be like them, but to me, she's really good. Anyway, my bad day has nothing to do with her."

"Then what is it?"

We reach the park and head over to the swing set. I sit in one seat, Reece in the other. Pushing my legs on the ground, the swing starts moving back and forth ever so lightly. "It was just a bad day."

"But why, what happened for it to be a bad day?"

"I'm not sure I know how to explain it."

"You've got a voice, use it."

Looking down at the dirt slightly flicking up, I try and concentrate on what I can say about my day without revealing anything about the police. "I think I had an anxiety attack today. That's how it was explained to me. My mind hasn't been ready to deal with the fallout of this, so it turned off. But when it decided to comprehend it all, I went into a meltdown, and I couldn't deal with it."

"But you're dealing with it now. Aren't you?"

"How? I'm a mess, Reece. Today people were talking to me and I had no idea what they were saying. I was eating without even knowing what I was eating. Everything looked like it was one color. I couldn't see anything." I look everywhere but at Reece, because I know my words aren't making sense. It's almost like I'm talking for the hell of it. "I lost it today. I lost myself, and I didn't know how to move forward."

"You think moving forward will be as easy as a few sessions with your counselor, a couple of hugs and a 'there, there'? 'Cause it won't be. There'll come a time in your future where you'll notice you've gone an hour without being consumed by thoughts or images of what happened. And then it'll be two hours, and three hours until one day, you've learned to live it and you won't let it stop you from moving forward."

"Are you saying I can't move forward because *I'm* stopping it?" Suddenly, I'm pissed off.

"No, I'm saying it's natural to feel like that now, it's raw and you're still trying to find your bearings. But one day, you'll be able to live with it, and to say 'this happened, but I won't let it rule my life.' That day won't come easily. Hell, there'll be a lot of days in between where you'll break down and want to hide away from everyone."

"That's how I feel now. I want to lock myself away in my safe haven, and never come back out again."

"That's normal, Dakota. I see my aunt and how she is. She's old and she still has days where she struggles. There are days she can barely get out of bed, she'll call my Mom all weepy and crying, and Mom goes to her. But at the same time, she knows she may have those days, but she manages to work through them and the next day she's okay."

"You think one day I'll be okay? Maybe even normal?"

Reece chuckles and flicks me on the leg. "You've never been normal, Dakota. No need to try to be normal now." His cheeky smile makes me happy.

"I just want to feel like I did before prom," I whisper.

"Unfortunately I don't think that'll ever happen. But it doesn't mean you can never feel good and strong. It just means you'll have down days every now and again. You'll have to learn the signs and prepare for them."

"Oh God, why does this have to be so difficult?" I sigh.

"Dakota, you have so much support and love all around you. We'll all help you through it." He reaffirms his words by squeezing my knee. "I'm going to push you." He hops off the swing, and starts pushing me. Leaning back, I close my eyes and tilt my head up toward the darkened sky. The wind gliding through my hair makes me feel alive. His warm hands on my back spark a longing inside me. I want to be better, mentally.

We hear a car drive by the park slowly and when I open my eyes, we're hit with an incredibly bright spot light. "What's going on?" I question. Suddenly red and blue lights start flashing lights on top of the car. Reece stops pushing me, and heads over toward the car.

I jump off the swing, and go with Reece. "It's late. What are you two doing here?" A female police officer asks, shining the bright light in our direction.

Both Reece and I hold our hand up over our eyes, shielding us from the powerful spotlight. "We were talking, and swinging."

She dims the light and gets out of her car. She looks us up and down, then shines her flashlight over toward where we were sitting. "You drinking?" she asks.

"No, Ma'am," Reece replies. "Just talking."

"On your way home." She flicks her head sideways, gets back in her car and turns it around. She follows us slowly all the way until we get home.

When we get inside, Mom and Dad are in the family room. "Did you have a good time?" Dad asks.

It's then I finally realize what's happened. It was a small intervention. A way to get me out of the house so I could take a step toward feeling like my old self again. "It was good, until the police showed up," I answer.

Both Mom and Dad's faces drop in shock. "Police?"

"Yeah, I think they thought we were drinking, so they made us leave," Reece chuckles. "It was good while it lasted. Anyway, I've got to get home. Walk me out?" he asks me.

"Sure."

We stand on the porch, holding hands and reliving the police situation. But really it makes me feel better knowing they're patrolling around here. It's comforting to know they're close by. "I don't think I'll be able to see you on the weekend. There are lots of things happening at home and with Miles away, I have to help out more."

"That's okay. I get it."

"I can't believe the summer is almost over. Back to school on Monday."

"Yeah, seniors too." I widen my eyes and purse my lips together. "I don't want to go. I can't imagine how I'll react if anything gets mentioned."

"You'll have me, Dakota. There's nothing to be scared of."

I nod, but I'm really freaking out. I don't want him to know how I'm feeling, so I bottle it away and keep it a secret. *I'm good at doing that.*

CHAPTER 43

N ERVOUSLY I PACE in the family room. Sam's still getting ready and Mom's impatiently yelling at her. "Hurry up, Samantha, we're going to be late."

I keep pacing, chewing my fingernails trying to distract myself.

"I'll only be another minute," Sam hollers back.

Mom goes to the door, and keeps an eye on me. "How are you doing, Dakota?" she asks. But she knows. I've been telling her since they found out what happened how petrified I am of going back to school. "You okay?"

I shake my head, and start on my next nail. "I don't know if I can do this."

"If you don't go now, it'll only get harder to go tomorrow. You have to face it. Your father said the social media group has been taken down and there haven't been any more pictures."

"It's social media, Mom. The moment it's on the web, that's it. It'll never be truly gone."

"I know. But I'm holding on to the hope not many people from your school saw it. And even if they did, you have nothing to be ashamed of. Don't let them affect you."

"What if they're horrible? Or I end up crying all day?"

"Call me, and I'll come pick you up right away." She walks over and rubs her hands up and down my arms. "You'll be okay. You can do this."

"Alright," I reply, though I have a feeling I'm going to be the furthest thing from okay.

Sophie, Reece and I are sitting in the cafeteria eating our lunch. Well, they're eating while I'm pushing my food around, distracted by my anxiety.

"You okay, doll?" Reece asks as he leans over to give me a peck on the cheek.

"Doll? You've never called me that before."

"You're cute, and little. And cute."

"You already said cute."

"I'll say it again, you're cute." He bumps my shoulder with his and gives me a beautiful smile. Aw, he makes my heart flutter.

Sophie laughs and then chokes. "You two are cute," she manages to spit out between coughs. "So cute you're making me choke."

Lindsey walks past us, and snidely says, "Wow, look who's sitting at the loser table." She makes an L with her hand and lifts it to her forehead.

"How old are you, Lindsey? Even the freshmen don't do that," I angrily spit at her.

"Whatever, loser." She happily walks away.

"Skank," I yell back.

"Calm down, Rocky." Reece reaches over and gently massages my shoulder. "I thought I was going to have to step in and referee for a second. Feisty."

"I'm sick of her bullshit. She was one of my best friends, and the minute Levi and I break up, she not only goes straight to him, she becomes a raving bitch."

"I hate to tell you, Dakota, she's always been a raving bitch," Sophie says as she picks up a piece of lettuce and munches away.

"Sophie's right, Dakota. She always has been," Reece agrees.

"Ugh," I moan loudly. How have I never seen this side of her before?

"That's her, the girl in those pictures," I hear someone whisper from behind me.

Reece's spine stiffens, as he turns to look at whoever whispered. "Have you got a problem?" he asks, standing from his seat and extending to his full, six-foot height. "You want to ask a question, come here and ask." He takes a menacing step forward, his chest puffed out and his hands balled into fists.

The air around us crackles as Reece moves into the space of the guy who whispered. He's another senior, someone I've never had anything to do with in the past.

"Nah man, not saying anything." He backs away, his hands held chest high, palms out as if conceding to Reece's anger.

"You gonna beat up everyone who says your little girlfriend is a slut and whore?" Levi appears and chest bumps Reece. It's a challenge, a dare to see who's toughest.

Reece's neck muscles tense, while he stands his ground, and pushes Levi. "You want another broken nose? I have no fucking problem busting it again." Reece steps forward, and Levi steps back.

"Hey," I jump up and get between the two before a fight breaks out. I put my palm to Reece's chest, and give him a pleading gaze. "Please, don't. He's not worth it," I whisper so only he can hear me. Reece's eyes are glaring at Levi, I can feel the anger rolling off him as he considers my plea. "Please, I need you," I beg. If he's suspended or thrown out for fighting, I won't have my support group around me.

"Listen to the whore. You don't want me messing up that pretty-boy face of yours." Levi's voice changes into a baby tone when he says 'pretty boy face'; it's a taunt to make Reece lose it so he throws the first punch.

And this pisses me right off.

I swiftly turn on my heel, and slap him so hard his head jerks to the side. "You're a fucking pig!" I yell.

Levi stands stock still, his hand rubbing his cheek and his mouth wide open. He wasn't expecting that from me, *nor was I*. He straightens his shoulders, arches a brow and smirks at me.

Levi moves closer, threateningly, toward me, and Reece grabs my arm and pushes me behind him, as he takes my place so they're toe to toe. "You'll get your own, whore," he spits at me from around Reece.

"Fuck off, before I lay you out on your ass," Reece says through a clenched jaw. His arm is behind him, smashing me to his body protectively.

"Watch your back, Hendricks," Levi warns Reece.

"Bring it," Reece quickly replies, his chest puffed out.

Levi backs away, taking a few steps backwards while he continues to watch us. When he's halfway across the cafeteria he yells, "Me and you, Hendricks. Me and you." Pointing a finger at Reece.

Reece's protective stance doesn't let up. He keeps a watchful eye on Levi even as his arm is wrapped around me, shielding me from any danger.

"Reece," I whisper trying to step away from him. But his arm tightens and he doesn't let me move. "Reece."

His shoulders are visibly shaking from the effort it's taking to control his anger, and the muscles in his arms are flexed, making the sleeve of his t-shirt cling to his arms. "You okay?" he asks as he turns to cup my face, making sure I'm not hurt or frightened.

"I'm okay," I answer staring into his wide brown eyes.

He grabs my hand and almost drags me over to our seats. Sophie's smiling at us, and she looks like she's got a secret she's busting to tell us. "You alright, Sophie?" Reece asks.

"I am. Wanna know what I heard?"

"What?" I ask, pushing my food away because now I've lost the little interest I did have. I fold my arms in front of me, waiting for Sophie to speak. "Well?"

"Lindsey was standing close to me, and when Levi walked away, I heard her say, 'it's so cute how Reece is so protective of Dakota.' He told her to shut up and stop being a bitch. Then he walked away. She ran behind him saying how sorry she was."

"I've come to the conclusion that Lindsey is not the smartest of people," Reece says joining his hands and steepling his fingers to tap on his lips. "Not smart at all."

"She's still a nasty piece of work," Sophie pipes up and says. "Real nasty."

The bell sounds for the end of lunch and we all head to the last few classes of the day.

Mrs. Walker's English class is the last of the day. As I head there, Aaron and Jordan cross paths with me in the hallway. I decide to be the bigger person here and say hello to Jordan. "Hi," I say as I pass her. She looks me up and down, and she ignores me. "I'm well, thanks," I sarcastically add while she's beside me.

"I didn't ask," she snaps bitchily.

"I was talking to someone who actually has a heart, clearly that isn't you." I flip my hair and walk away from her. I wouldn't normally be horrible like this, but she deserves it.

I head into Mrs. Walker's class, and Reece is sitting at the back, with a spare seat beside him. He smiles at me the moment he sees me, and he winks.

And my heart jumps.

CHAPTER 44

"**S**AM, WANT TO walk this morning?" I ask as we have breakfast. Last night's counseling session went really well. I didn't break down, and surprisingly I didn't cry. It feels like that's all I've been doing lately, is crying.

"Yeah, let's walk," Sam eagerly answers.

Mom hears us and smiles.

"Be ready in ten. Okay?" I quickly finish my breakfast and go to brush my teeth and grab my bag. I'm not so nervous about school today, I handled the events of yesterday better than I'd thought I would and I know each day will get easier.

There were a few slurs, murmurs and even-name calling, but I know what the truth is, so it didn't bother me as much as I'd expected.

"Ready?" Sam calls from the front door.

I grab my bag and head out. "Bye, Mom," both Sam and I yell out at the same time. We start walking toward school and Sam says to me, "A few of the kids were talking about that group yesterday. They asked me if I knew about it."

"What did you say?" I kick a small pebble down the road and watch it go skittering across the asphalt.

"Told them I hope when they pee it feels like razor blades."

"Oh my God, you didn't really say that, did you?"

"Hell yeah, I did! They stopped asking when I told them I was going to flush their heads down the toilet and see how they like walking through school with pee on their head." She smiles at me triumphantly, and adds a swagger to her walk.

"You're one of a kind. Never change, Sam, never."

"I've got sparkle, and if you're lucky, I may share it with you."

We round the corner to get to school and a white car slows down and drives beside us. "Who the hell is that?" I ask, pushing Sam off the sidewalk and further away from the white car.

When I duck to see who it is, they take off down the street do a U-turn. On the way back, I see it's Mr. C, and the hair on my body stands to attention as he slows again, looking at us.

"What the hell is that about?" I ask.

"Creepy, there's something seriously wrong with this. Come on, let's go." She starts toward school at a faster pace.

I head over to my locker the period before lunch to grab my math book. Mr. C's class. *Cringe.* Thank God both Reece and Sophie are in this class, and I don't have to sit there on my own.

Reluctantly, I head to class, and when I get there, I spot Mr. C is sitting on the edge of his desk. He has his phone in his hands and he's looking down at the screen. Reece isn't here yet, but Sophie is, and she's got her head down in a book, reading. "Hey," I whisper as I walk past Mr. C and shudder as I feel his beady eyes flick over my body.

"Mr. C's class." She gives me a wicked smile, hiding the truth of how we both feel about him.

Everyone filters in slowly, and Mr. C watches as we all take our seats. He looks agitated, like something's wrong. He gazes down at his phone, types something, then looks around the class again. Standing, he heads over to the door and closes it, but not before he steps out to the hall looking to see if anyone else is coming.

"What's going on with Mr. C?" Reece asks me and Sophie.

"No idea. He's acting weird, though. This morning he drove past me and Sam on our walk to school, then turned around and came back again. Now he's been sitting on his desk, probably playing Candy Crush on his phone. He looked up, then went out there."

The door slams shut and Mr. C re-enters the classroom. "I trust you all had a good vacation?" he asks us all.

Excited murmurs and whispers burst forth from the class. Then the door swings open, and Levi strolls in like he thinks he's a goddamn king. His eyes flick to me and he winks. *Sleaze.*

I know why he's acting like this. It's obvious he's seen those pictures and he thinks I cheated on him. I get it, really I do. I'd be beyond hurt and humiliated to think that someone had cheated on me. and I hope once the police's solid lead pans out, he'll understand what really happened. Hopefully, we can at least be civil. I don't ever expect an apology for him acting like an idiot; I just don't want to be on the receiving end of his hurtful comments.

I look up at the front of class, and Mr. C is still on his phone. "I'll be with you in a minute, class; I've got to send this urgent text message," he says.

"He's so weird," I whisper to Sophie.

"Tell me about it."

The class starts and we've already begun working on calculus. We're half-way through the lesson, with Mr. C showing examples and breaking them down, when suddenly everything changes.

The door opens, and two uniformed police officers walk into the room. Mr. C steps back, then quickly regroups and steps forward toward the police.

Students are moving, scraping their chairs, and a lot of gasping noises as these police officers invade our room. They take a moment to look through the room, and walk toward the back . . . toward Levi.

"Levi Matthews, you are under arrest. You have the right to remain silent . . ."

Levi is pulled up from his desk by one of the police officers. He turns Levi around and quickly handcuffs him.

"What . . . ?" I whisper as I watch this incredibly intense exchange happen in a matter of seconds. The police are in our room, and out before anyone has a chance to get their head around what's happening.

The two burly officers leave with each holding one of Levi's arms, still reading him his rights.

I look around the class. Some girls crying, some guys' mouths are hanging open. "What just happened?" Sophie asks loudly.

We all look to Mr. C, who's standing at the front of the class, looking as disconcerted as we all are. Our principal appears and stands at the front of the class. "Mr. Collins, I'll take the class. Go grab a coffee."

Mr. C slowly nods his head, apparently still in shock. He grabs his phone and his briefcase and leaves the room.

We're all looking around us, still trying to figure out what happened.

"Class." Mr. Preston, our principal claps his hands twice to get our attention.

Sophie puts her hand up.

"Yes." He points to her.

"What just happened?"

"I'm not at liberty to discuss it. Now, where did Mr. Collins leave off in your lesson?" Sophie sticks her hand up again. "Yes?"

"Two police officers just disrupted our class, handcuffed Levi, and read him his Miranda Rights. And you can't tell us what's going on?"

"That's correct. Where are we up to?" Sophie is tenacious. "Yes," he says with a frustrated sigh.

"You can't expect us to concentrate on work, when Levi was just handcuffed."

"Miss . . ." He waits for her last name.

"Sophie Masters."

"Ah, yes, Miss Masters. That's exactly what I expect of you. To concentrate on your work."

Sophie rolls her eyes and mumbles something under her breath. She looks at me and mouths, 'What happened?'

"I don't know," I whisper in response.

The class goes by quickly, everyone itching to know what happened. By the time the bell sounds, the corridors are filled with people and the only thing anyone can talk about is how Levi got arrested. We head to the cafeteria and people are stopping Reece, Sophie, and me, asking us what we know.

When we head to our table, Sam and Taylor are already here, huddled together talking in a hushed tone. They see us approach and look straight at us. "What happened?" Sam pounces the moment we sit.

"No idea. Seriously, we were sitting there and the next thing two cops come in, grab Levi, handcuff him, and take him out. It happened so fast. Mr. C tried to ask them what was going on, but they had Levi so quick. I've never seen anything like it," Reece says.

"Was it like those movies where they come in and extract someone and everyone's left stunned?" Taylor asks Reece.

"That's exactly how it was. Mr. Preston showed up and told Mr. C to go. Man, I have no idea what the hell happened," Reece replies.

Sam leans over to me, Reece and Taylor leaning back, talking to each other. "Did anything weird happen in class?" she questions me.

"Nope. Did you see anything weird in class, Sophie?" I ask her.

"Nothing. We were half way through when they came in. They were huge, too."

Lunch is spent not eating, but listening to what everyone's saying. When the bell sounds, Reece and I walk to our lockers so we can get our

English books out.

I feel a tap on my shoulder, and turn to see Lindsey who's clearly been crying. "What happened, Dakota?" she asks through her tears.

I almost feel sorry for her. Her boyfriend's been dragged out of class, and no one knows what's going on. "I don't know, Lindsey."

"Did you do this?"

I frown at her and shake my head. "Me? People can't be arrested for being assholes, or you'd be right there with him."

Her shoulders slump and she looks down at her feet, embarrassed. "Sorry, I didn't mean to say that. I'm really upset because I can't get any answers from anyone."

"I'm sure whatever it is, it'll be sorted out."

She gives me the first hint of friendliness she has in a long time. She half smiles at me, her eyes soft with hurt. "Thank you. If you hear anything, will you let me know?"

"Um." I bring my shoulders up in a shrug. "Sure."

"Thank you."

She walks away and Reece stares at me, completely surprised. "You could've told her to piss off."

"I'm not like that."

"I know, and I really love that about you." He gives me a small kiss on the cheek.

He said love.

I smile. And do a little internal dance.

As we walk to English, Jordan, Aaron, and Mariah all stop us. They're asking the same question as everyone else: do we know what happened. Our replies are the same, and by the time the end of the day gets here, Sophie, Reece, and I are glad we're on our way home.

"God, I don't think I can deal with any more surprises. That's it! I declare this month to be 'no more surprise' month. I'm really not sure I can handle any more," I say with a sigh.

"Come on, doll, I'll take you home. Grab Sam and I'll wait for you by the car. Need a lift Sophie?"

"No, Mom's waiting. See you guys tomorrow."

"See ya."

I may have declared this month is surprise free, but something is telling me, there's more to come.

CHAPTER 45

"**I**T'S ALL ANYONE is talking about," Sam says.

"I know, I can't believe it myself. I wonder what happened," Dad says. "Pass the potato salad please, Sam." Sam hands him the bowl.

I look down at my plate and pick at my dinner. I lean an elbow on the table, not really concentrating on anything. My head's fuzzy with the day's events. "Are you okay, sweetheart?" Mom asks.

"Yeah, I'm good. I've never seen anything like that scene today. It literally happened in less than two minutes. But it felt like it was forever. I've never experienced anything like it."

"And pray to God you never experience it again," Dad says. "When I was a young man, probably about twenty or so, I had a job in a small convenience store to help put me through college. I had the night shift, working until about midnight, before the next guy came to replace me. Anyway, one particular night had been so busy, it was Christmas Eve. We were getting hammered. I had help until about nine, then the guy who was helping me had to leave as his mom had been involved in a car accident. So there I was, twenty years old, weighed maybe a hundred and twenty pounds and getting swamped with the volume of people coming in to stock up on things like milk and bread, that kind of stuff. Anyway, when it got to eleven, and the store finally slowed down. I had a lot of money in the till, but because it had been so busy, I hadn't had a chance to deposit any in the safe."

"I don't like where this is going, Dad." Sam's stressed. She's tapping her fingers on the table, while her eyes are wide as she leaning in listening to Dad.

"This guy came in, fired a shot over my head, made me open the till, and took all the money. Then he ran."

"Oh." I gasp, shocked and terrified at the same time. "What happened?" I ask.

"He was in and out in under thirty seconds. The store had surveillance and recorded him. It was under thirty seconds, but to me everything stopped. I was terrified. I had no idea what happened, my heart rate shot up through the ceiling, I swear I thought he was going to kill me."

"You could've died, Dad," Sam says, big fat tears forming in her eyes and spilling over.

"Aw, pumpkin, he didn't want me dead, he just wanted whatever was in the till." He stands and goes straight to Sam, comforting her.

"What do you think about that, Mom?" I ask.

"Your father told me that story soon after we met. He told me because I was working in a gas station and he told me he didn't want me doing that anymore because of what happened to him. He told me he'd feel better if he knew the love of his life was doing something safer."

"Did you really say that?" I ask Dad.

The tops of his ears are red, and the same color is spreading across his cheeks. "I may have said something similar. I don't recall the exact words." He tries to play it down.

"I remember, Owen. And those are the words you used."

"Thank you, darling." He leaves Sam who's smiling now and goes back to his seat, giving Mom a chaste kiss on her lips.

"My point is . . ." A knock on the door interrupts him before we get find out what the point was. Dad looks around the table at us. "Is anyone expecting guests?" he asks us. We all shake our heads and peer toward the door. "Okay, stay here. I'll see who it is."

Dad goes to the door and we're all quiet, trying to listen to his conversation, but we can't hear anything clearly. Dad's footsteps come into the family room and I hear at least two more sets of feet following him.

"Um, Dakota?" I turn around to see Tracey, Andrea, and Mr. C all standing in my living room.

"What's *he* doing here?" I demand, pointing at Mr. C, suspicious and appalled that he has the audacity to come to my home. Abruptly, I stand and move as far away as possible from him. With my back against the wall, I carefully watch him.

"Dakota, we need to talk to you," Tracey says.

Dad comes to me, and protectively slings his arm around my shoulders. My eyes are focused on Mr. C. His beady eyes are watching me and I can't help but bury myself into Dad's side. I want to be brave, but I can't when he's in my home and I can't avoid him.

"Come sit, Dakota," Andrea says and pats the sofa beside her. I opt to stay opposite her, where I can keep an eye on my math teacher.

"Dad," I whisper.

"I promise you, everything's okay."

We all sit, and I hold my breath waiting for the words Andrea or Tracey are going to speak, but I'm also cautious of Mr. C.

"We have some news to tell you," Tracey starts. "This is Detective Gary Pearce. He's been undercover at your school since last year."

"You're a cop?" I ask incredulously.

"Yes, Dakota, I am." He holds his badge out for me to look at.

"I don't get it. Why were you at our school?" I look to Sam, and her mouth is wide open, her eyes popping out of her head. I'm fairly certain she's as stunned by this as I am. "But you're creepy. You'd always show up where we were, checking us out."

"It's my job."

"This doesn't make sense. None of it does."

"About eighteen months ago, three girls came into the police station and reported they'd had their drinks spiked and had subsequently been raped. All separate occasions, all within a few weeks of each other, all in exactly the same circumstances."

"Okay," I skeptically say.

"We built a task force to try and find who this person was. With all the information we had, we were able to narrow it down to one of three schools. We put an undercover police officer in each of the schools, posing as a teacher to keep an eye on what was happening."

"Then you knew what was happening to me on the night of the prom."

"I suspected, and when you disappeared I tried to find you, I even drove around looking for you. I pulled cars off their beats to search for you, but no one could find you. With what happened to you, we pinpointed the abuser to be someone at your school."

"But when I woke up, I was out by the bleachers, you couldn't have looked too hard if you didn't find me there."

"We did look there. But when we searched it, you weren't there. You were taken away from the school, then brought back and dumped there."

"Shit," Mom whispers. "Sorry." She quickly retracts it and slaps her hand over her mouth.

"Now that we knew the school, we just had to figure who the students were. It could've been anyone. The night of the prom, I didn't know *who* to look at, so I had to keep an eye on everyone. But all three schools had their proms on the same night. We were stretched and had to monitor all three. The moment I saw you, I called in back-up and we started searching for you."

"What?" Disbelief floods me. From what he's said, and what I'm understanding, he's basically saying the police knew someone was going to be assaulted on the night of my prom.

"A few of the boys disappeared, about fifty of them, and I had no idea where they got to. I noted down their names, and we started investigating them all one by one."

"Oh." Words elude me. I'm stunned at the revelations Mr. C is making.

"Then the social media pictures started, and although at first they'd been deleted quickly, we finally were able to get an IP address."

"An IP address? You mean they were all sent from the same computer?" Dad asks, confused.

"Yes, he was extremely brazen, or stupid. Either way, it worked in our favor. But thanks to you, Dakota, the dress you provided, and your recollection of what happened to you, we have an ironclad case. We've got the person carrying out these assaults."

"Who?" I ask.

Mr. C looks remorseful, as if he doesn't want to tell me.

It hits me before he even opens his mouth.

Oh my God.

Levi raped me. "It was Levi," I gasp.

"Yes," he confirms. "Today in class, we had the warrant ready to arrest him. All the officers needed was confirmation from me he was in class."

A movie plays back in my head. I'm standing at the back of the class, watching everything from the moment I stepped into class. And I catch it. The small smile Mr. C gives his phone when he sends that 'important' text message. He was telling them, Levi was in class. "They came in quick, and got him out fast before anyone knew anything," I say.

"At the same time, there was a raid happening at his house. It had to be synchronized, and we had to make sure he was in my class so no other teacher was suspicious or put in the middle of it."

I sit quietly on the sofa. The bottom of my world has just fallen out from beneath me. To say I'm devastated is only the tip of the iceberg.

Betrayed, hurt, humiliated. All of that and so much more.

"I just . . . I need a drink," I say as I stand on wobbly legs and head into the kitchen.

Mom follows me in. "Dakota," she sighs sympathetically. I shake my head as I reach for a glass, I don't want to hear anything, I just want something to drink. Pouring some water from the faucet, I take a few minutes to process everything they've said.

I don't want to believe Mr. C, but deep down inside I know it's the truth. I count to ten in my head, breathing deep to settle my frazzled nerves and rapidly beating heart. I drink the water and place the glass in the sink, pull my shoulders back and return to the family room.

"He belongs in jail. Tell me the evidence you have is enough to send him there." My tone is eerily controlled; I'm not emotional or weepy. I'm furious. Goosebumps sweep my entire body as ice settles inside my veins.

"He's going to jail for a long time. His brother is, too."

"His brother? Levi doesn't have a brother," I say. "He told me he's an only child. I've been to his house many times, and there was never any mention of his brother." No photos, no name . . . nothing.

"Yes, he has an older brother, Robert. He dropped out of school and started running drugs for some low-level drug dealer. Then Robert started selling them on his own."

Every new piece of information I'm getting is filling in the overall puzzle. Everything fits. Finally everything is coming together. "He was getting the drugs from his brother," I say, realizing how intricate the web he'd spun was. "What other evidence have you got?"

"There was sperm on your dress."

I shiver, and cringe. Vomit wants to come up, but I push it down, I refuse to let my weakness show. "Is that all? If it is, is that enough? He can say we had consensual sex and that's how his sperm got on my dress."

"You're a smart young lady, Dakota. Don't ever let that go." Mr. C points to me. "But yes, there's more."

My jaw clenches as I move my neck from side to side to loosen the tension in my muscles. "What else?" I ask.

"We found his collection of trophies."

"Underwear, right?" He nods his head. "How many?" I hold my breath, because I know there are more than just mine.

"Including you, eight in total."

I expel the breath I've been holding. "Is Sophie one of them?"

"We can't tell you that. But it's best if you call her." That's all the confirmation I need. Sweat coats the palms of my hands as I ball them into fists.

"Why the pictures on social media? Why did he do it? Do you know? Did he say?"

"Levi became very forthcoming when we confronted him and his lawyer with what evidence we had. Our investigation is tight. There's no way he'll get out of going to jail."

"But why did he continue to humiliate me on social media?" I ask in a pained tone.

"His answer was that you deserved it for being a prick tease."

And there it is. My life was flushed down the toilet because he thought I was a 'prick tease.' Because he thought he was entitled to something from me, he altered the way I'll be for the rest of my life because I refused him sex.

I collapse to the sofa and suddenly I don't feel so strong. I have no energy left inside me to fight. I was nothing to him.

"I can't deal with any more tonight," I say to all three police officers.

"Dakota, I just want to say, your strength throughout all this has been amazing. It's because of you we were able to find him, and it's because of you, we'll be able to put him away. He won't be hurting anyone else," Andrea says.

"I'm proud of you, Dakota," Mr. C adds.

Mom and Dad talk to them for some time as they show them out, while Sam and I sit numbly on the sofa.

Neither of us is talking, because neither of us knows what to say. When Mom and Dad come back, they sit on the sofa, quiet too.

My world has collapsed. It's fallen apart and I'm not sure I know how to deal with this. It's bigger than I ever thought.

The man I trusted ended up betraying me.

The man I mistrusted ended up playing a key role in seeking justice on my behalf.

I come to the very real conclusion, that I'm lost. I'm broken. *Emotionless.* And I can't get out of this.

"I need to see Tara," I say. "I've been betrayed, humiliated, and raped. And I don't know what to do now."

Mom and Dad both look at me, and nod.

I need to learn how to become a survivor; I can't stay a victim any longer.

CHAPTER 46

"IT'S BEEN OVER a week since the police came to my house and hit me with all the truths I didn't want to know. I haven't returned to school yet. Instead, I've being seeing Tara daily and she's been helping me deal with this clusterfuck.

Sophie's come over today. Both of us are having difficulty adjusting to the knowledge my ex-boyfriend raped us both. "Do you want a drink?" I ask her as she comes into my house.

"Yeah, I think I do. Got a scotch?" she chuckles. I know she doesn't mean it, but with the information overload we've gotten, we've thankfully found strength in each other.

"How about a soda?"

"Sure, as long as it's mixed with scotch."

I chuckle at her and head over to the fridge to get us both a soda.

"Hi Sophie, how are you doing?" Mom asks with a smile. She walks into the kitchen, carrying a clean load of laundry.

"I won't say it's getting easier, but I'm thankful I have Dakota to talk to. Mom called Tara, and we have an appointment with her early next week. Dakota always tells me how much she's helping her, and I need to close off that part of my life and move forward." She opens the soda and takes a sip.

"You're both young, and although this will certainly change the way you look at things, it doesn't mean you can't live again. It's going to take time, a long, long time, before you can truly move forward. But I'm glad I called your mom and talked to her. She's a lovely lady. You should bring her over for dinner one night," Mom says to Sophie.

"Thank you, I'll let her know you've offered."

"I know your mom is busy, but anytime she's ready, so are we. Okay, girls, I'll leave you to it. Dakota, Tara's appointment from this afternoon has been moved to tomorrow morning. She called while I was taking the laundry out of the dryer."

"Okay," I respond and smile.

Mom takes the basket and heads into her room.

"I can't believe all the emotions I've been going through," Sophie says as she plops down on one of the stools in the kitchen. "When the police showed up. . . ." She goes quiet and shakes her head. "When they showed up, and told us, Mom thought she was being pranked because I'd never told her."

"I know you said she was really understanding when she first found out, but how is she now?"

"She wanted to pack up and leave, start new. But we talked about it. And we both have to face our past and move on with what future we can make for ourselves. I like it here, despite Levi raping me, despite the fact I only have a handful of friends. Mom said she can get a cleaning job anywhere, but I like it here and I don't want to move. I really think once I've got myself together, that I'd like to stay here."

"Good, 'cause I really want you in my life. I think we're meant to be friends."

"Yeah, I suppose, you'll do." She playfully shoulders me. "Do you wonder why he did what he did?"

"Every damn day. He gave the police his reason for raping me, but it doesn't make sense. You know the part that's most upsetting to me?" Sophie shakes her head. "How he had all those girls underwear, bagged and dated with their details or description. To me, that says he's a serial rapist. He never had any intention of stopping."

"And he never thought he'd be caught."

"Now that he's been caught, I'm not sure I really know how to deal with it all. I mean, Tara's helping me process it. Mom, Dad, Sam and Reece have all been so supportive, but there's still a part of me that can't quite grasp *why* he did it. Not only to me, but to all of us. What makes a person think to himself, 'hey, I'm going to rape her' to begin with? But not only that, how did he bring the conversation up to his brother?"

"His brother wasn't exactly a pillar of the community."

"I didn't even know he had a brother until the cops told us the night they came over. But now more and more information is coming out, it's no wonder he never mentioned him. The brother's last known address was their place although he didn't live there. His parents threw him out "when he turned to drugs and stole from them to support his habit."

"His parents put him through rehab many times, too." Sophie shakes her head. "Such a shame he preferred drugs to family."

"He's an addict. That's what drugs do to people. But I still want to know how the concept even got into Levi's head. We were in the back of the limousine and I told him I wasn't ready, I thought he took it well. To go from that, to drugging me . . . Even the fact he had drugs on him to start with, does that mean he was going to drug me regardless of whether I agreed to have sex with him or not? Or does it mean he had intentions of drugging someone else after we'd had sex?"

"I can't answer that, Dakota. And I doubt Levi will either."

"I know. I have this stupid, fairy tale thought. You know, he'll say he's sorry, I'll forgive him and get better and we all live happily ever after. But I'm not sure I can forgive him. His betrayal has really rocked me to my core. I mean, I haven't been back to school, and I'm not sure when I'll get back there. Thankfully, Reece is bringing me all my homework."

"I've missed a few days, but nothing like you. Did you hear Lindsey hasn't returned to school either?"

"Nope, I haven't. I've had loads of messages and phone calls. And every day Sam brings home cards and letters from people. I got one from Jordan, who said she was sorry for everything, including how she treated me. Mariah sent one saying she was sorry too."

"Are you going to forgive them? Everyone's treating me differently too. They're more accepting and not as judgmental as what they used to be. Jordan and Mariah both came over and sat with me and Reece, your sister, and Taylor at lunch, and they both had their heads down in shame."

"Sam told me about that. She said she gave them a hard time, and they ended up crying."

"She did. I had to tell her enough was enough and if she kept going than she was no better than them."

"She told me. And I agree with you. But at the same time, the only reason Sam was saying those things was to protect us two."

"I know. Which is why I tapped her leg with my foot and shook my head. She got me, 'cause she stopped and we talked about it later. She's a great sister to have on your side. I tell you, she'll have your back for life."

"Yeah, I know. I really can't wrap my head around it all. I can't."

"Tara will help you. I can already see how she's helped. You're not as jittery, or timid, and I want that for myself. Not that I'm those things, but I have my own demons I have to deal with. You know with Dad in jail, and Levi. I bottle my fears and issues differently, we all do. We're not all the same."

"I don't know, Sophie. I just don't think I'll ever be able to forgive him. How do I look at a guy who abused my trust by sexually assaulting me and say, 'It's okay, I forgive you'? I can't because then it's like telling myself I deserved what he did to me, like I'm telling *him* it's okay to do that."

"I don't think it's about telling him it's okay, it's more about looking him in the eye and telling yourself *you're* okay. You forgive yourself, not him."

"I get that, really I do. Because this humiliation is so reactive. Everyone at school now knows what happened—the teachers, parents, everyone. Those pictures were stored on his computer, with hundreds, if not thousands of pictures he took of all of us." I point to her and me, but indicate all the victims.

"I know, and when he has his day in court, they'll come out, and everyone will see them all over again. But once the trial's finished, we can finally move on with our lives."

"There's a lot of work ahead of us," I say, staring at my soda can.

"There are so many rumors flying around school," Reece says as we sit at the dining table. We begin going through the homework he's brought over. "Most I laugh at."

"What's being said?"

"There was one that said you've been kidnapped by an alien and the Secret Service is trying to find you."

I shake my head and roll my eyes. "Then there's one that Mr. C is SWAT,"

"No, he's a detective. Totally different."

"Another said you're really a mermaid and have gone back to the sea."

"Seriously, everyone has too much time on their hands."

"It may have been me who made that last one up and told one of the juniors to see how long it would take for it to get around the school." I stare at him, blankly. I don't even know what to say. "It didn't take long. Though by the time it came back around it had morphed into you being a two-headed mermaid." I laugh and slap my hand to my forehead. "I'm being serious."

"I don't doubt it." I chuckle.

Reece laughs too, and when the happy sound dies down, his face falls into an intense, warm stare. "How you doing today?"

"Better than yesterday, and not as good as tomorrow."

"Why aren't you at Tara's?"

"She had to change my appointment to tomorrow morning."

"So you're going tomorrow morning?"

"Uh-huh." I nod my head.

"Dakota?" Mom appears and sits opposite Reece and myself. Her face is pale, and she's clutching her phone to her chest.

Instantly, I know something's wrong. "What is it?" I ask in a panic. *Oh God,* please don't tell me Levi's escaped and disappeared. There's no way I'm ready to handle the threat of him being out there. My hands grip the edge of the chair so tightly, they're starting to ache. Shifting my body, I'm literally sitting on the edge of my seat.

"Lindsey's mom just called me."

Momentarily I let my stress levels fall. "What's happened?"

"She tried to kill herself. She's been admitted into the hospital and she's undergoing treatment."

I turn my head and stare at Reece, who's obviously as shocked as I am. "What?" we both ask.

"Kill herself?" Reece murmurs.

Mom nods her head. "When?" I ask, still dazed and stunned.

"Lindsey's mom said three nights ago. She's asked to talk to you."

"Lindsey's mom wants to talk to me? Why? I have nothing to say to her, or even Lindsey."

"No, Lindsey asked if you could go see her at the hospital. She wants to talk to you."

My mind spins. I can't think of a reason why Lindsey would want to talk to me. "I'm not sure I want to see her or hear what she has to say."

"In my opinion, Dakota, you owe it to yourself. Not to her, but to yourself, to know what it is she wants to tell you. It may be another piece you need to move forward and heal or it may be nothing. But if you don't want to go, then you're well within your rights to say no. Either way, you have my support."

"What do you think?" I ask Reece.

"It's not up to me, Dakota. But I have to say, I agree with your mom. Even if she yells and screams at you, you might find something in that to help you deal with all of this. I can be there with you too, if you like?"

he offers. He gently takes my hand in his, and his thumb softly strokes the back of my hand.

I sit and consider the alternative. If I don't go, then I can't tell her what I need to tell her for my own self-preservation. If I do go, then I could be a total mess from whatever she's going to say to me. Weighing up the options, my heart tears at both scenarios. Either way, I'm grateful I have Tara in the morning. She'll help me through it.

"Okay, I'll go," I timidly say. "Mom, is it okay if Reece takes me?" Mom looks a little hurt when I ask. "It's not that I don't want you there, but Reece knows the dynamic at school, and he may have an insight I'm unaware of because I've missed a weeks' worth."

A small, though strained smile pulls at Mom's lips. "I understand. Of course he can take you."

I stand and round the table, hug Mom, and give her a peck on the cheek. "Thank you."

"If she looks like she's starting to fall, it's your responsibility to get her out of there and bring her home." Mom points a finger to Reece.

"I promise you, I'll protect her with my life."

Mom's concern is completely justified. This has the potential to become a huge mess. There's so much that's happened, and I'm sure even more will happen before it's through.

"I'll grab my jacket," I say to Reece and head to my room.

Lindsey looks terrible. Her face is pasty white, her lips are cracked, and she looks like she's lost a lot of weight from her already slender body. I sit in the chair beside her bed, waiting for her to tell me whatever it is she called me here to say. Her mom is on the other side of the bed. Her eyes are red-rimmed and it's obvious she's been crying.

"Thanks for coming," Lindsey says in a small, strangled voice.

Reece is standing behind me with his hands on my shoulders. Lindsey's eyes travel from mine to Reece's then she looks back down at her hands which are sitting on her lap.

"What do you want to say to me?" I cut to the chase. If all she wants is sympathy from me, then she's going to be sorely disappointed.

"You know I tried to kill myself?" she asks.

"Yes," I respond in a flat tone.

"Do you know why?"

"No, but I have a feeling you want to tell me."

Her mom moves forward, and clutches Lindsey's hand. I see the encouragement she's giving her, and I try and dial back my anger.

"I've loved him ever since I can remember. When you two broke up, and he came to me, I thought it was finally my chance to be with him. But he only really wanted me for sex, and he was still hung up on you."

Reece's hands tense on my shoulders. He quickly eases off when I tense reactively. He's angry, and he has every reason to be. "Okay," I respond, encouraging her to continue.

"He was so rough with me. Whenever we had sex, he wasn't gentle, or loving. He would hurt me, and when I'd tell him, he'd laugh. So I tried being more like you, but he'd get even rougher." I draw my brows together and fidget in the seat. "But I still loved him. Then when he told me about the pictures, he made out like you cheated on him, and you'd done something wrong. He told me you'd always been a bitch about me to him, which drove the envy I had even further."

"You were working on information he told you, instead of asking me yourself."

"Yes." She looks at me, her eyes brimming with tears, and looks back down at her hands twisting together. "The more he told me, the more I wanted you to pay for treating him badly and bitching about me."

"And that's why you were so horrible to me? To Sophie?" She nods her head. Her mom is crying quietly and Lindsey is crying too. "Was the end result worth it, Lindsey?"

"If I could go back in time, and make everything right, I would."

I nod my head. "I don't know why, but I actually believe you."

"I'm so sorry, Dakota. What you've been through, I can't ever imagine."

"Why did you hurt yourself?" I ask.

"Because I can't live with everything I've said and done. And the way he treated me, he was beyond brutal. He told me he liked it rough, I thought he meant hair pulling and stuff like that. But when he said he liked it rough, I never in a million years thought he meant *that* rough."

I sit for a moment and let Lindsey and her mom cry. It must be difficult to hear this from your daughter, and not want to go and find him and rip his damn head off. But that was Lindsey's choice to make. She could have left him, instead of letting him treat her like that. "By staying with him while he treated you so poorly, you were telling him you weren't worth anything more than being his fuck buddy," I say.

Her mom's eyes widen at my blunt words, but Lindsey nods in agreement. "I know. Dakota, I can never apologize enough. And I hope one day you'll find it in your heart to forgive me."

Lindsey's crime was her inability to see the truth. She allowed him to abuse her, enabling him, giving him permission to continue. Willingly giving him her power. He took mine away the moment he decided to drug and rape me.

He, in turn, brainwashed her to think what they had was normal.

My heart hurts for Lindsey, because her road will be difficult too. She's going to need help to overcome this, and I'm not going to be the cause of her not moving forward.

I stand and take Reece's hand. "I forgive you, Lindsey," I say, because I really do. "I forgive you for everything you've said and done to me."

Her face lights up and she has her Lindsey vibe back. "Thank you, Dakota. Maybe, when this is all over, we can hang out again?" There's so much hope in her voice.

But I look her dead in the eye and shake my head. "No," I say with assertiveness. "We'll never hang out again; we'll never be friends again. I need to move on, and I pray to God you do too. I hope you get the help you need, and I really hope you find some strength in yourself. But we will never be friends again."

Her chin drops to her chest, her shoulders visibly shaking while she tries to control the crying. "I understand," she finally croaks.

"Find some peace, Lindsey."

Reece and I turn and leave the hospital. He slings his arm around my shoulder and kisses my temple. "God, you're so damn strong," he announces proudly.

"Not yet, but one day I will be."

EPILOGUE

"IT'S FREEZING OUTSIDE. It's also my birthday. Sophie couldn't be here tonight because she's helping her mom with a cleaning job. Her mom wouldn't hear of it, but she's also been working really hard trying to save money so they can move out of the small apartment above the store and into a house.

It's been seven months since Levi was arrested, and last week I got my final blood results back. I'm happy to report, I don't have HIV or any other sexually transmitted disease.

Levi's trial is set for another year, and because of the severity of what he did, and number of girls he sexually assaulted, he's already serving time behind bars. His parents were offered bail, but the amount was so high they couldn't raise the capital.

I like knowing he's behind bars, and I'm hoping he continues to stay there. The District Attorney trying his case has spoken to us and asked me to testify. It took me about four seconds to say yes, and Mom and Dad to say no. They don't want me reliving the horror of what he did. But like I explained to them, if I don't take a stand, who will?

Sophie also agreed to testify, to help secure his sentence behind bars.

It's not because I'm strong, because trust me, I'm not. But if I can stop him from getting out and hurting anyone else, then I'm going to do everything in my power to make sure he's there for a very long time.

"Who's ready for cake?" Mom asks as she stands and starts stacking the dishes on top of each other.

"Here, I'll do that," Reece offers.

"Thank you, Reece." Mom smiles at him and lets him take the dishes into the kitchen while she sets the table for cake.

"I'll help too," Taylor adds. "Can't let Mr. and Mrs. B think you're the only nice one," he smacks Reece on the back of the head.

Luckily Reece's hands are full, or I could see a rough tussle in our near future.

"Boys," my father adds. "Last time you two wrestled, it cost you a new TV."

"Oh yeah," they both grumble together. They'd been trying to outdo each other, one saying their kicks were high than the other. Taylor fell on his ass, his left leg going from under him, his right leg going straight through the TV.

Taylor got Reece a job at his work and they both worked their butts off to buy another TV for Dad, and since then Dad likes them even more. He says they have good values and show responsibility.

Life is progressing at a snail's pace. I still see Tara, though not as intensively. I see her once a week, but when I have bad days, I call her myself and book in an appointment. Those days are rare but I doubt they'll ever completely disappear. I push past them, and thanks to my family, Reece, and Sophie, I get through it.

"Happy birthday to you." Mom brings out my birthday cake, starting off the singing celebration.

She sets it down in front of me, and when everyone's done singing I blow out the seventeen candles on top.

"Do you ever wonder, when a person blows out the candles, how much of their spit ends up on the cake? Yet, we happily eat it," Sam pipes up.

"Oh yuck," we all moan.

Dad scrunches up his napkin and pegs it at her head. "Really, Samantha?" he teases her. "Where is your mind? Or at least the filter to not say everything that pops into your head?"

Sam beams at Dad and lifts her shoulders. "I'm still going to eat it," she says happily.

Mom cuts up the cake and gives each of us a slice.

When we finish eating, Taylor hands me an envelope. "Happy birthday," he says. Opening it up, there's a gift card for Hollister's.

"Thank you, Taylor, that's great."

"Here you go, big sister." Sam hands me a small box. "There's no card. I couldn't be bothered getting you one."

Smiling, I roll my eyes at her. "Thanks." I open the box and it's a silver bracelet with a plaque. The engraved plaque says, '*Sisters forever.*'

"Oh my God!" I jump up and go give her a hug. "Thank you, it's so beautiful. I love you so much."

"I love you too," she echoes my words.

When I let her go, Sam helps me put it on. I jiggle it around a bit, letting the overhead light catch the sparkle. "It's so pretty," I say happily.

When I sit down Reece hands me a long dark green box. "Happy birthday, doll."

I open it up and there's a gorgeous silver chain inside it. "Oh wow," I say. "That's gorgeous! Will you put it on me?" I ask.

"Not yet. Later." He winks at me, and now I'm suspicious of him. He nervously shifts in his seat and looks at Mom and Dad. I'm watching him though, because I know he's up to something.

"Now it's our turn." Dad gets off his chair, and heads over to where Mom is. He drapes his arm over her shoulder, and she shifts in her seat to get something out of her pocket. Mom's got the biggest smile on her face as she hands me a small box.

"What's this?" I shake the box but nothing sounds inside of it.

"Open it," Dad encourages me.

I open the box and there's a key inside. "It's a key? I already have a house key, but it's pretty? Thank you." Am I missing something?

"It's not a house key, Dakota. It's a key to your new car."

All the blood drains from my face, while I blink crazily at Mom and Dad. "You bought me a car?"

"Don't get too excited. It's not new and flashy, but it is reliable. We're picking it up next week. You need to learn to drive, and to become more independent. This is our present to you."

I look down at the key in the palm of my hand, turning it over and over. "You're giving me my independence. You're telling me I'll be okay."

Mom cries, and Dad nods.

"Thank you. I'm not sure I would have been able to survive these past few months if it wasn't for all of you. My life was turned upside down, and not once did you doubt or even question me. I really don't know how I could've gone through it all without your support." I close my hand around the key. "This is so much more than just a key."

Mom nods, tears streaming down her cheeks.

"We'll always be here for you and your sister. You both have our unwavering love and support," Dad says.

I look around the table, Sam is crying, Taylor's wiping a tear away, too. "You crying, Taylor?"

"Nah, man, it's my damned allergies."

"The ones you never had until now?" Sam lightly punches him in the arm.

"Yeah, they only play up every now and then. Can't help it."

Mom starts clearing the table, and everyone moves away, clearly affected.

I turn to Reece, who's staring at me. "Grab your coat and scarf, Dakota. Let's go sit out back for a while."

"It's cold."

"So what? You'll be warm." He stands and grabs his coat, and I go to my room to get mine too.

We meet by the back slider and head out to sit near the pool. It's cold, really cold. We don't get snow here but this year's winter has seen the threat of it for the first time since I can remember. "I have another present for you," Reece says.

"Yeah? The necklace is more than enough. You really shouldn't have."

"Dakota, since I was nine years old, I've loved you. And every year that passes I fall more and more in love with you."

Oh . . . wow. My heart melts at his words. "Reece," I whisper.

He takes a small pouch out of his pocket and hands it to me. I open it and out slides a gorgeous silver bottle-shaped pendant with a brilliant green emerald cut into the shape of a heart in the center of it. "My heart belongs to you. Keep it close, because it only beats for the love of my life. I'm more in love with you now than I was when I was nine."

"Reece." I choke up, my throat dries, and I'm fighting back tears.

"When you're ready, I want you to know I'll be waiting. Never give my heart back, because it'll only ever belong to you."

I turn to Reece, move forward and cup his cheeks. I lean in and brush my lips slowly, carefully, across his.

"I love you," I whisper.

Tonight a silent promise is made.

My heart already belongs to Reece, and when I'm ready, my body will too.

THE END

FIND YOUR STRENGTH

Statistics quoted are accurate as at June 2016
from RAINN—Rape, Abuse & Incest National Network.

Hotline US   ~ 800.656.HOPE (4673)

Hotline AUS ~ 1800 737 732

Hotline UK   ~ adults: 0844 847 7879
             ~ under 18s: 0808 802 0808

ACKNOWLEDGEMENTS

Dakota's story is something we hear about often. Sometimes, we may even know someone who's experienced it; or you maybe a survivor yourself.

Please, find your strength and know there's always help.

I need to say thank you to the most incredible people who've been through this journey with me.Debi Orton, for being a terrific editor and fixing all my Aussie slang I tend to use.

Mel Lazar, you're so much more than my friend. You're my beautiful friend who did first round edits of Mistrust and gave me the most honest of feedback.

Shaneen Murphy, my first proofreader, I hope you love Dakota and Reece as much as I do.

Cheryl Riddell, my second proofreader and someone who's invested so much time in me.

Mandy Furneyvall, my third proofreader who's been terrific in catching the last of the errors.

Book Cover by Design. Kellie always makes the most beautiful of covers for me. Mistrust is of no exception. Perfect.

Give Me Books, Kylie always finds the time to give me to promote my cover reveals and release day blitz.

Integrity Formatting. Tami is so accommodating in everything I need. She goes out of her way to help.

Jodi Perry. My sounding board. Whenever I get stuck or whenever I just need to vent, she's always there and has my back.

My family. The support you've given me on my journey is nothing short of beautiful.

But most importantly, to my readers. Every time I release a book, I'm always nervous on the response I'll get from you. I wait for aftermath, but all I'm shown is the most beautiful of messages and reviews. Thank you. It's because of you, I know that I can write any subject and you'll accept it.

ALSO BY MARGARET McHEYZER

Ugly

*This is a dark YA/NA standalone, full-length novel.
Contains violence and some explicit language*

If I were dead, I wouldn't be able to see.
If I were dead, I wouldn't be able to feel.
If I were dead, he'd never raise his hand to me again.
If I were dead, his words wouldn't cut as deep as they do.
If I were dead, I'd be beautiful and I wouldn't be so...ugly.
I'm not dead...but I wish I was.

Chef Pierre

Holly Walker had everything she'd ever dreamed about – a happy marriage and being mum to beautiful brown-eyed Emma - until an accident nineteen months ago tore her world apart. Now she's a widow and single mother to a boisterous little 7-year-old girl, looking for a new start. Ready to take the next step, Holly has found herself a job as a maître d' at Table One, a once-acclaimed restaurant in the heart of Sydney. But one extremely arrogant Frenchman isn't going to be easy to work with...

Twenty years ago, Pierre LeRoux came to Australia, following the stunning Aussie girl he'd fallen in love with and married. He and his wife put their personal lives on hold, determined for Pierre to take Sydney's culinary society by storm. Just as his bright star was on the upswing, tragedy claimed the woman he was hopelessly in love with. He had been known as a Master Chef, but since his wife's death he has become known as a monster chef.

Can two broken people rebuild their lives and find happiness once more?

Smoke and Mirrors

Words can trick us.

Smoke obscures objects on the edge of our vision.

A mirror may reflect, but the eye sees what it wants.

A delicate scent can evoke another time and place, a memory from the past.

And a sentence can deceive you, even as you read it.

Grit

Recommended for 18 years and over

Alpha MC Prez Jaeger Dalton wants the land that was promised to him.

Sassy Phoenix Ward isn't about to let anyone take Freedom Run away from her.

He'll protect what's his.

She'll protect what's hers.

Jaeger is an arrogant ass, but he wants nothing more than Phoenix.

Phoenix is stubborn and headstrong, and she wants Jaeger out of her life.

Her father lost the family farm to gambling debts, but Jaeger isn't the only one who has a claim to the property.

Sometimes it's best to let things go.

But sometimes it's better to fight until the very end.

Yes, Master

**** This prologue contains distressing content. It is only suited for readers over 18. ****
Also contains M/M, M/M/F, M/F and F/F scenes.

My uncle abused me.

I was 10 years old when it started.

At 13 he told me I was no longer wanted because I had started to develop.

At 16 I was ready to kill him.

Today, I'm broken.

Today, I only breathe to survive.

My name's Sergeant Major Ryan Jenkins and today, I'm ready to tell you my story.

A Life Less Broken
Contains distressing content. 18+

On a day like any other, Allyn Sommers went off to work, not knowing that her life was about to be irrevocably and horrifically altered.

Three years later, Allyn is still a prisoner in her own home, held captive by harrowing fear. Broken and damaged, Allyn seeks help from someone that fate put in her path.

Dr. Dominic Shriver is a psychiatrist who's drawn to difficult cases. He must push past his own personal battles to help Allyn fight her monsters and nightmares.

Is Dr. Shriver the answer to her healing?

Can Allyn overcome being broken?

My Life for Yours

He's lived a life of high society and privilege; he chose to follow in his father's footsteps and become a Senator.

She's lived a life surrounded with underworld activity; she had no choice but to follow in her father's footsteps and take on the role of Mob Boss.

He wants to stamp out organized crime and can't be bought off.

She's the ruthless and tough Mob Boss where in her world all lines are blurred.

Their lives are completely different, two walks of life on the opposite ends of the law.

Being together doesn't make sense.

But being apart isn't an option

HiT Series Box Set

HiT 149

Anna Brookes is not your typical teenager. Her walls are not adorned with posters of boy bands or movie stars. Instead posters from Glock, Ruger, and Smith & Wesson grace her bedroom. Anna's mother abandoned her at birth, and her father, St. Cloud Police Chief Henry Brookes, taught her how to shoot and coached her to excellence. On Anna's fifteenth birthday, unwelcome guests join the celebration, and Anna's world is never the same. You'll meet the world's top assassin, 15, and follow her as she discovers the one hit she's not sure she can complete – Ben Pearson, the current St. Cloud Police Chief and a man with whom Anna has explosive sexual chemistry. Enter a world of intrigue, power, and treachery as Anna takes on old and new enemies, while falling in love with the one man with whom she can't have a relationship.

Anna Brookes in Training

Find out what happened to transform the fifteen-year-old Anna Brookes, the Girl with the Golden Aim, into the deadly assassin 15. After her father is killed and her home destroyed, orphan Anna Brookes finds herself homeless in Gulf Breeze, Florida. After she saves Lukas from a deadly attack, he takes her in and begins to train her in the assassin's craft. Learn how Lukas's unconventional training hones Anna's innate skills until she is as deadly as her mentor.

HiT for Freedom

Anna has decided to break off her steamy affair with Ben Pearson and leave St. Cloud, when she suspects a new threat to him. Katsu Vang is rich, powerful, and very interested in Anna. He's also evil to his core. Join Anna as she plays a dangerous game, getting closer to Katsu to discover his real purpose, while trying to keep Ben safe. Secrets are exposed and the future Anna hoped for is snatched from her grasp. Will Ben be able to save her?

HiT to Live

In the conclusion to the Anna Brookes saga, Ben and his sister Emily, with the help of Agent rescue Anna. For Anna and Ben, it's time to settle scores…and a time for the truth between them. From Sydney to the Philippines and back to the States, they take care of business. But a helpful stranger enters Anna's life, revealing more secrets…and a plan that Anna wants no part of. Can Anna and Ben shed their old lives and start a new one together, or will Anna's new-found family ruin their chances at a happily-ever-after?

Binary Law (co-authored)

Ellie Andrews has been receiving tutoring from Blake McCarthy for three years to help her improve her grades so she can get into one of the top universities to study law. And she's had a huge crush on him since she can remember.

Blake McCarthy is the geek at school that's had a crush on Ellie since the day he met her.

In their final tutoring session, Blake and Ellie finally become brave enough to take the leap of faith.

But, life has other plans and rips them apart. Six years later Blake and his best friends Ben and Billy have built a successful internet platform company 3BCubed, while Ellie is a successful and hardworking lawyer specializing in Corporate Law.

3BCubed is being threatened with a devastatingly large plagiarism case and when it lands on their lawyers desk, it's handed to the new Corporate Lawyer to handle and win.

Coincidence or perhaps fate will see Blake and Ellie pushed back together.

Binary Law will have Blake and Ellie propelled into a life that's a whirl wind of catastrophic events and situations where every emotion will be touched. Hurt will be experienced, happiness will be presented and love will be evident. But is that enough for Blake and Ellie be able to live out their own happily ever after?